THE WOMAN OF ROME

THE WOMAN OF ROME

a novel by

ALBERTO MORAVIA

LONDON
SECKER & WARBURG
1959

Martin Secker & Warburg, Ltd.,
7 John Street, Bloomsbury,
London, W.C.1.

Translated by

LYDIA HOLLAND

0436 287137

First published July 1949
Reprinted before publication
Reprinted July 1949
Reprinted August 1949
Reprinted September 1949
Reprinted January 1950
Reprinted September 1950
Reprinted March 1952
Reprinted May 1953
Reprinted May 1956
Reprinted January 1959

Printed and bound in Great Britain by
Butler & Tanner Ltd., Frome and London

AUTHOR'S PREFACE

Some readers of *La Romana* may bring forward the objection that a simple and uneducated woman of the people would be incapable of telling her own story in the first person in the correct literary style I have lent her. This, in fact, was the problem that faced me from the outset. Two ways were open to me in relating the imaginary autobiography of the character I had chosen to portray—I could either adopt a realistic, photographic, spoken style of language, typical of a woman of Adriana's class and profession, a clumsy, poor dialect, incapable of expressing more than a limited number of feelings and incidents; or I could make my characters speak in my customary style, as I have in all my other books. I chose the second course for two reasons : firstly, I did not see any necessity to change my style because I had changed my characters, and, secondly, the language of literature is always truer and more poetically expressive than the spoken language. I cannot deny that women like Adriana do not usually speak as Adriana does, nor do they express the feelings and ideas she expresses. Nevertheless, I have attributed to her only those feelings and ideas which women like Adriana would express if they had the verbal and mental power to do so. In other words, although not all men possess the same intellectual capacity and the same knowledge, they all, even the most wretched, have their own moral world in its entirety. All I have tried to do is to represent Adriana's moral world, by doing her the same service the public letter-writers perform when they interpret and commit to paper on the street corners the unformulated sentiments of illiterate servant-maids.

PART ONE

CHAPTER ONE

At sixteen years of age I was a real beauty. I had a perfectly
oval face, narrow at the temples and widening out a little
below; my eyes were large, gentle and elongated; my nose
formed one straight line with my forehead; my mouth was
large, with beautiful full red lips, and when I laughed I showed
very white, regular teeth. Mother used to say I looked like
a Madonna. It struck me that I resembled a certain film-star
who was very popular at the time and I began to do my hair
as she did. Mother said that although my face was beautiful,
my figure was a hundred times more beautiful; she said there
was not a figure like mine in all Rome. In those days I did
not trouble about my figure, I thought a beautiful face was
all that mattered; but today I must admit mother was right.
I had firm, straight legs, curving hips, a long back, narrow
waist and broad shoulders. My abdomen was rather prominent, as it always has been, and my navel was so deeply
hollowed in my flesh that it almost disappeared; but mother
said this was an additional beauty, because a woman's abdomen
ought to be rather prominent and not flat as is the fashion
today. My bosom, too, was well-developed, but firm and
resilient, so that I did not have to wear a bust-bodice; but
when I used to complain that it was over-developed, mother
said it was really beautiful and that women's bosoms nowadays
were non-existent. When I was naked I seemed tall and
well-proportioned, modelled like a statue, they told me later
on; but when fully clothed I looked like a slim young girl,
and no one could have guessed that I was built as I was.
This was due to the proportion between the various parts
of my body, I was told by the artist for whom I first began
to pose.

Mother discovered this painter for me. Before she married

and became a shirtmaker, she had been a model; one day an artist gave her some shirts to make and, remembering her old profession, she suggested I should pose for him. The first time I went to his studio mother insisted on coming with me, although I protested that I could easily go alone. I felt ashamed, not so much at having to undress in front of a man for the first time in my life, as at the things I guessed mother would say to persuade him to employ me. And in fact, after she had helped me to slip my clothes over my head and had made me stand naked in the middle of the room, she began to talk enthusiastically to the artist. " Just look what a bosom ! What hips ! Look at her legs ! Where else will you find legs and hips and a bosom like these ? " As she said these things, she kept on prodding me, just like they prod animals to persuade people to buy them in the market. The painter was laughing and I grew ashamed and, since it was winter, I felt very cold. But I realised mother was not talking in this way out of spite and that she was proud of my beauty because she was my mother, and if I was beautiful I owed it all to her. The artist, too, seemed to understand her feelings and laughed from no ulterior motive but with genuine friendliness, so that I felt reassured and, overcoming my shyness, walked on tiptoe to the stove to warm myself. This artist must have been about forty and was a stout man with a cheerful, easy-going manner. I felt that he looked at me without desiring me, as he would an object, and this reassured me. Later on, when he knew me better, he always treated me with kindness and respect, as a human being and no longer as a mere object. I was attracted to him immediately, and I might even have fallen in love with him out of sheer gratitude, just because he was kindly and affectionate towards me. But he never let himself go with me; he always behaved like an artist and not like a man, and our relationship remained as correct and distant the whole time as it was on the first day I posed for him.

When mother had come to an end of my praises, the painter, without saying a word, went over to a heap of papers piled up on a chair and after having looked through them he pulled out a coloured print and showed it to mother. "There's your daughter," he said in an undertone. I moved over from

8

the stove to look at the print. It showed a naked woman lying on a bed covered with magnificent stuffs. A velvet curtain hung behind the bed and two winged cherubs, like two little angels, floated in the air in the folds of the curtain. The woman really did resemble me; only, although she was naked, the stuffs and the rings she was wearing on her fingers showed clearly that she must have been a queen or someone important, whereas I was only a common girl. At first mother did not understand and stared in consternation at the print. Then she suddenly seemed to see the resemblance. " She's exactly like that ! It's Adriana ! You see how right I was ? Who is this woman ? " she exclaimed excitedly.

" It's Danae," replied the artist with a smile.

" Danae who ? "

" Danae—a pagan goddess."

Mother, who had expected to hear the name of a real person, was rather disconcerted, and in order to hide her embarrassment began to explain to me that I had to do what the artist wanted; lie like the figure in the print, for instance, or stand, or sit, and keep still all the time he was working. He said laughingly that mother knew more about it than he did; and mother immediately began to talk of when she was a model and was known all over Rome as one of the handsomest models, and the harm she had done herself by marrying and giving up being a model. Meanwhile the artist had made me lie down on a sofa at the end of the studio and take up a pose, arranging my arms and legs in the position he required. But he did it with an abstracted, thoughtful gentleness, hardly touching me, as if he had already seen me in the attitude in which he wanted to paint me. Then, although mother continued to chatter, he began to sketch in the preliminary outlines on a white canvas standing on an easel. Mother noticed, he was no longer listening to her, since he was absorbed in drawing me.

" How much will you give this daughter of mine an hour ? " she asked.

Without lifting his eyes from the canvas the painter named a sum. Mother picked up the clothes I had arranged on a chair and threw them at me.

" Come on ! Get your clothes on—we'd better be going,"
she said to me.

" Now what's the matter ? " asked the painter in astonishment, stopping his work.

" Nothing," answered mother, pretending to be in a great
hurry. " Come on, Adriana—we've got such a lot to do."

" But, look here," said the painter, " if you want to come
to terms, make an offer—what's the meaning of all this ? "

Then mother began to make a dreadful scene, shouting at
the top of her voice that he was mad if he thought he could
get away with paying me so little ; that I was not one of
those old models nobody wants ; that I was sixteen and was
posing for the first time. When mother wants something
she always starts shouting and pretends she is furiously angry.
But she is not really angry at all and I, who know her through
and through, know that she is as calm as oil underneath. But
she shouts like the women in the market when a purchaser
offers too little for their goods. She shouts most of all at
well-mannered people because she knows their manners will
always make them yield to her.

And in fact even the artist gave way in the end. While
mother was making a scene, he kept on smiling and making a
gesture from time to time with one hand as if he wished to
say something. At last mother stopped to get her breath
and he asked her again how much she wanted. But she
wouldn't say straight out. " I'd like to know just how much
the painter who did that picture you showed me gave his
model ! " she shouted unexpectedly.

The artist began to laugh. " What's that got to do with
it ? Those were other days—he probably gave her a bottle
of wine or a pair of gloves."

Mother seemed as much put out as she had been when he
told her the print represented Danae. The artist was having
a little quiet fun at her expense, without any malice, of course,
but she did not realise it. She started shouting again, calling
him mean and boasting about my beauty. Then she suddenly
pretended to calm down and told him how much she wanted.
The artist argued the point for a while and at last they agreed
on a sum that was only a little less than mother had asked.

10

The artist walked over to a table, opened a drawer and paid her. She took the money, looking highly delighted, gave me a few more hints and left. The artist shut the door and then, returning to his easel, spoke to me.

" Does your mother always shout ? "

" Mother loves me," I replied.

" I got the impression that she loves money more than anything else in the world," he said quietly, as he proceeded with his drawing.

" No, no, that's not true," I retorted eagerly, " she loves me best of all; but she's sorry I was born poor and she wants me to earn a good living."

I've related this matter of the artist in detail, first of all because this was the day when I began work, although later on I chose another profession, and then because mother's behaviour on this occasion explains her character and the nature of her affection for me.

When my hour's sitting was over, I went to meet mother in a milk-bar where she had told me to pick her up. She asked me how it had gone and made me tell her every detail of the conversation which the artist, who was rather a silent fellow, had carried on with me during the sitting. In the end she told me I would have to be very careful, perhaps this artist had no dishonourable intentions, but many of them employed models with the idea of making them their mistresses. I was to repel their advances at all costs. " They are all penniless," she explained, " and you can't expect to get anything out of them. With your looks you can aim much higher, much higher."

This was the first time mother had ever spoken to me in this way. But she spoke decisively, like someone saying things they have been meditating for some time.

" What do you mean ? " I asked her in astonishment.

" Those people have plenty of talk but no money. A lovely girl like you ought to go with gentlemen," she answered rather vaguely.

" What gentlemen ? I don't know any gentlemen ! "

She looked at me. " You can be a model for the time being," she said even more vaguely, " then we'll see—one thing leads to another." But the reflective, grasping look on her face alarmed me. I asked her nothing more on that occasion.

But in any case mother's advice was unnecessary, because I was very serious even for my extreme youth. After this artist, I met others and soon became well enough known among the artists. I must say that they were usually tactful and respectful, although more than one showed me what his feelings were towards me. But I repelled them all so harshly that I soon had the reputation of being unapproachably virtuous. I have already said that most of the artists were nearly always respectful; this was probably due to the fact that their aim was not to make love to me but to draw and paint me, and all the time they were drawing and painting they saw me, not with the eyes of a man, but of an artist, as if I were a chair or any other object. They were accustomed to models, and my naked body, although it was young and fully developed, made as little impression upon them as upon a doctor. But the artists' friends often embarrassed me. They used to come in and begin to chat with the artist. But I soon noticed that, although they did their utmost to appear indifferent, they were unable to keep their eyes off me. Some were quite shameless and used to begin wandering around the studio so that they could examine me from every angle. These glances, as well as mother's veiled allusions, roused my sense of coquetry and made me conscious both of my beauty and of the advantages I might draw from it. At last I not only became accustomed to their tactlessness, but after a while, I could not help feeling delighted when I saw how excited the visitors became and disappointed when they were indifferent to me. And so my vanity led me unawares to think that whenever I chose to I could improve my situation by making use of my looks, just as mother had said.

My chief thought at that time, however, was to get married. My senses were still dormant and the men who watched me while I was posing aroused no other emotion in me but vanity. I used to give mother all the money I earned and, when I was not posing, I stayed at home with her and helped her cut and sew shirts, our only means of livelihood since my father, who had been a railwayman, had died. We lived in a small flat on the second floor of a long, low building, erected specially for the railwaymen fifty years earlier. The house was situated on one of the suburban avenues, pleasantly shaded with plane-trees. On one side was a row of houses similar to ours, all alike, with two floors, brick façades without any stucco, twelve windows, six to each storey, and a central door; on the other side, the city walls extended from tower to tower, intact at that point and smothered in greenery. There was a gate in the city walls not far from our house. Near this gate, running along inside the walls, stretched the enclosed site of an amusement park, Luna Park, whose illuminations and music enlivened the summer months. If I looked out sideways from my window I could see the festoons of coloured lamps, the beflagged roofs of the various booths and the crowd packed round the entrance under the branches of the plane-trees. I could hear the music quite clearly and I often stayed awake at night listening to it and half-dreaming, with my eyes wide open. It seemed to come from a world out of reach, at least for me, and this feeling was heightened by the darkness and narrowness of my room. The whole population of the city seemed to have come together at Luna Park and I was the only one left out. I longed to get out of bed and join them, but I did not move, and the music, which kept up an uninterrupted jangle of sound the whole night through, made me conscious of a definite loss, due to some sin I did not even know I had committed. Sometimes while listening to this music I even began to cry, so bitter was it to be left out. I was very sentimental at this time and any little thing—a friend's snub, a reproach from mother, a touching scene at the cinema— made tears well up in my eyes. Perhaps I would not have been conscious of a forbidden, happy world if mother had not forbidden me to go near Luna Park or have any other amusement when I was a child. But her widowhood, her poverty, and above all her hostility to all those distractions fate had denied her, made her refuse to let me go to Luna Park or any other place of entertainment, except much later, when I was fully grown up and my character was already formed. I

13

owe to this, in all probability, the suspicion that has remained with me all my life through of somehow being shut out from the gay, brilliant world of happiness, a suspicion I am unable to shake off, even when I know for certain that I am happy.

I have already said that at this time I thought only of getting married and I can also say how it was that this thought occurred to me. The suburban avenue where our house stood led a little further on to a more prosperous district. Instead of the long, low railwaymen's houses, that looked like so many dusty, worn-out old carriages, there were a number of little houses surrounded by gardens. They were not luxurious—clerks and small shopkeepers lived in them—but in comparison with our sordid dwelling they gave an impression of a gayer and easier life. First of all, each house was different; then, they were not all cracked and stained, with the plaster peeling off, an appearance which made our house and others like it seem as though their inhabitants had long neglected them through sheer indifference; and finally, the narrow, blossoming gardens which surrounded them created an impression of jealous intimacy, remote from the confusion and promiscuity of the street. In the building where I lived, on the contrary, the street penetrated everywhere: into the huge hall that was like a warehouse, into the wide, bare, dirty staircase, even into the rooms, where the rickety, casual furniture was reminiscent of junk-shops, where the same sort of pieces are exhibited for sale on the pavements.

One summer evening, when I was out walking with mother, I saw a family scene through a window in one of those villas; it impressed me deeply and seemed to tally in every respect with the idea I had of a normal, decent life. It was a clean little room, with flowered wallpaper, a sideboard and a central lamp hanging over a table laid ready for a meal. Around the table sat five or six people, among them three children between the ages of eight and ten, I suppose. A soup-tureen stood in the middle of the table, and the mother was standing up to serve the soup. It may seem strange, but what struck me most of all was the central lamp, or rather, the extraordinarily peaceful and normal look everything had in that light. As I turned the scene over in my mind later on, I told myself positively that I ought to make it my aim in life to live one day in a house like that, have a family like that, and live in that same light, which seemed to reveal the presence of innumerable firm and constant affections. Perhaps many people will think my ambitions very modest. But my situation at that time must be taken into account. That little house had the same effect on me, born in the railwaymen's houses, as the grander, wealthier dwellings in the luxury districts of the city had on the inhabitants of the little villa themselves. One man's Paradise is another's Hell.

But mother had made elaborate plans for my future; I soon realised they were plans that put entirely out of the question any such arrangements as the one I had most at heart. What she imagined was that with my beauty I might aim at any kind of success, but not at becoming a married woman with a family, like everyone else. We were extremely poor and my beauty seemed to her our only available capital, and, as such, it was not mine only but hers too, if for no other reason than that she it was who had given me birth, as I have said before. I was to draw on this capital as she decreed, without any consideration for appearances, in order to improve our situation. Probably the whole scheme was due chiefly to a lack of imagination. In a situation like ours, the idea of capitalising my beauty was the first to occur to her. Mother stopped short at this idea and did not bother to look beyond it.

At that time I had a very imperfect understanding of what mother's plans were. But even later, when they were quite clear to me, I never dared to ask her why, with such ideas, she had been reduced to such poverty, she, the wife of a railwayman. I understood from various hints that I myself was the cause of mother's failure, since she had had me so unwillingly and unexpectedly. In other words, I was conceived by accident; and mother, who did not dare to prevent my birth (as she ought to have done, she said), had been obliged to marry my father and accept all the consequences of such a marriage. When she referred to my birth she often used to say: "You were the ruin of me," a phrase that at one time hurt me and was obscure, but whose meaning I understood fully later on. The phrase meant: "If it had not been for you, I would not have married that man, and by now I'd have had my own car." Obviously, as she pondered over her own life in this way, she did not want her daughter, who was so much more handsome, to make the same mistakes and incur the same fate. Today, seeing things from a certain distance, I really cannot bring myself to say she was wrong. A family for mother had meant poverty, slavery, and a few rare pleasures which came to an abrupt end with the death of her husband. Naturally she considered a decent family life as a great misfortune, and was ever on the lookout for me not to be attracted by the same mirages which had led to her own downfall.

In her own way mother was very fond of me. As soon as I began to go the rounds of the studios, for instance, she made me a couple of dresses, a two-piece skirt and jacket, and a frock. As a matter of fact, I would have preferred some underwear, because every time I had to undress I was ashamed of the coarse, threadbare, often soiled lingerie I displayed, but mother said it did not matter if I wore rags underneath, what was important was to look presentable. She chose two cheap pieces of cloth, with striking colours and patterns, and cut out the dresses herself. But since she was a shirtmaker and had never made dresses before, she made them both up wrongly. The frock, I remember, pouched in front so that my breasts showed and I always had to pin it up. The jacket of the two-piece was too short and too tight; it pulled across my bosom and hips, and the sleeves did not cover my wrists; the skirt, on the other hand, was too wide and made creases in front. But I thought they were splendid because until then I had been dressed even worse, in jumpers, short little skirts showing my thighs, and skimpy little scarves. Mother bought me two pairs of silk stockings as well: I had always worn short socks and had bare knees before. These presents filled me with joy and pride; I never grew tired of looking at them and thinking about them, and used to walk self-consciously along the streets, holding myself upright, as if I were wearing a priceless dress made by some fashionable dressmaker, and not those poor rags.

16

Mother was always thinking about my future and before long she began to be dissatisfied with my profession as a model. According to her my earnings were too small; then the artists and their friends were poor and there was little hope of making useful acquaintances in their studios. Mother suddenly conceived the idea that I might become a dancer. She was always full of ambitious schemes, while I thought of nothing but a peaceful life with a husband and children. She got hold of this idea of dancing when the promoter of a variety company, who put on turns between films, ordered some shirts from her. She did not think the profession of a dancer would prove very profitable in itself, but, as she often said: " One thing leads to another," and simply appearing on a stage would provide an opportunity of meeting some gentlemen.

One day mother told me she had had a talk with this producer and he had encouraged her to take me along to see him. One morning we went to the hotel where he lodged with the whole company. I remember the hotel was an enormous old palace near the station. It was nearly midday, but still quite dark in all the corridors. The impression of sleep being wooed in a hundred rooms filled the air and took one's breath away. We went along several corridors and at last reached a kind of murky ante-chamber where three girls and a musician were practising in the sparse light as if they were on the stage. The piano was wedged into a corner near the opaque-glass window of the lavatory; in the opposite corner stood a huge pile of dirty sheets. The musician, a broken-down old man, was playing from memory, as though he were thinking of something else or drowsing. The three dancers were young and had taken off their jackets; they stood in their skirts, their breasts and arms bare. They had their arms round each other's waists and, when the musician struck up an air, they all three advanced towards the pile of dirty sheets, kicking their legs high, waving them to right and left, and finally turning their backs and waggling their behinds with provocative movements that contrasted most strangely with such a dim and squalid setting. My heart stood still as I watched them and saw how they beat time with their feet in a dull and heavy thudding on the floor. I knew well enough that although I had long, muscular legs, I had no gift for dancing. I had already had some dancing lessons with two girl friends in a dancing academy in our district. They knew how to keep time and kick their legs and swing their hips like two experienced dancers after the first few lessons, but I could only drag myself about as if I were made of lead from the waist down. I didn't seem to be built like other girls, there was something massive and heavy about me which even music was unable to dispel. Besides, feeling an arm round my waist had filled me with a kind of languorous abandon the few times I had danced, so that I dragged my legs rather than moved them. The artist, too, had said to me : " Adriana, you ought to have been born four centuries ago ! They had women like you then. It's fashionable nowadays to be thin, you're a fish out of water. In four or five years' time you'll be a Juno." He was mistaken there, though, because today, five years later, I am no stouter or more Junoesque than before. But he was right in saying that I was not made for these days of slim women. My clumsiness made me wretched and I would have given anything to be slim and able to dance like other girls. But although I ate little I was always as solidly built as a statue, and when I danced I was quite incapable of grasping the rapid, jerky rhythms of modern music.

I told mother all this because I knew the interview with the producer of the variety show would only be a fiasco and I was humiliated by the idea of being turned down. But mother began shouting at once that I was far handsomer than all the wretched girls who showed themselves off on the stage and the producer ought to thank Heaven if he could get me for his company, and so on. Mother knew nothing about modern beauty, and honestly believed that the more fully developed her bosom, and the rounder her hips, the more beautiful a woman must be.

The producer was waiting in a room that led out of the ante-chamber ; I suppose he watched his dancers' rehearsals from that room through the open door. He was sitting in an armchair at the foot of the unmade bed. There was a

18

tray on the bed and he was just finishing his breakfast. He was a stout old man, but the excessive smartness of his clothes, his brilliantine, his impeccable tidiness, made a strange effect against those tumbled sheets, in the low light of that stuffy room. His florid complexion looked painted to me, because unhealthy, dark, uneven patches showed underneath the rosy flush on his cheeks. He was wearing a monocle and puffed and panted all the time, showing such extremely white teeth that they were probably false. He was dressed very smartly, as I said. I still remember his butterfly-tie of the same pattern and colour as the handkerchief tucked into his breast-pocket. He was sitting with his belly sprawling forwards and, as soon as he had finished eating, he wiped his mouth and said in a bored, complaining voice : " Come on, show me your legs."

" Show the gentleman your legs," repeated mother anxiously.

I was no longer shy after the studios, so I pulled up my dress and showed him my legs, then stood still, holding my dress up and leaving my legs exposed. My legs are magnificent, long and straight, but just above the knees my thighs begin to swell out round and solid, broadening gradually to my hips. The producer shook his head as he looked at me. " How old are you ? " he asked.

" She was eighteen in August," replied mother readily.

He got up in silence, panting a little, and walked over to a gramophone standing on a table among a heap of papers and clothes. He wound it up, carefully chose a record and put it on the gramophone.

" Now try to dance to this music—but keep your dress up," he said.

" She's only had a few dancing lessons," said mother. She realised that this would be the decisive moment and, knowing how clumsy I was, she feared the result.

But the producer signed to her to be silent, set the record going, then with another gesture invited me to begin dancing. I did as he requested, holding my skirt up. Actually I only moved my legs, first left and then right rather slowly and heavily, and I knew I was not keeping time. He was still standing by the gramophone, leaning his elbows on the table and looking in my direction. He suddenly stopped the gramophone and went to sit down again in the armchair, with an unmistakable gesture towards the door.

" Won't it do ? " asked mother anxiously, already on the warpath.

" No, it won't do," he replied, without looking at her, while he felt about in his pockets for his cigarette-case.

I knew that when mother had a certain note in her voice she was going to make a scene and therefore I pulled her by the arm. But she jerked herself free and repeated in a louder voice, while she fixed the producer with gleaming eyes : " It won't do, eh ? And why, if I may ask ? "

The producer, who had found his cigarette-case, was now hunting for his matches. He was stout and every movement was a great effort.

" It won't do," he replied calmly but panting as he spoke, " because she's got no gift for dancing and because she hasn't the right figure for the job."

Just as I had feared, mother began to shout out her usual arguments at the top of her voice—that I was a real beauty, my face was like a Madonna's, and just look at my bosom, my hips, my legs ! He remained quite unmoved, lit his cigarette and went on smoking and watching her while he waited for her to finish.

" Perhaps your daughter may make a good wet-nurse in a year or two—but she'll never be a dancer," he then pronounced in his bored and plaintive voice.

He did not know the frenzy mother was capable of ; it so astonished him that he took his cigarette out of his mouth and stood gaping at her. He wanted to speak but she would not let him. Mother was thin and breathless and it was difficult to tell where all that noise came from. She said a number of insulting things to him in person and to the dancers whom we had seen in the corridor. At last, she snatched up some lengths of silk shirting he had entrusted to her and threw them at him, exclaiming : " Get these shirts of yours made by anyone you like . . . perhaps your dancing-girls will do them for you . . . I wouldn't touch them for all the gold in the world ! " He was completely disconcerted by this unexpected conclusion and stood there, amazed and apoplectic, with his body enveloped in his shirt material. Meanwhile I kept pulling at mother's sleeve and was almost crying with shame and humiliation. At last she yielded and, leaving the producer to extricate himself from his lengths of silk, we went out of the room.

Next day I told the artist, who had become my confidant to some extent, all that happened. He laughed a great deal at the producer's phrase about my potentialities as a wet-nurse, and then observed : " Poor Adriana—I've told you time and again ! You ought not to have been born in the present age. You ought to have been born four centuries ago. What today is a fault was then considered an asset, and vice-versa. The producer was quite right, from his own point of view. He knows the public wants fair, slim girls, with tiny breasts, tiny behinds, and cunning, provocative little faces. But you're well covered, without being exactly plump, you're dark, with a fully developed bosom—ditto for your behind !—and yours is a sweet and gentle face. What can you do about it ? You're absolutely what I want ! Go on being a model . . . then one day you'll get married and have a lot of dark, plump children just like yourself, with sweet and gentle faces."

" That's exactly what I want," I said emphatically.

" Good ! " he replied. " And now, lean over a little to one side . . . like that . . ." This artist was very fond of me in his way ; and perhaps, if he had stayed in Rome and had gone on letting me confide in him, he might have given me some good advice and many things would not have happened. But he was always complaining that he could not sell his pictures, and at last took the opportunity of an exhibition that was being organised in Milan to go and settle there permanently. I went on being a model, as he had advised me to do. But the other artists were not so kind and affectionate as he was and I did not feel inclined to talk to them about my life—which was, after all, an imaginary life made up of dreams, aspirations and hopes. Because at that time nothing ever happened to me.

So I continued being a model, although mother grumbled because she considered that I was earning too little money. At that time mother was almost always in a bad temper; and, although she did not say so, I knew that I was the chief cause of it. As I have already said, she had counted on my beauty to bring me unimaginable success and wealth. The career of a model was to be only the first step, after which, as she usually put it, one thing would lead to another. Seeing I was still nothing more than a model she grew embittered and irritated towards me, as if lack of ambition had cheated her of certain gain. Of course, she never put her thoughts into words, but allowed her hints, her rudeness, her sighs, the long faces she pulled and all the rest of her transparent play-acting to speak for her. It was a kind of never-ending blackmail; and I understood then why many girls, who are constantly badgered in this way by ambitious, disappointed mothers, end up by running away from home and giving themselves to the first man they meet, if only to escape from such an unbearable state of things. Naturally mother behaved like this because she loved me, but it was the kind of love the housewife feels for a laying hen: if it stops laying she begins to examine it, weigh it in her hand and reckon whether she would not do better to wring its neck.

How patient and ignorant we are when we are very young! I was leading a wretched life at this time and really never noticed it. I used to give mother all the money I earned by posing for long, wearisome, boring hours in the studios; and the rest of the time, when I was not naked, stiff and aching from allowing myself to be drawn and painted, I sat bent over the sewing-machine, never lifting my eyes from the needle, in order to help mother in her work. Far into the night I would still be sewing, and in the morning I would rise at daybreak, because the studios were a long way off and the sittings started very early. But before I went to work I made my bed and helped mother clean up the flat. I was really indefatigable, docile and patient, and at the same time serene, cheerful, and even-tempered; envy, bitterness and jealousy had no place in my heart; rather I was filled with the gentle, unceasing gratitude which blossoms so spontaneously in youth. And I never noticed the squalor of our flat.

One huge, bare room served as our workroom, furnished with a large table in the middle, always covered with bits and pieces, while other oddments hung from nails in the dark walls where the plaster was peeling off, and a few broken straw-bottomed chairs; then a bedroom where I used to sleep with mother in her double bed, immediately above which a huge patch of damp stained the ceiling, and in bad weather the rain used to drip down on us; and also a dark little kitchen cluttered up with the plates and saucepans which mother, being shiftless, never managed to wash up properly. I never noticed what a sacrifice my life really was, with no amusements, love or affection. When I think of the girl I was, and remember my goodness and innocence, I cannot help feeling deeply sorry for myself, in a powerless, poignant sort of way, as you do when you read of some charming person's misfortunes in a book and would like to be able to ward them off, but know you cannot. But there you are! Men have no use for goodness and innocence; and perhaps this is not the least of life's mysteries—that the qualities praised by every-one, of which nature is so prodigal, in point of fact serve only to increase the sum of unhappiness.

I imagined at that time that my longing to get married and set up a family life would one day be satisfied. Every morning I used to take the tram in the square not far from our house, where among a number of newly erected buildings, I noticed one long low construction against the city walls which was used as a garage. At that hour there was always a young man about the place, either washing or cleaning his car, who used to stare at me most pointedly. His face was sallow, thin and perfectly shaped, with a straight small nose, dark eyes, a most beautiful mouth, and white teeth. He closely resembled an American film-star much in vogue in those days and that is why I noticed him and, in fact, why I took him at first for something different from what he was, since he wore good clothes and had the air of being well

23

educated and decently behaved. I imagined that the car must be his and that he was well-to-do, one of the gentlemen mother talked so much about. I rather liked him, but I only thought of him when I saw him, then on the way to the studios he slipped out of my memory. But, without my realising it, his looks alone must have bewitched me, because one morning while I was waiting for the tram I heard someone obviously trying to attract my attention by making the sort of noise people make to call a cat, so I turned round; and when I saw him beckoning to me from the car I did not hesitate at all but, with a thoughtless docility which astonished me, walked over to him. He opened the door and as I got in I saw that his hand on the open car window was coarse and roughened, with black, broken nails and the first finger tobacco-stained, like the hands of manual workers. But I said nothing and got in all the same. " Where would you like me to take you ? " he asked as he shut the door.

I told him the address of the studio. I noticed he had a quiet voice and I thought him rather pleasant, although I could not help feeling there was something false and affected about him.

" Well, let's go for a run round—it's early—then I'll take you wherever you like," he answered. The car started up.

We left my neighbourhood by the avenue running along the city walls, went along a wide road with warehouses and little hovels on each side, and at last reached the country. Then he began to drive like a madman down a by-pass between two rows of plane-trees. Every now and again he said, without turning round : " We're doing eighty, ninety, a hundred, a hundred and twenty, a hundred and thirty kilometres an hour." He wanted to impress me with the speed, but I was chiefly anxious because I had to go and pose and was afraid that for some reason or other the car might break down in the open country. Suddenly he braked, switched off the engine and turned to me.

" How old are you ? "

" Eighteen," I answered.

" Eighteen—I thought you were older." He really did speak in an affected voice, which occasionally, in order to

24

emphasise some word, dropped as if he were talking to himself
or telling a secret.

" What's your name ? "

" Adriana.   What's yours ? "

" Gino."

" What do you do ? " I asked.

" I'm in business," he replied quickly.

" Is this your car ? "

He looked at the car with a kind of disdain.

" Yes, it's mine," he said.

" I don't believe you," I said openly.

" You don't believe me !   Well, well," he repeated in an
astonished, mocking tone, without turning a hair.   " Well,
well, well—why not ? "

" You're the chauffeur."

His ironic amazement became even more apparent.

" Now really, what extraordinary things you say !   Just
think of that, now.   Really . . . the chauffeur !   What on
earth makes you think that ? "

" Your hands."

He looked at his hands, without flushing or being em-
barrassed.   " Can't hide anything from the young lady, can
I ?   Smart girl, aren't you ?   Very well—I'm the chauffeur.
Is that all right ? " he said.

" No, it's not," I retorted sharply, " and please take me
back to town at once."

" Why ?   Are you cross with me because I told you I was
in business ? "

I really was cross with him at that moment ; I didn't know
why, it was as though I could not help it.

" Don't talk about it any more—take me back."

" It was only a joke.   Why not ?   Can't we even joke
any more ? "

" I don't like that kind of joke."

" Oh what a nasty character !   I was only thinking : this
young lady may even be a princess—if she finds out I'm only
a poor chauffeur she won't even look at me—so I'll tell her
I'm in business."

These words were very clever because they flattered me

and at the same time showed me what his feelings were towards me. In any case, he said them with a kind of grace that quite won me over.

"I'm not a princess—I work as a model, like you do as a chauffeur, to earn my living," I answered.

"What do you mean, a model?"

"I go to artists' studios, take off my clothes and they paint or draw me."

"Haven't you got a mother?" he asked pointedly.

"Of course I have ! Why?"

"And your mother lets you get naked in front of men?"

It had never crossed my mind that there was anything to be ashamed of in my profession, and in fact there was not; but I was glad he felt like that about it, it showed he had a serious moral sense. As I have already said, I was thirsting for a normal way of life and in his astuteness he had guessed (even now I don't know how), what he ought to say to me and what not. Any other man, I could not help thinking, would have made fun of me or would have shown an indelicate kind of excitement at the idea of my being naked. So unconsciously I modified the first impression his lying had given me and thought that after all he must be a decent, honest kind of fellow, just the man I had imagined for a husband in my dreams.

"Mother found me the work herself," I answered simply.

"Then it means she doesn't love you."

"No, it doesn't," I protested. "She does love me—but she was a model herself when she was a girl, and really, there's nothing wrong in it; lots of girls like me do it and are decent girls."

He shook his head, unconvinced, and then, placing a hand over mine, said: "Do you know—I'm glad I've met you. Really glad."

"So am I," I said ingenuously.

At that moment I felt a kind of impulse towards him and I almost expected him to kiss me. Certainly if he had kissed me then I would not have protested. But instead he said in an earnest voice, protectively: "If I had any say, you wouldn't be a model."

26

I felt I was a victim, and a feeling of gratitude swept over me. " A girl like you," he continued, " ought to stay at home and work if she likes, but at some decent job, that doesn't expose her to the risk of losing her honour—a girl like you ought to be married, have a house of her own, children, and stay with her husband."

That was exactly my way of thinking and I cannot say how happy I was to find that he thought or appeared to think as I did.

" You're right—but all the same, you mustn't think badly of mother. She wanted to make a model of me because she loves me," I said.

" No one would say so," he answered earnestly with indignant pity.

" Yes, she does love me—but she doesn't understand certain things."

We went on talking like this, seated behind the windscreen in the closed car. It was May, I remember, the air was soft, the shadows of the plane-trees were playing on the surface of the road as far as the eye could see. No one passed us except an occasional car at high speed, and the green, sunny countryside all around us was deserted, too. At last he looked at his watch and said he would take me back to town. In all that time he had not done anything but touch my hand once. I had expected him to try to kiss me at least, and was both disappointed and pleased by his discretion. Disappointed because I liked him and in fact could not help being attracted to gaze at his thin, red lips; glad because it strengthened my opinion that he was a serious-minded young man, just as I had hoped he would turn out to be.

He took me as far as the studio and told me that from that day on if I were to be at the tram-stop at a certain time he would always take me along since he had nothing to do just then. I was delighted to accept, and all that day my long hours of posing passed on wings. I seemed to have found a purpose in my life, and I was glad I could think about him without resentment or regret, like a person who not only attracted me physically but had the moral qualities I considered essential.

I did not mention him to mother; I was afraid she would not have allowed me to become involved with a poor man who had only a modest future. Next morning he came to pick me up as he had promised and this time took me straight to the studio. The following days, when it was fine, he took me out sometimes along the avenues or thinly populated streets on the outskirts of the city, so that he could talk to me at his ease; but he was always earnest and serious in his speech and had a most respectful manner calculated to charm me. I was very sentimental at that time and anything connected with goodness, virtue, morality, family affection, stirred me strangely, even to the point of tears, which welled up in my eyes on the slightest pretext and gave me an overwhelming and intoxicating feeling of consolation, trust and sympathy. So little by little I came to believe him absolutely perfect. Really, I asked myself sometimes, what faults had he? He was handsome, young, intelligent, honest, serious-minded, he really could not be said to have any flaw. I was astonished at these thoughts, because we do not encounter perfection every day of our lives, and I was almost frightened. What sort of a man is this, I asked myself, who has no fault, no shortcomings, however much I examine him? In fact, without knowing it I had fallen in love with him. And we all know love is a glass which makes even a monster appear fascinating.

I was so deeply in love that the first time he kissed me, in the avenue where we had had our first talk together, I felt a sense of relief, as if I had progressed in the most natural way possible from the stage of mature desire to that of its first satisfaction. But nevertheless, the irresistible impulse which joined our lips in this kiss frightened me a little, because I realised that my actions no longer depended on myself but on the exquisitely powerful force that drove me so urgently towards him. But I was completely reassured when he told me, as soon as we separated, that from now on we were to consider ourselves engaged. I could not help thinking that this time, too, he had read my innermost thoughts and had said the very words I wanted to hear. The uneasiness my first kiss had caused me therefore faded at once; and for the rest of the time we stayed there on the roadside I kissed him without any reserve, with a feeling of utter, violent and legitimate abandon.

Since then I have given and received many kisses, and God knows I have given and received them without participating in them, either emotionally or physically, as you give and receive an old coin that has been handled by many people; but I shall always remember that first kiss because of its almost painful intensity, in which I seemed to be expressing not only my love for Gino but a lifelong state of expectation. I remember that I felt as if the whole world were revolving round me and the sky lay beneath me, the earth above. In fact I was leaning back slightly, his mouth on mine, so that the embrace would last longer. Something cool and living pressed against my teeth and when I unclenched them I felt his tongue, that had caressed my ears so long with the sweetness of his words, now penetrating wordlessly into my mouth to reveal to me another sweetness I had never suspected. I did not know people could kiss in that way for so long, and I was soon breathless and half-intoxicated, so in the end, when we broke away from each other, I was obliged to lean back against the seat with my eyes closed and my mind hazy, as if I were going to faint. And so I discovered there were other joys in the world than merely living peacefully in the bosom of one's family. But I did not dream that in my case these joys were to exclude the more normal ones I had aspired to until then; and after Gino's promise of an engagement I felt sure that in the future I would be able to taste the delights of both, without sinning and without remorse.

I was so convinced of the rightness and the lawfulness of my behaviour that that very evening I told mother everything, perhaps with too much trepidation and delight. I found her at her sewing-machine by the window, sitting in the blinding light shed by an unshaded bulb.

"Mother, I'm engaged," I said, my cheeks burning as I did so.

I saw her whole face screw up in an expression of annoyance as if a trickle of icy cold water were running down her back.

"Who to?"

29

" A young man I met recently."

" What is he ? "

" A chauffeur."

I wanted to continue, but had not the time. My mother stopped her machine, jumped off her chair, and seized me by the hair. " Engaged, did you say ? . . . without telling me anything—and to a chauffeur ! Oh dear, oh dear . . . You'll be the death of me ! " She was trying to hit me as she said this. I protected myself as best I could with my hands and at last broke away from her, but she followed me. I rushed round the table in the middle of the room but she was after me, shouting desperately. I was utterly terrified by her thin face thrust out towards me with an expression of agonised rage. " I'll kill you ! " she shouted. " I'll kill you this time." Every time she said " I'll kill you " her fury seemed to increase and the threat appeared more actual. I kept to the end of the table and watched every movement she made, because I knew she was quite uncontrolled when she had these fits, and was really capable of hurting me with the first thing that she happened to pick up, even if she did not murder me. And in fact, she suddenly began waving her dressmaking scissors, the large ones, and I was only just in time to dart aside as the scissors passed me and hit the wall. She was frightened herself at this and suddenly sat down at the table, her face buried in her hands, and burst into a nervous, choking fit of crying, in which there seemed more anger than sorrow.

" I had made so many plans for you," she said between her sobs. " I wanted you to be rich, with all your good looks—and now you're engaged to a penniless fellow."

" He's not penniless ! " I interrupted timidly.

" A chauffeur ! " she exclaimed, shrugging her shoulders. " A chauffeur—you're unlucky, and you'll end up like me." She said these words slowly as if to savour all their bitterness. Then she added after a moment : " He'll marry you, and you'll become his servant, and then the servant of your children—that'll be the end of it."

" We'll get married when he has enough money to buy his own car," I said, telling her one of Gino's plans.

30

" Some hopes ! But don't bring him here," she suddenly shouted, raising her tear-stained face. " Don't bring him here—I don't want to see him. Do what you like, see him wherever you like—but don't bring him here."

That evening I went to bed supperless, feeling very unhappy and depressed. But I told myself that mother was carrying on in this way because she loved me and had made all sorts of plans for my future that were being upset by my engagement to Gino. Later on, even when I knew what these plans were, I could not really blame her. She had received in exchange for her honest, hard-working life, nothing but bitterness, travail and poverty. How could anyone wonder at her hoping for an entirely different life for her daughter ? I ought to say, perhaps, that they were not so much cut and dried plans as vague, scintillating dreams, which could be cherished without much remorse because of their very brilliance and vagueness. But that is only my own idea ; and perhaps, instead, mother really had reached the conclusion, through the life-long dulling of her conscience, of setting me one day on the path that later I was in any case destined to follow on my own account. I do not say this out of spite towards my mother but because I still do not quite understand what was in her mind at that moment, and experience has taught me that the most contradictory things may be thought and felt at one and the same moment, without your noticing the contradiction or choosing one in preference to another.

She had vowed that she did not want to meet him and for some time I respected her wish. But after Gino had kissed me the first few times, he seemed anxious to have everything open and above-board, as he put it ; and every day he insisted that I ought to introduce him to my mother. I did not dare to tell him mother did not want to know him because she thought his employment too humble, so I tried to postpone the meeting with various excuses. At last Gino realised I was concealing something from him, and he pressed me so much that I was obliged to tell him the truth.

" Mother doesn't want to know you because she says I ought to have married a gentleman and not a chauffeur."

We were in the car in the usual suburban avenue. He looked at me sadly and heaved a sigh. I was so infatuated with him that I did not notice how faked his sorrow really was.

"That's what comes of being poor," he exclaimed pointedly, and was silent for some time.

"Do you mind?" I asked him at last.

"I'm humiliated," he replied, shaking his head. "Any other man in my place would never have asked to meet her, would never have mentioned an engagement—that's all you get for trying to do the right thing."

"Why worry?" I said. "I love you—that's all that matters."

"I ought to have come with my pockets full of money, but no talk of an engagement, of course! And then your mother would have been delighted to welcome me."

I did not dare to contradict him, because I knew that what he was saying was absolutely true.

"Do you know what we'll do?" I said after a while. "One day I'll take you along and we'll surprise her. She'll have to meet you, then—she can't shut her eyes."

We arranged a day and in the evening, as we had agreed, I took Gino into the living-room. Mother had just finished her work and was clearing the end of the table in order to lay the cloth.

"This is Gino, mother," I said, as I led him in.

I had expected a scene and had put Gino on his guard. But to my surprise mother said shortly: "Glad to meet you," glancing at him aside. Then she left the room.

"You'll see it'll be all right," I said to Gino. I went close to him and putting my face up, said: "Give me a kiss."

"No, no," he replied in a low voice as he pushed me off, "your mother would be right in thinking badly of me."

He always knew how to say the exact words for every situation, and always said them at the right moment. I could not help admitting to myself that he was right. Mother returned and spoke without looking at Gino.

"There's only enough food for the two of us, really— you didn't tell me—I'll go out and——"

32

She did not finish what she was saying. Gino stepped forward and interrupted her.

"Good gracious! I didn't come here to invite myself to supper. Let me invite the two of you, you and Adriana."

He spoke politely like an educated person. Mother was unaccustomed to being talked to in that way and to being invited out, and for a moment she hesitated and stood looking at me.

"As far as I'm concerned, if Adriana wants to——" she then said.

"Let's go to the wine-shop down below," I suggested.

"Wherever you like," replied Gino.

Mother said she had to go and take off her apron so we were left alone. I was full of innocent joy; I felt I had won an important battle, whereas it was only a comedy and the only person not acting a part was myself. I went up to Gino and before he could push me away I kissed him impulsively. The relief from all the anxiety which had troubled me for so long, the conviction that from now on the way was open for my marriage, my gratitude to Gino for his polite attitude to my mother, were all expressed in this kiss. I had no hidden purpose, I was entirely whole-hearted in my love for Gino, and in my affection for my mother, I was sincere, trusting and naïve, like any eighteen-year-old before disillusionment has brushed off the bloom. I did not learn until much later on that very few people like this kind of candour or are moved by it; for it appears ridiculous to most people and above all induces in them the desire to do it hurt.

We all three went out to the pub round the corner, just beyond the city walls. Gino took no further notice of me when we were seated, but gave himself up entirely to my mother, with the obvious intention of winning her over. This desire of his to ingratiate himself with mother seemed perfectly just to me, and I therefore paid little heed to the grossest forms of flattery and adulation he was expending upon her. He called her *signora*, a mode of address that was quite new to mother, and he was careful to repeat it as often as he could, at the beginning or in the middle of his sentences, like a refrain. And then quite casually he would say:

33

" You're so clever, you'll understand . . ." " You've had experience, there's really no need to tell you some things . . ." or again, even more briefly : " With your intelligence . . ." He even managed to tell her that at my age she must have been handsomer than I. " How can you tell ? " I asked him, a little annoyed. " Oh ! It's quite plain to see . . . there are some things one just doesn't need to be told," he replied, in a general and flattering tone. Mother, poor thing, stared at him with her eyes popping out of her head as he buttered her up in this way, and her face became quite radiant and all her suspicions were lulled to sleep. Then again I would see her lips moving as she silently repeated to herself the nauseating compliments he showered upon her. It was obviously the first time in all her life that anyone had talked to her like this ; and her thirsting heart seemed to be able to drink in his words for ever. As for myself, as I have said already, these falsehoods seemed to show nothing else but affectionate respect for my mother and kind regards for me ; and so I only had to add one more stroke to the already over-charged picture of Gino's perfections.

Meanwhile a group of young men had come in and sat down at a table near ours. One of them, who seemed to be rather tipsy and kept on staring at me, gave voice to an obscene but at the same time flattering remark about me. Gino heard it and got up immediately and went over to the young man.

" Would you mind repeating what you said ! " he exclaimed.

" What the hell's it got to do with you ? " asked the young man, who was obviously tight.

" This lady and this young girl are with me," said Gino, raising his voice, " and as long as they're with me their business is my business. Do you get my meaning now ? "

" I see, keep calm . . . it's all right, it's all right . . ." answered the young man, slightly intimidated. The others seemed to be hostile to Gino, but did not dare to take their friend's side ; while he, pretending to be even drunker than he was, filled a glass and offered it to Gino, who refused it with a wave of his hand. " Won't you drink ? " shouted the young tippler. " Don't you like wine ? You're wrong

34

. . . it's good wine. I'll drink it myself," and he gulped it down in one breath. Gino stared at him sternly for a moment, then returned to us.

"Ill-mannered people," he said as he sat down and straightened his jacket with nervous gestures.

"You shouldn't have troubled," said my mother, highly flattered. "They're only rough lads."

But Gino was overwhelmed by this opportunity of parading his chivalry. "How could I have done otherwise?" he replied. "It would have been a different matter had I been with one of those . . . you, *signora*, will know what I mean . . . quite a different matter, although . . . But since I happen to be with two ladies, in a public place, in a restaurant . . . anyway he realised I was in earnest and dried up at once."

Mother was completely won over by this incident. Also because Gino had made her drink, and she found the wine as intoxicating as the flattery. But as so often happens to those who have drunk too much, beneath her surrender to Gino's charm, she continued to foster her ill feelings about our engagement. And she seized the first opportunity of making it plain to him that, in spite of everything, she had not forgotten.

Her opportunity came during a conversation about my profession as a model. I no longer remember how it was that I came to speak about a new artist for whom I had been posing that morning.

"I may be stupid, I may be old-fashioned, anything you like, but I really can't swallow the fact that Adriana takes off all her clothes in front of these artists every day," interrupted Gino.

"Why not?" asked mother in a thick voice which warned me, knowing her as I did, of the storm that was brewing.

"Because, in a word, it isn't moral."

I shall not give my mother's reply in its entirety because it was sprinkled with the oaths and shocking expressions she always used when she had drunk too much or was overcome with anger. But even when I've toned it down her speech reflects her ideas and feelings about the matter.

"It isn't moral, isn't it?" she began to shout at the top

of her voice, so that all the people at the other tables stopped eating and turned towards us. "Not moral—what *is* moral, I'd like to know? Perhaps it's moral to work your fingers to the bone all day, wash up, sew, cook, iron, sweep, scrub floors and then have your husband turn up in the evening, so deadbeat that as soon as his meal is done he goes to bed, turns his back on you and sleeps? That's what you call moral, is it? It's moral to sacrifice yourself, never have time to breathe, to grow old and ugly, then croak? Do you want to know what I think? It's that you only live once, and when you're dead, you're dead, and you and all your morality can go to the devil. And Adriana's perfectly right to show herself naked if people will pay her for doing it, and she'd do even better if——" A string of obscenities followed that made me writhe with shame because she shouted them all in the same piercing voice as the rest. "And if she were to do these things I wouldn't lift a finger to prevent her—not only that, but I'd help her to it—yes, I would—as long as they paid her, of course," she added, as if struck by an afterthought.

"I'm sure you wouldn't really be able to bring yourself to do it," said Gino, without appearing at all ruffled.

"Wouldn't I? That's what you say! What the devil do you think? Do you think I'm glad Adriana's engaged to a ne'er-do-well like you, a chauffeur? Wouldn't I have been a thousand times happier if she had gone on the streets? Do you think I like the idea that Adriana with all her beauty, which could earn her thousands, is going to be your servant for the rest of her life? You're wrong, utterly wrong."

She continued to shout, and with everyone turning their attention on us, I felt dreadfully ashamed. But Gino, as I have already said, was not at all disconcerted. He seized the moment when mother, panting and exhausted, was obliged to stop for lack of breath, to pick up the wine-bottle and fill her glass, saying as he did so: "A little more wine?"

Poor mother could not help saying "Thanks," and she accepted the glass he offered her. People who saw us drinking together as if nothing had occurred, despite her vehement outburst, went on with their own conversations.

"Adriana, with all her beauty, ought to lead the sort of life my mistress does," said Gino.

"What sort of life?" I asked eagerly, being anxious to lead the conversation away from myself.

"In the morning," he said in a vain and fatuous voice, as if bathing in the reflected glory of his employers' wealth, "she gets up at eleven or twelve. She has her breakfast taken up to bed on a silver salver with heavy silver-ware. Then she has a bath, but first the maid puts some salts in the water to make it smell nice. At midday I take her out in the car—she goes to have a vermouth, or to do some shopping. Then she goes home, has her lunch, lies down and then spends a couple of hours dressing. You ought to see how many dresses she's got! Cupboards full of them. Then she goes out visiting, in her car, or receives people. They play cards, drink, have music. They're awfully rich people! She must have several millions' worth of jewels alone——"

Mother's thoughts were as easily distracted as a child's, whom a trifle will put into a good mood. She had now forgotten all about me and the hardness of my fate, and was staring at the picture of so much splendour.

"Millions!" she repeated greedily. "And is she beautiful?"

Gino, who was smoking, spat out a shred of tobacco scornfully. "Beautiful? She's real ugly—thin, looks like an old witch."

They went on talking about the wealth of Gino's mistress, or rather, Gino went on singing the praises of her wealth as if it were his own. But mother had fallen once more into a depressed and dissatisfied mood, after her moment of curiosity, and did not utter another word all evening. Perhaps she was ashamed of her outburst; perhaps she was envious of all that wealth and was thinking resentfully of my engagement to a poor man.

Next day I asked Gino apprehensively whether mother had offended him; he replied that although he did not share her ideas he understood them perfectly, inspired as they were by a wretched life of deprivation. She was to be pitied, he said, and anyway, obviously she only spoke like that because she loved me. This was my impression, too, and I was grateful to Gino for having understood her so well. I had been afraid that mother's outburst might have spoilt everything for us. Gino's moderation not only filled me with gratitude but was one more item to be added to the list of his perfections. If I had been less blinded and inexperienced I would have reflected that only calculating deceit can aim at creating such a sense of perfection; and that real sincerity gives a picture of many faults and shortcomings, together with a few good qualities.

The fact of the matter is that I now found myself, in comparison with Gino, in a constant state of inferiority. I seemed to have given him almost nothing in exchange for his patience and understanding. Perhaps my state of mind, as one who had received many kindnesses and felt called upon to reciprocate them, explains why I made no resistance, as I would have done earlier, when his love-making became even bolder. But I must also admit, as I have already said about our first kiss, that I felt impelled to give myself to him by a most powerful yet, at the same time, most exquisite force; it was something akin to the power of sleep, which occasionally, in order to conquer our contrary will, induces us to drop off by means of a dream that we are still awake; and so we yield, being convinced that we are still resisting.

I remember all the phases of my seduction perfectly, and because I desired and at the same time repelled each advance made by Gino, it gave me both pleasure and remorse. Each step, too, was taken with calculated gradualness, neither hurriedly nor impatiently, as if he were a general invading a country rather than a lover carried away by desire, as he explored my passive body, from my lips down to my thighs. I do not mean to imply, however, that Gino did not really fall in love with me later on, when his scheming and calculation did give place to a deep, insatiable desire, even if it was not love.

During our outings in the car he had been content so far to kiss my mouth and neck. But one morning, while he was kissing me, I felt his fingers fumbling with the buttons of my blouse. Then I had a feeling that I was cold, and looking over his shoulder towards the mirror over the windscreen I saw that one of my breasts was uncovered. I was ashamed but did not like to cover myself again. It was Gino, who hastily guessing the cause of my embarrassment, pulled the edges of my blouse together again over my bosom and himself did up all the buttons. I was grateful to him for this gesture. But later, when I thought it over at home, I felt excited and attracted. Next day he repeated the gesture and this time I felt more pleasure and less shame. From that time I became accustomed to this demonstration of his desire and I think that if he had not repeated it I would have been afraid he no longer loved me so much.

Meanwhile he talked ever more frequently of the life we would lead when we were married. He also spoke about his family who lived in the provinces and were not really poor, since they even owned some strips of land. I believe he really came, like most liars, to believe his own lies in the end. Certainly his feelings for me were very strong and probably, since we became more intimate every day, they became more sincere as well. As for myself, his talk lulled my uneasiness and gave me a feeling of perfect, naive happiness such as I have never experienced at any time since then. I loved, I was loved, I imagined I would shortly be married, I thought I wanted nothing more on earth.

Mother realised at once that our morning trips were not exactly innocent and let me see she knew it by such phrases as: "I don't know what you and Gino get up to when you're out in that car, and I don't want to know, either . . ." or: "You and Gino are up to some mischief, worse luck for you," and so on. But I could not help noticing that this time her scolding seemed surprisingly mild and ineffective. She not only seemed resigned to the idea that Gino and I were lovers, but also, at heart, to desire it. I am sure now that she was on the lookout for an opportunity to break off my engagement.

One Sunday Gino told me that his employers had left for the country, that the maids had all gone off on holiday to their own villages, and that the villa had been left in charge of himself and the gardener. Did I want to see over it? He had spoken about it so often and in such glowing terms that I was longing to visit it and I therefore accepted gladly. But in the very instant of accepting, a yearning excitement inside me made me realise that my curiosity to see the villa was nothing more than an excuse, and that the real motive behind my visit was something quite different. Nevertheless, I pretended to myself and to Gino that I believed my own excuse, as we always do when we long for something and at the same time try not to.

"I know I ought not to come," I warned him as I got into the car, "but we shan't stay long, shall we?"

I was conscious of saying these words in a provocative and at the same time rather scared manner.

"Just long enough to see over the house—then we'll go to the flicks," said Gino reassuringly.

The villa stood among other villas in a little street on a slope, in a new and well-to-do district. It was a peaceful day and all those villas outlined on the hillside against the blue sky, with their red brick or white stone façades, their loggias adorned with statues, their sun-traps, terraces and verandahs blooming with geraniums, and the tall, leafy trees in the gardens between each house, gave me a sense of novelty and discovery, as if I were entering a freer and more beautiful world, where it would have been pleasant to live. I could not help remembering my own district—the road running along the city walls, the railwaymen's houses, and I said to Gino: "I was wrong to come here."

"Why?" he asked coolly. "We shan't stay long—don't worry."

"You don't see what I mean!" I replied. "I was wrong, because afterwards I shall be ashamed of my own house and neighbourhood."

"You're right there," he said with relief, "but what can you do about it? You ought to have been born a millionaire—only millionaires live up here."

He opened the gate and led the way down a gravel path between two rows of little trees trimmed into the shape of cubes and rounds. We entered the villa by a plate-glass door and found ourselves in a bare, gleaming entrance-hall, with a black and white check marble floor, polished like a mirror. From here we went into a light and spacious larger hall, with the ground-floor rooms leading out of it. At the end of the hall a white staircase led to the upper floor. I was so scared at the sight of this hall that I began walking on tiptoe. Gino noticed me and told me, laughing, that I could make as much noise as I liked, since nobody was at home.

He showed me the drawing-room, a huge place with many mirrors and sets of armchairs and sofas; the dining-room, which was a little smaller, with an oval table, chairs and sideboard made of a beautiful dark and polished wood; the linen-room, full of white varnished wall-cupboards. In a smaller sitting-room there was even a bar arranged in a niche in the wall, a real bar with shelves for the bottles, a nickel-plated coffee-machine and a zinc counter; it was like a little chapel, especially on account of a little gilded gateway that shut it off. I asked Gino where they did the cooking and he told me the kitchen and servants' rooms were in the basement. It was the first time in my life that I had been in a house of this kind, and I could not help fingering things, as if unable to believe my own eyes. Everything looked new to me and made of precious materials—glass, wood, marble, metals, stuffs. I could not help comparing those walls and that furniture with the dirty floors, blackened walls and rickety furniture in my own house, and I told myself my mother was right when she said money was the only thing that mattered in the world. I supposed the people living among all those lovely things could not help being lovely and good themselves, they could not possibly drink or swear or shout or hit one another, or do any of the things I had seen done in my own flat and others like it.

Meanwhile, for the hundredth time, Gino was explaining

with extraordinary pride the way life was lived in a place like that, as if he were bathing in the reflected glory of all that luxury and ease. " They eat off china plates, but they have silver ones for dessert and sweets. The knives and forks are all silver. They have five different courses and drink three kinds of wine. The mistress wears a low-necked dress in the evening and the master a black dinner-suit. When dinner's over the parlourmaid hands round seven kinds of cigarettes, foreign brands, of course, on a silver tray. Then they go out of the dining-room and have coffee and liqueurs wheeled in on that little table over there . . . they always have guests . . . sometimes two, sometimes four . . . the mistress has got some diamonds as big as this ! and a marvellous pearl necklace . . . she must have some millions' worth of jewels ! "

" You told me that before," I interrupted him peevishly.

But he was so carried away he did not notice my irritation. " The mistress never goes down into the basement—she gives her orders by 'phone. Everything in the kitchen is electric. Our kitchen's cleaner than most people's bedrooms. But not only the kitchen ! Even the mistress's dogs are cleaner and better off than many people." He spoke with admiration of his employers and with scorn of poor people ; and partly because of the comparison I kept on making between that house and my own, and partly because of his words, I felt very poor.

We went up the staircase to the next floor. Gino put his arm round my waist and hugged me tight. And then, I don't know why, I almost felt as if I were the mistress of the house just going upstairs with my husband, after some reception or dinner, on my way to spend the night with him in the same bed, on the next floor. As if he had guessed what I was thinking (Gino was always having these intuitions), he said : " And now let's go to bed together—tomorrow they'll bring us our coffee in bed." I began to laugh, but almost hoped it would come true.

I had put on my best dress that day to go out with Gino, and my best shoes, blouse and silk stockings. I remember the dress was a two-piece, a black jacket and a black-and-white

42

check skirt. The stuff wasn't too bad, but the dressmaker in our neighbourhood who had cut it was not much more experienced than mother. She had made a very short skirt, shorter at the back than in front, so that although my knees were covered my thighs could be seen from behind. She had made the jacket extremely close-fitting, with wide revers and such tight sleeves that they hurt my armpits. I felt as if I were bursting out of that jacket; and my bosom stuck out as if a piece of the jacket were missing. My blouse was a very plain one, made of some cheap pink stuff, without any embroidery, and my best white cotton petticoat showed through it. My shoes were black and shiny, the leather was good but the shape old-fashioned. I had not got a hat and my wavy chestnut-brown hair hung loose over my shoulders. It was the first time I had worn the dress and I was very proud of it. I thought myself very smart and could not help imagining everyone turned round in the street to look at me. But as soon as I entered the bedroom of Gino's mistress and saw the enormous downy bed with its embroidered silk coverlet, embroidered linen sheets and all those gossamer draperies floating down over the head of the bed, and saw myself reflected three times over in the triple mirror standing on the dressing-table at the end of the room, I realised I was dressed like a scarecrow; my pride in my rags was ridiculous and pitiful; and I thought I would never again be able to call myself happy unless I could dress well and live in a house like that. I almost felt like crying; and I sat down on the bed in bewilderment, without saying a word.

"What's the matter?" asked Gino, sitting down beside me and taking my hand.

"Nothing," I said, "I was looking at a country cousin of my acquaintance."

"Who?" he asked in amazement.

"That," I said, pointing to the mirror in which I could see myself seated on the bed beside Gino; and really, we both looked like a couple of hairy savages who had wandered into a civilised house by mistake, but I looked worse than he did.

This time he understood the feeling of depression, envy and jealousy that was tormenting me.

43

"Don't look at yourself in that mirror," he said, as he put his arms round me. He feared for the outcome of his plans and did not realise that nothing could have been more favourable to them than my present feeling of humiliation. We kissed one another and the kiss revived my courage, because I felt that after all I loved and was loved.

But a little later when he showed me the bathroom, which was as big as an ordinary room, with its white, shining tiles and the built-in bath with nickel-plated taps; and when he opened one of the cupboards and showed me his mistress's dresses, packed tight together, the sensation of envy and of my own poverty returned and made me feel quite desperate. I was suddenly overcome by a desire to think no more about these things; and for the first time I wanted, consciously, to become Gino's mistress, partly so as to forget my own condition and partly in order to persuade myself that I too was free and capable of doing what I liked, despite the sense of slavery that was weighing me down. I could not wear beautiful clothes nor have a house like that, but at least I could make love like the rich do, and perhaps better than they do.

"Why show me all these clothes?" I asked Gino. "What do they matter to me?"

"I thought you'd be curious to see what they're like," he replied, rather disconcerted.

"I'm not at all interested in them," I said, "they're lovely, but I didn't come here to look at clothes."

I saw his eyes light up as I spoke.

"I'd rather see your room," I added carelessly.

"It's in the basement," he replied eagerly; "shall we go down?"

I looked at him in silence for a moment and then asked him with a newly-found, straightforward kind of manner I disliked in myself: "Why are you playing the fool with me?"

"But I——" he began uneasily in surprise.

"You know better than I do that we didn't come here to look over the house or admire your mistress's dresses, but to go to your room and make love—well, then, let's get on with it and make no more bones about it."

In this way, all in a moment, through having seen the house, I changed from being the shy, ingenuous girl I had been when I entered it; and I was amazed at the change and hardly recognised myself. We left the room and began to go down stairs. Gino put his arm round my waist and kissed me on every step—I do not think anyone ever went down a stairway so slowly. When we reached the ground floor Gino opened a doorway concealed in the wall and still kissing me and holding me by the waist, led me down the back stairs into the basement. It was evening, and dark in the basement. We reached Gino's room at the end of a long passage, without putting on any lights, our arms still round one another, his mouth on mine. He opened the door, we entered, I heard him close it behind us. We stood there in the dark for some time, kissing one another. It was an endless kiss; every time I wanted to stop he started again and every time he wanted to stop it was I who went on. Then Gino pushed me towards the bed and I let myself fall on to it.

Gino kept on whispering in my ear, most provocatively, sweetnothings and persuasive little phrases with the obvious purpose of bewildering me and preventing me from noticing that meanwhile he was trying to undress me. But this was quite unnecessary, first of all because I had made up my mind to give myself to him, and then because I hated all those clothes I had liked so much before, and was dying to be rid of them. Naked, I thought, I would be as beautiful, if not more beautiful, than Gino's mistress and all the other rich women in the world. In any case, my body had been waiting for this moment for months now, and I felt that despite myself, it was quivering with impatience and repressed desire like a chained and starving animal, which finally, after a long fast, is set free and given food.

For this reason the act of love seemed entirely natural to me, and my physical pleasure was not accompanied by any feeling that I was doing something unwonted. On the contrary, I seemed to be doing things I had already done; I did not know where nor when, maybe in another life, just as sometimes certain landscapes seem familiar whereas you are really seeing them for the first time in your life. This did

45

not prevent me from loving Gino passionately, fiercely, kissing him, biting him, crushing him in my arms almost to the point of suffocation. He, too, seemed to be swept away by the same rage of possession. And so we embraced one another violently in that dark little room, buried beneath two floors of the empty, silent house, goading our bodies in innumerable ways like two enemies struggling for life and trying to hurt each other as much as possible.

But as soon as our desire was satisfied and we lay beside one another, drowsy and exhausted, I became terribly afraid that now Gino had possessed me he would no longer want to marry me. So I began to talk about the house we would live in after the wedding.

The villa belonging to Gino's mistress had made a deep impression upon me, and I was quite convinced now that there could be no happiness except among beautiful, clean things. I realised we would never be able to own a house or even a single room like that house; but nevertheless I insisted on trying to overcome this difficulty by explaining to him that even a humble flat could appear well-to-do if it shone like a mirror. The brightness of the villa even more than its luxury had given me a welter of ideas. I tried to convince Gino that cleanliness could make even ugly objects look beautiful; but what I really wanted was to convince myself, since I was in despair at the idea of my own poverty and I knew that marrying Gino would be the only way out of it. "Even two rooms can be beautiful," I said, " if they're properly kept, with the floors washed down every day, all the furniture dusted and the brass polished and everything kept tidy, the plates in their proper places, the dusters in their proper places, clothes and shoes all in their proper places. The main thing is to sweep thoroughly and wash the floors and dust everything every day. You don't have to judge by the house where mother and I live—mother's untidy and anyway, she never has the time, poor thing. But our house'll shine like a mirror, I can promise you that much."

"Yes, yes," said Gino, " cleanliness comes first. Do you know what the mistress does if she finds a speck of dust in some corner? She calls the chambermaid, makes her go down on her knees and pick it up with her hands—like you make dogs when they've been dirty in the house. And she's quite right."

"I'm sure my house'll be even cleaner and tidier than that," I said. "You'll see."

"But you're going to be an artists' model," he said to tease me. "And you won't bother with the house at all."

"A model!" I replied sharply. "I'm not going to be a model any more . . . I'll stop at home all day and keep it clean and tidy for you and cook for you . . . mother says that means I'll be your servant . . . but if you love someone even being a servant can be a pleasure."

So we stayed chatting for a long time; and little by little my fear dwindled, giving way to my usual charmed and innocent trustfulness. How could I doubt him? Gino not only agreed to all my plans, but discussed the details, improved on them, added others of his own. I think I have already said that he must have been fairly sincere at the time; being a liar he had ended by believing his own lies.

After we had chatted and prattled for a couple of hours, or thereabouts, I dropped off to sleep and I think Gino also slept. We were wakened by a ray of moonlight which came in through the semi-basement window and lit up the bed and our bodies lying there. Gino said it must be very late; and in fact the alarm-clock on the night-table showed that it was a few minutes past midnight. "What on earth will mother do to me!" I exclaimed, jumping out of bed and beginning to dress in the moonlight.

"Why?"

"I've never stayed out so late in all my life—I never go out in the evening."

"You can tell her we went out for a run in the car," said Gino as he too got up, "and it broke down right out in the country."

"She won't believe it."

We hurried out of the villa and Gino took me home in the car. I was sure mother would not believe the tale about the car having broken down; but I did not imagine that her intuition would have led her to guess exactly what had happened between Gino and me. I had the keys of the front door and of the flat. I went in, raced up the two flights of stairs and opened the flat door. I hoped mother was already in bed, and my hope was strengthened by finding the house in pitch darkness. Without turning on the light I started to go on tiptoe towards the bedroom, when I felt myself seized violently by the hair. In the dark my mother, for it was she, dragged me into the living-room, threw me on to the sofa and began to strike me with her fists, in a tempest of fury, without once giving vent to a single word. I tried to defend myself with my arm, but mother, as if she could see what I was doing, always found a way of getting in a nasty blow from underneath that struck me full in the face. At last she grew tired and I felt her sit down beside me on the sofa, panting heavily. Then she got up, went and lit the lamp in the middle of the room, and came to sit beside me, with her hands on her hips, staring at me. I felt full of shame and embarrassment as she watched me, and tried to pull down my dress and tidy myself up after the state a struggle of that kind had left me in.

"I bet you and Gino have been making love," she said in her usual voice.

I wanted to say yes, it was true; but I was afraid she would hit me again; and now there was light I was more afraid of the precision of her blows than of the pain itself. I hated the idea of walking about with a black eye, especially before Gino.

"No, we haven't—the car broke down during the trip and made us late," I replied.

"And I say you've been making love."

"We haven't."

"Yes, you have—go and look at yourself in the mirror—you're green!"

"I'm tired—but we haven't been making love."

"Yes, you have."

"We haven't."

What astonished and rather worried me was that she showed no indignation while she kept on insisting like this, but only a strong and by no means idle curiosity. In other words, mother wanted to know whether I had given myself to Gino,

48

not in order to punish me or reproach me with it but because, for some hidden motive of her own, she simply had to know. But it was too late; and although I was sure by now that she would not hit me again, I continued obstinately to deny it. All at once mother stepped forward and made as if to take me by the arm. I raised my hand to protect myself, but she only said: "I won't touch you—don't be afraid. Come along with me."

I did not understand where she wanted to take me, but being scared out of my wits I obeyed her all the same. Still holding me by the arm, she led me out of the flat, made me go downstairs and accompanied me into the street. It was deserted at that time of night, and I realised immediately that mother was hurrying me along the pavement towards the little red light burning outside the chemist's shop where the first-aid station was. I made a last effort to resist her when we were on the chemist's doorstep, and dug my feet in, but she gave me a push and I entered all of a heap, almost falling on my knees. Only the chemist and a young doctor were in the shop.

"This is my daughter. I want you to examine her," mother said to the doctor.

The doctor made us go into the backroom where the first-aid bed was.

"Tell me what's the matter—what must I examine her for?" he asked mother.

"She's been making love with her fiancé, the little bitch, and she says she hasn't," shouted mother. "I want you to examine her and tell me the truth."

The doctor began to be amused, his lips twitched as he smiled and said: "But this isn't a diagnosis—it's a matter for a specialist——"

"Call it what you like," answered mother, shouting at the top of her voice all the time, "I want you to examine her— aren't you a doctor? Don't you have to examine the people who ask you to?"

"Calm yourself. What's your name?" he turned to me.

"Adriana," I answered. I was ashamed but not deeply.

Mother's scenes were as well-known as my own mildness of temper throughout the whole neighbourhood.

" And suppose she has ? " continued the doctor, who seemed aware of my embarrassment and was trying to avoid making the examination. " What's the harm ? They'll get married later on, and it'll all end well."

" Mind your own business."

" Keep calm, keep calm ! " repeated the doctor pleasantly. Then turning to me : " You see your mother really wishes it—so take your things off. I won't be a moment and then you can go."

I summoned up all my courage. " All right, then," I said, " I have made love—let's go home, mother."

" Not at all, my dear ! " she said authoritatively. " You've got to be examined."

Resignedly I let my skirt fall to the ground and stretched myself on the bed. The doctor examined me.

" You were right," he then said to mother. " She has— now are you satisfied ? "

" How much ? " asked mother, taking out her purse. Meanwhile I slipped off the bed and put on my clothes again. But the doctor refused to take the money.

" Do you love your fiancé ? " he asked me.

" Of course," I replied.

" When are you getting married ? "

" He'll never marry her," shouted mother. But I replied calmly : " Soon—when we've got our papers ready." There must have been so much ingenuous trust in my eyes that the doctor laughed indulgently, gave me a little pat on the cheek and then pushed us out.

I expected mother to cover me with insults as soon as we reached home and perhaps even hit me again. But instead there she was, silently lighting the gas and beginning to cook me something. She put on a saucepan, then came into the living-room and, having removed the usual bits and pieces from the end of the table, she laid a place for me. I was sitting on the sofa on to which she had dragged me by the hair a little while before and was watching her in silence. I was very much surprised, not only because she did not scold me, but because her whole face reflected some strangely un-repressed and bubbling satisfaction. When she had finished laying the table she went back into the kitchen and after a while returned with a dish.

" Now eat."

As a matter of fact I was very hungry. I got up and went to sit down, rather awkwardly, on the chair mother was urging me to take. There was a piece of meat and two eggs in the dish, an unusual dinner.

" It's too much," I said.

" Eat—it'll do you good—you need something," she answered. Her good temper was quite extraordinary, per-haps a little malicious but in no way hostile.

" Gino didn't think of giving you anything to eat, eh ? " she added after a while, almost without bitterness.

" We fell asleep," I answered, " and afterwards it was too late."

She said nothing but stood watching me while I ate. She always did this—served me and watched me while I ate, then went to eat on her own in the kitchen. For a long time now she had never eaten with me at the same table; and she always ate less, either my leavings or some other food not so good as mine. I was a delicate, precious object in her eyes, someone to be treated with every care, the only one she had ; and for some time now her flattering and admiring servility had ceased to astonish me. But this time her calm satisfaction gave me an uneasy sense of anxiety.

" You're angry with me because we made love—but he's promised to marry me. We'll get married very soon," I said after a while.

" I'm not angry with you," she replied immediately. " I was at the moment because I'd been waiting for you all evening and I was worried—but don't think about it any more—eat."

Her deceptively reassuring and evasive tone, like the tone people use in speaking to children when they don't want to answer their questions, made me even more suspicious.

" Why ? " I insisted. " Don't you believe he'll marry me ? "

"Yes, yes, I believe it, but go on, eat."

"No, you don't believe it."

"I do, don't worry—eat."

"I won't eat any more," I said, driven to the point of exasperation, "until you tell me the truth—why are you looking as pleased as Punch?"

"I'm not."

She picked up the empty dish and took it into the kitchen. I waited until she came back and then repeated: "Are you glad?"

She looked at me for a long time in silence, and then answered in a threatening, serious tone: "Yes, I'm glad."

"Why?"

"Because I'm quite sure now that Gino won't marry you, and he'll chuck you."

"He won't. He said he'll marry me."

"He won't marry you; he's had what he wanted already —he won't marry you and he'll chuck you."

"But why shouldn't he marry me? There must be some reason."

"He won't marry you and he'll leave you—he'll have some fun with you, but he won't give you even a pin, penniless as he is, and then he'll leave you."

"Is that what you're so glad about?"

"Of course! Because now I'm quite sure you won't marry each other."

"But what does it matter to you?" I exclaimed, hurt and irritated.

"If he wanted to marry you, he wouldn't have made love to you," she said suddenly. "I was engaged to your father for two years and until a few months before we were married he only gave me a kiss or two—he'll have a good time with you and then leave you, you can bet your boots on that! And I'm glad he'll leave you, because if he were to marry you he'd be the ruin of you."

I could not help admitting to myself that some of the things mother was saying were true, and my eyes filled with tears.

"I know what it is," I said, "you don't ever want me to have a family; you'd rather see me begin to lead a life like Angelina's!" Angelina was a girl in our neighbourhood who had begun openly to be a prostitute after two or three broken engagements.

"I want you to be comfortably off," she replied gruffly. And then, picking up the plates, she took them into the kitchen to wash them up. When I was alone I began to think over her words at some length. I compared them with Gino's promises and behaviour and I did not feel that mother could possibly be right. But her certainty, her calm, the cheerful way in which she looked ahead disconcerted me. Meanwhile she was washing up the plates in the kitchen. Then I heard her put them on the dresser and go into her bedroom. After a while I went to join her in bed, feeling tired and depressed.

Next day I wondered whether I ought to mention mother's doubts to Gino; but after much hesitation I decided not to. As a matter of fact, I was so afraid that Gino would leave me, as mother had insinuated, that I dared not mention her opinion to him in case I put the idea into his head. For the first time I realised that by giving herself to a man, a woman places herself in his hands and no longer has any means of forcing him to behave as she wishes. But I was still convinced that Gino would keep his promise; and his behaviour, as soon as I met him, strengthened me in this conviction.

Certainly I was looking forward to his many pettings and caresses; but I was afraid he would not mention marriage or would only speak of it in a general way. But instead, as soon as the car stopped in the usual avenue, Gino told me he had fixed the date for the wedding in five months' time, not a day longer. I was so delighted that I could not help bursting out, as though mother's ideas had been my own: "Do you know what I thought?—I thought that after what happened yesterday you would leave me."

"What on earth——!" he said with an offended look. "Do you take me for a cad?"

"No, but I know lots of men behave like that."

"Do you know," he continued, dwelling on my reply, "I might have been offended by what you imagined about me? Whatever do you think I am? Is that the way you love me?"

"I do love you," I said ingenuously. "But I was afraid you wouldn't love me any more."

"Have I shown you in any way so far that I don't love you?"

"No—but you never know."

"Look," he said suddenly, "you've put me into such a bad temper that I'm going to take you straight to the studio." And he made as if to start the car up at once.

Terrified, I threw my arms round his neck and begged him not to. "No, Gino, what's come over you? I was only talking—forget it," I pleaded.

"When you say certain things it means you think them—and if you think them it means you aren't in love."

"But I do love you."

"I don't love you, though!" he said sarcastically. "I've only been playing with you, as you say, with the idea of leaving you—funny thing you didn't notice it until now."

"But Gino," I exclaimed, bursting into tears, "why do you talk to me like this? What have I done to you?"

"Nothing," he said, starting up the car, "but now I'm going to take you to the studio."

The car started off, with Gino sitting bolt upright and serious at the wheel; and I let myself go entirely, sobbing as I watched the trees and milestones slipping past the window, and saw the outline of the first houses in the town on the horizon, beyond the fields. I imagined how mother would crow over our quarrel if ever she came to know of it, and found out that Gino, as she had prophesied, had left me, and driven by despair I opened the door and leaned out.

"Either you stop or I'll throw myself out of the car!" I cried.

He looked at me, the car slowed down, and then turning up a side-road he brought it to a standstill behind a little hillock topped by ruins. He switched off the engine, put on the brake and then turned to me.

"All right," he said impatiently, "say what you have to say—go on——"

Believing he really meant to leave me, I began to speak with a passion and ardour that seem both ridiculous and touching as I look back on them today. I explained how much I loved him; I even eached the point of telling him I did not care whether we were married or not, so long as I could continue to be his mistress. He listened to me, sullen-faced, shaking his head and repeating every now and again: "No, no—it's no use today—perhaps I'll have got over it by tomorrow." But when I said I would be content to be his mistress, he retorted firmly: "No, it's got to be marriage or nothing." We continued arguing in this way for some time and by his perverse logic he often drove me to despair and made me cry again. Then little by little he appeared to change his inflexible attitude; and at last, after I had kissed him and caressed him in vain, I seemed to have won a great victory when I persuaded him to leave the front seat of the car and make love to me on the back seat, in an uncomfortable posture which in my anxiety to please him was too quick for me and bitterly exhausting. I ought to have realised that by behaving like this I was not the victor in any sense but on the contrary was placing myself even more in his hands, if only because I showed I was ready to give myself to him not merely because I loved him but in order to coax and persuade him when words failed me—which is just what all women do when they love without being sure that their love is reciprocated. But I was completely blinded by the perfect behaviour his cunning had taught him to assume. He always did and said the very things he ought to do and say; and my lack of experience did not teach me that such perfection belonged rather to the conventional figure of a lover I carried in my own mind than to the man who stood in flesh and blood before me.

But the date of the wedding had been fixed and I immediately began to concentrate on my preparations. I decided with Gino that at first we would go to live with my mother. In addition to the living-room, kitchen and bedroom, there was a fourth room in the flat, which mother had never furnished for want of money. We kept useless, broken junk in it; and you can imagine what useless, broken junk was in a house like ours where everything seemed useless and broken. After discussing the matter endlessly, we fixed our minimum requirements—we would furnish this one room and I would make myself something of a trousseau. Mother and I were very poor; but I knew she had saved something and that she had scraped and saved for me, in order to be prepared, as she said, for any eventuality. What exactly this eventuality was supposed to be, could never be quite clear but it was certainly not my marriage to a poor man with an unsettled future. I went to mother, and said to her: "That money you've put by is for me, isn't it?"

"Yes."

"Very well, then, if you want me to be happy, give it to me now to furnish the room where Gino and I can live—if you've really saved it for me, now is the time to spend it."

I expected argument, discussion and a blunt refusal in the end. But instead mother welcomed the suggestion eagerly, showing once more the same sardonic calm that had so disconcerted me the evening after I had been to the villa with Gino.

"And isn't he going to give anything towards it?" was all she asked.

"Of course he is," I lied; "he's already said so—but I must give something too."

She was sewing by the window and had stopped her work in order to talk to me. "Go into my room," she said, "open the top drawer in the cupboard, where you'll find a cardboard box. My savings book is in it and also my bits of gold. Take both the book and the gold. You can have them."

The bits of gold did not amount to much—a ring, two ear-rings, a little chain. But ever since I was a baby that little treasure concealed among rags and only glimpsed in extraordinary circumstances, had aroused my imagination. Impulsively I hugged mother. She pushed me away, not roughly but coldly, saying: "Mind—I've got a needle—you'll prick yourself."

But I was not pleased. It was not enough to have got what I wanted and even more; I also wanted mother to share my happiness. "Mother," I said, "if you're only doing it to please me, I don't want it."

" Of course I'm not doing it to please him," she replied, taking up her sewing again.

" You don't really believe I'll marry Gino, do you ? " I asked her tenderly.

" I've never believed it, and today less than ever."

" Then why are you giving me the money to do the room up ? "

" That's not throwing money away. You'll always have the furniture and linen—money or goods, it's the same thing."

" Won't you come round the shops with me and choose the things ? "

" Good Lord ! " she shouted. " I don't want to have anything to do with it all ! Do what you like, go where you like, choose what you like—I don't want to know anything."

She was really quite unapproachable on the question of my marriage ; and I realised that her unreasonableness was not due so much to her idea of Gino's character, ways and means, as to her own way of looking at life. There was nothing spiteful in her attitude, but merely an utter rebellion against all accepted ideas. Other women hope eagerly that their daughters will get married ; mother hoped just as eagerly that I would not, and had done so for a long time now.

So there was a kind of silent wager on between mother and me : she wanted my marriage to fall through and me to become convinced of the excellence of her own plans, and I wanted the marriage to go on and mother to be persuaded that my way of looking at things was right. I therefore clung even more keenly to the hope of being married ; it was as though I was gambling my whole life desperately on a single card. I was bitterly conscious all the time that mother was watching my efforts and hoping to herself that they would fail.

I must mention here that Gino's perfect behaviour never broke down, not even during the preparations for our wedding. I had told mother that Gino had given me something towards the expenses ; but I had lied, because until then he had never hinted at such a thing. I was surprised and at the same time exaggeratedly delighted when Gino,

57

without my asking him, offered me a small sum of money to help me out. He apologised for the smallness of the sum by saying that he could not give more because he often had to send money home. Today, when I think over his offer, I can find no other explanation of it than that he gloried in being extremely faithful to the part he had decided to play. Perhaps this faithfulness had its origin in his remorse at having deceived me and his regret at not being in the position to marry me, as he really wanted to at that time. I hastened triumphantly to tell mother of Gino's offer. She contented herself with saying how small it was—not so little as to make him cut a poor figure, but just enough to throw dust in my eyes.

I was very happy during this period of my life. I used to meet Gino every day and we made love wherever we could —on the back seat of the car, or standing up in a dark corner in some deserted street, or in a field in the country, or at the villa again, in Gino's room. One night when he took me home we made love in the dark on the landing outside my front door, lying on the floor. Another time we made love at the flicks, huddled together at the back right underneath the projection-room. I liked joining the crowds in the trams and public places with him beside me, because people pushed me up against him and I took advantage of this to press my body to his. The whole time I wanted to squeeze his hand or ruffle his hair or caress him in some way, anywhere, even when others were present, and I almost tricked myself into believing it would not be noticed, as we always do when we give way to some irresistible passion. The act of love delighted me; perhaps I loved love itself even more than I did Gino, for I felt myself impelled to it, not only by my feelings for Gino but also by the pleasure I derived from it. Of course I did not imagine I could have had the same pleasure from any other man but Gino. But I realised in a dim way that the ardour, the skill, the passion I put into my caresses were not to be accounted for merely by the fact that we were in love. They had a character of their own, as if I had a gift for love-making which even without Gino would have shown itself sooner or later.

But the idea of my marriage took first place. In order to put some money by I helped mother all I could and often stayed up late. By day, if I was not posing in the studios, I went round the shops with Gino to choose our furniture and the material for my trousseau. I had little to spend and for this very reason I looked about all the more carefully and calculatingly. I made them bring out even things I knew I could not buy, and turned them over at my leisure, discussing their value and haggling over the price; afterwards I assumed a dissatisfied air or promised I would return, then left the shop without having purchased anything. I did not realise it, but these frantic expeditions to the shops, this exhausting handling of goods I could not afford, brought home to me the truth of what mother had said—that there was little happiness to be had without money. This was the second glimpse I had had, after my visit to the villa, of what a paradise of wealth could be, and since I felt excluded from it through no fault of my own, I could not help being rather embittered and upset. But I tried through love-making to forget the injustice, as I had done at the villa. Love was my only luxury, it alone made me feel I was the equal of many other women richer and more fortunate than I.

At last, after much discussion and shop-gazing, I decided on my extremely modest purchases; and I bought a suite of furniture in modern style, by hire-purchase because I had not enough money to pay for it outright—there was a double bed, a chest-of-drawers with a mirror, bedside-tables, chairs and a wardrobe. It was common stuff, cheap and roughly made, but no one would believe the passion I felt immediately for these few sticks of furniture. I had had the walls of the room whitewashed, the doors and windows varnished, the floor scraped, so that our room was a kind of island of cleanliness in the filthy sea surrounding us. The day the furniture came was certainly the happiest in my life. I could hardly believe that a clean, tidy, light room like that, smelling of whitewash and varnish, was my very own; and this incredulity was mixed with an endless feeling of satisfaction. Sometimes, when I was sure mother was not watching, I went into my room, sat down on the bare mattress and stayed there for hours looking round me. Still as a statue I gazed on my sticks of furniture as if I were unable to believe they were real and was afraid they might vanish into thin air at any moment, leaving the room empty. Or else I got up and lovingly dusted them and heightened their polish. I think that if I had really let myself give way to my feelings I would have kissed them. The curtainless window looked down on to a huge, dirty courtyard surrounded by other long, low houses like ours. It was like looking into the courtyard of a prison or hospital, but, entranced as I was, I no longer paid any attention to it, so to say; I felt as happy as if the room gave on to a beautiful garden filled with trees. I imagined the life Gino and I would lead there—how we would sleep, make love. I had in mind other things I intended to buy as soon as I could—a vase, a lamp, an ashtray over in the corner or some other ornament. My only regret was that I could not have a bathroom like the one I had seen at the villa, with white shining tiles and taps, or at least a new, clean one. I was determined to keep my room extremely tidy and clean. The visit to the villa had convinced me that a luxurious life began with tidiness and cleanliness.

CHAPTER FOUR

Somewhere about this time while I was still continuing to pose in the studios, I struck up a friendship with another model called Gisella. She was a tall, well-made girl, with a very white skin, dark curly hair, small, deep-sunk blue eyes and a large red mouth. Her character was quite the opposite of mine. She was quick-tempered, sharp and spiteful, and at the same time very practical-minded and on the make; and perhaps it took these very differences to unite us in friendship. I knew of no other work she had besides that of being a model, but she dressed far better than I could, and did not conceal the fact that she received presents and money from a man she introduced as her fiancé. I remember I envied her black jacket with collar and cuffs of astrakhan which she often wore that winter. Her fiancé's name was Riccardo; he was a tall, placid, heavily-built young man, with a face as smooth as an egg, which I thought very handsome at the time. He was always sleek and shining, smothered in brilliantine, and wore new suits; his father kept a shop for men's underwear and ties. He was simple to the point of silliness, good-natured, cheerful, and probably was quite a decent young fellow. He and Gisella were lovers and I do not think there was any talk of marriage between them as there was between Gino and me. But Gisella, like me, aimed at marriage, without setting too many hopes on it. As for Riccardo, I am sure the idea of marrying Gisella never crossed his mind. Gisella, who was very silly but far more experienced than I, had determined that she was going to look after me and put me wise about many things. In short, she had the same ideas as mother about life and happiness. All the same, in mother's case these ideas were expressed in a bitter and quarrelsome way, since they were the fruit of her disappointment and hardships, whereas in Gisella's case they were due to her obtuseness, allied with her stubborn self-sufficiency. Mother was content to formulate her ideas, you might say, as if the statement of her principles mattered more to her than the application of them; but Gisella, who had always thought in that way and did not even dream that anyone might think differently, was astonished that I did not behave as she did. Only when I showed my disapproval, because I really could not prevent myself, did her astonishment give way to rage and jealousy. She suddenly discovered that I not only refused her protection and advice, but that I might even be in a position to criticise her from the height of my own fond and disinterested aspirations, and it was then that she planned, perhaps unconsciously, to suppress my judgment of her by forcing me to become like herself as quickly as possible. Meanwhile she kept on telling me that I was a fool to keep myself pure; that it was a shame to see me going around so badly dressed, living such a hard life, and that, if I wanted to, thanks to my good looks, I could completely change my whole position. At last I told her of my relationship with Gino, because I felt ashamed to have her

61

think I knew nothing about men, but I warned her that we were engaged and were getting married shortly. She immediately asked me what Gino did and, on hearing that he was a chauffeur, she pulled a face. But she asked me, nevertheless, to introduce him to her.

Gisella was my best friend and Gino my fiancé : today I am able to judge them dispassionately, but at the time I was quite blind to their real characters. I have already said that I thought Gino was perfect : perhaps I realised that Gisella had some faults, but to offset them I believed she was warm-hearted and very fond of me and I attributed her anxiety for my future not to her spite at knowing I was innocent and her desire to corrupt me, but to an ill-advised and mistaken goodness. And so I introduced them to one another in some trepidation. In my naïveté I hoped they would be friends. The meeting took place in a milk-bar. Gisella maintained a guarded silence the whole time and was obviously hostile. It looked to me as though Gino, in the beginning, was putting himself out to charm Gisella, because as usual he began to talk about life, dwelling on his employers' wealth, as if he hoped to dazzle her with these descriptions and hide the poverty of his own life. But Gisella refused to unbend and maintained her hostile attitude. Then she remarked, I don't quite remember why : " You're lucky to have found Adriana."

" Why ? " asked Gino in astonishment.

" Because chauffeurs usually walk out with servant-girls."

I saw Gino change colour ; but he was not one to be taken by surprise. " You're quite right," he replied slowly, lowering his voice with the air of someone considering an obvious fact he had overlooked until that moment, " in fact, the chauffeur before me married the cook—naturally, why not ? I ought to have done the same. Chauffeurs marry maids and maids marry chauffeurs. Why on earth didn't it occur to me before ? Still," he added carelessly, " I'd have preferred Adriana to be a maid rather than a model. I don't mean," he added, raising his hand as if to ward off any objection Gisella might make, " I don't mean because of the profession itself—although to tell you the truth, I can't swallow this matter of getting undressed in front of men—but chiefly because being in that profession she's obliged to make certain acquaintances, friends who——" He shook his head and made a face. Then, offering her a packet of cigarettes: "Do you smoke?" he asked her.

Offhand Gisella did not know what answer to make, and contented herself with refusing the cigarette. Then she glanced at her watch. "Adriana, we've got to go, it's late," she said. It was late, as a matter of fact, and when we had said good-bye to Gino we left the milk-bar. When we were in the street Gisella said to me: "You're doing something perfectly crazy. I'd never marry a man like that."

"Didn't you like him?" I asked her anxiously.

"Not the least bit. First of all, you told me he was tall, but he's almost shorter than you—then, he doesn't look you straight in the face—he's not natural at all, and he speaks in such a fanciful way that you can tell a mile off that he isn't saying what he really thinks. Then all the airs and graces he gives himself, when he's only a chauffeur!"

"But I love him!" I protested.

"Very well. But he doesn't love you—and one day he'll leave you," she replied calmly.

I was taken aback by this forecast; it was so assured and so exactly like one of mother's. I can say today, that leaving aside her ill-will, Gisella had seen through Gino better in one hour than I did in many months. On his side, Gino's opinion of Gisella was also malicious, but I must confess that later on it turned out to be not ill-founded. To tell the truth, my fondness for both of them, together with my inexperience, rendered me blind: it's only too true that one's nearly always right in thinking badly of someone.

"That Gisella of yours," he said, "is what we'd call a pick-up girl where I come from."

I looked astonished. He explained. "A street-walker. She's got the manners and the character of one of them. She's stuck-up because she dresses well—but how does she pay for her dresses?"

"Her fiancé gives her them."

" A different fiancé every night, I'll bet . . . Now, listen. It's either me—or her."

" What do you mean ? "

" I mean you can do as you like—but if you want to go on seeing her, you can count me out. Either me or her."

I tried to dissuade him but was unsuccessful. He must have been hurt by Gisella's scornful contempt for him; but in his indignant dislike of her there must have been something of the same faithfulness to the part he was playing as my fiancé which had made him suggest contributing to the costs of our setting up house together. He was as perfect as ever in the expression of sentiments he did not feel. " My fiancée must have nothing to do with bad women," he repeated inflexibly. At last, being afraid our marriage would go up in smoke, I promised I would see nothing more of Gisella, although I knew in my own heart that I could not possibly keep my promise, because Gisella and I both worked at the same time and in the same studio.

From that day on, I continued to see her unknown to Gino. When we were together she seized every single opportunity of referring to my engagement in the most ironical and deprecating terms. I had been so naïve as to tell her all kinds of little things about my relations with Gino; whereupon she used these confidences to hurt me and to show me my present life and my future in a derisory light. Her friend, Riccardo, who seemed to make no distinction between Gisella and me, and looked on us both as easy prey and girls unworthy of respect, lent himself willingly to Gisella's game and doubled the dose of her mockery and cruelty. But he did it good-naturedly and stupidly because, as I have said, he was neither clever nor really bad. My engagement was only a joking matter for him—a pastime. But Gisella, who found my virtue a constant reproof and who wanted to have me become like herself in order to take away any right I had to condemn her, attacked me bitterly and insistently, trying in every way she could to mortify and humiliate me.

She touched me chiefly on my weakest point : my clothes. " Really," she used to say, " I feel quite ashamed of going about with you today." Or else : " Riccardo would never

64

let me go out in the kind of things you put on . . . would you, Riccardo? Love shows itself in these things, my dear!" I was ingenuous enough to rise immediately to this baiting. I began to lose my temper: I stood up for Gino and, though with less conviction, for my clothes, and always came off the worse, red in the face, and my eyes full of tears. One day Riccardo, moved to pity, said: "I'm going to give Adriana a present today. Come along, Adriana. I want to give you a handbag." But Gisella opposed him violently, saying: "No, Riccardo! No presents! She's got her Gino, let him give her presents." Riccardo, who had made the suggestion out of good nature, but without imagining the pleasure his gift would have caused me, yielded at once. And that very afternoon, out of pique, I went off to buy myself a handbag with my own money. Next day I met the two of them with my handbag under my arm, and told them it was a present from Gino. This was the only victory I had in all the deplorable squabbling. And it cost me very dear, because it was a nice bag and I gave a great deal for it.

When Gisella imagined that by dint of sarcasm, humiliation and sermonising she had worn me down sufficiently, she approached me and told me she had a suggestion to make. "But let me tell you the whole story," she added; "don't be your usual pig-headed self before hearing what I've got to say."

"Go on," I said.

"You know I'm fond of you," she began, "you're like a sister to me. With your good looks you could have everything you want. I hate seeing you go around so shamefully dressed that you look like a gutter-snipe. Now listen." She stopped and gazed at me in all solemnity. "There's a gentleman, a real gent, a very nice, decent fellow, who has seen you and takes an interest in you. He's married but his family lives in the provinces. He's a big pot in the police," she added in an undertone, "and if you want to get to know him I can introduce you. He's a very nice fellow, very serious, and you can be quite sure no one will ever get to know anything about it. He's very busy, anyway, and you'd only see him two or three times a month, if that. He doesn't

65

object to your continuing with Gino if you like—doesn't mind your marrying him, but in exchange he'll see to it that you live an easier life than you do now. What about it ? "

" Thank him very much," I said frankly, " but I can't accept."

" Why not ? " she asked. Her astonishment was sincere.

" Because I can't. I love Gino and if I accepted I couldn't look him in the face."

" Come off it ! When I tell you Gino needn't know anything about it ! "

" That's just why."

" To think," she said, speaking as if to herself, " that if someone had put me on to anything like this—— What am I to say to him ? That you'll think it over ? "

" No, no . . . tell him I can't accept."

" You're a fool," said Gisella, disappointed, " that's giving good luck a kick in the pants."

She said many other things of the same nature which I answered in the same way, and at last went away very dissatisfied.

I had refused the offer on an impulse, without thinking over what it implied. Then, when I was alone, I felt almost regretful : perhaps Gisella was right and that was the only way to obtain all the things I needed so desperately. But I drove the thought away at once, and clung even more closely to the idea of marriage and the regular if modest way of life I promised myself. The sacrifice I had apparently made now obliged me to get married at all costs, even more insistently than before.

But I could not repress a certain feeling of vanity and told mother of Gisella's offer. I thought I would be doing her a twofold pleasure ; I knew she was proud of my looks and still clung to her ideas : this offer flattered her pride and strengthened her convictions. But I was astonished at the state of agitation my tale threw her into. Her eyes kindled with a greedy light, her whole face flushed with pleasure.

" Who is it ? " she asked at last.

" A gentleman," I answered. I was ashamed to tell her it was someone in the police.

" Did she say he was very rich ? "

" Yes. Apparently he earns a lot."

She did not dare to say what she was obviously thinking, that I had been wrong to turn down the offer.

" He's seen you and takes an interest in you ? Why don't you let her introduce him to you ? "

" What's the point, since I don't want him ? "

" Pity he's already married."

" I wouldn't want to meet him even if he wasn't."

" There are so many ways of going about things," said mother. " He's rich, he likes you, one thing leads to another—he could help you, without asking for anything in return."

"No, no," I replied, " those people don't give anything for nothing."

" You never know."

" No, no," I repeated.

" It doesn't matter," said mother, shaking her head. " Still, Gisella's a jolly nice girl and is really fond of you. Any other girl would be jealous and wouldn't have mentioned it to you. You can see she's a real friend."

After my refusal Gisella did not talk of her gentleman friend any more, and she even stopped teasing me about my engagement, to my surprise. I continued to see her and Riccardo on the sly. But I mentioned her to Gino more than once in the hope that they would make it up, because I did not like these underhand dealings. But he never even allowed me to reach the end of what I was saying, and only repeated his expressions of hatred and swore that if ever he found out I was seeing her everything would be over between us. He meant what he said. And I had an idea that he would not have been sorry of an excuse to break off the engagement. I told mother of Gino's dislike for Gisella and she said, almost without spite : " He doesn't want you to see her because he's afraid you'll compare the rags you go about in with the clothes her fiancé gives her."

" No, he says it's because Gisella's a bad lot."

" He's a bad lot ! I wish he'd find out you're seeing Gisella and really would break off the engagement."

I was terrified. "But mother!" I exclaimed. "You'd never go and tell him!"

"No, no," she replied hastily, almost bitterly. "It's your business, and I've got nothing to do with it."

"If you were to tell him," I said passionately, "it would be the last you'd ever see of me."

It was St. Martin's summer and the days were mild and clear. One day Gisella told me she and Riccardo and a friend of his had planned an outing by car. They needed another woman to make up the foursome and had thought of me. I was delighted to accept because at that time I was always on the look-out for any pleasure to lighten the misery of my days. I told Gino I had to pose for a few extra hours; and in the morning, fairly early, went to the appointment on the other side of Ponte Milvio. The car was already waiting and when I drew near, Gisella and Riccardo, who were sitting in front, kept their places, but Riccardo's friend jumped out and came to meet me. He was young, of medium height, bald, with a sallow face, large, dark eyes, an aquiline nose and a wide mouth whose corners turned up as if he were smiling. He was smartly but quietly dressed, quite differently from Riccardo, with a dark grey jacket and lighter grey trousers, a starched collar and black tie with a pearl tie-pin. He had a kind voice and his eyes looked kind, too, but at the same time sad and disillusioned. He was very polite and even ceremonious. Gisella introduced him to me as Stefano Astarita, and I immediately felt sure that the gentleman whose gallant suggestions she had conveyed to me must be this man. But I was not sorry to meet him, because his suggestions had not really been offensive and from a certain point of view were even flattering. I gave him my hand and he kissed it with a strange sense of devotion, an almost painful intensity. Then I got into the car, he sat beside me and we set off.

While the car sped along the bare, sunny road between parched fields, we hardly spoke. I was happy at being in a car, happy over the trip, happy at the fresh air which caressed my cheeks, and never grew tired of looking at the country. It was only the second or third time in my life that I had been out for a trip by car and I was almost afraid of missing something. I opened my eyes and tried to see as many things as possible, haystacks, farmhouses, trees, fields, hills, woods, thinking all the time that months, perhaps years, would pass before I could go on another such trip, and that I ought to get all the details by heart so that I would preserve a perfect memory of it whenever I wanted to recall it. But Astarita, who was sitting stiffly beside me at a little distance, seemed to have eyes for me alone. His sad, longing gaze never left my face and figure, and his look had the effect on me of a finger touching me here and there. I do not say that this attention annoyed me, but it did embarrass me. Gradually I felt obliged to take some notice of him and talk to him. He sat with his hands on his knees and was wearing a wedding-ring and another with a diamond on one hand.

"What a lovely ring!" I exclaimed clumsily.

He lowered his eyes and looked at the ring without moving his hand. "It was my father's. I took it off him when he died," he said.

"Oh!" I said, as if to apologise. And added, pointing to the wedding-ring: "Are you married?"

"Indeed I am," he replied with grim complacency. "I've got a wife—children—everything."

"Is your wife beautiful?" I asked shyly.

"Not as beautiful as you," he replied without smiling, in a very low, emphatic voice, as if he were stating some important truth. And, with the hand on which he wore the ring, he tried to take my hand, but I pulled mine away at once.

"Do you live with her?" I asked at random.

"No," he answered. "She's living in ———"—and he mentioned a far-off provincial town—"and I'm living here—alone. I hope you'll come to visit me."

I pretended I had not heard the information he had given me in a tragic and almost convulsive fashion.

"Why? Don't you like living with your wife?" I asked.

"We are legally separated," he said, pulling a face. "I was only a boy when I got married. The marriage was arranged by my mother. You know how they do these things—a girl of good family, with a handsome dowry. The parents fix everything up and it's the children who have to get married.—Live with my wife? Would you live with a woman like this?" He took his wallet from his pocket, opened it and handed me a photograph. I saw two dark, pale children, looking like twins, dressed in white. A little dark, pale woman, with close-set eyes like an owl and a malicious expression, stood behind them placing her hands on their shoulders. I returned it to him. He put it away in his wallet.

"I'd like to live with you," he sighed.

"You don't know me at all," I said, disconcerted by his attitude of obsession.

"I know you very well, though!—I've been following you for a month. I know all about you."

He was seated a little way off as he addressed me respectfully, but the whole time he was speaking the depth of his feelings almost made his eyes roll.

"I'm engaged," I said.

"Gisella told me," he said in a strangled voice. "Don't let's talk about your fiancé. What does he matter?" He made a brief, jerky movement of feigned indifference with his hand.

"He matters a lot to me," I replied.

He looked at me. "I like you immensely."

"I noticed that."

"I like you immensely," he repeated; "perhaps you don't realise how much."

He talked like someone out of his mind. But the fact that he sat apart from me and made no further attempt to take my hand reassured me. "There's no harm in your liking me," I said.

"Do you like me?"

"No."

"I'm rich," he said contorting his features into a grimace; "I'm rich enough to make you happy—if you come to see me you won't regret it."

"I don't need your money," I replied calmly, almost kindly.

70

He did not seem to have heard.

"You're very lovely," he said, looking at me.

"Thanks."

"Your eyes are beautiful."

"Do you think so?"

"Yes—so's your mouth. I want to kiss it."

"Why do you say these things to me?"

"I want to kiss all of you—every bit."

"Why do you speak to me like this?" I protested. "It isn't right. I'm engaged and going to be married in a couple of months."

"Please forgive me," he said. "But I get such pleasure out of saying these things—imagine I'm not speaking to you."

"Is Viterbo far now?" I asked in order to change the subject.

"We're nearly there. We'll have a meal at Viterbo. Promise you'll sit beside me at lunch."

I began to laugh because this intense obsession of his was very flattering to me. "All right," I said.

"Sit beside me as you are doing now," he continued. "The scent of you is enough for me."

"I haven't any scent."

"I'll make you a present of some," he said.

We had reached Viterbo by now and the car slowed down as we entered the town. During the whole trip Gisella and Riccardo, who were sitting in front of us, had not said a word. But as we began to thread our way slowly along the crowded main street Gisella turned round.

"How are you two getting along? Do you think I didn't see you?" she asked.

Astarita said nothing. "You can't have seen anything. We were only talking," I protested.

"Come off it!" she said. I was utterly astonished by Gisella's behaviour and also rather annoyed by Astarita's persistent silence.

"But if I tell you——" I began.

"Come off it!" she repeated. "You needn't get the wind up—we shan't give you away to Gino."

Meanwhile we had reached the square, so we got out of the car and began to walk along the Corso among the crowd dressed up in their Sunday best under the mild and brilliant October sun. Astarita did not leave my side for one moment; he was still serious, gloomy in fact, carried his head stiffly above his high collar and kept one hand in his pocket, the other dangling at his side. He looked as though he were my keeper rather than my companion. Gisella, on the contrary, was laughing and joking with Riccardo and many people turned round to stare at us. We went into a confectioner's and took a vermouth standing at the bar. I suddenly noticed Astarita mumbling something threateningly and asked him what was the matter.

"There's an idiot over there by the door staring at you," he said heatedly.

I turned round and saw a slim, fair young man standing in the doorway of the café looking at me. "Why not?" I said cheerfully. "Suppose he does look at me?"

"It wouldn't take much to make me go over and hit him in the face."

"If you do I'll never look at you again and I won't say a single word more to you," I said, feeling rather annoyed. "You've no right to interfere—you're nothing to do with me."

He said nothing and went over to the cash-desk to pay for the drinks. We left the café and continued our walk along the Corso. The sun, the noise and the movement of the crowd, all those healthy, rosy faces of the country people, cheered me up. When we reached an isolated little square at the end of one of the roads crossing the Corso I suddenly said: "There, look!—if only I had a little house like that one over there I'd be delighted to live here," and I pointed to a simple little two-storeyed house in front of a church.

"God forbid!" said Gisella. "Fancy living in the provinces—in Viterbo, what's more! I wouldn't, even if I was smothered in gold."

"You'd soon be fed up with it, Adriana," remarked Riccardo. "When anyone's used to living in a big town they can't settle down in the provinces."

" You're quite mistaken," I said. " I'd be delighted to live here with a man who loved me—have four clean little rooms, an arbour, four windows—I wouldn't want for anything more." I was quite sincere in what I said because I imagined myself living in that little house in Viterbo with Gino. " What do you think ? " I asked, turning to Astarita.

" I'd stay with you," he replied in an undertone, trying to avoid being overheard by the others.

" The trouble with you, Adriana," said Gisella, " is that you don't aim high enough. Those who ask too little of life get nothing."

" But I don't want anything," I objected.

" You want to marry Gino, though," said Riccardo.

" Yes, that I do want."

It was late by now, the Corso was emptying itself and we entered the restaurant. The ground-floor room was packed, mostly with peasants in their Sunday best who had come to Viterbo for the market. Gisella turned up her nose, saying it stank enough to take your breath away and asked the manager if we could go up to the second floor to eat. He said we could and led the way into a long, narrow room with only one window that gave on to a side-street. He opened the shutters and closed the windows, then spread a cloth on the rustic table that filled most of the room. I remember the walls were covered with a faded wallpaper, torn in places, with a pattern of flowers and birds. Besides the table there was only a little glass-fronted sideboard full of dishes.

Meanwhile Gisella was walking round the room examining everything, even looking through the window that gave on to the side-street. At last she pushed open a door that lead apparently into another room and, after having peeped in, she turned towards the proprietor and asked him in a tone of assumed carelessness what room it was.

" It's a bedroom," he said, " if any of you want to rest a bit after lunch——"

" We'll have a rest, shall we, Gisella ? " said Riccardo with his silly giggle. But Gisella pretended she had not heard, and after having peeped once more into the room she carefully pulled the door to again but did not quite shut it.

The cosy little dining-room had cheered me up, and therefore I thought no more about the half-shut door and a glance of understanding that I imagined had passed between Gisella and Astarita. We sat down to table and I had Astarita beside me as I had promised, but he did not seem to notice, he was so absorbed he could not even speak. After a while the proprietor came back with hors-d'œuvres and wine, and I was so hungry I flung myself on the food and made the others laugh at me. Gisella took the opportunity to begin her usual teasing about my marriage.

"Go on, eat," she said, "you'll never get so much to eat with Gino, nor such good stuff."

"Why?" I asked. "Gino'll earn money."

"You bet, and you'll eat beans every day!"

"Beans are all right," laughed Riccardo; "in fact I'm going to order some at once."

"You're a fool, Adriana," went on Gisella; "you need a man with something behind him, a decent man, who does things properly, cares about you and doesn't oblige you to go without things, and makes it possible for you to set off your good looks. And instead of that you go and fix things up with Gino."

I kept a stubborn silence, my head bent over my plate while I went on eating. Riccardo laughed. "In Adriana's place I wouldn't give up anything," he said, "neither Gino, since she likes him so much, nor the seriously-intentioned fellow. I'd take both—and quite possibly Gino wouldn't have anything to say against the arrangement."

"He would," I said hastily, "if he even knew I'd gone this trip with you today he'd break off the engagement."

"Why?" asked Gisella, on her high horse.

"Because he doesn't want me to see anything of you."

"The dirty, penniless, ignorant good-for-nothing!" said Gisella furiously. "I'd like to prove it . . . to go and say to him: 'Adriana still goes on seeing me; she went out with me all day today. So now break it off!'"

"No, please!" I begged her, terrified. "Don't do it——"

"It'd be the best thing that could happen to you."

74

"Perhaps. But don't do it," I besought her again. "If you're fond of me, don't do it."

During this conversation Astarita said nothing and ate hardly a mouthful. He still kept his eyes on me the whole time, with an exaggerated, significant, desperate expression I found extremely embarrassing. I wanted to tell him not to stare at me like that, but I was afraid Gisella and Riccardo would make fun of me. For the same reason I did not dare to protest when Astarita seized the opportunity to squeeze my left hand, which I had placed on the bench where we were sitting, and obliged me to go on eating with one hand only. I ought to have protested because Gisella suddenly burst out laughing. "She's quite true to Gino in what she says ! But when it comes to deeds——! Do you think I can't see you and Astarita holding hands under the table ? "

I blushed awkwardly and tried to free my hand. But Astarita kept tight hold of it.

"Let them alone," said Riccardo. "What's the harm ? If they hold hands, let us do the same."

"I was joking," said Gisella ; "I don't mind, I'm glad."

When we had eaten our macaroni, we were kept waiting for the next course. Gisella and Riccardo kept on laughing and joking and drinking in the meantime and made me drink too. It was good red wine, very strong, and soon went to my head. I liked the warm sharp taste of it and in my state of intoxication did not feel at all drunk but able to go on drinking indefinitely. Astarita, serious and absorbed, went on holding my hand, and I now let him. I told myself I could at least let him hold my hand, after all. There was an oleograph stuck over the door, of a man and woman dressed in the fashion of fifty years ago, who were embracing one another in an artificial, awkward way on a rose-covered balcony. Gisella noticed it and said she could not imagine how they could possibly kiss one another in that position. "Let's try," she said to Riccardo, " let's see if we can copy them."

Riccardo stood up, laughing, and assumed the attitude of the man in the oleograph, while Gisella, giggling too, leant against the table in the same position as the woman in the picture against the rose-bedecked side of the balcony. With a tremendous effort they managed to bring their lips together ; but, almost at the very moment, they lost their balance and toppled over together on to the table.

" Now it's your turn ! " said Gisella, excited by the fun.

" Why ? " I asked, scared. " What's it got to do with me ? "

" Go on, you must have a try."

I felt Astarita put his arm round my waist and tried to free myself. " I don't want to," I said.

" Oh, what a spoilsport you are ! " said Gisella. " It's only a joke."

" I don't want to."

Riccardo was laughing and urging on Astarita to make me kiss him. " If you don't kiss her, Astarita, I'll never look you in the face again." But Astarita was in earnest and almost frightened me : for him, this was obviously something more than a joke.

" Let me alone," I said, turning from him.

He looked at me, then glanced at Gisella with a query in his eyes, as if he expected her to egg him on. " Go on, Astarita ! " exclaimed Gisella. She seemed far more keen than he was, in a way I could vaguely guess was merciless and cruel.

Astarita held me still more tightly by the waist, pulling me towards him. Now it was no longer a joke and he wanted to kiss me at all costs. Without saying a word, I tried to free myself from his grasp, but he was very strong, and the more I pushed with my hands against his chest, the closer could I feel his face little by little approaching mine. But perhaps he would not have succeeded in kissing me if Gisella had not come to his aid. Suddenly, with a triumphant squeal, she got up, ran behind me, grasped my arms and pulled them backwards. I did not see her but I felt her dogged determination in the way her nails buried themselves in my flesh and in her voice which kept on repeating, between bursts of laughter, in an excited, cruel and jerky way : " Quick, quick, Astarita ! Now's your chance ! " Astarita was now upon me : I did my best to turn my face away, the only movement I could make, but with one hand he took hold of my chin and forced my face towards his, then he kissed me hard and long on my mouth.

" There, that's that ! " said Gisella triumphantly, and went back to her place delighted.

Astarita let go of me. " I'll never come out with the lot of you again," I said, feeling annoyed and hurt.

" Oh, Adriana ! " said Riccardo, making fun of me, " and all for a single kiss ! "

" Astarita's covered in lipstick ! " exclaimed Gisella, ecstatically. " What would Gino say if he came in now ? "

Astarita's mouth really was covered with my lipstick, and even to me he looked ridiculous with a scarlet streak like that across his gloomy, sallow face. " Come on," said Gisella, " make it up, you two—rub off his lipstick with your handkerchief. Whatever will the waiter think, when he comes in, if you don't ? "

I had to put a good face on the matter, and wetting a corner of my handkerchief with my tongue I gradually wiped the rouge off Astarita's sullen face. I was wrong, though, in showing how easy-going I was, because immediately, as soon as I had put my handkerchief away, he put his arm round my waist. " Let go," I said.

" Come on, Adriana ! "

" What difference does it make ? " said Gisella. " If he likes it—and it doesn't do you any harm. He's kissed you anyway. Let him do as he likes."

So I yielded once again and we stayed beside one another, his arm round my waist while I sat there stiffly and unwillingly. The waiter came in with the second course. While we were eating my ill-humour faded, although Astarita held me close. The food was very good and, without noticing, I drank all the wine Gisella kept on pouring out for me. After the second course we had fruit and sweets. It was an excellent sweet ; I wasn't used to things like that and therefore, when Astarita offered me his share I could not say no, and ate that too. Gisella, who had also drunk a great deal, began to coax Riccardo in all sorts of ways, putting little quarters of tangerines into his mouth and giving him a kiss with each one. I felt pleasantly tipsy. And

77

Astarita's arm round my waist no longer troubled me. Gisella got up, more and more restless and excited every moment, and went to sit on Riccardo's knee. I could not help laughing when I heard Riccardo pretend to cry out in pain as if Gisella's weight were crushing him. All of a sudden, Astarita, who had not moved until then, content to have one arm round my waist, began to kiss me breathlessly on my neck, bosom and cheeks. I did not protest this time, first because I was too tipsy to struggle, and then because he seemed to be kissing another person, so little did I participate in his outburst, but kept as still and as stiff as a statue. In my state of intoxication, I had the impression that I was standing outside myself, in some corner of the room, looking on indifferently as a mere curious spectator at Astarita's wild passion. But the others took my indifference for love, and Gisella called out : " That's right, Adriana—that's the way ! "

I wanted to reply but changed my mind, I don't know why, and raising my glass full of wine I said clearly and resonantly : " I'm tight ! " and emptied it at one breath. I believe the others clapped their hands. But Astarita stopped kissing me, and looking fixedly at me, said under his breath : " Let's go into the other room."

I followed his eyes and saw he was looking at the half-open door of the next room. I imagined he must be drunk, too, and nodded my refusal, but gently, almost flirtatiously.

" Let's go into the next room," he repeated like a man in his sleep.

I noticed Gisella and Riccardo had stopped laughing and chatting and were watching us.

" Come on ! " said Gisella. " It's all right ! What are you waiting for ? "

I sobered immediately. I really was drunk, but not so drunk as to be unaware of the danger threatening me. " I don't want to," I said. And I stood up.

Astarita got up, too, and seizing me by one arm tried to drag me towards the door. The other two began to egg him on again. " Go on, Astarita ! " they urged.

Astarita half-dragged me as far as the door, although I struggled. Then I freed myself with a sudden jerk and ran

78

to the door that led out on to the stairway. But Gisella was quicker than I. "No, you don't, dearie!" she cried. She leapt up from Riccardo's knees and ran over to lock the door, before I could get there, then took the key out.

"I don't want to," I repeated, terrified, standing beside the table.

"What harm can it do you?" asked Riccardo.

"Idiot!" said Gisella harshly, pushing me towards Astarita. "Such a fuss—go along, now."

I realised that despite her cruelty and insistence Gisella did not understand what she was doing. The plot she had laid for me must have seemed to her most delightfully clever and entertaining. I was also amazed at the gay indifference of Riccardo, whom I knew to be kindly and incapable of doing anything he thought wicked.

"I don't want to," I repeated.

"Why not?" asked Riccardo. "There's no harm in it."

Gisella went on pushing me eagerly and excitedly.

"I didn't think you were so silly," she said. "Go on, Adriana, what are you waiting for?"

Up till now Astarita had not said a word, he stood motionless by the bedroom door, gazing at me. Then I saw him open his mouth as if to speak. "Come on," he said, speaking slowly and thickly, as though the words had a sticky consistency and he found it difficult to spit them out. "Otherwise I'll tell Gino you came out with us today and let me make love to you."

I understood at once that he really would carry out his threat. You may well doubt words themselves, but there is often no mistaking the tone of voice in which they are uttered. He would certainly have told Gino, and that would have meant the end for me before I had really begun. Thinking it over today, I suppose I could have withstood him. If I had shouted, if I had struggled violently, I would have persuaded him that his blackmailing was as ineffective as his revenge. But perhaps it would have been no good, because his desire for me was stronger than my disgust. At the time, of course, I felt entirely overcome, and thought more of avoiding a scandal than of opposing him. I found myself plunged into this situation quite unprepared for it, with my mind full of plans for the future which I desired to carry out at all costs. What happened to me at this time in such a crude way, must, I think, happen to all those who have as simple, law-abiding, innocent ambitions as I have. The world gets hold of us through our ambitions and sooner or later forces us to pay a high and painful price, and only outcasts and people who have renounced everything can ever hope to be let off this payment.

But at the very moment that I accepted my fate, I experienced a sharp and lucid sensation of pain. A flash of intuition seemed to light up the whole future path of my life, as a rule so dark and tortuous, and reveal it straight and clear before my eyes, and showed me in that single moment what I would lose in exchange for Astarita's silence. My eyes filled with tears and I began to cry, putting my arm over my face. I realised I was weeping from utter resignation and not in rebellion, and that, in fact, my legs were taking me towards Astarita in the midst of my tears. Gisella pushed me by the arm, repeating : " What are you crying for ? Anyone would think it was the first time ! " I heard Riccardo laugh ; and I felt, without seeing him, that Astarita's eyes were upon me as I came slowly towards him in tears. Then I felt him put an arm round my waist and the door of the room closed behind me.

I did not want to see anything, even feeling seemed too much. And so I kept my arm obstinately across my eyes although Astarita tried to draw it away. I suppose he wanted to behave like all lovers on such occasions, that is, to win me over gradually and almost unconsciously to his desires. But my obstinate refusal to take my arm away from my face obliged him to be more brutal and hurried than he wanted. So, after he had made me sit on the edge of the bed and had tried in vain to coax me with caresses, he pushed me back against the cushions and threw himself on me. My whole body from the waist down was as heavy and inert as lead, and no embrace was ever accepted with greater submission and with less participation. But I stopped crying almost immediately and, as soon as he lay breathless on my bosom, I removed my arm from my face and stared into the darkness.

I am convinced that at that moment Astarita loved me as much as a man can love a woman, and far more than Gino did. I remember that he could not stop running his hand again and again over my forehead and cheeks with a convulsive, passionate movement, trembling all over and murmuring words of love. But my eyes were dry and wide open, and my head, cleared now of the wine-fumes, was filled with an icy, eddying clarity. I let Astarita caress me and talk to me while I followed my own thoughts. Once more I saw my own bedroom, as I had arranged it, with the new furniture I had not quite finished paying for, and felt a kind of bitter consolation. I told myself that nothing now could prevent my marrying and living the kind of life I wanted. But at the same time I felt my spirit was entirely changed and that a new certainty and decision had replaced my once fresh and ingenuous hopes. I suddenly felt much stronger, although it was a tragic strength and shorn of love.

"It's time to go back into the other room," I said at last, speaking for the first time since we had entered the bedroom.

"Are you cross with me ?" he immediately asked in a low voice.

"No."

"Do you hate me ?"

"No."

"I love you so much," he murmured. And began once more tempestuously to cover my face and neck with rapid, passionate kisses. I let him have his way and then said : "Yes, but we must go."

"You're right," he answered. He broke away from me and began, as far as I could tell, to get dressed in the dark. I tidied myself as best I could, got up, and turned on the light over the bed. In that yellow light the room looked just as I had imagined from its stuffy, lavender-scented smell : the ceiling was low, the beams were whitewashed, the walls covered with French wallpaper, the furniture old and heavy. A marble-topped wash-hand-stand stood in one corner, and on it two jugs and basins with a green and pink flower pattern, and a large mirror in a gold frame. I walked over to the wash-hand-stand, poured a little water into the basin and, dipping the end of the towel in it, I sponged my lips which Astarita had bruised with his kisses, and my eyes still red from crying. The mirror threw back from its scratched and coruscating surface a painful image of myself, and for a moment I looked at it spellbound, my heart filled with pity and wonder. Then I pulled myself together, tidied my hair with my hands to the best of my ability and turned towards Astarita. He was waiting for me by the door, and as soon as he saw I was ready he opened it, avoiding my eyes and keeping his back turned to me. I switched off the light and followed him.

We were greeted cheerfully by Gisella and Riccardo who had been carrying on in the same gay, careless manner as when we had left them. They had failed to understand how upset I had been before, and now were just as incapable of understanding my present serenity.

"You're a nice one to play the innocent! You didn't want to, didn't want to, but as far as I can see you settled down to it very soon and very well," Gisella cried out. "In any case, if you like it, it's all right by me. . . . But it wasn't worth while kicking up such a fuss about it."

I looked at her; it seemed to me extraordinarily unfair that she, who had urged me to yield and had even held my arms so that Astarita could kiss me more easily, should now be the one to reproach me for my complacency.

"You aren't very logical, Gisella," remarked Riccardo with his rough common sense. "First you persuade her— and now you seem to be telling her she oughtn't to have done it."

"Of course," replied Gisella harshly, "if she didn't want to, she's been very wrong. If I didn't want to myself, nothing, not even force, could make me. But she wanted to," she added, looking at me in a disgusted and dissatisfied way, "she wanted to. And how!—I saw them in the car while we were coming to Viterbo. That's why she ought not to have kicked up such a fuss, that's what I say."

I did not utter a word, being almost lost in admiration of the refinement of her pitiless and unwitting cruelty. Astarita came near and tried clumsily to take my hand. But I pushed

82

him away and went to sit down at the end of the table. " Look at Astarita ! " exclaimed Riccardo. " He looks as if he's just come away from a funeral ! "

As a matter of fact, Astarita, with all his gloom and solemnity, seemed to understand me better than the others did. " You make a joke of everything," he said.

" Well, do you think we ought to burst into tears ? " cried Gisella. " Now you two just sit and twiddle your thumbs and wait, as we did. It's our turn now. Come on, Riccardo ! "

" Be careful," said Riccardo, getting up to follow her. He was obviously drunk and did not know himself what we had to be careful about.

" Come along, do ! "

So they left the room and Astarita and I were alone. I sat at one end of the table and he at the other. A ray of sunshine came in through the window and shone brightly on the untidy crockery, the fruit parings, half-empty glasses and dirty knives and forks. But Astarita's expression remained distressed and overcast, although the sun was shining full on his face. His desire had been appeased, but all the same the look of anguished intensity he had displayed at the beginning of our relationship was still present in his eyes. I felt sorry for him then, despite the harm he had done me. I realised he had been wretched before having me and now, when it was over, he was no less wretched. He had suffered before because he had wanted me, he suffered now because I did not return his love. But pity is love's worst enemy; if I had hated him he might have hoped that one day I would come to love him. But I did not hate him and since, as I have said, I felt sorry for him, I was sure I would never feel anything more towards him than an unwelcoming and frigid disgust.

We sat there a long time in the sunny room, waiting for Gisella and Riccardo to return. Astarita chain-smoked and he looked at me all the time through the clouds of smoke that enveloped him, with the eloquent gaze of a man who wants to say something but dare not. I was sitting sideways at the table, my legs crossed, and the only desire in my heart was to get away. I did not feel tired, nor ashamed of myself; if I wanted anything at all it was to be alone and think over what had happened, at my leisure. The longing I had to be away was side-tracked every now and again by silly things I noticed—the pearl in Astarita's tie-pin, the pattern on the wallpaper, a fly walking round the edge of a glass, a little drop of tomato-sauce that had splashed on to my blouse while I was eating, and I was annoyed with myself at being unable to think of anything more important. But this petty-mindedness was of some use when Astarita, after a long silence, overcame his shyness and asked me, in a choking voice: "What are you thinking about?" I thought for a moment and then said simply: "One of my nails is broken and I can't think when or how I did it." It was true. But he looked at me bitterly and incredulously and from that moment definitely gave up any further attempt to talk to me.

At last, in God's good time, Gisella and Riccardo came back, looking a little worn out, but as cheerful and easygoing as before. They were surprised to find us so silent and solemn; but it was late now and love-making had made them calmer, it had quite a different effect upon them from what it had on Astarita. Gisella had even become affectionate to me, and no longer showed the cruelty and excitement she had before and after Astarita's blackmailing coup. I found myself almost believing his blackmailing had contributed a new kind of sensual thrill to her dull relationship with Riccardo. She put her arm round my waist as we went downstairs. "Why are you looking so upset?" she whispered. "If you're worried about Gino, you needn't be—Riccardo and I won't mention it to a soul."

"I'm tired," I lied. I'm incapable of sulking, and her arm round my waist was enough to make my resentment fade.

"So am I," she answered. "I had the wind blowing in my face all the way here." A moment after, as we waited on the doorstep of the restaurant while the two men went towards the car, she spoke again.

"You aren't cross with me because of what happened?"

"Not at all," I answered. "What's it got to do with you?" Having got out of her little plot all the different kinds of satisfaction she could, she also wanted to be sure

84

that I was not peeved with her. I felt I understood her only too well. And for this reason, because I was afraid she might realise I understood her and be angry, I was anxious to dispel all her doubts and to make a show of affection towards her. I turned to her and kissed her on the cheek, saying : " Why should I be cross with you ? You always said I ought to give up Gino and take Astarita."

" That's it," she agreed emphatically, " I still think so. But I'm afraid you'll never forgive me——"

She seemed anxious ; and I, as if by some curious infection, was even more anxious than she was herself, from fear that she might discover what I really felt.

" Obviously you don't really know me," I answered simply. " I know you want me to leave Gino because you're fond of me and you're sorry I don't do the best I can for myself. I might even say," I added, telling one more lie, " that perhaps you're right."

She was evidently reassured and, taking me by my arm, said in conversational, but at the same time measured and confidential tones : " You must understand what I mean. Astarita or anyone else would do . . . but not Gino ! If you knew how it upsets me to see a lovely girl like you throwing yourself away ! Ask Riccardo. I keep on at him all day long about you." She was chatting to me now without any more embarrassment, as she usually did, and I was careful to agree with her whatever she said. And so we reached the car. We took the places we had had coming and the car started up.

None of us spoke during the return journey. Astarita went on gazing at me, but with a look of humiliation rather than of desire. But by now his gaze caused me no embarrassment and I felt no wish, as I had coming, to speak to him and be pleasant to him. I breathed in the air that blew on my face from the open window and automatically counted the milestones that measured the distance from Rome. But at a certain moment I felt Astarita's hand brush against mine and noticed he was trying to put something into it—a piece of paper, perhaps. I imagined that he had scribbled something to me because he did not dare to address me, but when

I glanced down I saw that it was a banknote folded in four.

He looked at me fixedly while he tried to make me close my fingers over the note, and for a moment I was tempted to throw it in his face. But at the same time it occurred to me that such behaviour would have been quite superficial, inspired by a spirit of imitation rather than by a deep impulse coming from the heart. The feeling I experienced at that moment bewildered me and, no matter how or when I have received money from men, I have never again experienced it so clearly and so intensely: a feeling of complicity and sensual conspiracy such as none of his caresses in the restaurant bedroom had been able to arouse in me. It was a feeling of inevitable subjection which showed me in a flash an aspect of my own nature I had ignored until then. I knew, of course, that I ought to refuse the money; but at the same time I wanted to accept it. And not so much from greed, as from the new kind of pleasure which this offering had afforded me.

But although I had decided to accept it, I made a movement as if my intention were to push back the note; I did this from instinct, with no shadow of calculation. Astarita insisted, still gazing into my eyes, and then I slipped the note from my right hand into my left. I felt strangely thrilled, my face was burning and my breathing laboured. If Astarita had been capable of guessing my feelings at that moment he might have imagined I loved him. Nothing could have been further from the truth; it was only the money and the way it was earned and the way it was given me which filled my mind. I felt Astarita take my hand and I let him kiss it, then pulled it away. We did not look at one another again until we reached Rome.

Once back in town, we parted from each other almost as if we had been fugitives, as if each of us knew we had been committing some crime and only wanted to get away and hide. As a matter of fact, something very like a crime had been committed that day, by all of us—by Riccardo through stupidity, by Gisella through envy, by Astarita through lust, and by me through inexperience. Gisella made a date with me for the following day to go and pose, Riccardo said

86

good-night, Astarita could only press my hand silently, still as earnest and distressed as ever. They took me as far as my own door. Despite my tiredness and remorse, I remember I could not help a feeling of satisfied vanity as I got out of the magnificent car at my own street-door, under the very eyes of the family of the railwayman, our neighbours, who were looking out of their window.

I went and shut myself up in my own room, and the first thing I did was to look at the money. I found that there was not one, but three notes of a thousand lire each, and for a moment I felt almost happy as I sat on the edge of the bed. The money would not only pay the rest of the hire-purchase for the furniture, but would be enough for me to buy one or two other things I needed. I had never had so much money in my life before, and I could not stop fingering the notes and staring at them. My poverty made the sight of them not only delightful but almost incredible. I had to keep on looking longingly at these notes, as I had at my pieces of furniture, in order to convince myself that they really belonged to me.

CHAPTER FIVE

My long night's deep sleep had obliterated, or so I thought, even the memory of my Viterbo adventure. Next day I awoke my usual calm self, determined to persist in doing all I could to achieve a normal family life. Gisella, whom I saw that morning, made no allusion to the trip, either out of remorse for what she had done or well-advised tact, and I was grateful to her for this. But I was becoming anxious about my next meeting with Gino. Although I was sure that I was not at all guilty, I yet knew that I would have to lie to him, and I felt displeased at having to do this and was not even sure whether I would be capable of doing it, because it would be the first time and until now I had been absolutely straightforward with him. Of course, I had not told him I had been seeing Gisella; my motives in this case had been so innocent that I had not even considered it as a lie, but much more, it so happens, as a resort to which I had been driven by his unreasonable dislike of Gisella.

I was so worried and, scarcely had we met on that very day, than I found it difficult to prevent myself from bursting into tears, telling him everything and begging his forgiveness. The whole story of my trip to Viterbo weighed heavily on me and I longed to free myself by talking about it. If Gino had been anyone else and I had known him to be less jealous, I would certainly have spoken of it, and then, in my opinion, we would have loved one another more than ever and I would have felt cherished and bound to him by a tie stronger than love itself. We were in the car as usual, in the usual suburban avenue in the early morning. He noticed my uneasiness and asked me what was the matter.

'Now I'll tell him all about it—even if he kicks me out of the car and I have to walk back into town,' I thought. But I had not the courage and asked him instead whether he loved me.

" What a question ! " he replied.

" Will you always love me ? " I continued, my eyes brimming over with tears.

" Always."

" Shall we be married soon ? "

He seemed irritated by my insistence.

" Upon my word ! " he exclaimed, " I might think you didn't trust me—didn't we say we'd get married at Easter ? "

" Yes, we did."

" Didn't I give you the money to set up house ? "

" Yes."

" Well, then—am I the kind of man to keep my word, or not ? When I say a thing I do it. I bet it's your mother egging you on."

" No, mother's got nothing to do with it ! " I denied, feeling alarmed. " Listen, shall we live together ? "

" Of course."

" And be happy ? "

" It depends on ourselves."

" Shall we live together ? " I repeated, unable to escape the recurrent thoughts my anxiety caused me.

88

" Oh, my God ! You've already asked me, and I told you."

" I'm sorry," I said, " but sometimes it hardly seems possible." Unable to control myself any longer, I began to cry. He was astonished at my tears, and also uneasy, but it was an uneasiness filled apparently with remorse, the reasons for which became clear to me only much later on. " Come on, now ! " he said. " What are you crying for ? "

I was crying really because of the bitterness and pain of being unable to tell him what had happened and so free my conscience of the burden of regret. I was also crying because I felt humiliated at the thought that I was not good enough for him, for anyone so fine and perfect as he was. " You're right," I said at last with an effort, " I'm a silly girl."

" I wouldn't say that—but I don't see what you've got to cry about."

But the burden remained with me. That very afternoon, after I had left him, I went to church to make my confession. I had not been for nearly a year ; I had known all along that I could go at any time and that had been enough for me. I had given up going to confession when I kissed Gino for the first time. I realised that according to the church my relations with Gino were a sin, but since I knew we were going to get married I did not feel any remorse and meant to get absolution once and for all before my wedding.

I went to a little church in the heart of the city, the one with its door between the entrance to a cinema and the window of a hosiery shop. It was almost pitch-dark inside, except for the high altar and a side-chapel dedicated to the Madonna. It was a dirty, neglected little church ; the straw-bottomed chairs were pushed here and there in the untidy way the congregation had left them when they went out, and this made you think of some boring meeting you'd heave a sigh of relief to get away from, rather than of going to Mass.

A feeble light falling from the apertures in the lantern of the dome showed up the dust on the paved floor and the white cracks in the yellow mottled varnish of the imitation marble columns. The numerous silver exvoto tablets in the form of flaming hearts that hung jostling each other on the walls created a gimcrack and melancholy impression. But a smell of stale incense in the air put heart into me. As a little girl I had breathed in the same smell; and the memories it awakened in me were all innocent and pleasurable. I seemed to be in a familiar spot; and, although I had never been there before, I felt as if I had been frequenting that same church all my life.

But before confessing I wanted to go into the side-chapel where I had noticed a statue of the Virgin. I had been dedicated to the Virgin ever since the day of my birth, indeed, mother always used to say I looked like her, with my regular features and large, dark, gentle eyes. I had always loved the Madonna because she carried a baby in her arms and because her Baby, who became a man, was killed; and she who bore him and loved him as any mother loves her son, suffered so when she saw him hanging on the Cross. I often thought to myself that the Madonna, who had so many sorrows, was the only one who could understand my own sorrows, and as a child I used to pray to her alone, as the only one who could understand me. Besides, I liked the Madonna because she was so different from mother, so serene and tranquil, richly clothed, with her eyes that looked on me so lovingly; it was as if she were my real mother and not the mother who spent her time scolding me, and was always worn-out and badly dressed.

So I knelt down, and hiding my face in my hands, with my head bent, I said a long prayer to the Madonna in person, begging her to pardon me for what I had done and beseeching her to protect me, my mother and Gino. Then I remembered it was my duty to bear no malice towards anyone so I called down the protection of the Madonna upon Gisella who had betrayed me through envy, on Riccardo who had backed her up through stupidity and in the end upon Astarita, too. I prayed longer for Astarita than for the others, just because I was full of resentment against him and I wanted to blot it out and love him as I loved the others and forgive him and forget the harm he had done me. At length I felt so deeply moved that tears came to my eyes. I raised my eyes to the statue of the Madonna, over the altar, and my tears were like a veil before me, and the statue was misty and quivering as if seen through water, and the candles that glittered all round the statue made so many little golden points, lovely to behold yet at the same time embittering, as are at certain times the stars we yearn to touch but know to be far beyond our reach. I remained thus for some time, in contemplation of the Madonna, almost without seeing her; then the bitter tears began to trickle slowly from my eyes and roll down my face, tickling me, and I saw the Madonna looking at me, her Baby in her arms, her face illuminated by the candle-flames. She seemed to be looking at me with sympathy and compassion, and I thanked her in my heart; then, rising to my feet, I found my peace of mind restored, and I went to confess.

The confessionals were all empty; but, while I wandered about looking for a priest, I saw someone come out of a little door to the left of the High Altar, pass in front of the altar, genuflect and cross himself, and make his way towards the other side. He was a monk, I did not know of what order, and summoning my courage I called out to him in a humble voice. He turned and came towards me at once. When he was nearby I saw that he was fairly young, tall and vigorous, with a rosy complexion, fresh and manly, a thin fair beard, blue eyes, and a high, white forehead. I could not help thinking him an extraordinarily good-looking man, of a kind rarely to be met with either in or out of church, and I was glad I was going to confess to him. I told him in an undertone what I wanted: then, making me a sign to follow him, he led the way to one of the confessionals.

He entered the box and I went to kneel down in front of the grill. A small enamelled plate nailed on to the confessional bore the name of Father Elia; and this name pleased me and inspired faith in me. When I was on my knees, he said a short prayer and then asked me how long it was since I had last been to confession.

"Almost a year," I replied.

"That's a long time—too long. Why?"

I noticed his Italian was not very good; he rolled his r's like the French do, and from one or two mistakes he made, trying to pronounce foreign words in an Italian way, I realised he was French himself. I was glad of the fact that he was a foreigner but I really could not have said why. Perhaps because when we are about to do anything we consider important, every unusual detail seems a sign of good omen.

I explained that the tale I was about to tell him would make it clear why I had gone so long without confession. After a short silence he asked me what I had to say. Then I began to tell him impulsively and trustingly of my relations with Gino, my friendship with Gisella, the trip to Viterbo, Astarita's threat. Even while I was talking I could not help wondering what impression my story would make on him. He was unlike most priests and his unusual appearance, as of a man of the world, set me thinking with curiosity what reasons could have led to his taking vows. It may seem strange that, after the extraordinary emotion my prayer to the Madonna had roused in me, I should be distracted to the point of asking myself questions about my confessor; but I do not think myself that there was any contradiction between my emotion and my curiosity. Both came from the bottom of my heart, where devotion and coquetry, sorrow and lust were inextricably mixed.

But little by little, even while I was thinking about him in the way I have described, I experienced a feeling of relief and a consoling eagerness to tell him more, to confess everything. I felt uplifted and freed from the heavy sense of anguish which had weighed me down until then, as a flower wilting in the heat is revived at last by the first drops of rain. At first I spoke hesitantly and with difficulty; then my words began to flow more easily; and at last I spoke with emphatic sincerity and swelling hopes. I omitted nothing, not even the money Astarita had given me, the feelings the gift had awakened in me and the use I intended to make of it. He listened without comment; and when I had finished said: "In order to avoid something you thought harmful, the breaking off of your engagement, you agreed to do yourself infinitely greater harm——"

"Yes, I know," I agreed, trembling, glad his sensitive fingers were probing my heart.

92

" As a matter of fact," he went on, as if talking to himself, " your engagement has nothing to do with it—when you gave way to this man you yielded to a feeling of greed."

" Yes, yes ! "

" Well, it was better for the marriage to be broken off than to do what you did."

" Yes, that's what I think now."

" That's not enough—you'll get married now, but at what cost to yourself ? You'll no longer be able to be a good wife."

The inflexible harshness of his words struck me to the quick. " No, it isn't like that ! " I exclaimed painfully. " It's as though nothing had happened, for me—I'm sure I'll be a good wife ! "

He must have liked the sincerity of my reply. He was silent for some time and then went on more gently. " Are you sincerely penitent ? "

" Yes, indeed I am," I replied impetuously. It suddenly occurred to me that he might oblige me to give the money back to Astarita and, although the idea of returning it was unpleasant in anticipation, nevertheless I imagined I would have obeyed him gladly, because the order came from someone I liked, who was able to dominate me in some strange way. But, without mentioning the money, he went on in his cold and distant voice, to which the foreign accent added such a curiously warm overtone; " Now you must get married as soon as possible—you must put things straight—you must make your fiancé understand that you can't go on with him on the present terms."

" I have already said that."

" What was his answer ? "

I could not help smiling at the idea of him, so fair and handsome, asking me such a question from the depths of the confessional.

" He says we'll get married at Easter," I replied with an effort.

" It would be better to get married at once. Easter's a long time yet," he replied after a moment's reflection, and this time he did not seem to be speaking as a priest but as a polite man of the world, who was a little bored at having to busy himself with my affairs.

"We can't any earlier. I've got to make my trousseau, and he has to go home and tell his people."

"Anyway," he continued, "he must marry you as soon as possible, and until the wedding-day you must give up all physical relations with your fiancé. This is a grave sin. Do you understand me?"

"Yes, I'll do it."

"You will?" he repeated doubtfully. "In any case, strengthen yourself against temptation through prayer—try to pray."

"Yes, I'll pray."

"As for the other man," he continued, "you mustn't see him for any reason whatsoever. This should not be difficult, since you don't love him. If he insists, if he comes to see you, send him away."

I told him I would do that; and, after much further advice pronounced in his cold and distant voice, which was nevertheless so charming to listen to, with its foreign pronunciation and the impression it gave of an educated person, he instructed me to say a number of prayers every day as a penance, and then gave me absolution. But before sending me away he made me say a paternoster with him. I gladly agreed because I was sorry to go away and had not yet heard enough of his voice.

"Our Father who art in Heaven," he said.

"Our Father who art in Heaven," I repeated.

"Thy kingdom come."

"Thy kingdom come."

"Thy will be done on earth as it is in Heaven."

"Thy will be done on earth as it is in Heaven."

"Give us this day our daily bread."

"Give us this day our daily bread."

"And forgive us our trespasses as we forgive them that trespass against us."

"And forgive us our trespasses as we forgive them that trespass against us."

"And lead us not into temptation, but deliver us from evil."

94

"And lead us not into temptation, but deliver us from evil."

"Amen."

"Amen."

I have given the prayer in full in order to recapture my feelings when I said it after him. It was as if I were a tiny girl again and he was leading me by the hand from one phrase to the next. Meanwhile, however, I was thinking of the money Astarita had given me and felt almost disappointed that he had not told me to return it. I really would have liked him to order me to do so, because I wanted to give him a concrete proof of my obedience and repentance and wanted to do something for him that would have been a real sacrifice. I got up when the prayer was at an end and he, too, came out of the confessional and made to go away, without looking at me and with only the very slightest nod in farewell. Then, without thinking what I was doing and almost despite myself, I pulled him by the sleeve. He stopped and looked at me with his clear, calm, inexpressive eyes.

I thought he was even handsomer than ever and a thousand crazy ideas passed through my mind. I imagined I might quite easily have fallen in love with him and wondered how I could manage to let him understand that I liked him. But at the same time my conscience warned me that I was in church and he was a priest and my confessor. My mind was in a whirl with all these thoughts and images, which took hold of me at one and the same time, so I was unable to speak for a moment.

"Is there anything else you want to tell me?" he asked, after waiting for as long as might reasonably be expected.

"I wanted to know whether I ought to give that man his money back?" I asked.

He glanced rapidly at me, a look that seemed to penetrate to the depths of my soul, it was so sharp and direct, then answered shortly: "Do you need it very much?"

"Yes."

"Well, then—you need not give it back—but in any case, do as your conscience tells you."

He said this in a particular tone, as if he meant to imply

that our meeting was over, and I stammered my thanks without smiling, gazing into his eyes as I did so. I had really lost my head at that moment and almost hoped he would show me by some gesture or word that he was not indifferent to me. He certainly understood the meaning of my look, and a slight expression of amazement crossed his face. He made a little gesture of farewell and went away, turning his back on me, and left me standing by the confessional, confused and thoroughly upset.

I did not tell mother anything about my confession, just as I had told her nothing of the Viterbo trip. I knew she had very firm ideas about priests and religion; she said they were fine things, but the rich stayed rich and the poor stayed poor all the same. " The rich know how to pray better than we do, you can see that," she used to say. Her ideas on religion were like her ideas about family and marriage. She had been religious herself once, used to go to church, but everything had gone badly for her all the same, so she did not believe in it any more. Once I told her our reward would come in the next world, and she became furious, telling me she wanted hers in this one, now, immediately, and if she didn't get it, that meant the whole thing was a tissue of lies. Still, as I have already said, she gave me a religious upbringing, because she had been religious herself once upon a time. Only her trials during recent years had embittered her and had made her change her mind.

Next morning as I got into the car Gino told me his employers were going away and we would be able to meet at the villa for a few days. My first impulse was one of joy, because I liked love-making and liked it with Gino, as I believe I have already made clear.

But all at once I remembered my promise to the priest.

" I can't," I said.

" Why not ? "

" It's out of the question——"

" All right, then," he said forbearingly with a sigh, " to-morrow then——"

" No, not even tomorrow—never again."

" Never ! " he repeated in a low voice, pretending to be

amazed. "That's how it is now, is it? Never! You might at least explain why."

His face was full of jealous suspicion. "Gino," I said hurriedly, "I love you and haven't ever loved you so much as I do now—but just because I love you, I've made up my mind that there oughtn't to be anything like that between us again until we're married—I mean no love-making."

"Now I see through the whole thing!" he said scornfully. "You're afraid I shan't want to marry you."

"No, I'm sure you'll marry me. If I thought that I wouldn't be preparing everything and wouldn't spend mother's money that she's been saving all her life."

"What a tale you make of your mother's money!" he said. He had become really unpleasant and I could hardly recognise him. "Why then?"

"I went to confession and the priest told me I mustn't make love to you any more until we're married."

He made a gesture of disappointment and a word escaped him which sounded to me like an oath. "What business has that priest to stick his nose into our affairs?"

I preferred to remain silent.

"Why don't you say something?" he insisted.

"I haven't anything more to say."

I must have seemed absolutely determined, because he suddenly changed his mind. "All right," he said, "as you say—do you want me to take you back into town?"

"If you will."

I must say this was the only time he was unpleasant and unkind to me. By the following day he seemed resigned and was his usual affectionate self, full of polite attention. So we continued to meet every day as before; except that we did not make love any more, but only talked to one another. Every now and again I gave him a kiss, although he had made it a point of honour not to ask me for one. I did not feel kissing him was really a sin because, after all, we were engaged and soon to be married. When I think over that time nowadays I imagine Gino was led to resign himself so quickly to his new part as a respectful fiancé by the hope of gradually diminishing the warmth of our relationship and

97

bringing me little by little to a kind of rupture, almost without my being aware of the fact. You hear constantly of girls who unwittingly find themselves free once more after long and exhausting engagements, with no harm done except that the best part of their youth has fled. All unawares I had given him the excuse he was probably seeking to ease up on our engagement, when I told him of the priest's injunction. He certainly would never have had the courage by himself, since he was a weak, selfish character, and the pleasure he derived from our relationship was greater than his desire to jilt me. But the confessor's intervention gave him an opportunity to put forward a hypocritical and apparently disinterested solution.

After some time he began to meet me less often, only every other day. And I noticed that our trips in the car were briefer each time and he was always more absent-minded when I talked of our plans for getting married. But although I vaguely sensed this change in his attitude I was not at all suspicious, because they were only puffs of smoke, trivialities, and he continued to behave in his usual kindly affectionate way to me. One day he told me, with an apologetic look on his face, that for family reasons he would have to postpone the date of our marriage until after the summer.

"Are you awfully upset?" he added, seeing that I made no comment on what he had said, and only looked in front of me with a bitter, blank expression.

"No, no——" I said, pulling myself together. "It doesn't matter—it can't be helped. It'll give me time to make my trousseau."

"You're lying. You do mind a lot." It was odd how he wanted me to be upset at the postponement of our wedding.

"I don't."

"Very well then, if you aren't upset it means you don't really love me and at the bottom of your heart perhaps you wouldn't mind if we never got married at all."

"Don't talk like that!" I exclaimed, in alarm. "It would be dreadful for me. I don't want even to think of it."

At that time I failed to understand the expression that flitted

98

across his face. Actually he had wanted to test my affection and had realised to his dismay that it was still very strong.

Although the postponement of my marriage was not enough to rouse my own suspicions, it strengthened mother's and Gisella's original convictions. Mother made no comment on the news at all, a manner she sometimes had (a strange fact this, given her violent and impulsive nature). But one evening while she was giving me my supper as usual, standing silently watchful for what I might need, I made some reference to the wedding.

" Do you know what they used to call a girl like you, in my time, a girl who keeps on waiting to get married and never does ? "

I went pale and felt faint. " What ? "

" A girl on the shelf," said mother placidly. " He's keeping you on the shelf like left-over meat. But sometimes meat goes bad through being kept and then it gets thrown away."

I felt furious. " It isn't true ! " I said. " It's the first time we've put it off, and only for a few months. The fact is you're wild with Gino because he's a chauffeur and not a gentleman."

" I'm not wild with anyone."

" Yes, you are—and because you had to spend money on the room for us, but you needn't worry——"

" My dear child—love's gone to your head ! "

" Don't worry, I tell you—he'll pay back all the rest of the hire-purchase, and we'll give you every penny you've spent. Look." Carried away by passion I opened my bag and showed her the banknotes Astarita had given me. " That's money of his," I went on, and I was so infatuated that I almost believed my own lies, " he gave me this—and he'll give me more."

She gaped at the money and put on a sorry, disappointed look which filled me with remorse. I had not been so unkind to her for a long time now ; and I also realised that I had been lying and that Gino had not really given me the money at all. She did not utter a word, cleared away, took up the plates and went out of the room. After a moment's angry reflection I got up and followed her. I saw her from the back, standing upright in front of the tap busy washing the plates which she put down one by one on the marble draining-board, her head and shoulders slightly bowed, and I felt a rush of pity for her. Impulsively I threw my arms round her neck. "Forgive me for what I said," I pleaded, "I didn't really think it. But when you speak about Gino you make me wild."

"Get along—leave me alone," she answered, pretending to struggle with me to free herself from my embrace.

"But you've got to understand!" I added passionately. "If Gino doesn't marry me I'll either kill myself or go on the streets."

Gisella took the news that my marriage had been postponed in much the same way as mother had done. We were in her furnished room when I told her, I was sitting fully clothed on the edge of the bed and she was in her nightdress combing her hair in front of the dressing-table. She let me get to the end without comment, then said calmly and triumphantly: "You see I was right?"

"Why?"

"He doesn't want to marry you and won't ever marry you. Now it isn't going to be at Easter but at All Saints'— then it'll be put off until Christmas—and then one day you'll get it into your head at last and you'll be the one to leave him."

Her words made me angry and unhappy. But I had already let myself go with mother, so to say, and anyway I knew that if I were to say what I thought I would have to break off my friendship with Gisella and I did not want to do this because she was, after all, my only friend. I ought to have said what I thought, that she did not want me to get married because she knew Riccardo would never marry her. This was the truth, but it was too spiteful a thing to say and I did not think it was fair to hurt Gisella just because she gave way, despite herself, to her own feelings of envy and jealousy when she spoke of Gino. "Don't let's talk about it any more, shall we? It doesn't really matter to you whether I get married or not—and it hurts me to talk about it," I contented myself with saying.

She suddenly left her place at the dressing-table and came to sit beside me on the bed. " How do you mean—it doesn't matter to me ? " she protested. " It matters a lot to me to see you being led by the nose like this," she added, putting her arm round my waist.

" But I'm not ! " I said in a low voice.

" And I'd like to see you happy," she continued. She was silent for a moment. " By the way," she then said casually, " Astarita is always bothering me because he'd like to see something more of you—he says he can't live without you— he's head over heels in love ! Do you want me to make a date for you with him ? "

" Don't mention Astarita to me," I said.

" He realises he behaved badly on that trip we took to Viterbo," she continued, " but at bottom it was because he loves you—he wants to make it up to you."

" The only way of making it up is not to show himself again," I said.

" Come on, now ! He's a serious chap and he really loves you—he insists on seeing you, speaking to you. Why shouldn't you meet in a café, for instance, with me there, too ? "

" No," I replied decisively. " I don't want to see him."

" You'll be sorry."

" You go out with Astarita ! "

" Like a shot, my dear. He's very generous and he doesn't care what he spends—but he wants you, he's stuck on you."

" Yes, I know, but I don't want him."

She continued arguing in Astarita's favour, but I would not let myself be persuaded. I was then at the height of my desperate desire to get married and have a family of my own, and was determined not to let myself be won over by reasoning or by money. I had even forgotten the shudder of pleasure Astarita had been able to rouse in me when he had forced me to take his money on the return journey from Viterbo. Just because I was afraid Gisella and mother might be right and for some reason or other my marriage might come to nothing, I clung to the idea of marriage with an even greater and more tenacious hope.

Meanwhile I had paid off all the instalments on the furniture and had begun to work even harder than ever to earn more money and pay for my trousseau. In the morning I posed in the studios, in the afternoon I shut myself in the living-room with mother and sewed till nightfall. She worked at the sewing-machine, by the window, and I sat a little way off at the table sewing by hand. Mother had taught me to be a seamstress and I have always been very quick and good at it. There were always a number of buttonholes and eye-holes to make and reinforce, and every shirt had to have its initials, and these I knew how to do particularly well, raised, firm, so that they seemed to stand out against the material. We specialised in men's wear, but sometimes we made a nightdress or a pair of cami-knickers or ladies' knickers, too, but only cheap stuff because mother did not know how to embroider and did not know any ladies who would give her orders. While I was sewing, my mind wandered off after Gino, marriage, the Viterbo trip, mother, my own life, in fact, and the time passed quickly. What mother used to think about I never knew; but she certainly thought about something, because when she was working the machine she always looked furious and, if I spoke to her, usually answered crossly. Towards evening, as soon as it began to get dark, I got up, shook off the ends of cotton and, after I had put on my best clothes, I used to go out and meet Gisella or, when he was off duty, Gino. I wonder today whether I was really happy. In a certain sense I was, because I was longing for something which I thought was near and attainable. Since then I have discovered that real unhappiness comes when all hope is gone; and then it is no use being well-off and in need of nothing.

More than once at this time, I noticed that I was being followed through the streets by Astarita. This used to happen very early in the morning when I was on my way to the studios. Astarita usually waited for me to come out, standing in a recess in the city wall on the opposite side of the road. He never crossed over, and while I walked hurriedly towards the square, skirting the houses, he contented himself with following me at a slower pace, hugging the walls. He was watching me, I suppose, and that was enough for him : the behaviour typical of a man so deeply in love. When I reached the square, he went and stood at the tram halt, just facing me. He continued to watch me; but I had only to look at him for him to grow embarrassed and pretend to be gazing up the road to see if the tram were coming. No woman can remain indifferent in the face of love of this nature; and even I, although I was determined never to speak to him, sometimes felt a flattered kind of pity for him. Then Gino came along or else the tram, and I either got into the car or the tram and Astarita was left at the tramstop watching me as I vanished in the distance.

One evening when I reached home I found Astarita standing hat in hand in the living-room, leaning against the table and chatting with mother. I forgot all pity and was filled with anger at seeing him in my house, when I thought what he might be saying to mother to win her over to plead with me on his side. "What are you doing here?" I asked.

He gazed at me and his face began to twitch convulsively as it had in the car on the way to Viterbo when he told me he liked me. But this time he was unable even to speak. "This gentleman says he knows you," began mother confidentially, "he wanted to see how you were." I realised from her tone that Astarita had talked to her exactly as I had thought he would, and probably had even given her money. "Please go away, mother," I said to her. She was alarmed by my frantic voice and went out into the kitchen without replying. "What are you doing here? Go away !" I repeated. He looked at me, appeared to move his lips, but said nothing. His eyelids drooped right over his eyes and I could almost see the whites; he looked to me as though he might fall right down in a fit. "Go away," I repeated aloud, stamping on the floor, "otherwise I'll call out for help—I'll call a friend of ours who lives below."

I have often asked myself why Astarita did not try to blackmail me a second time by threatening to tell Gino what had happened at Viterbo if I did not yield to him. He could have blackmailed me with more likelihood of success this time because he really had had me, and there were witnesses and I could not deny it. I have come to the conclusion that the first time he only desired me and the second he loved me. Love longs to be reciprocated, and now Astarita loved me he must have felt how unsatisfactory his possession of me had been that day at Viterbo, when I lay dumb and inert like a corpse. But this time I was determined at all costs to let the truth come out; after all, if Gino loved me he ought to understand me and forgive me. My determination convinced Astarita that a second attempt at blackmail would certainly be useless.

When I threatened to call for help he said nothing, but dragging his hat along the table he went off towards the door. When he had reached the end of the table he stopped, lowered his head, looked as though he were pulling himself together in order to speak to me. But when he raised his head once more and moved his lips, his courage seemed to fail him and he remained silent, staring at me. This second gaze seemed endless. Then with a nod he left me, shutting the door behind him.

I immediately went out to mother in the kitchen.

" What did you tell that man ? " I asked furiously.

" Nothing ! " she replied in a fright. " He asked me what work we did, he told me he wanted me to make him some shirts."

" If you go to him I'll kill you ! " I cried.

She looked at me in terror. " Who says I'm going there ? He can get someone else to make his shirts for him ! " she replied.

" Didn't he speak about me ? "

" He asked me when you were getting married."

" What did you tell him ? "

" I said you were getting married in October."

" He didn't give you any money ? "

" No, why ? " She looked at me, feigning astonishment. " Should he have done ? "

I was sure from the tone of her voice that Astarita had given her money. I ran to her and seized her violently by the arm.

"Tell me the truth ! Did he give you any money ? "

"No, he didn't give me a penny."

Her hand was in her apron pocket. I seized her wrist violently and a banknote folded in two fell out of her open hand. Although I still had hold of her, she bent down and picked it up so greedily and so jealously that my fury subsided all at once. I remembered the agitation and delight Astarita's money had caused me the day we went to Viterbo and I felt I had no right to condemn mother because she had the same feelings and yielded to the same temptation. Now I wished I had not questioned her, had not seen the banknote. I contented myself with saying in a normal tone : " You see, he did give you something," and without waiting for her explanation I left the kitchen. From some hints she let fall at dinner, I understood that she wanted to begin to talk again about Astarita and the money, but I changed the subject and she did not insist.

Next day Gisella came without Riccardo to the tea-shop where we used to meet.

"I have to tell you something very important today," she said without any preliminaries as soon as she sat down.

A kind of presentiment made me grow pale. " If it's bad news, please don't tell me," I said faintly.

"It's neither good nor bad," she said eagerly; " it's just a piece of news, that's all. I've already told you who Astarita is———"

"I don't want to hear anything about Astarita . . ."

"Now listen ! Don't be such a child ! Astarita's a very important chap, as I told you before, one of the high-ups. He's a big pot in the political police."

I felt a little reassured, since after all I had nothing to do with politics. "It doesn't matter a scrap to me what Astarita is, even if he's a minister."

"Oh, you're so . . . !" exclaimed Gisella. "Just listen, instead of butting in all the time. Astarita told me you simply must go to see him at the Ministry. He's got to talk to you —not about love," she added hurriedly, seeing I was about to protest. "He's got to tell you something very important —something that concerns you."

"Something that concerns me?"

"Yes. Something for your own good. At least, that's what he said."

What made me decide that this time I would accept Astarita's invitation, after so many refusals, I do not know myself. "Very well, I'll go," I said, feeling more dead than alive.

Gisella was rather disconcerted by my passive state. For the first time she noticed how pale and frightened I was.

"What's the matter?" she asked. "Is it because he's in the police? He's not after you! What are you scared of? He doesn't want to arrest you!"

I got up, although I felt dizzy. "All right," I said, "I'll go. Which Ministry is it?"

"Home Office. Just in front of the Super cinema. But listen——"

"At what time?"

"Any time in the morning. But listen——"

I slept very little that night. I could not understand what Astarita wanted of me, outside his own passion; but an intuition that seemed infallible to me told me it could not be anything good. The place he summoned me to led me to think it must be something to do with the police. I knew on the other hand, like all poor people do, that when the police get going it is never for your good, and after I had examined my own behaviour in every detail I came to the conclusion that Astarita wanted to blackmail me again by using some information he had obtained concerning Gino. I did not know anything about Gino's life and it might be that he was politically compromised. I had never troubled myself with politics, but I was not so ignorant as not to know that there were a number of people who had no liking for the Fascist government, and that men like Astarita had the task of hunting out such enemies of the government. My imagination depicted for me in vivid colours the dilemma Astarita would place me in: I would either have to give in to him again or let Gino go to prison. My dismay was caused by the fact that I did not at all want to satisfy Astarita and did not want Gino to go to gaol either. I felt no further pity for Astarita as I pondered over these matters, but only hatred. He seemed a vile and rotten creature to me, unfit to live, who deserved only merciless punishment. And, it so happened, that among other projected solutions to my problem that night, I even contemplated assassinating Astarita. But this was a morbid, half-waking fantasy rather than a solution; and, in fact, it kept me company until morning, like any fantasy which never properly develops into an objective and firm determination. I saw myself putting into my handbag a sharp, pointed clasp-knife which mother used for peeling potatoes, going to Astarita, hearing the invitation I feared, and then plunging the knife into his neck with all the strength of my muscular arm, just between his ear and his white starched collar. I saw myself leaving the room, pretending to be absolutely calm, and then running to hide at Gisella's or at some other friend's place. But although I went over these bloodthirsty scenes in my imagination, I knew all the time that I would never be capable of doing anything of the kind. I have a horror of blood and hurting people, and am more inclined to let myself be bullied than to bully anyone else.

I dozed off towards dawn and slept a little, then day broke, I got up and went to my usual appointment with Gino.

"I say," I said as soon as we met in the suburban avenue after the usual greetings, trying to make my voice sound as casual as possible, "have you ever had anything to do with politics?"

"Politics? How do you mean?"

"I mean doing anything against the government."

He looked at me knowingly. "Just a moment," he then said, "do you think I'm a damn fool?"

"No, but——"

"No, no, let's get this quite clear first! Do you think I'm a damn fool?"

"No," I said, "you don't look like one, but——"

"Very well, then," he said, "why the devil should you think I'd have anything to do with politics?"

"I don't know, but sometimes——"

"Nothing doing! You can tell whoever threw out any hints that Gino Molinari's not a damn fool."

At about eleven o'clock, after having wandered round the Ministry for more than an hour unable to make up my mind to enter, I approached the porter and asked for Astarita. First I had to go up a wide marble staircase, then a smaller but still extremely wide one, then I was accompanied along a number of passages into an ante-room with three doors leading into it. I was accustomed to associating the idea of the police with the mean, filthy offices of the local branches, and was therefore astonished to see the magnificence of the place where Astarita worked. The ante-room was vast, with a mosaic floor and old pictures such as you see in churches; leather chairs stood about against the walls and a huge table filled the centre of the room. Uneasy at such splendour, I could not help thinking that Gisella must be right—Astarita really must be someone important. His importance was impressed upon me by an unexpected occurrence. I had only just sat down when one of the doors opened and a tall and beautiful, if no longer so young lady came out, dressed all in black, very smart, with a little veil over her face; she was followed by Astarita. I got up, thinking it was my turn. But after Astarita had made me a sign with his hand as if to let me know that he had seen me, but that it was not quite my turn yet, he continued speaking to the lady in the doorway. Then, having accompanied her to the middle of the room, he bowed to her, kissed her hand, then left her, after making a sign to another person who was in the ante-room with me, an old man dressed in black with a little white beard and spectacles, who looked like a professor. When Astarita beckoned he rose immediately, and hastened after him, humbly and eagerly. The two of them disappeared into the room and I was left alone.

What had struck me most in Astarita's brief appearance had been the difference in his manner from what he had been on the Viterbo trip. Then I had seen him looking awkward, convulsed, dumb and half-crazed; now he seemed entirely master of himself, easy-mannered but precise, exuding an indefinable sense of discreet though authoritative superiority.

Even his voice had changed. During the trip he had spoken in low, warm, strangled tones, but while he was speaking to the lady with the veil his voice had sounded clear, cold, measured, calm. He was dressed as usual in dark grey with a high white collar which gave his head a rigid look, but on this occasion his suit and collar, which I had noticed during the trip without giving them any special significance, seemed as perfectly matched as a uniform to the huge room with its severe, heavy furniture, and the silence and order that reigned there. Gisella was right, I thought, he really must be someone who counted for a great deal, and only love could explain his awkward manner and sense of inferiority with regard to me.

These reflections took my mind off my earlier feelings of agitation, so that when the door opened after a few minutes and the old man came out, I felt sufficiently mistress of myself. But this time Astarita did not come to beckon to me from the doorway. A bell rang, a servant went in to see what Astarita wanted and shut the door behind him, then returned, and after having asked my name in a low voice he said I could go in. I got up and went casually towards the room.

Astarita's office was a room not much smaller than the anteroom. It was empty except for a sofa and two leather armchairs in one corner, and a large table, at which Astarita was seated, in another. Two windows with white curtains let in a cold, sunless light, so still and tragic that it reminded me of Astarita's voice when he was talking to the lady with the veil. There was huge soft carpet on the floor and two or three pictures hung on the walls. I can remember one of them : it was of an expanse of green fields bounded on the horizon by a chain of rocky mountains.

As I have said, Astarita was sitting behind a huge table, and when I entered he did not even look up from the papers he was reading or pretending to read. I say 'pretending' because I felt sure that this was all a show intended to intimidate me and fill me with a sense of his authority and importance. In fact, when I drew near to the table, I saw that the paper he was studying so attentively contained only three or four lines with a scribbled signature below them.

Besides, the hand on which he was leaning his forehead, between two fingers of which he held a lighted cigarette, revealed his state of agitation and was visibly trembling. This trembling caused some of the ash to fall on the sheet of paper he was examining so closely and with such artificial attention.

I placed my hand on the edge of the table, and said : " Here I am."

At these words, as if at a signal, he stopped reading, jumped to his feet and came round to greet me, taking my two hands in his. And all this was done in perfect silence and contrasted strangely with the authoritative and unconcerned attitude he was trying to maintain. As a matter of fact, as I soon learnt, my voice alone had been enough to make him forget the part he had prepared himself to play ; and his usual state of agitation had then irresistibly overwhelmed him. He kissed my hands, first one then the other, gazed at me while rolling his melancholy and love-lorn eyes, and made as if to speak, but his lips trembled and he was forced to remain silent.

" You've come," he said at last in the low, strangled voice I recognised as his.

Now I, perhaps, by contrast with Astarita's attitude, felt full of self-assurance. " Yes, I've come," I said. " I ought not to have, really—what have you got to tell me ? "

" Come and sit down over here," he murmured. He had never let go of my hand, and still pressing it tightly, he led me by the hand to the sofa. I sat down, and all at once he knelt in front of me, put his two arms round my legs and pressed his forehead against my knees. He did all this without saying a word and trembling from head to foot. He pressed his forehead so hard against me that he hurt me, and after remaining for a long time like this he lifted his bald head upwards as though he wanted to lay it on my lap. I then made as if to get up. " You had something important to tell me—say it, or I'll go away," I declared.

With an effort he got to his feet, sat beside me and took my hand.

" It's nothing," he murmured, " I wanted to see you again."

I made to get up once more but he caught hold of me. "Yes," he added, " but I also wanted to tell you that you and I ought to come to an understanding."

" In what way ? "

" I love you," he said hurriedly. " I love you so much——— Come and live with me in my house ; you can be mistress there as much as if you were my wife—I'll buy clothes, jewels, anything you like for you———"

He seemed crazed, the words poured confusedly out of his mouth while his lips remained almost motionless and twisted. "And was it for this," I asked coldly, " you made me come up here ? "

" Didn't you want to ? "

" I won't even discuss it."

Oddly enough, he said not a word after I replied like this. But he raised his hand, and almost hypnotising me with his crazy, fixed stare, he caressed my face as if he wanted to memorise its shape. His fingers were light and I could feel them trembling while the tips traced my face from the forehead to the cheek and back again. It was the gesture of a man in love. And love is so deeply persuasive, even when it is not reciprocated, that for a moment I was almost moved by compassion to say something less final and chilling to him. But he gave me no time, because as soon as he had finished caressing me, he got up and spoke in halting and precise tones, a curious mixture of suppressed desire and some new and unknown sense of duty.

" Just a minute, though," he said. " I really have got something important to tell you." Meanwhile he went back to the table and picked up a red folder.

It was my turn to become agitated when I saw him coming towards me with this red folder. " What is it ? " I asked him faintly.

" It's—it's—" it was strange how the authoritative and official note in his voice became all mixed with his excitement—" it's some information about your fiancé."

" Oh ! " I said, and for a moment, frightened to death, I shut my eyes. Astarita did not notice, he was turning over the pages and in his agitation was crumpling them.

" Gino Molinari, isn't he ? "

" Yes."

" You're getting married in October, aren't you ? "

" Yes."

" But Gino Molinari appears to be married already," he continued, " and, to be precise, to Antonietta Partini, the daughter of the late Emilio and Diomira Lavagna . . . and that four years ago . . . they've got a child called Maria . . . at the present time his wife is living in Orvieto, with her mother."

I said nothing, but got up from the sofa and made for the door. Astarita remained standing in the middle of the room, with the papers in his hand. I opened the door and went out.

I can remember that when I found myself in the street, among the crowds, on a fine and cloudy day of that mild winter, I felt with bitter certainty that my life, like a river that has been artificially turned from its course for a brief period, had begun once more to flow in its usual direction, without change or novelty, after an interruption caused by my hopes and the preparations for my marriage. Perhaps this sensation was due to the fact that in my bewilderment I was looking around me with an attention shorn of its original gaiety, and the crowds, the shops, the streets, appeared to me for the first time for many months in a pitilessly normal light, neither beautiful nor ugly, neither interesting nor dull, but just as they were, as they must appear to a drunkard when his state of intoxication is past. But more probably it derived from my realisation that the normal things in life were not, as I had supposed, my plans for happiness, but the exact opposite—I mean, all those things that are inimical to all planning and programmes, are casual, faulty and unforeseen, agents of disillusionment and sorrow. If this were true, as I thought it must be, I had undoubtedly begun that morning to live again, after a state of intoxication lasting several months.

This was the only thought the discovery of Gino Molinari's deceit aroused in me. I did not dream of blaming him and did not really feel any deep sense of injury towards him.

I had not been led astray without my own complicity. And the memory of the pleasure I had enjoyed in his arms was too recent for me not to try to find excuses, if not justification, for his lying. I supposed he had been weak rather than wicked, carried away as he was by desire, and that the fault, if fault there was, lay with my beauty which made men lose their heads and forget all their scruples and obligations. In the long run Gino was no more to blame than Astarita, only he had used fraud whereas Astarita had used blackmail. Both of them loved me extremely, and certainly would have preferred to possess me by legal means if they could, and would have secured for me that modest form of happiness which I had set my heart on. Fate, on the contrary, had led me with all my beauty to meet the very men who could not obtain that kind of happiness for me. Unfortunately, even if there was no one to blame there was most decidedly a victim, and that was myself.

This way of reasoning and arguing may seem feeble to some, after such a betrayal as Gino's. But every time I have been hurt—and I often have because of my poverty, innocence and loneliness—I have always tried to find excuses for the wrongdoer and to forget the harm done me as quickly as possible. If the hurt changes me at all I do not show it in my conduct and outward appearance, but far more deeply in my soul which closes in upon itself like healthy flesh attempting as soon as possible to heal a wound. But scars remain and these almost unconscious wounds in the soul are always permanent.

With Gino the same thing happened. I bore him no grudge, not even for a moment, but within me I felt many things were shattered for ever—my respect for him, my hopes of establishing a family, my desire not to admit that Gisella and mother were right, my religious faith or at least the kind of belief I had held until then. I compared myself with a doll I had had when I was little—after I had beaten her and dragged her about all day long I felt a kind of lump inside her, a sinister creaking, although her face was still as rosy and smiling as ever. I screwed off her head and then little scraps of china, string, screws and the works that made her talk and

113

move her eyes about all tumbled out of her neck, together with odd pieces of wood and shreds of stuff whose function remained a mystery to me.

Stunned but calm I returned home and that afternoon went about my usual business without telling mother what had happened nor the conclusions I had reached as a result. But I realised that I could not pretend to the extent of sewing my trousseau as I had done on other days. I picked up the things I had already made and those I still had to do and locked them away in the wardrobe in my room. Mother could not help noticing I was unhappy, which was unusual, because I am nearly always gay and thoughtless. But I told her I was tired, as indeed I was. Towards evening, while mother was machining, I left my work, went into my room and stretched myself on the bed. I realised I was looking at the furniture which I had finished paying for and was really mine, now, thanks to Astarita's money, with a very different expression from before, without pleasure or hope. I did not feel unhappy but only tired and indifferent as you do after some enormous but entirely useless effort you have made. I was physically tired, anyway, aching in all my limbs, with a deep longing for rest. Thinking in a confused way about my furniture and how impossible it would be to use it now as I had hoped, I fell asleep fully dressed on the bed. I slept soundly for about four hours, a deep, sorrowful sleep, woke up very late and called mother out of the darkness that surrounded me. She ran in to me at once and told me she had been unwilling to wake me because she had seen me sleeping so peacefully and contentedly. "Supper's been ready for an hour," she added, standing there and looking at me; "what are you doing? Won't you come and have something to eat?"

"I don't want to get up," I answered, covering my dazzled eyes with one arm. "Why don't you bring it in to me?"

She went out and returned shortly afterwards with a tray bearing my usual supper. She put the tray on the edge of the bed and I pulled myself up and leaning on one elbow began to eat, without any appetite. But after the first few mouthfuls I stopped eating and flung myself back on the pillows again. " What's the matter? Aren't you eating anything?" mother asked.

" I'm not hungry."

" Aren't you well?"

" I'm perfectly well."

" I'll take it away then," she grumbled. She lifted the tray off the bed and went to put it on the table near the window.

" Don't wake me tomorrow morning," I continued after a moment.

" Why?"

" Because I've made up my mind I'm not going to be a model any more—you work too hard and earn too little."

" What'll you do?" she asked anxiously. " I can't keep you—you're not a child and you need a lot. I've got so much on my shoulders—your trousseau——" She began to wail and moan.

" Don't bother me now," I said slowly and wearily, without removing my arm from my face; " don't worry, there'll always be enough money."

A lengthy silence followed. " Don't you want anything?" she asked at last, humiliated and anxious, like a maid who has been reprimanded for being too familiar and is trying to get herself forgiven.

" Yes, please. Help me to undress. I'm so tired and I'm still half asleep."

She obeyed and sitting on the bed took off my shoes and stockings, which she placed tidily on a chair at the foot of the bed. Then she took off my dress and helped me slip into my nightdress. I kept my eyes shut all the time and as soon as I was under the covers I curled up and hid my head in the sheet. Mother wished me good-night from the doorway when she had switched off the light, but I did not reply. I fell asleep again at once and slept all night well into the morning.

Next morning I should have gone to my usual appointment with Gino, but when I woke up I realised I did not want to see him until the pain had passed and I was able to consider his treachery objectively from a distance, like something that had happened to someone else, not to myself. Then, as always, I mistrusted the things that are said and done under the stress of emotion, especially when this emotion, as in my case, was not one of liking and affection. Certainly I did not love Gino any longer, but I did not want to hate him exactly, because I thought that in doing so I would only burden my soul with a painful emotion, unworthy of me, and this in addition to the harm he had already done me through his betrayal.

In any case, I felt so tired that morning, a kind of sensuous laziness, and was less unhappy than I had been the evening before. Mother had gone out very early and I knew she would not come back before midday. So I lingered on in bed, and this was my first pleasure at the beginning of a new phase in my life, which from now on was to be one solely of pleasure. Every day since I was born I had got up in the early hours, and lying idly in bed without doing anything was a real luxury for me. I had never yielded to it, but now I had made up my mind to lie in bed whenever I felt like it, and I thought I would act in the same way about all the things I had rejected up till now on the grounds of my poverty and my dreams of a normal family life. I thought how I enjoyed love-making and money and the things money can bring, and I told myself that from now on I would never refuse love or money or what money could bring, if I had the chance. Do not imagine that I thought these things heatedly, in resentment and a spirit of revenge. I was quite calm as I lay there caressing the idea and enjoying it in antici- pation. Every situation, no matter how unpleasant, has its reverse side. For the moment I had lost marriage and all the modest advantages I had contemplated, but in return I had regained my freedom. My deepest hopes remained unchanged, certainly; but still, an easy life attracted me very much and the glittering prospect concealed from me all the sadness and resignation that lay behind my new resolve. Gisella's and mother's sermons began to bear fruit. The whole time, although I had been living a virtuous life, I had known that my beauty was such as to be able to earn me anything I wanted, if I would only make up my mind. That morning was the first time I looked on my body as a very convenient means for achieving the aims which hard work and honesty had not enabled me to attain.

These thoughts, or rather daydreams, made the morning pass like lightning and I was astonished when I heard the church bells next door chiming midday and saw that a long ray of sunshine had come through the window and lay across the bed. The bells and the ray of sunshine, like my idleness that morning, seemed unusual, precious luxuries. The rich ladies who lived in villas like Gino's mistress must lie in their beds dreaming in just the same way at that very same moment, hearing the chimes and watching the ray of sunshine with astonished eyes. With a feeling that I was no longer the same busy, needy Adriana of yesterday but quite a different Adriana, I got out of bed at last and took off my nightdress in front of the wardrobe mirror. I looked at myself naked in the mirror and for the first time understood my mother's pride when she said to the artist : ' Look at her bosom ! Her legs—her hips——' I thought of Astarita, whose whole character, manner and voice, even, were changed by his desire for my bosom, my legs, my hips, and I told myself I would certainly find other men who would give me as much money and even more than he did, if they could have pleasure from me.

I dressed lazily in my new character, drank some coffee and went out. I went to a nearby bar and 'phoned Gino's villa. He had given me the number, telling me with characteristic servility to use it very sparingly because his employers did not like the phone to be used by the servants. I spoke first of all to a woman who must have been the parlourmaid and then Gino came almost immediately. He asked me at once whether I was feeling ill, and I could not help smiling, since I recognised in his anxiety his old perfection of manner, which perhaps was not entirely assumed, and had done so much to deceive me. " I'm perfectly well," I replied, " I've never been so well in my life."

" When shall I see you ? "

" When you like," I said, " but I'd like to see you as I did the first time—at the villa if your employers go away."

He realised what I meant at once. "They're going away in about ten days' time, for Christmas," he replied eagerly, "not earlier."

"All right, then," I replied carelessly, "I'll see you in ten days' time."

"Why?" he asked in amazement.

"I'm busy."

"What's the matter?" he asked suspiciously. "Are you cross with me?"

"No," I replied. "If I were cross with you I wouldn't want to see you at the villa, would I?" It had occurred to me that he might become jealous and pester me. So I added: "Don't be scared—I love you as I always did. Only I've got to help mother with some extra work because of the holidays—and since I won't be able to get away from home until late and you're never free late at night, I'd rather wait until your employers go away."

"But what about the morning?"

"I'll be sleeping in the morning," I answered. "By the way—you know I'm not a model any more?"

"Why?"

"I got tired of it—you're glad, aren't you? I'll see you in ten days' time, then. Shall I give you a ring?"

"Very well."

He said 'very well' without much conviction. But I knew him well enough to be sure that despite his suspicions he would not turn up before the ten days had passed. Rather, just because he was suspicious he would not turn up. The idea that I might have discovered his treachery must have filled him with terror and dismay. I hung up the receiver and realised I had spoken to Gino in a calm, good-natured and even affectionate voice, and I congratulated myself. By and by my feelings for him would also become calm, good-natured and affectionate and I would be able to see him without any fear of plunging him, myself and our relationship into the false and trying atmosphere of hatred.

In the afternoon of that very day, I went straight off to see Gisella in her furnished room. As was usual with her at that hour, she had only that moment got out of her bed, and was dressing for her date with Riccardo. I sat down on the unmade bed and, while she wandered about in the semi-darkness of the untidy room, full of clothes and knick-knacks, I told her in the most matter-of-fact tone of voice how I had gone to call on Astarita and how he had told me that Gino had a wife and child. On hearing this news, Gisella exploded into an exclamation, I don't know whether of joy or surprise, came to sit on the bed facing me, and, putting her two hands on my shoulders, gazed into my eyes.

" No, no . . . I can't believe it . . . a wife and daughter ! Is it really true ? "

" The daughter's called Maria."

Obviously she wanted to get to the bottom of the story and discuss it as fully as possible, and my peaceful attitude disappointed her.

" A wife and daughter . . . and the daughter's called Maria . . . can you talk about it like that ? "

" How should I talk about it ? "

" Aren't you upset ? "

" Of course I'm upset."

" But how did he break the news ? Did he say ' Gino Molinari's got a wife and daughter,' just like that ? "

" Yes."

" What did you say ? "

" Nothing. What could I say ? "

" But how did you feel ? Didn't you burst into tears ? After all, it's a disaster for you."

" No, it didn't occur to me to cry."

" Well, now you can't marry Gino," she exclaimed after a moment's thought, and cheerfully. " What a business, all the same ! That man's got no conscience—a poor girl like you, who lived only for him, as you might say. Men are all scoundrels."

119

" Gino doesn't yet know I know everything," I said.

" In your place, my dear," she said eagerly, " I'd tell him what I think of him . . . and he wouldn't get off without a flea in his ear."

" I've got a date with him in ten days' time," I answered. " I think we'll go on making love."

She drew back, staring straight at me. " Why on earth ! . . . Do you still like him . . . after what he's done ? "

" No," I answered, and I could not help lowering my voice, " I don't like him so much, but "—I hesitated, and then lied deliberately—" scenes and a flea in the ear aren't always the best way of getting your own back."

She looked at me a moment with half-shut eyes, standing back as painters do while scrutinising their pictures:

" You're quite right . . ." she exclaimed. " I hadn't thought of that . . . but do you know what I'd do in your place ? I'd let him stew in his own juice, calmly, quite sure of himself—and then one fine day I'd leave him."

I didn't reply. She continued after a moment, in a less excited voice but always just as lively and expressive. " Still, I can hardly believe it . . . a wife and daughter . . . and he was so finicky about you ! And made you buy all that furniture and a trousseau. It's a bad business, a bad business ! "

I remained silent. " But I knew all along ! " she cried triumphantly. " I saw through him. You must admit that. What did I tell you ? He doesn't mean what he says. Poor Adriana ! " She threw her arms round my neck and kissed me. I let her kiss me.

" Yes, but the worst of it is, he's made mother spend her money," I then said.

" Does your mum know ? "

" Not yet."

" Don't be worried about the cash," she cried. " Astarita is so much in love with you—you only need to make up your mind and he'll give you every penny you want."

" I don't want to see anything more of Astarita," I answered. " Any man but Astarita."

I must say Gisella was no fool. She realised immediately

that for the moment it was better not to mention Astarita, and she also knew what I meant by the phrase, 'any other man but Astarita.' She pretended to think for a while.

"You're right." Then she continued: "I see what you mean. I'd feel rather queer myself if I went with Astarita after what has happened—he wants things at all costs—and he told you about Gino to get his own back." She was silent again. "Leave it to me," she went on seriously. "Do you want to meet someone who'll be willing to help you?"

"Yes."

"Leave it to me."

"But," I added, "I don't want to be tied up with anyone, I'd rather be free."

"Leave it to me," she repeated for the third time.

"Now I want to give mother her money back," I continued, "and buy some things I need. And I don't want mother to have to work any more," I added.

Meanwhile Gisella had got up and had seated herself at the dressing-table. "You've always been too good, Adriana," she said as she hastily dabbed on some powder. "Now can you see what happens to people who are too good?"

"Did you know I didn't go to pose this morning?" I said. "I've made up my mind to give up being a model."

"You're quite right," she replied. "I only pose myself for ——," and she named a certain artist, "just to do him a favour. But when he's finished, I'm through with it."

I felt very fond of Gisella at that moment, and thoroughly consoled. The sound of her saying 'Leave it to me' was reassuring, like a cordial and maternal promise to attend to my needs as soon as possible. I realised, of course, that Gisella was not inspired to help me by any affection she had for me, but rather by the almost unconscious desire, as in the Astarita affair, to see me reduced as quickly as possible to her own condition. But no one ever does anything for nothing and, since in this case Gisella's envy coincided with my own convenience, I saw no reason to turn down her help merely because I knew it was given from interested motives.

She was in a great hurry because she was already late for

her date with her fiancé. We left the room and began to descend the steep, narrow staircase of the old house.

"You know, I'm beginning to think Riccardo wants to play me the same trick as Gino has you," she said on the way down, spurred on by her state of excitement and perhaps by the desire to soften the bitterness of my disillusionment by showing me I was not the only unfortunate one.

"Is he married, too?" I asked innocently.

"No, but he spins me such a yarn—I think he wants to make a fool of me. But I told him straight out: 'Look here, my dear boy, I don't need you, and if you want you can stay, if not, clear out!'"

I said nothing, but I did think that there was a great difference between me and her and between my relationship with Gino and hers with Riccardo. At heart she had never had any illusions about Riccardo's intentions, and had not thought twice on occasion, as I well knew, about playing him false. I, on the contrary, had placed all the hopes of my inexperienced heart on becoming Gino's wife and had always been faithful to him, because the favour Astarita had obliged me to do him at Viterbo by his blackmailing could not really be called infidelity. But I thought she would probably be offended if I said this to her, so I did not speak. At the street door she arranged to meet me the following evening at a confectionery shop, warning me to be punctual because probably she would have someone with her. Then she ran off.

I realised I ought to tell mother what had happened, but I did not dare. Mother really loved me; and being the opposite of Gisella, who saw in Gino's treachery only the triumph of her own ideas and did not even try to conceal from me her cruel delight, mother would feel more sorrow than joy at seeing how right she had been in the end. At heart she desired only my happiness and did not care how I achieved it, but she was sure Gino would not be able to give it me. After much hesitation I decided not to tell her anything. I knew that on the following evening deeds, not words, would open her eyes; and although I realised it was a brutal way of showing her the great change that had come about in my life, yet I liked the idea that by so doing I would avoid a lot of explanation, reflections and comments, or at least, the kind of explanation, reflections and comments Gisella had poured out so generously when I had told her the tale of Gino's deceit. To tell the truth, I felt a kind of disgust now for the whole question of marriage and wanted to talk about it as little as possible and make others avoid the subject, too.

The following day I pretended to have an appointment with Gino and stayed out all afternoon so that mother, who was already suspicious, would not pester me all the time. I had had a new dress made for the wedding, a grey costume, which I had intended to put on immediately after the ceremony. It was my best dress and I hesitated a long time before putting it on. But then I thought that one day or other I would be obliged to do so, and it would not be on any purer or happier day than today, and that, on the other hand, men judge by appearances and it would suit my books better to show myself at my best in order to get more money; and I laid my scruples aside. And so I put on, not without certain misgivings, my best dress which today, when I think of it, seems very plain and simple like all my clothes at the time, did my hair carefully and painted my face, but no more than usual. And while on this subject, I must say I have never understood why so many women in my profession plaster their faces so thickly and promenade about the streets looking as if they were wearing carnival masks. Perhaps it is because, with the life they lead, they would otherwise look too pale; or perhaps because they are afraid that if they did not paint so crudely they would not attract men's attention and would not be able to show them that they are approachable. However tired I am and however much I overdo it, I never lose my healthy, bronzed look, and I can say without blushing that my looks have always been enough to make men turn their heads to stare at me when I pass down the street, without the aid of too much make-up. I don't attract men by using lipstick or eye-pencils or by peroxiding hair, but by my majestic bearing (at least, that's what lots of them have told me), the sweet serenity of my expression, my perfect teeth when I laugh, and the girlish mass of my dark, wavy hair.

Women who dye their hair and paint their faces probably do not realise that men, judging them for what they are from the very outset, feel a kind of disillusionment in anticipation. But I, being so natural and restrained, have always left them in doubt about my real character, and in this way have given them the illusion of adventure, which when all is said and done is what they want far more than the mere satisfaction of their senses.

When I was dressed and made up, I went to a cinema and saw the same film through twice. I left the cinema when night had fallen and went straight to the confectionery shop where I had the appointment with Gisella. It was not one of the usual cheap places where we used to meet Riccardo on other occasions; it was a smart shop and I had never been there before. I realised that the choice of this place was entirely due to her desire to provide a background worthy of me and to raise the price of my favours. Such attention to detail and other things, which I will mention later, really can lead a woman of my kind, if she is young and beautiful and knows how to use these gifts intelligently, to a steady comfortable position, which is what we all aim at in our hearts. But not many do it; and I was never one of them. My humble origin has always made me look suspiciously at luxury places. I have always felt ill-at-ease in restaurants, tea-shops, and bourgeois cafés, ashamed to smile or make eyes at the men, as if I were running the gauntlet amid all those glittering lights. I have always felt a deep, warm attraction for the city streets, with their palaces, churches, monuments, shops, doorways, which make them more beautiful and welcoming that any room in a restaurant or tea-shop. It has always been a favourite habit of mine to go down into the street, about the time of sunset, and, while walking slowly along beside the lighted shop windows, to watch the twilight gradually darken the sky above the roofs; I have always liked to wander among the crowds and to listen without turning round to the amorous suggestions which the most unexpected passers-by, with the sudden excitation of their senses, risk whispering on the spur of the moment; I have always loved to pace up and down the same street again and again, feeling almost worn out at the end but as fresh and eager in my heart as at a fair when the surprises are inexhaustible. The street has always been my restaurant, my drawing-room, my café, and this is due to the fact that I was born poor and the poor are known to get their entertainment cheap by gazing in at shop windows where they cannot afford to buy and at the façades of palaces where they cannot afford to live. For the same reason I have always loved the churches, of which there are so many in Rome, a luxury within everyone's reach since they are always open, where the ancient, humble stench of poverty is often stronger than the smell of incense among the marble, the gold and the precious ornaments. But a rich man, of course, does not walk through the streets or go to church ; at most he crosses the city in his car, leaning back against the cushions and occasionally reading a newspaper ; and, by preferring the street to any other spot, I immediately cut myself off from all those introductions I ought to have sought, according to Gisella, at the sacrifice of my own most deeply rooted tastes. I was never disposed to make such a sacrifice and all the time I was Gisella's partner my inclinations were a subject of heated discussion between us. Gisella did not like the street ; churches meant nothing to her, and crowds only disgusted her and filled her with scorn. What she aimed at were the expensive restaurants where attentive waiters anxiously watch their clients' slightest gesture, fashionable dance-halls, with a band in uniform and dancers in evening dress, the smartest cafés and gambling-halls. She became quite a different person in such places, changed her gestures, carriage and even the tone of her voice. She affected to behave like a real lady, in fact ; and this was the ideal she aimed at, which later, as we shall see, she did attain to some degree. But the most curious aspect of her success in the end was that she met the person fated to fulfil her ambitions not in a fashionable haunt but through me, in the streets she loathed so heartily.

I found Gisella at the confectionery shop with a middle-aged man, a commercial traveller, whom she introduced as Giacinti. When seated, he appeared to be of normal height, because his shoulders were very broad ; but when he stood up, he turned out to be almost a dwarf, and his broad shoulders made him appear even shorter than he was. His thick, white hair, gleaming like silver, was brushed straight up off his forehead, perhaps to make him seem taller, and his face was red and healthy, with the regular and noble features of a statue; he had a handsome smooth forehead, large dark eyes, a straight nose and well-shaped mouth. But an unpleasing expression of vanity, of conceit and false benevolence made his face, which at first sight seemed attractive and majestic, absolutely repellent.

I felt rather shy and sat down without saying a word after the introductions were over. Giacinti, as though my arrival were only an unimportant incident whereas it was really the whole purpose of the evening, went on with what he had been saying to Gisella. "You can't complain of me," Gisella," he said, and placed a hand on her knee, keeping it there all the time he was talking; "how long did our—let's call it alliance—last? Six months? Well, can you say, with your hand on your heart, that in all those six months I sent you away dissatisfied?" His speech was clear, slow, accented, emphatic, but he obviously spoke in that way, not so much to make himself understood, as to listen to his own voice and enjoy every word he uttered.

"No, no," said Gisella in bored tones, lowering her head.

"Get Gisella to tell you, Adriana," went on Giacinti in his clear, emphatic voice. "Not only have I never tried to cut down her—shall we call them professional earnings?— but every time I came back from Milan I always brought her a present. Do you remember the time I brought you a bottle of French perfume, now? And the other time I gave you some silk-and-lace cami-knickers? Women like to say men don't understand anything about lingerie—but I'm an exception to the rule!" He laughed softly, showing perfect teeth but so curiously white that they seemed false.

"Give me a cigarette, do," said Gisella shortly.

"At once!" he replied with ironic courtesy. He offered me one, too, took one himself, and after he had lit it continued. "Do you remember the handbag I brought you another time—

126

a big leather one—that was something to write home about !
Don't you use it any more ? "

" It's a morning bag," said Gisella.

" I like giving presents," he continued, turning to me,
" but not for sentimental reasons, you understand "—he
shook his head, puffing smoke from his nostrils—" but for
three clear reasons. One—I like to be thanked. Two—
there's nothing like a present for getting yourself properly
treated. In fact, anyone who has once had a present from
you always hopes for another. Three—because women like
an illusion and a present makes them feel there's some senti-
ment even when there isn't."

" You're a deep one, you are," said Gisella indifferently,
without even looking at him.

He shook his head, showing all his teeth in a handsome
smile. " No, I'm not deep—I'm simply a man with some
experience of life who has been able to learn from his experience. I know you have to do certain things with women,
others with your clients, others with your servants, and so on.
My mind's like an extremely tidy card-index. For instance
—a woman in the offing !—I take down my notebook, look
through it, find that certain measures obtained the desired
effect, others didn't, I put the notebook back in its place and
act accordingly. That's all there is to it." He stopped and
smiled again.

Gisella was smoking with a bored look, I said nothing.

" And I find women are grateful to me," he continued,
" because they realise at once that they won't have any disap-
pointments with me, I know what they expect, their weaknesses
and their whims, just as I'm grateful myself to a client who
understands me at a glance, one who doesn't waste my time
chatting, knows what he wants and what I want—I've got an
ashtray on my desk in Milan with the words : ' The Lord
bless those who don't waste my time.' " He threw his
cigarette down and looking at his watch added : " It's about
time to go and have a meal."

" What's the time ? "

" Eight. Excuse me a moment—I'll be right back."

He got up and went out at the end of the room. He really

was very short, with his broad shoulders and thick white hair standing up on top of his head. Gisella crushed out her cigarette on the ashtray. "He's an awful bore and talks of nothing but himself," she said.

"I noticed that."

"Just let him talk and say yes all the time," she went on, "you'll see he'll tell you heaps of things—he thinks he's God knows what—but he's very free with his money and really does give you presents."

"Yes, but then he keeps on reminding you——"

She did not reply, but shook her head as if to say : 'What can you do about it?' We were silent for a while, then Giacinti came back, paid, and we left the confectioner's.

"Gisella," said Giacinti, when we were in the street, "this evening is Adriana's—but would you like to come to supper with us?"

"No, no, thanks," Gisella replied hurriedly, "I've got a date." She said good-bye to Giacinti and went off.

"What a nice girl she is," I remarked to Giacinti as soon as she had gone.

He made a face. "Not bad," he said ; "she's got a good figure."

"Don't you like her?"

"I don't require of anyone that they should be likeable," he said, walking beside me and holding my arm tight, high up, almost under the armpit, "but that they should do well whatever they do—I don't ask a typist to be likeable, for instance, but to be able to type quickly without making mistakes—and I don't ask a girl like Gisella to be pleasant but to know how to do her job, that is, to give me a nice time for the hour or two I spend with her. Now Gisella doesn't know how to do her job."

"Why?"

"Because she's always thinking about money—and she's always afraid she won't be paid or won't get enough—I don't expect her to love me, but it's part of her profession to behave as though she loved me really, and give me an illusion—that's what I pay her for—but Gisella makes it too obvious she's only doing it for her own interest—she doesn't even give you

128

time to get your breath before she starts haggling.   It's too much of a good thing ! "

We had reached the restaurant, a noisy place, crowded with men of Giacinti's sort—commercial travellers, stock-brokers, shopkeepers, business men on their way through town.   Giacinti entered first.

" Is my usual table free ? " he asked as he gave the boy his hat and overcoat.

" Yes, Mr. Giacinti."

It was a table in the window.   Giacinti sat down, rubbing his hands together.

" Got a good appetite ? " he then asked me.

" I think so," I answered awkwardly.

" Good, I'm glad.   I like people to eat when they're at table. Gisella, for instance, never wanted to eat anything, said she was afraid of getting fat.   Lot of nonsense !   There's a time for everything.   At table you eat." He seemed full of resentment towards Gisella.

" But you really do get fat if you eat too much," I said timidly, " and some women don't want to put on weight."

" Are you one of those ? "

" No, I'm not.   But as a matter of fact they tell me I'm on the heavy side."

" Don't you listen to 'em—it's all envy.   You're all right, as you are.   I say so, and I know what I'm talking about." He patted my hand in a fatherly way as if to reassure me.

The waiter came.   " First of all," said Giacinti, " take these flowers away, they're a nuisance to me.   Then bring the usual, you know—double quick ! "

Then he turned to me.   " He knows me and knows what I like.   Leave it to him.   You'll see you won't have anything to complain of."

In fact I had nothing to complain of.   All the courses that were served were delicious and plentiful, even if not very choice.   Giacinti had a huge appetite and ate with concen-tration, his head lowered, his knife and fork firmly gripped, without looking at me or talking, as if he were by himself. He really was entirely engrossed in the act of eating and in his greed even lost his much vaunted calm, his gestures were

129

confused, as if he were afraid he would not be done in time and would have to go hungry. He pushed a piece of meat into his mouth, with his left hand hurriedly broke off a morsel of bread, bit it, with his other hand poured himself a glass of wine and began to drink before he had finished chewing. All the time he kept on smacking his lips, rolling his eyes and shaking his head every now and again like a cat when it has got hold of too big a mouthful. I was not at all hungry, though, unlike my usual self. For the first time in my life I was going to make love to a man I didn't love and didn't even know and I looked him over carefully, noting my own feelings and trying to imagine how I would go through with it. After this first time I used to pay no attention to the appearance of the men I went with; perhaps because being driven by necessity, I quickly learnt to pick out at a first glance the one good, pleasing aspect in each man which would make intimacy bearable. But that evening I had not yet learnt the trick of my profession, which consists in knowing how to discover immediately some underlying attraction to make the act of love less unpleasant, and I was seeking it instinctively, as you might say, without realising what I was doing. I have already said that Giacinti was not ugly; in fact, as long as he kept his mouth shut and did not reveal the consuming passion of his soul, he might even have been called handsome. This was saying a great deal, because, after all love is very much a matter of physical contact; but it was not enough for me, because I have never been able to stand a man, let alone love him, for his mere physical qualities. Now when supper was over and Giacinti, after a belch or two, had begun to talk again, once his ill-mannered greed was satisfied, I realised there was nothing in him, at least, nothing I could discover, which would make him even tolerable. Not only did he talk about himself the whole time, as Gisella had said, but he did it in a most unpleasant way, was a conceited bore, telling me most of the time things that did him no credit at all and only strengthened my first instinctive feeling of repulsion. There was absolutely nothing in him that I could like ; and all the things he boasted of and enlarged upon as qualities seemed dreadful faults to me. Later I met other men, though not many, who were just as worthless, with nothing good in them at all to cling to, that might make them likeable; and I have always marvelled at their existence and asked myself whether it was not perhaps my own fault if I was unable to discover at first sight the qualities they must undoubtedly possess. In time, however, I have become accustomed to such unpleasant companions, and I pretend to laugh, joke and be what they believe I am and want me to be. But that evening my first discovery filled me with gloomy reflections. While Giacinti went on talking, fiddling at his teeth with a toothpick, I was telling myself I had taken up a very hard profession—the simulation of passionate love for men who actually roused the most contrary feelings in me, as in Giacinti's case; I told myself no money could repay such favours—that it was impossible in such cases not to behave like Gisella, who thought only of the money and showed it. It also occurred to me that that evening I would be taking this hateful Giacinti back to my poor little room I had intended to use so differently. And I thought how unfortunate I was and how fate had meant me to be under no illusions from the very beginning, by leading me to meet Giacinti and not some artless youth in search of adventure, or some decent unpretentious fellow like hundreds of others; and that Giacinti's presence among my furniture would put the seal on my renunciation of all the old dreams of a respectable, normal life.

He talked all the time, but still, he was not so dull as not to notice that I was hardly listening to him and was not cheerful. "Feeling glum, kiddy?" he suddenly asked me.

"No, no," I replied hurriedly, pulling myself together, but half-tempted by his deceptively affectionate tones to confide in him and talk a little about myself since I had allowed him to talk of himself for so long.

"That's better!" he went on. "I don't like gloomy folks. And I didn't invite you here to be glum—you may have your reasons, mind, I don't doubt it, but as long as you're with me leave your glum feelings behind—I don't want to know anything of your affairs, I don't want to know who you are, what's happening to you, nor anything else—

I'm not interested. We've got a deal on, you and I, even if it's not in writing. I guarantee to give you a certain sum of money and you in return guarantee to make me pass the evening pleasantly. Nothing else matters." He said these words seriously, perhaps a little irritated by the fact that I had not appeared to be listening to him attentively enough.

" But I'm not unhappy ! Only it's so smoky in here and noisy—I feel a bit giddy," I answered, without showing anything of the feelings that had stirred me.

" Shall we go ? " he asked anxiously. I said yes. He called the waiter immediately, paid the bill and we left.

" Shall we go to a hotel ? " he asked me when we were out in the street.

" No, no," I answered hurriedly. I was frightened at the idea of having to show my papers ; and anyway, I had already made up my mind in another sense : " Come to my place."

We got into a taxi and I gave my home address. As soon as the taxi started, he threw himself upon me, pawing me all over and kissing my neck. I could tell from his breath that he had had a lot to drink, and that he must be tight. He kept on calling me ' kiddy,' the usual term for young children, and on his lips it irritated me and sounded ridiculous and out of place. I let him have his way for a while then, pointing to the chauffeur's back, said : " Hadn't we better wait until we get there ? "

He did not reply but fell heavily back against the cushions, red and congested in the face, as though suddenly attacked by a fit of apoplexy. Angrily he muttered : " I pay him to take me where I want to go and not to busy himself with what's going on in his taxi." He was obsessed by the idea that money could shut anyone's mouth, and more especially his money. I did not answer and for the rest of the entire journey we sat stiffly beside one another without touching. The city lights flashed through the taxi windows, lit up our faces and hands for a moment, then were swallowed up again ; and it seemed queer to me to be beside that man whose very existence I had been unaware of a little time before, and to be hurrying with such a man towards my own flat, to give myself to him as I would to my beloved. These reflections shortened the journey. I pulled myself together, amazed to see the taxi stop in the usual street before my door.

"Don't make a noise going in, because I live with my mother," I said to Giacinti in the dark on the way upstairs.

"Don't worry, kiddy," he answered.

When we reached the landing I unlocked the door. Giacinti followed me; I took his hand and, without switching on the light, led him across the passage to the door of my room which was the first on the left. I made him enter first, turned on the bedside lamp, and standing in the doorway gave a kind of farewell look round at my furniture. Giacinti, delighted at finding a new, clean room when he had probably been afraid he would find himself surrounded by filthy, ramshackle furniture, sighed with satisfaction and threw his overcoat down on a chair. I told him to wait for me and went out of the room.

I walked straight to the living-room and found mother there sewing at the centre table. Seeing me, she put down her work at once and made to get up, probably imagining she would have to get my supper as on other evenings.

"Don't get up," I said. "I've already had my supper. I've got someone in the next room. Don't come in on any account."

"Someone there?" she asked in astonishment.

"Yes," I answered quickly. "Not Gino—a gentleman." Without waiting for her to question me further I left the living-room.

I returned to my own room and locked the door. Giacinti, red in the face and impatient, came to meet me in the middle of the room and took me in his arms. He was much shorter than I and bent me back against the end of the bed in order to reach my face with his lips. I tried not to let him kiss me on the mouth, and by turning my face away as if I were shy and then throwing my head back as if in ecstasy, I succeeded in my intention. Giacinti made love exactly as he ate, greedily, without discrimination, beginning in one place then another, afraid he was missing something, blinded by my body as he had been by the food at the restaurant. After he had embraced me he seemed to want to undress me as we were, still standing up. He uncovered one of my arms

133

and a shoulder, and then began to kiss me again, as if the sight of my bare flesh had put his head in a whirl. I was afraid his clumsy gestures would tear my dress and at last I said : " Come on, get your clothes off," but without pushing him away.

He left me at once and began to undress, sitting on the edge of the bed. I did the same on the other side.

" Does your mother know ? " he suddenly asked.

" Yes."

" What does she say about it ? "

" Nothing."

" Does she disapprove ? "

These details were obviously nothing more to him than an additional thrill in his adventure. This trait is common to all men. Few can resist the temptation of mingling physical pleasure with some other kind of interest or even pity. " She neither approves nor disapproves," I said shortly, standing up and slipping my petticoat over my head. " I'm my own mistress and can do what I like." When I was naked I put my clothes tidily on a chair and then stretched myself on the bed, flat on my back, one arm under my head and the other across my bosom to cover it. I do not know why but I remembered this was the position of the pagan goddess who resembled me in the coloured print the stout painter had given mother ; and suddenly I felt resentfully angry at the thought of the great change in my life since that day. Giacinti must have been astonished at the shapely, firm beauty of my body, which was not apparent when I was fully dressed, for he stopped taking his clothes off and stared at me in amazement, his mouth half-open and his eyes bursting out of his head.

" Hurry up," I said. " I'm cold."

He finished undressing and threw himself upon me. I have mentioned his way of making love already ; it was exactly like him, and I think I have described him adequately. I need only add that he was one of those men who become fearfully exacting at the thought of the money they have spent or are going to spend, as if they are afraid of being cheated if they don't take everything they think they have a

134

right to. I have already said that he was very greedy, but not so greedy as to be able to forget his money; he wanted to get all he could for it. His aim, I soon realised, was to make our meeting last as long as he could and to get out of me all the enjoyment to which he thought he was entitled. With this in mind he laboured over my body like someone over an instrument that requires much preparation before being played and urged me all the time to do the same with his. But although I obeyed him I soon began to be bored and to watch him coldly, as if his obvious calculations had set a distance between us, and I were seeing not only him but also myself from a great way off, through a mirror of dislike and disgust. This was the very opposite of the feeling of liking I had tried instinctively to encourage at the beginning of the evening. Suddenly a wave of shameful remorse swept through me and I closed my eyes.

In the end he grew tired and we lay beside one another on the bed.

"You must admit," he said in self-satisfied tones, "that although I'm not so young as I was I'm an exceptional lover."

"Yes, you are," I said indifferently.

"All the women say so," he went on, "and do you know what I think? Little bottles hold good wine. Some men twice my size aren't up to anything!"

I began to feel cold and sitting up pulled a corner of the blanket over us both. He interpreted this as sign of affection.

"Good girl," he said, "now I'm going to have a little sleep." Then he curled up against me and dropped off.

I kept still, lying on my back, his white head against my breast. The blanket covered us both to the waist and as I looked at him, at his hairy chest with the flaccid folds of middle age, at first I felt once more that I was with an utter stranger. But he was asleep; and sleeping he no longer talked, looked, moved. Given his unlovable character sleep revealed only the best of him; that is, he was just a man like all the rest, with no name or profession, no qualities or faults, simply a human being whose breast rose and fell as he breathed. It may seem odd, but as I looked at him and watched him trustfully sleeping beside me I felt almost affectionate towards

him, and what I felt was brought home to me by the care
I took to avoid waking him by some movement. This was
the impulse of sympathy I had been seeking in vain until that
moment; the sight of his white head leaning heavily against
my young bosom aroused it in me. This sensation comforted
me and almost made me feel less cold. For a moment, in
fact, I experienced a kind of amorous exaltation which brought
tears to my eyes. In reality my heart was full to the brim
of affection, then as always—an affection which for lack of
lawful objects I poured out even on unworthy things and
people, rather than leave it unused and unwanted.

After twenty minutes or so he woke up. "Did I sleep
long?" he asked.

"No."

"I feel fine," he said, getting out of bed and rubbing his
hands together. "How fine I feel! I feel at least twenty
years younger!" He began to dress, exclaiming continually
in his joy and relief. I dressed in silence.

"I'd like to see you again, kiddy," he said when he was
ready. "How do I set about it?"

"Just ring up Gisella," I replied, "I see her every day."

"Are you always free?"

"Always."

"Long live freedom!"

Then, taking out his wallet he asked me: "How much
do you want?"

"What you think," I answered. "If you give me a lot
you'll be doing a good deed, I need it," I added sincerely.

"If I give you a lot," he retorted, "it's not in order to
do a good deed—but because you're a handsome girl and
have given me a nice evening's entertainment."

"As you like," I said, shrugging my shoulders.

"Everything's got its own price and should be paid for
according to its worth," he continued, taking the money
from his wallet. "Good deeds don't exist. You've supplied me with certain things of a better quality than Gisella,
for instance, would have supplied. And it's only fair that
you should get more than Gisella. Good deeds have nothing
to do with it. Here's a piece of advice. Don't ever say:

136

' Give me what you think.' Leave that to the street-hawkers. If anyone says : ' Give me what you think,' I'm always tempted to give them less than they deserve." He made an expressive face and held out the money.

As Gisella had said, he was generous, and the money was far more than I had expected. Once more as I took it I had the same powerful feeling of sensual complicity which Astarita's money had caused me during the Viterbo trip. I thought this must mean I had a vocation and was really born for that profession, even if I longed for something different in my heart of hearts. "Thanks," I said, and before realising what I was doing a grateful impulse made me kiss him on the cheek.

" Thanks to you," he replied, getting ready to go. I took his hand and led him in the dark through the hall to the front door. For a moment, when the bedroom door was shut and the front door not yet open, we were completely in the dark. And then some almost physical instinct told me that mother must be hiding in a corner of the hall, in the dark where I was wandering with Giacinti. She must be squatting behind the door or in the other corner between the sideboard and the wall, and was waiting for Giacinti to leave. I remembered the other time I had done the same, the night I had returned late after being with Gino in his employers' villa ; and I became very nervy at the idea that as soon as Giacinti had gone she might jump at me, seize me by the hair, drag me to the sofa and rain down blows upon me. I could feel she was there in the dark ; I felt as if I could almost see her, and had a kind of shrinking sensation behind me, as if her hands were hovering over my head, ready to grip me by the hair. I had Giacinti by one hand and the money in the other. Then I thought that as soon as she sprang at me I would put the money in her hand. This would be a silent way of reminding her that she had been the one to urge me the whole time to earn money in this way ; and it would also be an attempt to shut her mouth by appealing to the passionate love of money ever uppermost in her soul. Meanwhile I had opened the door.

" Bye-bye, then," said Giacinti. "I'll ring up Gisella."

I watched him go downstairs, broad-shouldered, his white hair standing straight up on his head, waving his hand in farewell without turning round. And I shut the door. Immediately, as I had foreseen, mother was upon me. But she did not seize me by the hair as I had feared, but tried in a clumsy way I did not understand at first to embrace me. Faithful to my plan, I sought her hand and thrust the money into it. But she pushed it away and it fell to the ground. I found it on the floor next morning when I left my room. All this happened breathlessly, but without a word said on either side.

We went into the living-room and I sat down sideways at the table. Mother sat in front of me and looked at me. She seemed worried and I felt awkward.

"Do you know, while you were in there, I suddenly felt scared for a moment?" she said unexpectedly.

"Scared of what?"

"I don't know," she replied. "First of all, I felt lonely . . . I felt cold all over . . . not myself at all . . . everything was spinning round me, like when you've had too much to drink . . . everything seemed queer. I found myself thinking: 'That's the table, that's the chair, that's the sewing-machine,' but I couldn't really believe they were the table, the chair, the sewing-machine. I didn't seem to be myself, even, I said to myself: 'I'm an old seamstress, I've a daughter called Adriana.' But I wasn't sure . . . I started to go over the past to convince myself, to think what I had been, when I was little, when I was your age, when I got married, when you were born . . . And I was afraid because it all flashed past like a single day and I had suddenly grown old from being young as I was, and I hadn't noticed the change. . . . And when I'm dead it'll all be as though I had never been born," she said with an effort, looking at me.

"What makes you think like that?" I said slowly. "You're still young. What's death got to do with it?"

She did not appear to have heard me and continued in her emphatic speech which I found painful and artificial. "I tell you, I was afraid. And I thought: 'Suppose someone didn't want to go on living, would they have to all the same ?' . . . I don't say you ought to kill yourself, you need courage to do that, but suppose you didn't want to live any more, like you don't want to eat or walk, maybe . . . Well, I swear by your dead father . . . I don't want to go on living——"

Her eyes were full of tears and her lips trembled. I felt like crying, too, and I got up and put my arms round her and went to sit on the sofa with her at the end of the room. We stayed there, holding one another close, both crying. I felt bewildered, because I was very tired and mother's talk, with its disconnected and troubled logic, increased my bewilderment. But I was the first to pull myself together because, after all, I was only crying out of sympathy with her. I had given up crying about myself long since. " Come come," I said, patting her on the shoulder.

" Adriana, I mean it . . . I don't want to go on living," she repeated through her tears. I patted her shoulder and let her cry to her heart's content without speaking. Meanwhile I could not help thinking that her tears were a sure sign of her remorse. She had always lectured me, saying I ought to follow Gisella's example and sell myself to the highest bidder, indeed she had. But there is a great difference between saying and doing. And when she saw me bringing a man home, felt me put the money in her hand, it must have been a heavy blow to her. Now she had the result of her lecturing before her eyes and she could not help being horrified. But at the same time she must have been incapable, somehow, of recognising that she had been mistaken, and perhaps she felt a bitter kind of complacency at the uselessness now of any such recognition. And so, instead of telling me straight out : ' You've done wrong—don't do it again,' she preferred to talk to me of things that did not concern me, her life and her desire to die. I have often noticed that many people, in the very instant when they perform some action they know to be wrong, try to cover themselves and restore their position by talking of higher things which show them to themselves and to others in a disinterested, noble light, that is in no way connected with what they are doing or allowing to be done. This is how it was in mother's case—except

139

that the majority act in this way quite consciously, while mother, poor dear, did it all unawares, as her heart and circumstances taught her.

But her phrase about her wish to die rang true to me. I supposed that I, too, had not wanted to live after I had discovered Gino's deception. Only, my body went on living on its own, unconcerned with my will. My bosom, my legs, my hips, which gave men such pleasure, went on living; my hidden sex between my thighs went on living and made me desire love even when my will opposed it. It was no use stretching myself out on the bed determined to live no longer, not to wake in the morning—while I was asleep my body went on living, the blood flowed in my veins, my stomach and intestine went on digesting, the hair grew again under my arms where I had cut it, my nails grew, my skin was bathed in sweat, my strength was renewed; and at a certain time in the morning my eyelids would open, without my conscious will, and my eyes would once more light upon the reality they hated, and I would realise that despite my desire to die I was still alive and had to go on living. So one might as well make the best of life and not think any more about it, I concluded.

But I said nothing of all this to mother because I realised such thoughts were just as sad as her own and would not have cheered her up at all. Instead, when she seemed to stop crying I left her side, saying: "I'm hungry." It was true, because in my nervousness I had hardly touched anything at the restaurant.

"There's your supper," said mother, glad I was suggesting something useful she could do, which she did every evening. "I'll go and get it ready for you." She went out and I was left alone.

I sat down at the table in my usual place and waited for her to return. My head was empty of thoughts, and nothing was left of all that had happened except the sickly-sweet odour on my fingers and the salty streak of dry tears on my cheeks. I kept still and watched the shadows flung on the long bare walls of the living-room by the hanging lamp. Then mother returned with a plate of meat and vegetables.

"I haven't warmed up the soup, it wouldn't be good by now—and there wasn't much of it."

"It doesn't matter, this will do."

She poured me out a glass of wine full to the brim and stood as usual in front of me, motionless and attentive, while I ate.

"Is the steak all right?" she asked anxiously after a while.

"Yes, it's nice."

"I told the butcher specially he was to give me a tender one." She seemed herself again and everything was exactly like it was on other evenings. I ate slowly and when I had finished I stretched my arms, yawning. I suddenly felt splendid, and this movement gave me a sense of pleasure because my body felt young, strong, satisfied.

"I'm very sleepy," I said.

"Wait a bit, I'll go and make up the bed," said mother eagerly, and made as if to go out. But I stopped her. "I'll do it myself," I said.

I got up and mother picked up the empty plate. "Let me sleep on tomorrow morning," I said, "I'll wake myself."

She replied that she would do as I wanted and when I had said good-night and kissed her I went into my room. The bed was still as Giacinti and I had left it. I simply pulled the pillows and the blanket into place, then got undressed and slipped into bed. I lay there with my eyes wide open in the dark for a while, my mind a blank.

"I'm a whore," I said aloud at last, to see what effect the words would have on me. They did not seem to have any effect, so shutting my eyes I fell asleep almost immediately.

CHAPTER EIGHT

I saw Giacinti every evening during the next few days. He rang up Gisella the next morning and, as soon as she met me in the afternoon, she gave me his message. Giacinti had to leave for Milan the evening before the day I had arranged to meet Gino and this was why I agreed to see him every evening.

Otherwise I would have refused, because I had vowed to myself that I did not want ever again to have a settled relationship with any one man. I thought it was better, if I was taking up this profession, to do it in earnest, with a different lover each time, rather than deceive myself into thinking I was not taking it up by letting one man keep me; with the added danger of growing fond of him or he of me, and thereby losing not only my physical liberty but also my emotional liberty as well. In any case, my ideas about normal married life had remained unchanged; and I thought that, if I were to marry, it would never be to a lover who had kept me and in the end had decided to make a business relationship legal, if not moral; but rather to a young man who would love me and whom I would love in return, one out of my own class of life, with my own tastes and ideas. What I wanted, in fact, was to keep the profession I had chosen completely separate from my own earlier ambitions, without any contacts or compromises, since I felt I was equally well cut out to be a good wife and a good harlot, but was quite incapable of maintaining a cautious and hypocritical middle way between the two. Also, when all was said and done, there was probably more to be made out of the scruples of many men than out of the generosity of one man alone.

Every evening Giacinti took me to have supper in the same restaurant and then came home with me, remaining with me until well on in the night. By now mother had quite given up any attempt to talk to me about my evenings, and contented herself with asking me whether I had slept well when she brought me my coffee on a tray late next morning. Previously I used to go and sip my coffee in the kitchen, very early, without sitting down even, in front of the stove, feeling the biting cold of the water I had washed in still on my hands and face. Now instead mother brought it to me and I drank it in bed, while she opened the shutters and began to tidy up the room. I never said anything to her that I had not already said in the past; but she had understood on her own that everything was changed in our life and she showed by her behaviour that she realised perfectly well what the difference was. She acted as if we had a tacit agreement and seemed by her attentions to be begging me humbly to allow her to continue to serve me and make herself useful in our new way of life as she had done in the past. But I must say this habit of bringing me my coffee in bed must have reassured her to some extent, because many people, and mother was one of them, endow habits with a positive worth even when they are not positive, as in the present case. With the same zeal she introduced many little changes of the kind into our daily life. For instance, she used to prepare a great bowl of boiling water for me to wash in as soon as I got up, used to put flowers in a vase in my room, and so on.

Giacinti always gave me the same amount and without telling mother I used to put it in a drawer in the box where she had placed her savings until now. I only kept a little small change for myself. I suppose she must have noticed the daily additions to our capital, but we never mentioned it to one another. I have noticed in the course of my life that even people who earn their livelihood by recognised means prefer not to speak about it, not only to strangers but not even to friends. Probably money is linked with a sense of shame or at least modesty which prevents it being included in the list of ordinary topics of conversation and places it among those secret and inadmissible things which it is better not to mention ; as if it is always wrongfully earned, no matter what its origin may be. But perhaps it is also true that no one likes to show the feeling money rouses in his soul, since it is a most powerful feeling and hardly ever dissociated from a sense of sin.

One evening Giacinti said he would like to sleep in my room with me, but with the excuse that the neighbours would notice him in the morning when he left I managed to send him away. As a matter of fact my intimacy with him had not made one single stride since the first evening, through no fault of mine. Until the day he left he behaved exactly as he had on the first evening. He was a man of little or no worth, at least in his emotional relationships, and all the feeling I was able to muster I had experienced that first day while he was asleep—a general feeling which probably was not even connected with him. The idea of sleeping with a man like that disgusted me. And I was also afraid of being bored, because I was sure he would keep me awake half the night talking confidentially about himself. He never noticed my boredom or my dislike of him, however, and left me convinced that in those few days he had made himself extremely pleasant in my sight.

The day of my appointment with Gino came at last and so much had happened in those ten days that I felt as if a hundred years had passed since I used to see him on my way to the studio and used to work to save money and set up house and considered myself an engaged girl soon to be married. He was there most punctually at the appointed time, and as I got into the car he seemed very pale and upset. No one likes to have a deception flung in his teeth, not even the boldest deceiver, and he must have thought a great deal and have had his suspicions during the ten days that had interrupted our usual meetings. But I showed no resentment, and, as a matter of fact, I was not even pretending, because I felt perfectly calm; and when the bitterness of the first moment's disillusionment had passed I felt a kind of indulgent and sceptical fondness for him. After all, I still liked Gino, as I knew from the first glance I gave him, and this was saying a lot.

"So your confessor's changed his mind?" he asked me after a while, as the car sped towards the villa. His tone was mocking but at the same time uncertain.

"No," I answered simply, "I've changed my mind."

"Have you finished all your work with your mother?"

"For the time being."

"Queer."

He did not know what he was saying but he was obviously testing me to discover whether his suspicions were justified.

"Why is it queer?"

"I was only saying it for something to say."

"Don't you believe I've been busy?"

"I don't believe anything."

I had decided to show him up, but in my own way, by playing with him a little, like a cat with a mouse, without

144

the brutal scenes Gisella had advised, which did not chime in with my temperament.

"Are you jealous?" I asked him coquettishly.

"Me jealous? Good Heavens!"

"Yes, you are—if you were sincere you'd admit it."

He took the bait I was offering. "Anyone in my place would be jealous," he said.

"Why?"

"Oh, come off it! Who d'you think would believe you? Such important work that you can't spare five minutes to see me!"

"It's true, though," I said calmly. "I've worked very hard." And it was true; what else was it but work, and very tiring work, that I had been doing with Giacinti every evening? "And I've earned enough to pay off the rest of the hire-purchase and buy my trousseau," I added, making fun of myself. "So at least we'll be able to get married without any debts."

He said nothing; he was clearly trying to persuade himself of the truth of what I was saying, and was slowly abandoning his earlier suspicions. At that moment I made a movement I usually made in the past: I flung my arms round his neck while he was driving and kissed him hard below the ear, whispering: "Why are you jealous? You know you're the only person in my life."

We reached the villa. Gino drove the car into the garden, shut the gate and went towards the tradesmen's entrance with me. It was twilight and the first lights were already gleaming in the windows of the houses round about, red in the bluish mist of the winter evening. It was nearly dark in the underground passage and there was a smell of slops and stuffiness. I stopped.

"I don't want to go to your room this evening," I said.

"Why not?"

"I want to make love in your mistress's room."

"You're off your head!" he exclaimed in scandalised horror. We had often gone into the upper rooms, but had always made love in his room, in the basement.

"It's just a whim," I said. "What does it matter to you?"

"It matters a lot—something might get broken—you never know—and if they notice, what'll I do?"

"Oh, what a tragedy!" I exclaimed lightly; "you'll get the sack, that's all."

"And you can speak of it in that tone!"

"How should I speak of it? If you really loved me, you wouldn't think twice about it."

"I do love you, but I can't hear of this—don't let's even talk of it, I don't want any trouble, I don't."

"We'll be careful. They won't notice."

"No."

I felt perfectly calm. "I, who am your fiancée, ask you this one favour," I exclaimed, continuing to pretend what I did not really feel, "and you refuse, because you're afraid I'll put my body where your mistress puts hers and lay my head where she lays hers . . . but what are you thinking? That she's better than I am?"

"No, but——"

"I'm worth a thousand of her sort," I went on, "but so much the worse for you . . . You can make love to your mistress's pillows and sheets . . . I'm going."

As I have already said, his respect and his subservience to his employers went very deep. He was nauseatingly proud of them, as if all their wealth were his, too. But seeing me speak in that way and turn away impetuously with a determination I had not accustomed him to find in me in the past, he lost his head and ran after me.

"Wait a bit! Where are you? I was only talking! Let's go upstairs, if you like!"

I let him plead with me a little more, pretending to be offended. Then I agreed and we went to the upper floor, our arms round one another, and stopping on each step for a kiss, just like the first time, but with a change of heart—at least, speaking for myself. In his mistress's room I walked straight over to the bed and turned the covers down. He protested, once more mastered by fear. "You don't mean to get right into the bed?"

"Why not?" I replied calmly. "I don't want to get cold."

146

He said nothing, visibly upset. When I had prepared the
bed I went into the bathroom, lit the geyser and turned on
the hot-water tap, just a trickle, so that the bath would not
fill too rapidly. Gino, uneasy and dissatisfied, followed me
and protested once more.

" Having a bath, too ? "

" They have a bath after they've made love, don't they ? "

" How should I know what they do ? " he answered with
a shrug. But I could see that in point of fact my boldness
did not really displease him, he merely found it difficult to
swallow. He was not a brave man and he liked to be on the
right side of the law. But law-breaking attracted him all
the more since he hardly ever allowed himself to slip.
" You're right, after all," he said with a smile after a moment's
pause, wavering between temptation and reluctance, as he
felt the mattress with his hand. " It's comfortable here—
better than in my room."

" Didn't I say so ? "

We sat down together on the edge of the bed. " Gino,"
I said, throwing my arms round his neck, " think how lovely
it will be when we have a house of our own, just for the two
of us . . . it won't be like this . . . but it'll be our own."

I do not know why I said this. Probably because I knew
for certain by now that all those things were out of the
question ; and I liked to worry the very spot where my
mind was most constantly pierced. " Yes, yes," he said,
and kissed me.

" I know the kind of life I like," I continued with the cruel
feeling that I was describing something lost and gone for
ever, " not a fine place like this . . . two rooms and a kitchen
would be enough for me. But everything would be my
own . . . and it would be as clean as a new pin . . . and
we'd be peaceful. We'd go out on Sunday together, eat
together, sleep together. Oh, Gino, just think how lovely
it'll be ! "

He said nothing. As a matter of fact, I remained quite
unmoved as I said all this. I felt I was playing a part, like
an actor on the stage. But this made it all the more bitter,
because the cold, superficial part I was playing, which awoke

not the slightest echo in my own mind, was what I had really been only ten days before. Meanwhile, while I was speaking Gino undressed me impatiently. And I noticed once more, as I had when I got into the car, that I still liked him; perhaps my body, always ready to take pleasure from him, rather than my soul, which was by now estranged, made me so good-natured and quick to forgive. He caressed me and kissed me, and his caresses and kisses troubled my mind and the pleasure of my senses overcame the reluctance in my heart. "Oh Gino—you make me feel like dying!" I murmured at last sincerely, as I fell back on the bed.

Later on I put my legs under the sheets and so did he, and we lay together with the embroidered sheet of that magnificent bed pulled up to our chins. Over our heads was suspended a kind of baldachin, with a cloud of white, gossamer veilings floating down over the head of the bed. The whole room was white, with long, fine curtains at the windows, beautiful low furniture against the walls, bevelled mirrors, ornaments of glittering shining glass, marble and silver. The exquisitely fine sheets were like a caress against my body; and if I moved ever so slightly the mattress yielded gently to my limbs and induced a deep desire for sleep and rest. Through the open door I could hear the quietly querulous sound of the water flowing into the bath. I felt utterly content and not in the least resentful against Gino any longer. This seemed the best moment to tell him that I knew everything; because I was sure I would say it kindly, with no shadow of bitterness.

"So, Gino," I said in most caressing tones after a long silence, "your wife's called Antonietta Partini."

Perhaps he was drowsing, because he jumped violently as if someone had clapped him unexpectedly on the shoulder. "What's that you said?"

"And your little girl's called Maria . . . isn't that right?"

He would have liked to protest again, but he looked into my eyes and realised it was useless. Our heads lay on the same pillow, our faces side by side, and I was speaking with my mouth almost on his. "Poor Gino," I said, "why did you tell me so many lies?"

148

"Because I loved you," he answered violently.

"If you really loved me you ought to have thought how unhappy I'd be when I learnt the truth. But you didn't think of that, Gino, did you?"

"I loved you," he interrupted me, "and I lost my head . . . and . . ."

"That'll do," I said. "I was wretchedly unhappy for a while . . . I didn't think you capable of such a thing . . . but it's all over now . . . don't let's mention it again . . . I'm going to have a bath now." I pushed off the sheets, slipped out of bed and went into the bathroom. Gino stayed where he was.

The bath was full of hot water, a bluish colour, lovely to see among all the white tiles and shining taps. I stood in the bath and slowly let myself down into the steaming water. Lying in it I shut my eyes. There was no sound from the next room. Gino must be thinking over what I had said and was trying to work out some plan whereby he could avoid losing me. I smiled at the thought of him in the big double bed, with my news still like a slap in the face. But my smile was not spiteful, it was the sort of smile caused by something comical which has nothing to do with us, because, as I have said, I felt no resentment towards him, but rather, knowing him for what he really was, only a kind of fondness for him. Then I heard him walking about, probably dressing. After a while he peeped in at the bathroom door and looked at me like a whipped dog, as if he did not dare to enter.

"So we shan't see anything more of each other," he said humbly, after a long silence.

I realised that he really loved me in his own way, although not enough to make lying to me and deceiving me utterly repulsive. I remembered Astarita and thought that he, too, loved me in his own way. "Why shouldn't we?" I replied, while I soaped one of my arms, "if I hadn't wanted to see you I wouldn't have come today—we'll still meet, but not so often as before."

His courage seemed to return at these words. He came into the bathroom. "Shall I soap you?" he asked.

I could not help thinking of mother who was also so full of

attention and care for me each time after she had renounced her parental authority.

"If you like," I said shortly. "Soap my back where I can't get at it." Gino picked up the soap and sponge, I stood up and he washed my back. I looked at myself in a long mirror opposite the bath and imagined I was the lady who owned all those lovely things. She, too, must stand up like that, and a maid, some poor girl like myself, had to bend over and soap her and wash her, taking care not to scratch her skin. I thought how lovely it must be to be waited on by somebody else and not do everything with your own hands : to keep still and limp while she bustles about full of respectful attention. I remembered the simple idea I had had the first time I went to the villa : that without my shabby clothes, naked, I was the equal of Gino's mistress. But my fate, most unjustly, was quite different.

"That'll do," I said to Gino in irritation.

He picked up the bath-robe and I got out of the bath ; he then held it out behind me and I wrapped myself in it. He wanted to embrace me, perhaps to see whether I would repel him, and I let him kiss my neck as I stood there, motionless, wrapped in the bath-robe. Then he began to dry me all over, in silence, starting with my feet, going up to my breast, eagerly and able as if he had never done anything else in his life, and I shut my eyes and imagined once again that I was the mistress and he the maid. He took my passivity for acquiescence and I suddenly discovered that instead of drying me he was caressing me. At that I pushed him away, let the bath-robe fall and went on tiptoe barefooted into the next room. Gino stayed in the bathroom to let the water out.

I dressed quickly and then walked round the room looking at the furniture. I stopped in front of the dressing-table dotted with pieces of gold and tortoise-shell. Among the hairbrushes and perfume-bottles I noticed a gold powder-compact. I picked it up and looked at it closely. It was heavy, apparently made of solid gold. It was square, of rolled gold in stripes, and a large ruby was set in the catch. I had a feeling of discovery, rather than of temptation : now

I could do anything, even steal. I opened my bag and put the compact into it; being heavy it slipped right down into the bottom among my loose change and keys. In taking it I also felt a kind of sensual pleasure, not unlike the sensation accepting money from my lovers caused me. As a matter of fact I did not know what to do with such a valuable compact, it did not match my clothes and the kind of life I led. I was sure I would never use it. But in stealing it I seemed to be obeying the logic which now governed the course of my life. I thought I might as well be hanged for a sheep as a lamb.

Gino returned and, with servile attention to detail, began to tidy the bed and all the things he did not think were in their proper places. "Come on!" I said scornfully as I saw him looking around anxiously when he had finished, in order to make sure everything was in its usual place; "come on! Your mistress won't notice a thing—you won't be sacked this time!" I saw a flash of pain cross Gino's face at this and I was sorry I had said it, because it was spiteful and not even sincere.

We said nothing on the way downstairs nor in the garden as we got into the car. Night had fallen some time since. And as soon as the car began to thread its way through the twisted streets of that fashionable district I began to cry gently, as if I had been waiting only for that moment. I did not even know myself why I was crying and yet I was filled with bitterness. I am not made to play disillusioned, angry parts and the whole afternoon, although I had done my utmost to appear calm, disillusionment and anger had nevertheless underlain many of my deeds and words. Now for the first time, while I was still crying, I really felt resentful towards Gino, who through his betrayal of me had aroused emotions I found unpleasant, which did not suit my character. I thought how good and sweet I had always been and how perhaps I was not going to be so any more from that moment, and the thought filled me with despair. I would have liked to ask Gino heartbrokenly: 'Why did you do all this? How can I ever forget it and think no more about it?' But instead I said nothing, swallowed my tears and shook my head a little to make them run down my cheeks, like one shakes a branch to rid it of its ripest fruit. I hardly noticed that meanwhile we were driving right across the city. When the car stopped, I got out and held out my hand to Gino. "I'll give you a ring," I said. He looked at me with an expression of hope that changed to amazement when he saw my face bathed in tears. But he had no time to say a word, for I ran off with a wave of the hand and a forced smile.

CHAPTER NINE

And so life continued to revolve for me always in the same direction and with the same people, like the merry-go-rounds of Luna Park, where the flashing lights used to fill my heart with gaiety when I watched them from the windows of our flat as a child.

Merry-go-rounds, too, have very few figures and these are always the same. The swan, the cat, the car, the horse, the throne, the dragon, and the egg swing past time and time again to the sound of a wailing, strident, clashing music, to be followed once again by the swan, the cat, the car, the horse, the throne, the dragon, and the egg, the whole night through. The figures of my lovers began to revolve for me in just the same way; no matter whether they were men I had already met or newcomers, they were all alike. Giacinti returned from Milan with a pair of silk stockings as a gift and I saw him every evening for some time. Then he went away again and I took up with Gino, seeing him once or twice a week. On other evenings I went with men I picked up in the street or had introduced to me by Gisella. There were young men, older men and some quite old ones; some were charming and treated me kindly, others were unpleasant and regarded me merely as an object to be bought or sold; but, since I had made up my mind never to become attached to any of them, it was always the same story in the end. We used to meet in the street or in a café, sometimes had supper together, then hurried back to my place. There we shut ourselves up in my room, made love, chatted a little; and then the man paid up and left, and I joined mother in the living-room where she was waiting for me. If I was hungry I had a meal, and then went to bed. Very occasionally, if it was early, I slipped out again down-town to find another man. But days and days passed when I saw no one and stayed at home doing nothing. I had become very lazy; it was a sad, voluptuous idleness in which I indulged the desire for rest and peace I shared with mother and all the poor hard-working people around me. Sometimes the mere sight of the empty savings-box was enough to drive me out into the streets in the heart of the city to seek company; but quite often my laziness triumphed and I preferred to borrow money from Gisella or send mother to do her shopping on credit.

And yet I really cannot say I disliked this way of life. I soon realised that my passion for Gino had not been anything particularly unique and that in my heart of hearts I liked all men, for some reason or another. I do not know whether this happens to all the women who take up my profession or whether it means that I had a special vocation for it; I only know that each time I felt a thrill of curiosity and expectation which were rarely deceived. I liked the long, slim, adolescent bodies of the young men, their clumsy gestures, their shyness, their sentimental glances, the coolness of their hair and lips; I liked the muscular arms, the broad chests, the indefinable weight and power in the shoulders, abdomen and legs of virile men in their prime; I even liked old men because men are different from women in that they are not limited by age, and even in old age keep their charm or acquire a new one of a particular kind. The fact that I changed my lover every time helped me to notice qualities and defects at first sight, with that precise and keen observation which can only be obtained by experience. The human body, besides, was an inexhaustible source of mysterious, insatiable delight; and I often found myself gazing at the limbs of my companions of a single night, or touching them with my finger-tips as if I yearned to reach beyond the superficial relationship between us and discover the meaning of their physical beauty and

153

explain to myself why I felt so deeply attracted. But I tried to hide my attraction as much as possible because these men might have mistaken it for love in their perpetual vanity, and have imagined I was in love with them ; whereas, as a matter of fact, love, at least as they understood it, had nothing to do with my feelings, which were more like the reverent trepidation I used to feel when I performed certain religious duties in church.

The money I earned in this way, however, was not as much as might be supposed. First of all, I was incapable of being so mercenary and greedy as Gisella. I wanted to be paid, of course, because I was not going with men for amusement ; but my own nature led me to give myself to them more out of physical exuberance than out of convenience and I did not think about the money until the time came to be paid, that is, when it was too late. I always had a dim conviction that I was supplying men with goods that cost me nothing, something usually not paid for. I felt I received money as a gift rather than as a due. I felt love either should not be paid for or else could never be paid for dearly enough ; and between my modesty and my vanity I was unable to fix any price that did not seem purely arbitrary to me. Therefore, if they gave a lot, I thanked them too gratefully ; if they gave me little, I could never persuade myself that I had been cheated and I did not protest. Only later, after much bitter experience, I decided to copy Gisella who used to come to terms beforehand. But at first I always felt ashamed and was quite unable to mention any sum except in an undertone, so quite often they failed to understand me and I had to repeat it.

There was another reason why my earnings were insufficient. This was the fact that, since I was far less careful about what I spent than I had been before, and had spread myself on buying a few dresses, some perfume, toilet articles and other things that I needed professionally, the money my lovers gave me never went very far : very much like the money I had earned as a model and by helping mother with her sewing. I seemed no better off than before, despite the sacrifice of my honour. There were days when there was not a penny in the house, just as before and even oftener than before. I was tormented by my anxiety at having no settled future, just as before and even worse than before. I am rather carefree and phlegmatic by nature, and my anxiety never became an obsession like it does in other people who are not so well-balanced and indifferent as I am. But the thought was always at the back of my mind, like a worm in a piece of old furniture, and it was always warning me that I possessed nothing and that I could neither forget my condition and rest, nor improve it once for all by means of my chosen profession.

Mother no longer felt at all anxious, or at least, if she did, she did not show it. I had told her straight away that she need no longer ruin her sight by sewing all day long; and she immediately gave up most of her work, as if she had been waiting for this moment all her life : she kept only a few orders which she did when she felt like it, more as a pastime than as a livelihood. It was as if the effort she had made for so many years, beginning when she was little and had worked as a maid in a clerk's family, had suddenly failed without leaving any trace or any possibility of recuperation, like old houses that tumble down in a heap upon themselves, and leave no outside wall standing but only a pile of rubble. For someone like mother, money meant chiefly eating and resting to her heart's content. She had more to eat than before and allowed herself all those little comforts which to her mind distinguish the rich from the poor, such as getting up late, sleeping after lunch, going out for a walk occasionally. I must say that the effect of these innovations was the most unpleasant part of my new life. Probably people who are accustomed to slaving all their life ought never to give it up ; idleness and comfort ruin them even when their source is an accepted and legitimate one, as was not the case with us. As soon as our conditions improved mother began to put on weight, or rather, so rapidly did her anxious, breathless thinness vanish, that she began to swell out in an unhealthy fashion, in a way I felt was significant although I could not tell what it signified. Her bony hips put on flesh, her thin shoulders filled out, her cheeks which had always seemed drawn in as though she were panting, became puffed and florid. But the saddest detail in mother's gain in weight was her eyes. In the past they had been large, wide-open, with an ever-alert and apprehensive expression; now they had become smaller, had an indefinable, ambiguous gleam. She had grown stouter, but was no handsomer or younger-looking. She, rather than myself, seemed to bear the visible traces of our changed way of life in her face and figure, and I was unable to look at her without a painful feeling of remorse, pity and disgust. She increased my embarrassment by letting herself go in manifestations of greedy, ecstatic satisfaction. The fact was, she could hardly believe she need no longer work her fingers to the bone and her manifestations were those of a person who has never eaten enough or slept enough all her life.

Of course I did not let her have any inkling of my feelings. I did not want to upset her and in any case I realised that before reproaching her with anything I ought to reproach myself. But every now and again some gesture of annoyance escaped me, and I seemed to love her less, now she was stout, swollen and walked with a waddle, than I had when she shouted at me, rushed up and down moaning and groaning all day, was thin and distraught. 'I wonder if mother would have grown stout in the same way if I had fallen on clover through a good marriage?' I often asked myself. I believe she would, now I think of it; and I attribute the disgust her stoutness aroused in me to the way I could not help looking at her, full of remorse and complicity.

I did not conceal my new condition of life from Gino for very long. In fact I had to tell him almost immediately, the first time I saw him again, about ten days after we had made love at the villa. One morning mother came to wake me. "Do you know who's come and wants to speak to you?" she said in a hushed and conspiratorial voice. "Gino!"

"Let him in," I replied simply.

Rather disappointed by the brevity of my reply she opened the window and went out. A moment later Gino entered and I saw at once that he was angry and worried. He said nothing in greeting, walked round the bed and came to a standstill in front of me where I was lying sleepily watching him.

156

" I say—you didn't pick up anything from my mistress's dressing-table by mistake the other day, did you ? " he asked.

' Now it's coming ! ' I thought. I noticed that I did not feel at all guilty. But Gino's servile submissiveness impressed me in the usual painful way.

" Why ? " I asked.

" An extremely valuable powder-compact has disappeared. A gold one with a ruby. The mistress has turned the house upside-down. Since I was in charge of the villa I know they suspect me, although they haven't said anything. Luckily she only noticed it yesterday, a week after she got back, so it's possible one of the maids stole it. Otherwise they'd have given me the sack already, or charged me, had me arrested, something or other——"

I was afraid some innocent person might have got into trouble through me. " They haven't done anything to the maids ? " I asked.

" No," he replied nervily. " But a policeman came and questioned us all. There's been no peace in the place for a couple of days."

I hesitated a moment. Then I said : " I took it."

He stared at me, twisting his face into a disagreeable expression. " You took it ! And that's how you tell me ? "

" How should I tell you ? "

" But that's what's called stealing."

" Yes."

He looked at me and suddenly became furious. Perhaps he feared the consequences or perhaps he guessed in a dim fashion that I considered him responsible for the theft, when all was said and done.

" Out with it ! What's up with you ? " he said. " That's why you wanted to go into the mistress's bedroom ! Now I see through the whole thing ! But I, my dear girl, am not going to be mixed up in anything of that sort. If you want to steal, do it anywhere you like, I don't care a damn, but not in the house where I'm employed. A thief ! I'd have been nicely caught if I'd married you—I'd have married a thief——"

157

I watched him carefully while he let off steam. I was amazed now that I could have thought him perfect for so long. He was anything but perfect. At last when I thought he had come to an end of all he could say in reproach I began to speak. "Why get into such a state, Gino? They aren't accusing you of having stolen it! They'll talk about it for a day or two more and then the whole thing will die down. And the Lord knows how many powder-compacts your mistress has."

"But why on earth did you steal it?" he asked. Obviously he wanted to force me to say what he dimly guessed, as I have already said.

"Because," I answered simply.

"Because! That's not an answer."

"If you really want to know then," I answered calmly, "I stole it, not because I wanted it or needed it, but because now I can even steal if I feel like it."

"What are you getting at?" he began.

But I did not let him continue. "At night I walk about the streets picking up men; I bring them here and they pay me. If I do this I can steal, too, if I want to, can't I?"

He understood and his reaction was typical of him. "You can steal, too—that's all right. But I'd have been caught if I'd married you!"

"I wouldn't have done it, in that case," I said. "I've done it since I found out you've got a wife and child."

He had been waiting for this phrase all along and answered promptly. "No, my dear—that won't do! Don't try to put the blame on me. No one has to be a whore and a thief if she doesn't want to."

"Obviously I was one without knowing it then," I answered. "You gave me my chance to become it."

He realised from my calmness that there was nothing to be said, so he changed his tactics. "Very well—what you are and what you do aren't my business. But I've got to have that compact back. Otherwise sooner or later I'll lose my job. You've got to give it me back and I'll pretend I've found it in the garden or somewhere."

I answered immediately. "Why didn't you say so before?

158

If it's so that you won't lose your job, take it. It's in the first drawer in the wardrobe."

He hurried over to the wardrobe at once in his relief, opened the drawer, took out the powder-compact, put it in his pocket. Then he looked at me with a different expression in his eyes, a hint of shame and a desire for reconciliation. But I really could not face the embarrassing scene his look promised.

" Have you got the car outside ? " I asked.

" Yes."

" Well, it's late and you'd better not wait. We'll talk it all over next time we meet."

" Are you cross with me ? "

" No, I'm not cross with you."

" Yes, you are."

" No, I'm not."

He sighed, bent over the bed and I let him kiss me.

" You'll phone me ? " he asked as he reached the door.

" Don't worry."

And in this way Gino learnt of my new way of life. But the day we met we did not mention the compact or my profession; they were like uninteresting, commonplace matters, whose only importance had been their novelty. He behaved more or less like mother, in fact, except that he did not appear to feel even for one moment the shock mother had felt the first time I took Giacinti home, and which, from time to time, I couldn't help seeing beneath her satisfaction and even in the unhealthy, puffy look she had. Gino's chief characteristic was a kind of honied and shortsighted cunning. I imagine that when he learnt of the changes brought about in my life by his betrayal of me he simply shrugged his shoulders and said to himself : " Oh, well—two birds pecking at one cherry—as things are, she can't point a finger at me and I can go on being her lover all the same." There are men who think themselves lucky if they can keep what they have, whether it is money or women or life itself, even at the expense of their own dignity. And Gino was one of them.

I continued to see him because, as I have said, I still liked him despite everything and there was no one I liked more.

And also because, although I believed everything was over between us, I was not anxious for an abrupt, unpleasant break. I have never liked a clean break or sudden interruptions. I think things in life die as they are born, by themselves, through boredom, through indifference or even through habit, which is in itself a kind of steady and faithful boredom ; and I like to be conscious of them dying in this way, naturally, without it being my fault or anyone else's, and slowly giving place to other things. After all, we never get clear, positive changes in life ; and those who do make hurried changes risk seeing their old habits come to the fore once again, still alive and as deeply-rooted as ever. I wanted to reach the stage when Gino's caresses would leave me as indifferent to him as did his words, and I was afraid that, if I did not let things take their own time, he would continually keep cropping up in my life and oblige me, despite myself, to renew our old relationship.

Another person who came back into my life at this period was Astarita. It was far simpler in his case than in Gino's. Gisella used to see him secretly and I suppose he made love to her just to be able to talk about me. Anyway, Gisella was on the look-out for an opportunity to mention him to me, and when she thought enough time had passed and I had recovered my good temper, she took me aside, and, after beating about the bush a bit, at last told me she had met Astarita and he had asked for news of me. "He didn't say anything exactly," she continued, "but I could see he's still in love with you. As a matter of fact I felt sorry for him—he looks wretched. Of course he didn't say anything to me—but I'm positive he'd like to see you again—and after all———"

"Look here, it's no use you going on talking in this way ! " I interrupted her.

"In what way?"

"Beating about the bush like that ! Why don't you say straight out that he sent you to me, that he wants to see me again and you've undertaken to give him my reply ? "

"Suppose I have," she said, rather taken aback, "what then ? "

"Then," I said calmly, "you can tell him I've nothing

against seeing him again—like I do the others, of course, from time to time, without committing myself."

She was extremely astonished by my calmness; she thought I hated Astarita and would never have agreed to meet him again. She did not understand that by now love and hatred had ceased to exist for me and thought, as usual, that I had some hidden motive.

"You're right," she said after a moment's reflection and with a certain slyness. "In your place I'd do the same. You have to overlook your dislikes in some cases—Astarita really loves you and might even have his marriage annulled and marry you. Still—you are a sharp one! And I thought you such an innocent!"

Gisella had never understood the least thing about me and I knew by experience that I would be wasting my breath if I tried to explain to her. So I therefore agreed. "That's just how it is," I said, feigning nonchalance, and left her in a state of mingled admiration and envy.

She gave Astarita my reply and I met him at the same confectioner's where I had met Giacinti for the first time. As Gisella had said, he still loved me passionately and in fact, as soon as he saw me he went as white as a sheet, lost his self-possession and did not say a word. His emotion must have been stronger than himself and I believe some of the simple women of the people must be right when they say, like mother, that some men have been bewitched by their lovers. I had cast a sort of enchantment over him, without any desire or intention on my part; and although he realised it and did all he could to break free he was quite incapable of doing so. Once and for all time I had rendered him inferior, dependent, subject to me; once and for all I had disarmed him, hypnotised him and placed him at my mercy. He explained later that sometimes he used to rehearse to himself the cold, scornful part he would play, and even learned his phrases by heart; but as soon as he saw me he grew pale, his breast was filled with anguish, his mind became a blank and his tongue refused to speak. He even seemed unable to face me, he lost his head and felt driven irresistibly to throw himself on his knees before me and kiss my feet.

161

He really was different from all the others; I mean he was quite obsessed. The evening we met he begged me, as soon as we had had a meal at a restaurant in tense and nervy silence and had reached my place, to tell him every single detail of my life from the day we went to Viterbo until the day I broke with Gino. "Why does it interest you so much?" I asked him in astonishment.

"There's no real reason," he replied, "but what difference does it make to you? Don't think about me, just talk."

"As far as I'm concerned," I said, shrugging my shoulders, "if it'll give you any pleasure——" So I told him precisely everything that had happened after the trip: how I had had a talk with Gino, had followed Gisella's advice and had met Giacinti. The only thing I did not mention was the matter of the compact, perhaps because I did not want to embarrass him, since he was in the police professionally. He asked me a number of questions, especially about my meeting with Giacinti. He never seemed to tire of the details, it was as if he wanted to see and touch everything, take part in it, not only hear about it. I can't tell you how often he interrupted me with: "And what did he do?" or, "And what did you do?" When I had finished he embraced me. "It was all my fault," he stammered.

"No, it wasn't," I said, rather bored by the discussion. "It wasn't anyone's fault."

"Yes, it was my fault. It was I who ruined you. If I hadn't behaved as I did at Viterbo, everything would have been different."

"You're absolutely wrong," I said quickly, "if it's anyone's fault it's Gino's—it has nothing to do with you. You, my dear, wanted to have me by force and things taken by force don't count. If Gino hadn't deceived me I'd have married him, then I'd have told him all about it and it would have been as if I had never met you."

He seemed to cling to the idea that he was to blame, not because he was sorry but because it pleased him, on the contrary, to think he had corrupted me and led me astray. But to say that it pleased him is too feeble an expression: I should say the idea excited him, and perhaps this was the chief

162

cause of his passion for me. I understood this later on when I noticed that he often insisted on my telling him, when we met, all that had happened between me and my bird-of-passage lovers in the interval. While he listened to my account he had a troubled, taut and tense expression on his face which embarrassed me and filled me with shame. And immediately afterwards he threw himself upon me, and while he possessed me he kept on passionately repeating obscene, brutal, offensive words I won't mention, but which would be insulting to even the most depraved women. How he could reconcile this extraordinary attitude with his adoration of me I never could fathom; in my opinion it is impossible to love a woman and at the same time fail to respect her, but in Astarita love and cruelty were mixed, the one lent the other its own colour and strength. I have sometimes thought that his strange excitement at imagining me degraded by his own fault had been suggested to him by his profession as a member of the political police; his function, as far as I could understand, was to find the weak point in the accused, and corrupt and humiliate them in such a way that they would be harmless ever afterwards. He told me himself, I cannot remember in what connection, that every time he succeeded in persuading an accused man to confess or break down, he felt a peculiar kind of satisfaction, like the satisfaction of possession in love. "An accused man's like a woman," he used to say, "as long as she resists she can hold her head up. But as soon as she has given way she's a rag and you can have her again how and when you like." But more probably his cruel, complacent character was natural to him and he had chosen his profession simply because that was his character, and not the other way round.

Astarita was not happy; in fact, his unhappiness seemed the most utter and incurable I had ever known, because it was not due to any external cause, but originated in some weakness or twist I never succeeded in fathoming. When he was not obliging me to tell him my professional adventures he usually knelt in front of me, put his head in my lap and stayed like that, motionless, even for a whole hour. I had only to stroke his head lightly every now and again, like mothers stroke their children. From time to time he uttered a moan, perhaps he was even crying. I never loved Astarita, but at such moments he roused a feeling of immense pity in me, because I could see he was suffering and there was no way of alleviating his sufferings.

He used to talk very bitterly about his family; his wife, whom he hated, his little girls whom he did not love, his parents who had given him a difficult childhood and had obliged him to make a disastrous marriage while he was still an inexperienced youth. He hardly ever referred to his profession. Only once he told me, with an expression of peculiar distaste : " There are lots of useful things in a house, even if they aren't all clean. I'm one of them—a garbage-can for rubbish." But I formed the impression that on the whole he considered his profession an honourable one. He had a great sense of duty and was a model official, as far as I could judge from my visit to him at the Ministry and his way of talking, being zealous, secretive, sharp-sighted, incorruptible and inflexible. Although he formed part of the political police force he declared he knew nothing about politics. " I'm a cog in a wheel," he said to me another time, " what they say, I do."

Astarita would have liked to meet me every evening but besides the fact that I did not wish to be tied up to any one man, as I have already said, he bored me and his convulsive, jerky seriousness and strange ways made me feel uneasy, so that every time I left him I heaved a sigh of relief, although I pitied him. For this reason I tried to avoid seeing him more than once a week. The rareness of our meetings certainly helped to keep his passion for me ever wakeful and burning. If I had agreed to live with him, on the other hand, as he continually suggested, he would gradually have become accustomed to my presence and in the end would have seen me for what I really am—a poor girl like dozens of others. He gave me the number of the phone on his desk at the Ministry. It was a secret number, known only to the chief of police, the head of the government, the minister and a few other important people. When I phoned he used to reply at once, but as soon as he found it was me his voice, which had been

164

clear and calm a moment before, became troubled and he began to stutter. He really was completely conquered and under my thumb, like a slave. I remember that once I absent-mindedly stroked his cheek, without having been asked. He immediately seized my hand and kissed it passionately. On other occasions he asked me to repeat my impulsive caress; but caresses cannot be given to order.

Quite often I had no desire to go down into the streets to pick up men, so I stayed at home. I did not want to stay with mother because although we had a tacit agreement not to mention my profession our conversation always came round to it, in awkward allusions, and I would almost have preferred to talk of it openly without concealment. Instead, I used to shut myself up in my room, warning mother not to disturb me, and stretched myself out on the bed. My room looked on to the courtyard, through the closed window no noise reached me from outside. I used to doze for awhile, then got up and wandered round the room, busy with some little task, such as tidying my things or dusting the furniture. These jobs were nothing more than a stimulus to set my mind working, an attempt to create an atmosphere of intense and secluded intimacy. I used to become more and more deeply immersed in my reflections, until in the end I hardly thought at all, and was content with feeling alive after so much wasted time and exhausting ways.

At a certain moment a profound feeling of bewilderment always overcame me during the hours I spent in such solitary seclusion; I suddenly seemed to see the whole of my life and all of myself from all sides, with icy clearsightedness. The things I was doing were doubled, lost the substance of their meaning, were reduced to mere incomprehensible, absurd externals. I used to say to myself: " I often bring home a man who has been waiting for me in the night, without knowing me. We struggle with one another on this bed, clutching each other like two sworn enemies. Then he gives me a piece of printed, coloured paper. Next day I exchange this piece of paper for food, clothes and other articles." But these phrases were only the first step in a process of deeper bewilderment. They served to clear my mind of the

165

judgment always lying in wait there about my profession, and they showed me my profession as a series of meaningless gestures, similar in every way to the gestures of other professions. Immediately afterwards a distant sound in the city or the creaking of some piece of furniture in the room gave me a ludicrous and almost hectic realisation of my existence. I said to myself : " Here I am and I might be elsewhere—I might exist a thousand years ago or in a thousand years' time— I might be a negress or an old woman, fair or short——" I thought how I had come out of endless night and would soon go on into another endless night and that my brief passing was marked only by absurd and casual actions. I then understood that my distress was caused not by what I was doing but more profoundly by the bare fact of being alive, which was neither good nor evil but only painful and meaningless.

My dismay used to make my flesh creep with fear for a few moments ; I used to shudder uncontrollably, feeling my hair stand on end, and suddenly the walls of my flat, the city and even the world seemed to vanish, leaving me suspended in dark, empty, endless space—suspended, what's more, in the same clothes, with the same memories, name and profession. A girl called Adriana suspended against nothingness. Nothingness seemed to me something terrible, solemn and incomprehensible, and the saddest aspect of the whole matter was my meeting this nothingness with the manners and outward appearance I bore in the evening when I used to meet Gisella in the confectioner's where she waited for me. I found no consolation in the idea that other people also acted and moved in just as futile and inadequate a way as I did when faced with this nothingness, within this nothingness, surrounded by this nothingness. I was only amazed at their not noticing it, or not making their observations known, not referring more often to it, as usually happens when many people all at once discover the same fact.

At these times I used to throw myself on to my knees and pray, perhaps more through a habit contracted in childhood than from a conscious will. But I did not use the words of the usual prayers, which seemed too long for my sudden mood.

I used to throw myself on to my knees so violently that my legs hurt for some days afterwards, and used to pray aloud in a voice filled with despair, saying: " Christ have mercy upon me," just these few words. It was not really a prayer but a magic formula which I thought might dispel my anguish and bring me back to reality. After having cried out impulsively in this way, with all my strength, I remained for some time with my face in my hands, utterly absorbed. At last I used to become aware that my mind was a blank, that I was bored, that I was the same Adriana as ever, that I was in my own room ; I touched my body half-astonished at finding it whole, and getting up from my knees I slipped into bed. I felt very tired and aching all over, as if I had fallen down a rocky slope, and I went to sleep immediately.

These states of mind, however, had no influence on my daily life. I went on being the same Adriana, with the same character, who took men home for money and went about with Gisella and talked of unimportant things with my own mother and with everyone else. And I thought it was strange that I was so different alone from what I was in company, in my relationship with myself and with other people. But I did not flatter myself that I was the only one to have such violent and desperate feelings. I imagined everyone, at least once a day, must feel his own life reduced to a single point of absurd, ineffable anguish—except that their knowledge apparently produced no visible effect upon them, either. They left their houses as I did, and went around playing sincerely their insincere parts. This thought strengthened me in my belief that all men, without exception, deserve to be pitied, if only because they are alive.

PART TWO

CHAPTER ONE

By now Gisella and I were partners more than friends. We did not agree about the places to frequent, it is true, for Gisella preferred restaurants and fashionable haunts, while I preferred simple cafés and even the street; but we managed to come to an agreement even over this matter of a difference in taste: we used to go to the different places in turn. One evening, after we had dined fruitlessly at a restaurant, we were on our way home when I became aware that a car was following us. I tipped Gisella off with the warning that we might be accosted. She was in an angry mood that evening, because she had had to pay for her supper without getting anything out of it and she had been extremely hard-up for some time. "You can go if you like," she replied rudely, "I'm going home to bed." Meanwhile the car had come up close to the kerb and was keeping level with us at reduced speed. Gisella was near the wall and I was on the outside. I looked out of the corner of my eye and saw there were two men in the car. "What shall we do?" I asked Gisella in a whisper. "If you don't come, I shan't go either."

She in her turn cast a surreptitious glance at the car and, for a moment, she seemed to hesitate, still in a foul temper. "I'm not coming," she said finally. "You go. Are you scared?"

"No, but I'm not going unless you come, too."

She shook her head, glanced once more at the car, which was still keeping pace with us, and then, as if suddenly making up her mind, said: "All right. But pretend there's nothing doing and we'll lead them up the garden path a bit. I don't like picking them up here in the Corso."

We walked along for fifty yards or so, the car keeping alongside the whole time, then Gisella, on reaching a corner, turned up into a dark and narrow side-street with a narrow pavement running beside an old wall covered with posters. We heard the car turn into the side-street too, and then the blinding white rays from the headlights fell on us. We felt as though the light stripped us naked and nailed us both against the damp wall with its torn, faded advertisements; and we stood still. Gisella spoke to me in an undertone. " What sort of creatures are they? Didn't they get a good enough look at us in the Corso? I'm in half a mind to go home——"

" No, no, don't ! " I pleaded hastily. I did not know why myself, but I was extremely anxious to meet the two men in the car. " What does it matter? They all behave in this way."

She shrugged her shoulders, and at the same time the head lights wavered and went out and the car stopped by the pavement in front of us. The driver thrust a fair head out of the window.

" Good-evening ! " he said in a ringing voice.

" Good-evening," replied Gisella, on her dignity.

" Where are you going to all on your lonesome? " he continued. " Can't we keep you company? "

Despite the ironical tone of a person who thought he was being very witty, these were the hackneyed phrases and I had already heard them hundreds of times.

" That all depends——" replied Gisella, still on her dignity. She too always made the same replies.

" Oh, come on, now ! " insisted the man in the car. " Depends on what? "

" How much will you give us? " asked Gisella, going up to the car and putting her hand on the door.

" How much do you want? "

Gisella named a sum. " You're expensive," he chirped, " very expensive ! " But he seemed inclined to accept. His friend, whose face was concealed, leaned forward and whispered something in his ear. But the fair young man shrugged his shoulders and then turning to us, said : " All right—get in."

His friend opened the door, got out, and went to sit in the back of the car; he then opened the door on my side

170

and invited me to get in beside him. Gisella sat with the fair young man. He turned to her. " Where shall we go ? " he asked.

" To Adriana's," she answered and gave him the address.

" That's fine," said the fair young man, " let's go to Adriana's."

Usually when I was with one of these men whom I did not know, in a car or elsewhere, I kept still and silent, waiting for them to speak or do something. I knew from experience that they are impatient to take the initiative and do not need any encouragement. That evening too I kept still and dumb while the car made its way through the city. All I could see of my neighbour, whom the arrangement of places had designated as my lover for the night, were his long, thin, white hands lying on his knee. He did not speak or move either, and his head was in shadow. I thought perhaps he was shy and suddenly felt attracted to him. I had been shy, too, and shyness always moved me because it reminded me of what I had been like before I met Gino. Gisella was talking, though. She liked to talk politely of indifferent matters as long as she could, just like a lady in the company of men who respect her.

" Is this your car ? " I heard her ask at a certain moment.

" Yes," answered her companion. " I haven't pawned it yet. Do you like it ? "

" It's very comfortable," said Gisella composedly, " but I prefer a Lancia—they're quicker and the springs are better. My fiancé has a Lancia."

This was true, Riccardo had got a Lancia. Only he had never been Gisella's fiancé and Gisella and he had not been meeting for some time now. The young man began to laugh. " Your fiancé's got a Lancia that goes on two wheels ! " he said.

Gisella was very touchy and the slightest remark made her angry. " I say," she said resentfully, " what do you take us for ? "

" I don't know—tell me who you are," said the fair young man. " I don't want to make a false step."

Another of Gisella's obsessions was to pass herself off for

something she was not with her pick-up lovers : for a dancer, a typist or a respectable lady. She did not realise that her claims contrasted utterly with the fact that she let herself be so easily approached and always mentioned the money part of the business immediately. "We're two dancers in the Caccini company," she said haughtily, "we're not in the habit of going out with the first man who turns up. But since the company isn't properly set up yet we were just going for a little walk this evening. As a matter of fact I didn't want to accept your offer—but my friend said you looked such decent fellows. If my fiancé got to know I'd never hear the end of it . . ."

The fair man laughed again. "Of course we're two decent fellows ! But you're two street-walkers ! Why not ? "

My neighbour spoke for the first time. "Shut up, Giancarlo," he said in an even voice.

I said nothing. I did not like being given that name because of the malicious intention that prompted it, but after all, it was the truth.

"First of all, it isn't true," said Gisella, " and what's more, you're a cad."

The fair young man said nothing. But he slowed down at once and then brought the car to a standstill beside the kerb. We were in a deserted and dimly lit side-street with houses on either side. He turned to Gisella.

"I say, suppose I were to chuck you out of the car ? "

"Just try ! " said Gisella, drawing back. She was very spirited and was not afraid of anyone.

My neighbour leaned forward towards the front seat at this and I saw his face. He was dark, with a shock of hair falling over his high forehead, large, dark, bulging eyes, a clearcut nose, curving lips and an ugly, receding chin. He was very thin, his adam's apple showed above his collar. "Are you going to shut up or not ? " he said to the fair man, emphatically but patiently, as if he were intervening in some affair that did not really concern him at all, it seemed to me. His voice was neither deep nor very masculine, it sounded as though it might easily break into a falsetto squeak.

"What's it got to do with you ? " asked his friend, turning

172

round. He said it in an odd kind of voice, however, as if he were ashamed already of his own coarseness and was not sorry his friend had intervened. My neighbour continued. "What sort of behaviour is this? We invited them . . . they trusted themselves with us . . . and now we're insulting them!" He turned towards Gisella. "Don't take any notice of him," he added kindly, "perhaps he's had a drop too much to drink! I'm sure he didn't mean to offend you." The fair man made a gesture of protest but his companion stopped him by putting a hand on his arm and saying peremptorily: "You've had too much to drink, I tell you, and you didn't mean to insult her—now let's get along."

"I didn't come here to be insulted," said Gisella quaveringly. She, too, seemed grateful to the dark man for his intervention.

"Of course! No one likes to be insulted . . . of course they don't!" he said. The fair man was gazing at them with a stupid look on his red face, that seemed swollen and bruised in patches; he had round grey-blue eyes and his large red mouth looked greedy and uncontrolled. He gazed at his friend who was patting Gisella's shoulder soothingly, and finally burst into sudden laughter. "Upon my word of honour!" he exclaimed. "I don't know what's up. Where are we? Why are we squabbling? I can't even remember how it all began. Instead of all being friends together, here we are squabbling—it's enough to drive a fellow crazy!" He was roaring with laughter and, still laughing, turned to Gisella. "Come on, lovely . . ." he said, "don't be cross—we were really made for each other . . ."

"Actually, that's just what I was thinking," she said, forcing a smile.

"I'm the nicest chap in the world, aren't I, Giacomo?" he continued in a shrill voice, laughing with all his might. "I'm everything you could wish for. But you have to know how to take me, that's all. Come on—give me a kiss now." He leaned forward and placed an arm round Gisella's waist. She took a handkerchief out of her bag, wiped the lipstick off her mouth then kissed him apologetically on the lips.

While she was kissing him he twisted his fingers convulsively, pretending to suffocate and turning it all to burlesque. They broke apart almost immediately and he started the car up again with deliberate gestures. "Here we are again! I swear I won't give you any further reason to complain of me. I'll be very earnest, well-behaved, like a thorough gentleman. You can clout me if I don't behave properly." The car set off again.

He went on talking and laughing aloud and even taking his hands off the steering-wheel to gesticulate, to our imminent danger, all the rest of the way. My neighbour, on the contrary, had relapsed into silence in his dark corner, after his brief intervention. I now felt extremely attracted to him and curiously keyed up. As I think back I now see that this was the moment when I fell in love with him, or at least, began to associate him with all the things I liked which so far I had never had. Love, after all, needs to be complete and not a merely physical satisfaction; and I was still seeking the perfection I had once thought I could say I had found in Gino. Perhaps it was the first time, not only since I had gone into the profession but in all my life, that I had met anyone like him, with his manners and voice. The stout painter I had posed for in the beginning was like him in a way, of course, but was colder and more self-possessed and in any case, I would have fallen in love with him, too, if I had wanted to. His voice and manner aroused the same sensations I had felt the first time I had gone to the villa of Gino's employers, although in a different way. Just as I had felt extraordinarily charmed by the orderliness, comfort and cleanliness of the villa and had thought life did not seem worth living if you could not live in a house like that, so, now, his voice and kindly gestures and all they implied about his character attracted me passionately. At the same time my physical desire was aroused, so that I longed to be caressed by his hands and kissed by his lips; and I realised that the intense and ineffable mingling of old aspirations and present desire, which is the essence of love and its inevitable accompaniment, was already working in me. But I was also very much afraid he might notice what I was feeling and might

174

escape me. Driven by my fear, I stretched out my hand towards his in the hope that he would press it. But his hands were indifferent to the clumsy touch of my fingers that tried to entwine themselves in his. I was dreadfully embarrassed, because I did not want to pull my hand away, but at the same time I felt I ought to, since he gave no sign of life. Then as the car turned a corner sharply we were thrown against one another and I pretended I had lost my balance and let myself fall with my head on his knees. He shuddered but did not move. The motion of the car was a delight. I shut my eyes and thrust my face between his hands to separate them, like a dog does, and kissed them and tried to make him stroke my face in an affectionate caress I could have hoped was spontaneous. I realised I had lost my head and was dimly astonished that a few kindly words could have produced such a state of agitation. But he did not grant me the caress I so humbly begged for and after a while withdrew his hands. The car came to a standstill almost immediately.

The fair man leapt out and assisted Gisella with mock courtesy. We, too, got out; I opened the front door and we entered the courtyard. The fair man led the way upstairs with Gisella. He was short and stocky, he looked as though he would burst out of his clothes, but he was not fat. Gisella was taller than he. Half-way up, he dropped a step behind and taking hold of Gisella's dress by the hem he pulled it up, exposing her white thighs with the garters round them and her thin little buttocks. "The curtain's going up!" he exclaimed in a burst of laughter. Gisella merely pulled her dress down again with one hand. I thought my companion must dislike such coarse behaviour and I wanted him to know that I disliked it, too.

"Your friend's very cheerful," I said.

"Yes," he replied shortly.

"Obviously everything's going swimmingly for him."

We entered the house on tiptoe and I showed them straight into my room. Once the door was shut we all four stood there for a moment, and since the room was small there seemed to be even more of us. The fair man was the first to recover his self-possession, by sitting on the bed and beginning to undress at once, as if he were on his own. He was talking about hotel rooms and private rooms, and telling us of one of his recent adventures. " She says to me : ' I'm a real lady—and I don't want to go to a hotel.' So I told her the hotels were full of real ladies. ' But,' says she, ' I don't want to have to give my name.' ' I'll pass you off as my wife,' says I, ' one more or less doesn't matter.' Right, off we go to the hotel. I pass her off as my wife, we go up to our room—but when I really get down to things she begins a long tale—that she regretted it now, she didn't want to, she really was a lady. So I lost my patience and tried to force her. I wished I hadn't, then ! She opens the window, threatens she'll throw herself out. ' O.K.,' says I, ' it's my fault for bringing you here.' Then she sits down on the bed and begins to whimper, tells a long, moving story, enough to break your heart. But if you wanted to know what it was all about I couldn't tell you, I've forgotten it. I only know that in the end I felt so good and nearly went down on my knees to ask her forgiveness for having taken her for something she wasn't. ' Now we see eye to eye,' I said, ' we won't do anything, we'll just lie down and sleep each on our own.' So that was that and I fell asleep at once. But half-way through the night I woke up, looked over to her side. She'd gone ! Then I looked at my clothes and saw they were all untidy, so I hunted through my pockets and found my wallet had gone, too. She was a real lady ! " His burst of laughter was so infectious that Gisella and I were obliged by his boundless gaiety to laugh, too. He had taken off his suit, his shirt, socks and shoes and now stood there in a pair of dove-coloured woollen combinations, close-fitting from the ankles to his throat, which made him look like a tightrope walker or a ballet-dancer. His comical aspect was emphasised still further by this garment, which is usually worn by older men, and at the sight I forgot his cruelty and almost felt attracted to him, because I have always been attracted to cheerful people and am more inclined to cheerfulness myself than to gloom. He began to strut, short and bouncing, about the room, as proud of his combinations as of a uniform. Then, from the corner where the chest-of-drawers stood he suddenly leapt on to the bed, falling on top of Gisella, who squealed out in surprise, and threw her back as if to embrace her. But then, while still hovering on all fours over Gisella, he lifted his red, excited face with a comical gesture, as if struck by a thought, and looked back at the two of us, like a cat does before beginning to touch its food. " What are you two waiting for ? " he asked.

I looked at my companion. " Shall I take my clothes off ? " I asked.

He was still wearing his coat-collar turned up round his neck. " No, no," he answered with a shudder. " After them."

" Shall we go into the next room ? "

" Yes."

" Go for a run in the car," cried the fair man, still hovering over Gisella, " you'll find the keys there." But his friend pretended he had not heard him and we left the room.

We went into the outer room. I signed to him to wait for me and entered the living-room, where mother was sitting at the table in the middle, playing patience. As soon as she saw me she got up and went out into the kitchen without even waiting for me to speak. So I peeped through the door and told the young man he could come in.

I shut the door and went to sit down on the sofa in the corner by the window. I wanted him to sit down beside me and cuddle me; the others always did. But he did not even look towards the sofa and began to pace up and down the sitting-room, all round the table, his hands in his pockets. I thought that perhaps he was bored by waiting. " I'm sorry," I said. " I've only got one bedroom I can use."

He stood still. " Did I say I wanted a room ? " he asked me huffily but gently.

" No, but I thought——"

He took a few turns round the room. I could not control myself any longer. " Why don't you come and sit down here beside me ? " I asked, pointing to the sofa as I did so.

He looked at me, then appeared to make up his mind, and came to sit down. " What's your name ? " he asked.

" Adriana."

" I'm Giacomo," he said and took my hand. This was unusual and again the idea flitted across my mind that he was shy. I let him hold my hand and smiled at him to encourage him.

" So we're expected to make love in a little while ? " he said.

" Yes."

" And suppose I don't want to ? "

" Then we wouldn't," I replied lightly, thinking he was only joking.

" Very well," he replied emphatically. " I don't want to, I haven't the slightest desire to."

" All right," I said. But actually his refusal was something so new in my experience that I did not understand.

" You aren't offended ? Women don't like to be turned down."

At last I understood what he meant and shook my head, incapable of saying a single word. So he didn't want me. I suddenly felt desperate, on the point of bursting into tears. " I'm not offended at all," I stammered. " If you don't want to—let's wait till your friend's done and then you can go."

" I don't know," he protested. " I'm making you waste your time—you could have earned something with another man."

I thought perhaps he could not rather than would not. " If you haven't got the money," I said, " it doesn't matter. You can pay me another time."

" You're a good girl," he said, " but I've got the money. In fact—— Look—I'll pay you all the same—so it won't seem as though you had wasted an evening." He put his hand into his jacket pocket, took out a roll of notes that looked as though he had prepared them beforehand and went to put them down on the table, away from me, with a clumsy yet strangely elegant and scornful gesture.

" No, no ! " I protested. " Why should you ? Don't let's even mention it." But I said it weakly because I was not at all sorry at heart to accept his money—it was always

178

some kind of a link with him and since I was now in his debt I could always hope to pay him back. He took my wavering refusal as an acceptance, which in fact it was, and did not pick up the money which he had left on the table. He came and sat down on the sofa again, and I put out my hand to take his, although I felt it was an awkward, silly thing to do. We looked at one another for a moment. Then he suddenly twisted my little finger hard with his long, thin fingers. "Oh!" I said angrily. "What's come over you now?"

"I'm sorry," he replied. He looked so deeply embarrassed that I was sorry I had reproached him so harshly.

"You hurt me, you know," I said.

"I'm sorry," he repeated. Seized by sudden agitation he stood up again and began to walk up and down. Then he came to a standstill in front of me. "Shall we go out?" he asked. "This waiting about really gets on my nerves."

"Where shall we go?"

"I don't know—shall we go for a run in the car?"

I remembered the times I had been out with Gino in a car and replied hastily. "No, not in the car."

"Let's go to a café. There are some cafés round here, aren't there?"

"Not round here, exactly, but I believe there's a place just outside the gates."

"Let's go there, then."

I got up and we left the living-room. On our way down I tried to joke with him. "Mind you—that money you gave me gives you the right to come and see me any time you like. Is that all right?"

"All right."

It was a mild, dark, damp winter night. It had been raining all day and the paved road was covered with large, black puddles in which the unwavering lights of the rare street lamps were reflected. The sky was cloudless above the walls, but there was no moon and only a few stars shone dimly through the mist. From time to time unseen trams passed behind the walls, scattering vivid flashes from the electric lines, which for a brief moment lit up the sky, the ruined towers, and the buttresses covered with greenery.

When I was out in the street I remembered I had not been in the direction of the amusement park for months. I usually turned right towards the square where Gino used to meet me. I had not gone in the direction of Luna Park, I remembered, since I was a young girl and used to go out for walks with mother, and we climbed the wide road below the walls and went to enjoy the lights and the music without daring to enter because we had no money. On that side, on the main road, stood the villa with the little tower through whose open windows I had had a glimpse of the family seated round the table : the villa that had first made me dream of marriage, a house and a normal life of my own. I felt drawn to talk to my companion about that time, my youth, my hopes, not only from a sentimental impulse but also, I must confess, for interested motives. I did not want him to judge me from appearances, I wanted him to see me in a better light, which I believed to be a truer one. Some people put on their best clothes and fling open the finest rooms in their house in order to welcome honoured visitors ; the equivalent for me of those best clothes and guest-rooms were the girl I had been, my dreams and ambitions. And I counted on my memories, although they were so poor and uninteresting, to make him change his mind and bring him nearer to me.

"No one ever goes along this side of the road," I said as we walked along. "But in summer everyone in the district goes for walks here. I used to—a long time ago, now. It had to be you to bring me here again."

He had taken my arm and was helping me along the flooded roadway.

"Whom did you go with ?" he asked.

"Mother."

He began to laugh so unpleasantly that I was astonished. "Mother," he repeated, dwelling on the " m " sound. "There's always a mum-mum-mum. What'll mum say, what'll mum do ? Mum-mum——"

I thought that perhaps he had some hidden reason for feeling resentful towards his own mother. "Did your mother do anything to hurt you ?" I asked.

"No, she didn't do anything," he replied ; "mothers never

do anything. Can you tell me anyone who hasn't got a mother? Do you love your mother?"

" Of course—why? "

" Oh, nothing," he replied hastily. " Don't bother yourself about me. Go on. So—you used to go out with your mother——"

The tone of his voice was neither reassuring nor inviting. But still I felt impelled to continue my reminiscences to him, partly out of liking for him, partly out of self-interest.

" Yes, we used to go out together, especially in the summer because our flat is stifling in summer Look—you see the little villa over there? "

He stood still and looked. But the windows of the villa were shut, it looked quite uninhabited. It seemed smaller than I remembered it and rather ugly and forbidding, cramped between the long, low, railwaymen's houses. " Well, what about it? "

I felt almost ashamed now of what I was about to say.

" I used to pass by that villa every evening," I continued with an effort, " and the windows were open because it was summer, as I said—I used to watch a family sitting down to a meal, then——" I stopped, feeling suddenly embarrassed.

" And? "

" You aren't interested in all this," I said, and felt I was being both sincere and cunning in my shamefacedness.

" Why? Everything interests me."

" Well then," I went on hurriedly, " I got the idea firmly fixed in my head that one day I would have a little house like that and would do just the things I used to see that family doing."

" Oh, I see ! " he exclaimed, " a little house like that—you didn't aim very high."

" It's not so bad in comparison with the house we live in at present," I said, " and, you know, at that age you get so many ideas in your head."

He pulled me towards the villa by one arm. " Let's go and see if that family still lives there."

" What on earth are you driving at? " I said. " Of course they're there."

"Very well, let's see."

We were just outside the villa. The narrow, overgrown garden was dark, the windows, the little tower, all dark. He went up to the gate. "There's even a letter-box," he said. "Let's ring and see if anyone's in. Still—this little house of yours looks empty."

"No, don't!" I said laughing. "Don't do anything. What's got into you?"

"Let's try." He lifted his hand and pressed the door-bell. I felt like running away, afraid someone might turn up. "Let's go, let's go!" I begged him. "Now they'll look out and what sort of a figure do we cut?"

"What will mother say, eh?" he repeated like a refrain, letting me tug him away. "What will mother do?"

"You've got mother on the brain!" I said, walking hastily.

We had reached the Amusement Park. Last time I had gone there I remembered there had been a huge crowd of people jostling one another, festoons of coloured lamps, stalls with their acetylene lights, decorations in the pavilions, music and noise. I was a little disappointed at finding nothing of all this. The fence appeared to surround a dark, deserted dumping-ground for building materials, rather than an amusement park. The arches of the switchbacks, with an occasional seat still suspended here and there, appeared over the top of the fence, looking like gross-bellied insects whose flight had been suspended by a sudden paralysis. The low, pointed roofs of the rain-soaked, unlighted pavilions gave an impression of sleep. Everything seemed dead, and justly so, since it was winter. The open space in front of the amusement park was deserted and covered with puddles. One single street-lamp shed a faint light.

"This is Luna Park in summer," I said. "There's always a huge crowd. But it doesn't work in winter. Where shall we go?"

"What about that café over there?"

"It's a tavern, really."

"Let's go to the tavern, then."

We passed beneath the city gate and facing us saw an
182

illuminated glass door on the ground floor of a row of little houses. I only realised when I was inside that it was the café where I had had a meal with mother and Gino, and Gino had told the offensive, drunken youth to mind his own business. There were only two or three people seated eating food out of newspaper packets on the marble-topped tables, and drinking the host's wine. It was colder inside than out, the air smelt of rain, wine and sawdust, the stoves appeared to have gone out. We sat in a corner and he ordered a litre of wine.

"Who's going to drink a litre?" I asked.

"Why? Don't you drink?"

"Only a little."

He poured himself a glass full to the brim and tossed it down in one breath, but with an effort and no pleasure. This gesture confirmed me in what I had already noticed about him—he did everything from force of will, superficially, without taking any part in what he was doing, as if he were acting. We remained silent for awhile, he kept staring at me with his bright, intense gaze, and I looked round the room. The memory of that distant evening in the tavern with mother and Gino returned to me and I was uncertain whether what I was feeling was regret or irritation. I had been very happy then, certainly; but how self-deceived! At last I came to the conclusion inside myself that it was exactly like opening a drawer left untouched for years, and instead of finding in it all the lovely things you had hoped for, you find only a few rags, moth and dust. Everything had come to an end, not only my love for Gino but youth itself and all its disappointed dreams. The truth of this was shown by the fact that I had been able to make use of my memories, knowingly and calculatingly, in order to move my companion.

"I didn't take to that friend of yours who was with us," I said, apropos of nothing, "but now I almost feel a kind of liking for him—he's so cheerful."

"First, he's not a friend of mine," he answered abruptly, "and then, he's not at all likeable."

I was astonished at the violence in his voice. "Don't you think so?" I asked mildly.

He took a drink and continued. " You ought to avoid witty people like the plague. There's usually nothing underneath all their wit—you ought to see him in his office ! He's not witty there."

" What sort of an office ? "

" I don't know—a patent office——"

" Does he make a lot of money ? "

" Terrific ! "

" Lucky fellow ! "

He poured out some wine for me. " Why do you go about with him if you dislike him so much ? " I asked.

" He's a friend of my childhood," he said, pulling a face. " We went to school together. All childhood friends are like that."

He drank again and added : " Still, he's better than me in some ways."

" Why ? "

" When he does anything he does it in earnest, but in my case, first I want to do it and then "—his voice broke off suddenly into a falsetto and I started, amazed—" when it comes to the point I don't do it. This evening, for instance —he phoned me and asked me if I wanted to go out on the pick-up, as they say—I agreed, and when we met you I really wanted to make love to you. But then, when we got back to your place, all my desire vanished——"

" Vanished—— " I repeated, looking at him.

" Yes. You no longer seemed to be a woman in my eyes —you seemed an object, a thing—you remember when I twisted your finger and hurt you ? "

" Yes."

" Well—I did it to find out if you really existed—as you do—even by making you feel pain."

" Yes, I existed all right," I said, smiling, " you hurt me a lot." Now I began to understand, and it was a relief that it was not because he disliked me that he had not wanted me. But in any case, there is never anything strange about people. As soon as one tries to understand them one finds that their behaviour, however unusual, is always due to some perfectly plausible motive. " So you didn't like me ? "

184

He shook his head. " Not really—you or any other girl would have been just the same thing."

" I say," I asked after a moment's hesitation, " you aren't impotent by any chance ? "

" Good God, no ! "

I now felt a pressing desire to be intimate with him, to bridge the gap between us, to love him and be loved by him. I had denied that his refusal had offended me, but actually, if not offended I was indeed hurt and wounded in my pride. I knew I was handsome and attractive and I did not believe he had any valid reason for not desiring me.

" Listen," I said simply, " let's finish our wine and then go home and make love."

" No, it's out of the question."

" Then you mean I didn't attract you even when you saw me in the street the first time."

" It isn't that—but do try to understand——"

I knew no man can resist certain arguments. " Obviously, I don't attract you," I repeated calmly, feigning bitterness, and at the same time I stretched out my hand and caressed his face with my palm. My hands are long, large and warm ; and if it is true that a person's character can be seen in her hand there can be nothing vulgar about mine, as there is in Gisella's, whose hands are red, rough and shapeless. I began to stroke his cheek, his temples, his forehead beneath his hair, looking at him all the time with an insistent, yearning sweetness. I remembered Astarita had done this to me at the Ministry and I realised once more that I was truly in love, because Astarita loved me without any shadow of doubt and that was a gesture of love itself. At first he remained still and unmoved by my caresses ; then his chin began to tremble, a sign in him, as I noticed later, that he was excited and an extremely youthful expression of distress, just like a boy's, was stamped on his face ; I was filled with pity for him and was glad of this pity because it meant I was getting into touch with him. " What are you doing ? " he murmured. " We're in public."

" What do I care ? " I answered serenely.

My cheeks were burning despite the cold in the tavern,

and I was surprised at seeing a little cloud of steam issue from our mouths at every breath. " Give me your hand," I said. Unwillingly he let me take it and I lifted it to my face, saying : " Feel how my cheeks burn ? "

He made no reply, only looked at me, his chin quivering. Someone came in, making the glass doors rattle, and I withdrew my hand. He sighed with relief and poured himself some wine. But as soon as the intruder had passed us I stretched out my hand again, and slipping it between the edges of his jacket I unbuttoned his shirt and touched his bare chest near his heart. " I want to warm my hand," I said, " and I want to feel your heart beating." I turned my hand over, touched him with the back of it and then with the palm again. " Your hand's cold," he said, looking at me.

" It'll get warm now," I smiled. I stretched out my arm and slowly passed my hand over his chest and thin ribs. I felt profoundly happy because I knew he was near me and I was filled with love for him, so much love of my own that I had no need of his. " It won't be long before I kiss you," I warned him jokingly as I gazed at him.

" No, no ! " he objected, trying to laugh, too, but really alarmed. " Try to control yourself ! "

" Let's go away, then."

" All right, let's go, if you want to."

He paid for the litre of wine he had not finished drinking and left the tavern with me. He now seemed roused in his own way, but not through love, as I was, but rather through some strange ferment which the events of the evening had stirred up in his mind. Later, when I knew him better, I discovered that the same excitement always overtook him whenever for some reason or other he came across some hitherto unknown aspect of his character or was strengthened in his knowledge of it. For he was extremely egoistic, though in a charming way—or rather, he was self-absorbed. " It's always like this with me," he began, as if talking to himself, while I took him home almost at a running pace ; " I have a great longing to do something, am filled with enthusiasm, everything seems flawless, I feel sure I'll act as I mean to act and then, when I really have to act, everything collapses and I cease to exist, as it were—or rather, only my worse sides exist—I become cold, idle, cruel—like I was when I twisted your finger."

He was talking absent-mindedly in a kind of monologue, possibly with a kind of bitter complacency. But I was not listening to him because I was so full of joy and I sped across the puddles on winged feet. "You've already told me all this," I said gaily, "but I haven't told you what I feel—I want to hug you close, to warm you against my body, to feel you beside me, and make you do what you don't want to do—I shan't be happy until you have."

He said nothing, he did not seem even to hear what I was saying, he was so deeply absorbed in thinking over what he had said himself. Suddenly I slipped my arm round his waist. "Put your arm round my waist, won't you?" I said.

He appeared not to have heard me; so I took his arm and managing as best I could, like one does when slipping on a coat, I put his arm round my waist. We went on walking awkwardly because we were both wearing heavy winter coats and our arms could hardly reach round our waists.

When we were below the tower of the little villa I stood still. "Give me a kiss," I said.

"Later," he replied.

"Give me a kiss."

He turned and I kissed him violently, placing my two arms round his neck. His lips were closed but I thrust my tongue between them and then between his teeth, which he finally unclenched. I was not sure he would return my kiss, but as I have already said, I did not mind. Then we drew apart and I saw a great crooked red patch of rouge round his mouth, which made his serious face look odd and funny. I burst into happy laughter.

"Why are you laughing?" he murmured.

I hesitated, then decided not to tell him the truth, because I enjoyed seeing him hastening along beside me so earnestly, quite unaware of that patch on his face.

"Oh nothing," I said. "Because I'm happy—don't think about me," and I gave him another rapid kiss on the mouth, feeling on top of the world.

But when we reached the front door the car had gone.

" Now Giancarlo's left," he said ill-humouredly, " I'll have to walk miles to get home."

I did not let myself be annoyed by his unkindly tone of voice, because by now nothing could offend me. His faults appeared to me in a special light that rendered them lovable, just as they do when one is in love.

" There's the night service on the trams—and if you like you can stay and sleep with me," I said, with a shrug.

" No, no, not that," he replied hastily.

We entered and climbed the stairs. When we reached the hall I pushed him into my room and peeped rapidly into the living-room. It was dark, except for the window where a ray of light from a street-lamp lit up the sewing-machine and chair. Mother must have gone to bed and I wondered whether she had seen Gisella and Giancarlo and spoken to them. I closed the door again and went into my own room. He was walking about restlessly between the bed and the chest-of-drawers.

" Listen," he said. " It'd be better if I went."

I pretended I had not heard him, took off my coat and hung it up. I felt so pleased that I could not help saying with all the vanity of a housewife : " How do you like this room ? Isn't it comfortable ? "

He looked around him at last and made a grimace I did not understand. I took his hand, made him sit on the bed. " Now leave it all to me," I said. He looked at me as he sat there with his coat-collar still turned up, his hands in his pockets. I removed his coat, slipping it off carefully, then his jacket, and hung it with the coat on a hanger. In no hurry, I undid his tie and then took off tie and shirt in one and hung them over a chair. Then I knelt down and taking his foot on to my lap, like a shoemaker, I pulled off his shoes and socks and kissed his feet. I had begun slowly and methodic-ally, but little by little as I removed his clothes a kind of frenzy of humility and adoration grew upon me. Perhaps it was the same feeling I had when I knelt down in church ; but this was the first time I had ever felt it for a man and I was happy, because I was sure that this was pure love, far removed from all sensuality and vice. When he was naked I knelt down between his thighs and placed my arms around him, caressing his body as though I were holding a dark flower in my hands and for a moment I pressed my cheek and hair against him, hard, with my eyes shut. He let me do whatever I wanted and the bewildered expression on his face overjoyed me. Then I got up, went behind the bed and quickly undressed, letting all my clothes fall on the floor where my feet trampled them. He was still seated on the edge of the bed, shivering, with downcast eyes. I came up behind him and possessed by some gay fit of violence I seized him and pushed him over, his head on the pillows. He had a long, slim, white body; bodies, like faces, have their own expressions, and his was chaste and young. I stretched myself beside him, my own body running the length of his, and felt how ardent and strong and dark and well-covered my body was in comparison with his thinness, slightness, coldness and whiteness. I clung to him violently and pressed my body against his hips and threw my arms across his breast, my face on his with my lips to his ear. I felt as though I wanted to wrap my body round him like a warm covering and infuse my own ardour into him, rather than make love to him. He lay on his back with his head slightly raised, his eyes open, as if he wanted to watch everything I was doing. His keen glance swept down my spine and gave me a strange feeling of uneasy discomfort; however, for a while I paid no heed to it, being led on by my first impulse.

"Don't you feel better now?" I murmured suddenly.

"Yes," he replied in a distant, neutral tone.

"Wait," I said.

But at the very instant when I was about to embrace him with renewed ardour I felt his cold, steady gaze once more taut upon my back like a piece of wet wire, and I suddenly felt ashamed and bewildered. My ecstasy died down, slowly I slipped from him and let myself fall on my back, separate from him. I had made a great effort of love, I had put into it the whole impulse of an innocent and primitive despair; the sudden realisation that my effort was useless filled my eyes with tears, and I put my arm across my face to hide from him the fact that I was crying. Apparently I had been mistaken, I could not love him or be loved by him, and I also thought that he must be judging me without any illusions for what I really was. Now I knew I was living in a kind of cloud I had made about me in order to avoid seeing my reflection in my own mind. But he, on the contrary, had dispersed the cloud with his glances and had placed the mirror once more before my eyes. And I saw myself as I really was, or rather, as I must have been for him, because I knew and thought nothing about myself; as I have already said, I hardly believed in my own existence.

"Go away," I said at last.

"Why?" He raised himself on one elbow and looked at me in embarrassment. "What's the matter?"

"You'd better go," I said calmly, keeping my arm over my face. "Don't think I'm cross with you—but I can see that you don't feel anything for me, so——" I did not finish, but shook my head.

He did not answer, but I felt him move and leave my side; he was dressing. I then felt a stabbing pain as though I had wounded myself deeply and someone was probing into the heart of the wound with a thin, sharp knife. I was in pain as I listened to him dressing, in pain at the thought that in a few moments he would be gone for ever and I would never see him again, in pain at my suffering.

He dressed slowly; perhaps he expected me to call him back. I remember hoping at one moment to hold him there by exciting his desire for me. I had lain down beside him with the coverlet drawn over me. Now, with a coquettishness I knew to be desolate and despairing, I moved my leg so as to make the cover slip off my body. I had never offered myself in this way and for a while, as I lay there naked, with my legs apart and my arm over my eyes, I had the almost physical illusion that his hands were on my shoulders and his mouth on mine. But then almost immediately I heard the door close.

I stayed as I was, motionless on my back. I believe I passed from sorrow to a kind of drowsiness, and then fell asleep without being aware of having done so. But when

the night was well advanced I awoke and realised for the first
time that I was alone. During my first sleep the sense of
his presence had remained with me despite the bitterness of
his departure. Somehow, I fell asleep again.

CHAPTER TWO

The following day I was surprised to find myself feeling as
languid, melancholy and indifferent, as if I were just recovering from a month's illness. I have a cheerful nature and my
cheerfulness, which is due to my bodily health and vigour,
has always been stronger than any misfortune that has be-
fallen me, so much so that on occasion I have been irritated
at feeling cheerful despite myself, even when circumstances
did not really warrant it. Every day, for instance, as soon
as I got up I usually felt an impulse to sing or say something
amusing to mother. But that morning my involuntary light-
heartedness was entirely lacking; I felt aching, dull, quite
without the usual impetuous gusto for the coming twelve
hours of life the day had to offer. I told mother, who noticed
my unusual mood at once, that I had slept badly.

This was true; except that I interpreted as its cause only
one of the many effects of profound humiliation inflicted on
my spirit by Giacomo's rejection. As I said before, I no
longer minded being what I was; I could see no reason, in
my own eyes, why I should not be that. But I had hoped
to love and be loved; and Giacomo's refusal, despite the
complicated reasons he had given me for it, were, I thought,
all due to my profession, which suddenly became hateful and
intolerable to me on this account.

Self-love is a strange beast that may lie dormant under the
cruellest blows and then awaken, mortally wounded by the
slightest scratch. One memory above all others stung me
to the quick and filled me with bitterness and shame : the
memory of a phrase I had uttered the evening before while
I was hanging up my coat. " How do you like this room ? "
I had said. " Don't you think it's cosy ? "

I remembered he had not answered, but had looked round him, making some grimace I had not understood at the time. Now I realised it was an expression of disgust. Certainly he had been thinking to himself : " A street-walker's room." As I thought it over I writhed at having said it with such ingenuous pride. I ought to have realised that to anyone like him, so civilised and sensitive, my room must have seemed a sordid hovel, made even uglier by the extremely modest furniture and the use I put it to.

I wished I had never uttered that unfortunate phrase ; but now it had dropped from my lips and there was no more to be done about it. This phrase seemed like a prison from which I could never escape by any possible means. For I could be identified with that phrase, irrevocably, having made myself what I was of my own free will. To forget it, or pretend to myself that I had never said it, would be like forgetting my very self or pretending to myself that I did not exist.

These reflections had the effect on me of a slow poison making its harmful way through the most precious blood in my veins. Although in the morning I usually tried to prolong my state of idleness, the moment always came when the sheets revolted me and my body, as if moved by a will of its own, threw them off and leapt out of bed. But the contrary happened on that day ; the whole morning passed, it was lunchtime, and although I tried to urge myself to get up I could not stir. I felt tied down, inert, incapable and sluggish ; and at the same time I was aching all over as if my immobility had been won at the expense of some enormous, desperate effort. I felt as though I was one of those rotting old boats that are sometimes towed to moorings in a marshy inlet, their holds full of black, stinking water, and if anyone boards one of them the decaying planks give way instantly, and the boat, which had been there perhaps for years, sinks in a twinkling. I do not know how long I lay there in that way, uncomfortably wrapped up in the blankets, staring into the void with the sheets drawn up to my nose. I heard the bells chime midday, then one, two, three and four o'clock strike. I had locked my door ; every now and again mother came and knocked anxiously. I told her I would get up soon and that she was to leave me alone.

When the light began to fade, I summoned up my courage and with an apparently superhuman effort I threw off the blankets and got out of bed.

My limbs were heavy with inactivity and disgust; and I dragged myself about the room rather than walked as I washed and dressed. My mind was a blank: I only knew, with the whole of my body rather than my mind, that for that day at least I had not the slightest desire to go out and pick up a lover. As soon as I was dressed, I went and told mother we were going to spend the evening together. We would go out for a stroll in the town and later we would have a vermouth in a café.

Mother's delight at an invitation of this kind, to which she was not accustomed, irritated me, I did not know why myself; and once again I noticed without any tenderness what flabby swollen cheeks she had and what tiny eyes, filled with a wavering and uncertain light. But I restrained the impulse to make some sharp remark to her which might have destroyed her happiness and sat down at the table in the dimly-lit room, waiting for her to dress. The white light shed through the curtainless windows by the street-lamp shone on the sewing-machine and lit up one of the walls. I lowered my eyes to the table and in the half-light I glanced at the rows of gaily-figured patience cards with which mother used to relieve the boredom of her long evenings alone. At this I suddenly felt a strange sensation. I felt as if I were mother, mother herself in flesh and blood, waiting for her daughter Adriana in the next room to have done with one of her pick-ups. This sensation was probably due to the fact that I was seated in her chair, at her table, in front of her cards. Places do occasionally conjure up feelings in this way; and many people when they visit a prison, for instance, imagine they feel the same chill, despair and sense of isolation experienced by the prisoner who once languished there. But the living-room was not a prison and mother's sufferings were neither so weighty nor so easily imaginable. She was only living as, I suppose, she had always lived. Nevertheless, perhaps because a moment earlier I had felt a hostile impulse towards her, the intuitive sense of the life she lived was enough to produce in me a kind of bodily change. When good people want to excuse some blameworthy deed, they sometimes say : "Put yourself in her place." Well, at that moment I put myself in mother's place, to such an extent that I persuaded myself I was mother.

I was, but at the same time I was conscious of being her, as she certainly was not, otherwise she would have rebelled in some way. I suddenly felt shrivelled, wrinkled, crippled, and realised what old age was in that it not only changes the body but makes it weak and powerless. What was mother like ? I had seen her sometimes when she was undressing and without reflecting I had noticed her shrunken, flabby, greyish breasts, and her sallow, relaxed belly. I now felt in my own person those breasts which had given me milk, that belly which had given me birth ; I could touch them, and I seemed to experience the same regret and helpless anguish which the sight of her changed body must have caused mother. Youth and beauty make life beautiful and even gay. But when they are gone ? I shuddered with terror and, shaking off the nightmare for a moment, congratulated myself on being in fact Adriana, who was both young and beautiful ; and on having nothing in common with mother, who was neither young nor beautiful nor ever would be again.

At the same time, slowly, like some mechanism that has run down and gradually begins to pick up speed again, my mind began to formulate thoughts that must have come to her while, alone in the room, she waited for my return. It is not at all difficult to imagine what a person like mother must have thought in such circumstances ; only in most people such thoughts are necessarily the product of reproach and scorn ; and in point of fact they do not so much imagine, as fashion for themselves, a kind of puppet on which to vent all their hostility. But since I loved mother and was putting myself in her place through affection, I knew that her thoughts at such moments were not selfish, fearful or shameful, but were, in fact, unrelated in any way to what I did and was. I knew, rather, that her thoughts were incidental and insignificant, the kind a poor, ignorant old woman would have, since she had never been able to believe or think the same thing for two days running without being sharply contradicted by necessity. Great thoughts and deep emotions, even when they are melancholy and negative, need shelter and a period of growth, they are delicate plants that require time to give them strength and firm rooting. But mother had never been able to cultivate anything else in her mind and heart than the short-lived weeds of day-to-day reflections, resentments and worries. And so I was able, as in fact I did, to sell myself for money in my own room; but mother, as she sat in the living-room before her patience cards, went on revolving in her mind the usual nonsense, if the things she had lived for throughout her life, from childhood up to the present day, may justly so be called: such as the price of food, the tittle-tattle of the neighbourhood, the household chores, the fear of accidents, the jobs she had to do and other such trivialities. At most, perhaps, day in day out, she listened for the clock to strike in the neighbouring belfry, and, without attaching much importance to them, had some such thoughts as: "Adriana's being longer than usual this time," or, on hearing me open the door and say a word or two in the hall: "Adriana's finished." What else? Now, in my imaginings I had become mother herself, body and soul, and just because I was able to put myself so truly and nakedly in her place, I felt I loved her again even more than before.

The noise of the door being opened awoke me from my kind of daydream. Mother was lighting the lamp. "What are you doing in the dark?" she asked me, and I leapt to my feet, dazzled, and looked at her. She had put on brand new clothes: I took that in at the first glance. She had not put on a hat, because she never wore one, but was wearing an elaborately-cut black dress. On her arm she carried a large, black leather bag with a yellowish metal clasp, and had a short cat fur round her neck. She had damped her grey hair and combed it carefully, pulling it tightly piled on top of her head into a little knot stuck through with hairpins. She had even dabbed some pink powder on her dry, withered cheeks which now looked too florid. I could hardly help smiling when I saw her so dolled up and serious; and in my usual affectionate way I said as I rose: "We'd better be going."

I knew mother enjoyed ambling slowly along, when the traffic was at its height, through the main streets where the best shops in town are to be found. So we took a tram and got off at the top of Via Nazionale. When I was a little girl mother used to take me for walks along this street. She used to begin from Piazza dell'Esedra, on the right-hand pavement, and proceed slowly, looking attentively into every shop window until we reached Piazza Venezia. Then she would cross over and return to Piazza dell'Esedra, still looking at every single thing in the windows and dragging me along by the hand. Then, without so much as having bought a pin or having dared to enter one of the numerous cafés, she used to take me home, tired and sleepy. I remember I did not enjoy these walks myself because, unlike mother, who seemed content to feed her appetite on detailed and delighted window-shopping, I had wanted to enter the shops, buy and take home some of the many lovely new things offered for sale in so much light behind the gleaming plate-glass windows. But I realised very young that we were poor and I never expressed my feelings in any way. Only once—I cannot remember why—I did, as the saying goes, pick my fancy. And we rushed along the crowded street at twice our usual speed, mother dragging me by one arm while I tugged against her with all my might, bawling and weeping. Until at last mother lost her patience and boxed my ears instead of giving me the object I craved for; and, at each successive blow I forgot the pain of not being allowed to have what I wanted.

Here I was then, once more at the far end of the pavement opposite the Piazza dell'Esedra, on mother's arm, as if all the years had made no difference. Here the pavements were swarming with feet wearing shoes, boots, high boots, shoes with heels and shoes without, some in sandals, all which, merely to look at them, made one's head go round; the people were strolling up and down in couples, or in groups of men, women and children, or alone: some leisurely, some in a hurry, all alike, perhaps just because they all wanted to be different, with the same clothes, the same hair, the same faces, eyes and mouths; here were the furriers, shoe-makers, stationers, jewellers, watch-makers, book-sellers, florists, drapers, toy-shops, ironmongers, milliners, hosiers, glove-shops, cafés, cinemas, banks; here were the lighted windows of the big buildings, with people moving about the rooms or working at desks; the electric signs, always the same; on the street corners stood the newspaper kiosks, the chestnut-sellers, the unemployed selling Armenian paper, and rubber rings for umbrellas; here were the beggars; a blind man with black spectacles, cap in hand at the top of the street, his head thrown back against the wall, lower down an elderly woman suckling a child at her shrunken breast, and lower still an idiot with a shiny yellow stump like a knee-joint where his hand should have been. As I found myself once more in that street among such familiar objects, I had an impression of immobility, which made me shudder profoundly and feel momentarily naked, as if the icy breath of fear had passed between my body and my clothes. The clamorous, im-passioned voice of a woman singing came from the radio of a nearby café. She was singing *Little black-faced Babby*—it was the year of the Abyssinian war.

Mother naturally had no inkling of what I was feeling; and of course I did not show it. As I have already said, I look good-natured, docile, sweet-tempered, and other people cannot easily guess what is going on inside my head. But at a certain moment my feelings got the better of me (the woman's voice had now started on a sentimental song); my lips were trembling and I spoke to mother. "Do you remember when you used to take me up and down this street to look in the shop windows?"

"Yes," she replied, "but everything cost less in those days—this bag, for instance—you'd have got it for thirty lira then."

We passed on from the leather-shop to the jewellers'. Mother stopped to look at the jewellery. "Look!" she exclaimed ecstatically. "Just look at that ring! Heaven knows what it would cost—and that heavy gold bracelet! I'm not so keen on rings and bracelets myself—but I do like a nice necklace. I had a coral necklace once—but then I had to sell it."

" When ? "

" Oh, years ago now."

I do not know why, but I was reminded that so far, with all my professional earnings, I had never yet been able to buy myself even the simplest ring. " You know," I said to mother, " I've made up my mind not to bring men home any more. I've done with all that."

This was the first time I had mentioned my profession to mother in so many words. She had a look on her face that I failed to understand at the time. " I've told you time and again," she said. " Do what you like. If you're happy, I'm happy."

But she did not seem happy. " We'll have to take up the life we were living before. You'll have to start cutting out and sewing shirts again," I continued.

" I did it for years," she said.

" We won't have so much money as we have now," I insisted rather heartlessly. " We've been rather spoilt lately. I don't know what I'll do myself."

" What will you do ? " mother asked hopefully.

" I don't know," I answered. " Be a model again, perhaps, or help you with your work."

" What help will you be to me ! " she said discouragingly.

" Or else," I went on, " I can go into service. What *is* there to do ? "

Mother's face now looked sad and wretched, as if she had in a twinkling shed the creature-comforts of recent times, as trees their dead leaves at the first chill of autumn. " You must do what you want," she repeated; with conviction, however. " As long as you're happy, that's all I say."

I realised that two opposing passions were struggling within her : her love for me and her attachment to an easy way of life. I was sorry for her and I would have preferred her to have had the courage to give up one or the other of these two emotions for good and all : either all for love or all for lucre. But this happens very rarely and we spend our lives cancelling out the effects of our virtues with those

198

of our vices. " I wasn't happy before," I said, " and I shan't be happy now—only I can't go on any more in this way."

After this we said nothing more. Mother's face was quite grey and collapsed, and once more her old drawn look of thinness seemed to have come back underneath her recent florid appearance. She looked at the shop windows just as eagerly and with as much concentration as before; but mechanically now, with no delight or curiosity, as if her mind were engrossed with something else. Perhaps her eyes were unseeing even while she gazed; or rather, she saw, not the goods exposed in the windows, but her sewing-machine with its tireless treadle, and the needle thrusting madly up and down, the heaps of unfinished shirts lying on the table, the black cloth she used to wrap round the completed work before taking it across town to her customers. But there were no such visions between my eyes and the shop windows. I saw them perfectly and my thoughts were crystal-clear. I could make out all the objects behind the glass windows with their price tickets, one by one, and told myself I might not want to continue in my profession, did not want to, in fact, but there was actually nothing else I could do. I might, within certain limits, have purchased most of the objects I was contemplating, but the very day I returned to my employment as a model or anything of that kind I would have to give those things up for ever, and the usual cheese-paring, comfortless life full of repressed desires, useless sacrifice and profitless saving would begin all over again for mother and me. I might even aspire to owning some jewel, if I could find someone to give it to me. But if I returned to my old way of life, jewels would be as far out of my reach as the stars in the heavens. A rush of disgust for the old life, so stupidly harsh and hopeless, overwhelmed me, and at the same time I had a vivid sense of the absurdity of my reasons for wishing to change my profession. Simply because a student, with whom I had become infatuated, had refused to have anything to do with me ! Because I had persuaded myself that he despised me ! Because I would have liked to be something different from what I was, in fact. I told myself it was only pride and that I could not out of mere pride plunge myself, and mother in particular, back into the old, wretched conditions. I suddenly saw Giacomo's life, which for a brief moment had converged with mine and mingled with it, running off in another direction while my own continued along the path I was already treading. "If I found someone who loved me and wanted to marry me I'd change, even if he were poor," I thought, "but it wouldn't be worth while for a whim." My heart was filled with the sweet calm of liberation at this thought. I have often had the same feeling since, not only every time I have refused what fate seemed to have to offer me in life, but also when I have gone out to meet it. I was what I was, and I had to be that and nothing else. I might be either a good wife, although this may seem odd, or a woman who sells herself for money; but I could not be a wretched little creature toiling and moiling all her life long, with no other aim than the satisfaction of her own pride. Having made peace with myself, I smiled.

We were standing in front of a women's clothiers, that displayed silks and woollens. "Look what a lovely head-square!" mother said. "That's just what I want."

Feeling at peace and serene once more, I raised my eyes and looked at the square she meant. It really was lovely, in black and white, with a pattern of birds and foliage. The shop door was open and the counter in full view, and on the counter stood a tray divided into little sections all filled with squares like that, heaped untidily together. "Would you like it?" I asked mother.

"Yes, why?"

"Then you shall have it. But first give me your handbag and you take mine."

She did not understand and gaped at me. I said nothing, but took her large black leather bag and put my smaller one into her hands. I unfastened the clasps of her bag and keeping it open with my fingers I slowly entered the shop, like someone intending to make a purchase. Mother, who still did not understand but dared not question me, followed me in.

"We wanted to see some head-squares," I said to the assistant, as I walked up to the tray.

" These are silk . . . these cashmere . . . these wool . . . these cotton . . ." she said, tumbling the squares out before me.

I walked right up to the counter, and holding the bag level with my stomach I began to examine the squares with one hand, opening them and holding them up to the light, the better to see the pattern and colours. There were at least a dozen black and white ones, exactly alike. I let one slip on to the edge of the case, with an end hanging over the counter.

" I really wanted something brighter," I then said to the shop assistant.

" There's a better quality article," said the assistant, " but it's dearer."

" Let me see it."

She turned to lift down a case from the shelves. I was prepared for this and drawing away from the counter a little, I opened the bag. It only took a moment to pull the square down by one end and then press myself up against the counter again.

Meanwhile the assistant had lifted the case down from the shelf. She put it on the counter and showed me some larger and finer head-squares. I examined them, calmly, at my leisure, commenting on the colours and patterns, and even showed them to mother with little exclamations of approval which she answered by nods, feeling more dead than alive since she had seen what I had done.

" How much are they ? " I asked at last.

She told me the price. " You were right," I said regretfully. " They're too dear, for us, anyway—but thanks all the same."

We left the shop, and I walked hastily towards a nearby church because I was afraid the assistant might notice the theft and run after us through the crowd. Mother, hanging on to my arm, looked about her with a suspicious and bewildered air, like someone who is drunk and none too certain that what he sees wavering and shifting before his eyes is not drunk rather than he himself. I could not help laughing at her bewilderment. I did not know why I had stolen the square; it was not important in itself, because I had already stolen the compact in the house of Gino's employer and in such matters what counts most is the first step. But the sensual pleasure of the first time came back to me; and I felt I understood now why so many people steal. A few steps brought us to the church in a side-street. " Shall we go in for a moment? " I asked mother.

" If you like," she answered submissively.

We entered the little white church, circular in shape, which seemed like a dance-hall with its double ring of columns encircling the stone-flagged floor. A dull light poured down from the lights in the dome on to the two rows of pews polished by use. I raised my eyes and saw that the dome was frescoed all over with figures of angels with outspread wings, and I felt certain that those splendid, handsome angels would protect me, and that the assistant would not notice the theft before evening. The silence, the smell of incense, the shadow and sense of retirement in the church, all helped to reassure me after the confusion and excessively strong light in the street. I had entered the church hastily, almost knocking into mother, but I grew calmer at once and my fear subsided. Mother made as if to fumble inside my bag, which she was still holding. I held her own out to her. " Put your square on," I whispered to her.

She opened the bag and arranged the stolen square on her head. We dipped our fingers in the holy-water stoup and went to sit down in the first row of pews facing the High Altar. I knelt down and mother remained seated, her hands in her lap, her face shaded by the head-square that was too large for her. I realised she was distressed; and I could not help comparing my own calm with her distress. I felt I was in a sweet and conciliatory frame of mind and, although I knew I had done something forbidden by religion, I felt no remorse and was far nearer a religious state than I was when I had done nothing wrong and had worked my fingers to the bone to eke out a living. I remembered the shudder of bewilderment I had experienced a moment earlier while looking at the crowded thoroughfare, and I was comforted by the idea that there was a God who could see clearly into me and saw there was nothing bad, and that the mere fact of being alive rendered me innocent, as all men are, in fact. I knew this God was not there to judge and condemn me, but to justify my existence, which could only be good since it depended directly from Him. While I mechanically repeated the words of the prayer I was looking at the altar, where the dark image in a picture dimly visible behind the candle-flames appeared to be the Madonna, and I realised that between the Madonna and myself the question was not whether I should behave in such and such a way, but more essentially whether I should feel encouraged to continue living or not. The encouragement I was seeking suddenly seemed to me to be pouring out towards me from the dark figure behind the altar-candles, in the form of a sudden sensation of heat that flooded my whole being. Yes, I was encouraged to go on living, although I knew nothing about life nor why I was alive.

Mother sat there, sullen and bewildered, with the brand new head-square sticking out like a beak over her nose. When I turned round to look at her, I could not help smiling affectionately at her. " Say a little prayer—it'll do you good," I whispered. She shivered, hesitated, and then unwillingly knelt down, her hands joined. I knew she did not want to believe any more in religion, it seemed to her a kind of false consolation whose aim was to make her be good and forget the harshness of life. But nevertheless I saw her lips moving mechanically and the expression of suspicious ill-humour on her face made me smile again. I wanted to reassure her, tell her I had changed my mind, she had nothing to worry about, she would not be obliged to work as she had in the past. There was something childish about mother's sulkiness ; she was like a child when it is refused a sweet it had been promised, and this seemed to be the most important aspect of her behaviour to me. Otherwise I might have thought she counted on my profession to enable her to enjoy all her little comforts ; and I knew in my heart that this was not true.

Having said her prayers, she crossed herself angrily and rapidly, as if to show clearly that she had only done it to please me. I got up and signed to her to come out. On the doorstep she took off the square, folded it carefully and replaced it in her bag. We returned to Via Nazionale and I walked towards a confectionery shop. "Now we're going to have a glass of vermouth," I said. "No! Why should we? We don't need one," protested mother, in a voice that sounded both pleased and apprehensive. She was always like that—afraid from of old that I would spend too much. "What'll it cost?" I said. "One vermouth!" She was silent and followed me into the shop.

It was an old-fashioned place, with a counter and skirting board of polished mahogany and a number of glass cases filled with handsome boxes of sweets. We sat down in a corner and I ordered two vermouths. The waiter made mother feel embarrassed, and while I was ordering she sat there stock-still and awkward, her eyes cast down. When he had brought our drinks, she picked up the little glass, just took no more than a sip, put it down again, then said seriously as she looked at me: "It's good."

"Well, it's vermouth," I replied. The waiter had brought a metal and glass cake-stand with some cakes in it. I opened it. "Have one," I said to mother.

"No, no—for goodness' sake!"

"Go on—have one!"

"It'll spoil my appetite."

"One cake!" I looked at the cakes and chose a *millefeuilles* and gave it to her. "Eat this one," I said. "It's not heavy."

She took it and nibbled at it in little mouthfuls, perfunctorily, looking at the cake again after each bite. "It's really good," she said at last.

"Have another," I said. This time she did not need pressing and accepted another cake. When she had finished the vermouth we sat on without speaking, watching the customers coming and going in the shop. I could see that mother was glad to be sitting in a corner with two cakes and a vermouth inside her, that she was amused by the incessant movement of the people, and that she had nothing to say to me. This was probably the first time she had ever been in such a place and the novelty of the experience prevented any thoughts she might have on other subjects.

A young lady entered, holding by the hand a little girl who was wearing a fluffy white fur collar, a short little dress and white cotton gloves and stockings. The mother chose a cake from the stand on the counter and gave it to her.

" When I was a little girl you never took me into the cakeshops," I said to mother.

" How could I have afforded it ? " she asked.

" And now instead," I concluded in even tone, " it's I who bring you here."

She was silent for a moment, then said sullenly : " Now you're throwing it in my face because you brought me here— I didn't want to come."

I put my hand on hers. " I'm not throwing anything in your face," I said. " I'm glad I brought you here. Did granny ever take you to cake-shops ? "

She shook her head. " I never went outside our own district until I was eighteen."

" You see," I said, " you need someone in a family who will do certain things for the first time one day or other. You didn't do them, nor your mother, nor probably your mother's mother. So I do them. You can't go on like that for ever and ever amen ! "

She did not answer, and we stayed there for another quarter of an hour watching the people. Then I opened my bag, took out my cigarette-case and lit a cigarette. Women of my sort often smoke in public places in order to attract the attention of men. But I was not thinking of picking anyone up just then ; in fact, I had decided for that evening at least to have nothing to do with them. I wanted to smoke and that was all. I put the cigarette to my lips, inhaled the smoke, then blew it out of my mouth and nostrils, holding the cigarette between two fingers and watching the people.

But there must have been something provocative in my gesture, because I immediately noticed a man near the counter who was about to sip a cup of coffee he held in one hand, stop with the cup half-way to his lips and stare fixedly at me. He was a man in his forties, short, with thick curly hair and bulging eyes, and a lantern jaw. He was so stocky that he seemed to have no neck. He stood there with his cup half-way to his lips, staring at me, like a bull that has seen a red rag and stands motionless before lowering its head to attack. He was well, though not fashionably dressed, with a well-fitting overcoat which accentuated the breadth of his shoulders. I lowered my eyes and for a moment began to weigh up what there was for and against such a man. I knew his character was such that one glance from me would suffice to make the veins in his neck stand out and his face grow purple; but I was not at all sure that I liked him. Then I realised that the desire to attract him had set my whole body on edge, like the hidden sap which bursts forth from the rough bark in a number of tender flower buds, and I was obliged to renounce my reserved manner. And this was only one hour after I had decided to change my profession ! I said to myself that there was nothing to be done about it, it was stronger than I was. But my thoughts were quite light-hearted; for since I had left the church I had become reconciled to my fate, whatever it was, and I felt that my acceptance of it was worth more to me than any high-minded self-denial. So, after a moment's consideration, I raised my eyes and looked at him. He was still there, like a wild beast, his cup in his thick, hairy hand, his bovine eyes fixed on me. At that I took the initiative, as it were, and threw him a lengthy and caressing, ogling glance with all the suggestiveness I could summon. His eyes encountered mine and he grew purple as I had foreseen he would. He sipped his coffee, put the cup down on the counter, and, strutting in his close-fitting overcoat with stiff little steps, he went to the cash-desk and paid. He turned in the doorway and made me a definite, imperious sign of understanding. I looked my acceptance in reply.

" I'm going to leave you now," I said to mother. " You stay here, though, in any case I can't leave this place with you."

She was enjoying all the sights in the shop, and started in alarm. " Where are you going ? Why ? "

" There's a man waiting for me outside," I said as I got to my feet. " Here's the money . . . pay for everything and go home . . . I'll be there before you, I expect . . . but I won't be alone."

She looked at me in dismay, and, it seemed to me, with a kind of remorse. But she did not say anything. I nodded good-bye and went out. The man was waiting in the street. I was hardly out of the place when he was upon me, grasping my arm firmly. " Where shall we go ? "

" To my place."

So, after a few hours of anguish, I gave up the unequal struggle against what appeared to be my fate, indeed, I welcomed it with more affection, as one embraces a foe one cannot defeat ; and I felt liberated. Some may think it is far easier to accept an unworthy but profitable fate than to renounce it. But I have often wondered why misery and anger dwell in the hearts of those people who try to live according to certain precepts and to conform to certain ideals, and why those who accept their destiny—which is mainly emptiness, obscurity and feebleness—are so often gay and carefree. In such cases, the individual does not follow a precept but his own temperament, which appears to him in the guise of a real, genuine destiny. My temperament, as I have already said, was to be gay, amiable and serene, at all costs, and I accepted it.

CHAPTER THREE

I gave up Giacomo altogether by deciding to think no more about him. I felt I loved him and if he were to return I would be happy and would love him more than ever. But I also knew I would never let myself be humiliated by him again. If he came back I would stand there before him, enclosed in my own life as in a fortress, which would really be impregnable and unshaken until I left it of my own accord. " I'm a street-walker," I would say to him, " nothing more . . . if you want me, you've got to accept me for what I am." I had realised that my strength lay not in my desiring to be something I was not, but in my accepting what I was. My strength lay in my poverty, my profession, mother, my ugly house, my simple clothes, my humble origin, my misfortunes, and more profoundly in the feeling which made me able to accept all these things, a feeling as deeply embedded in my soul as a precious stone in the bowels of the earth. But I was quite sure I would never see him again; and this certainty made me love him in a melancholy, helpless way quite new in my experience, which had its own sweetness. As we love the dead who never will return.

At this time, I broke off my relationship with Gino once and for all. As I have already said, I dislike sudden breaks and I prefer things to live and die their own lives, their own deaths. My relations with Gino were a good example of my desires in this respect. They ceased because the life in them ceased, not through my fault and not even, in a certain sense, through Gino's. They ceased in such a way as to leave me no regrets or remorse.

I had continued to see him every now and again, two or three times a month. I liked him, as I have said, although I no longer respected him. One day he rang up and asked me to meet him at a milk-bar, and I told him I would be there.

The dairy was in my own neighbourhood. Gino was waiting for me in the inner room, a windowless little place, the walls covered with majolica tiles. As I entered I saw he was not alone. Someone was sitting beside him with his back towards me. I could only see that he was wearing a green raincoat and was fair, with his hair cut short on top of his head. I went up to them and Gino got to his feet, but his companion remained seated. "Let me introduce my friend Sonzogno," said Gino. Then he stood up, too, and I held out my hand. But when he took it I felt as though he were gripping me in a vice and a little cry of pain escaped me. He let go at once and I sat down smiling. "Do you know you hurt me?" I said. "Is that what you always do?"

He did not reply, did not even smile. His face was paper-white, his forehead hard and bulging, his eyes tiny and sky-blue in colour, he was flat-nosed and had a mouth like a slit. His hair was bristly and colourless, cut short, his temples squashed in. But the lower part of his face was broad, his jaw heavy and ugly. He seemed always to be grinding his teeth, as though he were masticating something; and it looked as if one of the nerves under the skin of his cheek were trembling and twitching all the time. Gino's attitude to him was one of admiring and respectful friendship.

" That's nothing ! " he said. " If you knew how strong he is ! He's got a killer's punch."

I thought Sonzogno regarded him with hostility.

" That's a lie," he said in his flat voice. " I haven't got a killer's punch. I might have——"

" What's a killer's punch ? " I asked.

" When you can kill a man with a single blow . . . then you're forbidden to use your fists . . . it's as fatal as a revolver."

" Feel how strong he is ! " insisted Gino excitedly, as if eager to ingratiate himself with Sonzogno. " Just feel. Let her touch your arm."

I hesitated, but Gino was keen and his friend also seemed to expect it. So I stretched my hand out, limply, to pinch his arm. He bent his forearm to flex his muscles, seriously, almost grimly. And then I felt beneath my fingers, through his sleeve, something that was like a bundle of iron cords, and I had a shock of surprise because he looked so slight. I withdrew my hand with an exclamation of mingled disgust and wonder. Sonzogno looked at me complacently, a slight smile playing on his lips.

" He's an old friend of mine," said Gino. " We've known one another quite a time, haven't we, Primo ? We're almost brothers, you might say." He patted Sonzogno on the shoulder, saying : " Good old Primo ! "

Sonzogno shrugged his shoulder as if to shake Gino's hand off. " We're neither friends nor brothers," he said. " We used to work together in the same garage, that's all."

Gino was not at all disconcerted. " Oh, I know you don't want it to look as if you're anyone's friend . . . always you're alone, on your own. No women, and no men."

Sonzogno looked at him. He had a fixed stare, incredibly insistent and unblinking ; Gino was obliged to turn his eyes away. " Who told you that rot ? " asked Sonzogno. " I go with anyone I like—men or women."

" I was only talking." Gino's cocksure air had vanished. " I've never seen you with anyone, that's all I can say."

"You've never known anything about my affairs."

"Well, I used to see you morning and evening every day."

"What if you did see me every day?"

"Well," said Gino disconcerted, "I've always seen you on your own, and I thought you never met anyone—if a man's got a girl or a friend you always get to know it."

"Don't be a fool," said Sonzogno brutally.

"Now you're calling me a fool," said Gino, flushing, and feigning his usual ill-humour. But he was obviously scared.

"Yes," repeated Sonzogno. "Don't act the fool or I'll knock your brains out."

I suddenly realised he was not only quite capable of doing it but that he actually intended to do so. Placing one hand on his arm I intervened. "If you want to fight it out, please do it when I'm not there. I can't stand violence."

"Here am I, introducing a young lady-friend to you," said Gino sulkily, "and you frighten her out of her wits with your ways! She'll think we're enemies!"

Sonzogno turned to me and smiled for the first time. When he smiled he screwed up his eyes, wrinkled his forehead and showed not only his little bad teeth but even his gums. "The young lady isn't frightened, are you?" he asked.

"Not a scrap," I answered briefly, "but I don't like violence, as I've told you."

A long silence ensued. Sonzogno remained motionless, his hands in the pockets of his raincoat, the nerves in his jaw twitching as he stared at nothing; Gino was still smoking with bent head and the smoke crept up his face and ears that were still crimson. Then Sonzogno got up. "Well—I'm off," he said.

Gino leapt eagerly to his feet. "All right then—we're as we were, eh, Primo?" he said as he held out his hand.

"As we were," repeated Sonzogno through clenched teeth. He shook my hand but without hurting me this time, and went away. He was slight and short; and it was really impossible to see where all his strength came from.

"You may be friends and even brothers—but the way he talked to you!" I said jokingly to Gino as soon as he had gone.

Gino had quite recovered by now. "He's made that way," he said, shaking his head. "But he's not a bad sort. It suits my books to be on the right side of him. He's useful to me sometimes."

"In what way?"

I noticed Gino was excited and all agog to tell me something. His face had suddenly become wildly excited and eager.

"You remember my mistress's compact?"

"Yes—well?"

Gino's eyes shone with delight. "Well, I thought it over and didn't give it back," he said, lowering his voice.

"You didn't give it back?"

"No. After all, I thought, she's rich and one compact more or less won't make any difference to her—specially since the deed was already done," he added characteristically, "and, when all's said and done, I wasn't the thief."

"I was the thief," I said in an even voice.

He pretended not to have heard me. "Still, later on there was the problem of selling it," he continued. "It was a showy thing, easy to identify, and I didn't dare. So I kept it in my pocket for a good while . . . until at last I met Sonzogno, told him the whole story . . ."

"Did you tell him about me?" I interrupted.

"No, not about you—I told him a girl-friend had given it to me, without mentioning any names—and he—— Just think, in three days he sold it and brought me the cash. Of course, he kept his share, like we agreed." He was trembling with joy and after having looked around him he pulled a bundle of notes out of his pocket.

I do not know why but at that moment I felt a deep aversion to him. It was not that I criticised what he had done, I had no right to do that at all, but his gloating irritated me; besides, I guessed he was keeping something back and what he had not told me was certainly far worse. "You were right," I said shortly.

"Here," he said, undoing the roll of banknotes, "these are for you—I've counted them."

"No," I replied immediately, "I want nothing, absolutely nothing."

" Why not ? "

" I don't want it."

" You're trying to insult me," he said. A shade of doubt and distress flitted across his face and I was afraid I really had offended him. I placed my hand on his. " If you hadn't offered it to me," I said with an effort, " I'd have been—well, not offended, perhaps, but surprised—but now it's done it's all right as it is. I don't want it because the matter's over and done with as far as I'm concerned, that's all—I'm glad you've got it, though."

He looked at me doubtfully, not understanding what I was saying, gazing at me as though he wanted to discover the hidden motive behind my words. I have realised since, when I have thought about him, that he was incapable of understanding me because he lived in a different world from mine. with different ideas and emotions. I do not know whether it was a worse world or a better one, I only know that some words did not mean the same for him as they did for me, and that most of the actions I criticised in him seemed to him both lawful and proper. He seemed to ascribe the utmost importance to intelligence, interpreted however, as astuteness. And in dividing mankind into two groups—those who were astute and those who were not—he always tried to place himself in the first category. But I am not at all astute myself, perhaps not even intelligent, and I have never been able to understand how a bad deed can be explained away, let alone accepted, merely because it was cunningly done.

The doubt that was tormenting him suddenly seemed to vanish. " I know what it is ! " he exclaimed. " You don't want to take the money because you're afraid—you're afraid the theft might be discovered. But you needn't worry. Everything's come straight."

I was not afraid, but I did not trouble to deny it because I had not understood the second part of his sentence.

" What do you mean ? " I asked. " Everything's come straight."

" Yes," he replied. " Everything's straight—you remember ! I told you they suspected one of the maids, didn't I ? "

"Yes."

"Well—I'd got my knife into that maid because she gossiped about me behind my back. A few days after the theft I could see things were looking bad for me—the police-officer had been back twice, I thought I was being shadowed. Mind you, they hadn't searched the house yet. So I got a brainwave to cause a search to be made on account of some other theft and then arrange for the blame for both thefts to fall on her."

I remained silent, and after having glanced at me with wide-open, glittering eyes as if to see whether I was admiring his cunning, he continued. "The mistress had some dollars in a drawer. I took them and hid them in the maid's room in an old suitcase. This time they searched the house, of course, the dollars were found and she was arrested. She swears she's innocent, naturally, but who'd believe it? They found the dollars in her own room."

"Where is this woman now?"

"In prison, and she won't confess. But do you know what the police-officer told the mistress? 'Don't worry, madam,' he said, ' by fair means or foul she'll own up in the end.' See what they mean? Fair means or foul? They'll beat her up."

I looked at him and, seeing him so proud of himself and worked up, I felt like ice and very bewildered. "What's her name?" I asked casually.

"Luisa Fellini—she's not so young, and she's very stuck-up. Her tale is that she'd become a maid through ill-luck and no one on earth was as honest as she!" He smiled, highly amused at the coincidence.

I made an effort as if I were heaving a deep sigh. "Do you know you're a cad?" I said.

"What? Why?" he asked me in amazement.

Now I had told him he was a cad, I felt freer and more determined. My nostrils quivered with rage. "And you wanted me to take that money!" I continued. "But I could feel it was money I oughtn't to take."

"What's all the fuss?" he said, trying to regain his composure. "She won't confess—and then they'll let her go."

213

"But you've just said yourself that they'll keep her in prison and beat her!"

"I was only talking."

"It doesn't matter. You've sent an innocent woman to gaol ... and then you've had the face to come and tell me all about it! You're a cad."

He suddenly grew furious, the blood left his face. He gripped my hand. "Shut up calling me cad!"

"Why? I think you're a cad and I'll say so."

He lost his head and made a curiously violent gesture. He twisted my hand in his as if he wanted to crush it and then suddenly bent his head and bit my hand hard. I freed myself with a jerk and stood up. "Are you crazy?" I exclaimed. "What's got into you now? Biting? It's no good ... you're a cad and you'll always be a cad." He did not reply but sunk his head on his hands as if he wanted to tear his hair out.

I called the waiter and paid for all the drinks, mine, his and Sonzogno's. "I'm going," I then said. "And I tell you ... everything's over between us. Don't show up again, don't look out for me, don't come ... I don't know you any longer." He said nothing but kept his head lowered. I left.

The milk-bar was at the top of the main road not far from the house where I lived. I began to walk slowly along on the side opposite the city walls. It was night, the sky was covered with clouds and a fine rain was falling like watery dust through the mild, unstirring air. The walls were in darkness as usual, except for an occasional rarely-spaced street-lamp. But I immediately noticed a man slip away from one of the street-lamps as I left the milk-bar and begin to follow along the walls at my pace in the direction I was going. I recognised Sonzogno, with his raincoat clipped in at the waist and his fair, shaven head. He looked short there beneath the walls, disappeared every now and again in the shadows, then reappeared in the gleam of a street-lamp. For the first time I felt sick of men, all men, always running after my skirt like a lot of dogs following a bitch. I was still trembling with rage; and as I thought of the woman Gino had sent to gaol I could not help being filled with remorse, because after all, I had been the one to steal the compact. But perhaps what I felt was revolt and irritation rather than remorse. Although I rebelled against injustice and hated Gino, yet I hated hating him and knowing injustice had been done. I am not really made for such things; I felt terribly distressed and not at all myself. I walked hurriedly, wanting to reach home before Sonzogno approached me, as he apparently intended doing. Then I heard Gino's voice calling me desperately from behind. "Adriana ! Adriana ! "

I pretended I had not heard and hastened on. He took me by the arm. " Adriana ! We've always gone together—we can't give one another up like this."

I freed myself with a jerk and went on walking. The clear-cut little figure of Sonzogno shot out of the darkness into the circle of light shed by a street-lamp on the other side of the road beneath the walls. " I love you, Adriana," Gino continued as he hurried along beside me.

I felt both pity and hatred for him, and this mixture of emotions was indescribably distasteful to me. I tried to think about something else, however. I suddenly had an illuminating flash, I don't know why. I remembered Astarita and how he had always offered me his assistance, and I thought he would almost certainly be able to have the poor woman released. This idea revived my spirits immediately; my heart was freed of its load and I even felt as if I did not hate Gino any more and was only sorry for him. I stood still and addressed him calmly. " Gino," I said, " why don't you go away ? "

" I love you."

" I loved you, too . . . but it's all over. Go away now, it'll be better for both of us."

We were standing in a dark stretch of the road where there were no shops or street-lamps. He took hold of me round the waist and tried to kiss me. I could have broken free easily enough because I am very strong and no one can kiss a woman if she doesn't want to be kissed. But some malicious whim put it into my head to call Sonzogno, who was standing motionless on the other side of the road under the walls, watching us, his hands in the pockets of his raincoat. I suppose I called him because now that I had discovered a way of undoing the harm Gino's action had done, my curiosity and coquetry were aroused once more. " Sonzogno ! Sonzogno ! " I cried out twice, and he immediately crossed the road. Gino was disconcerted and let me go.

" Tell him he's got to let me alone," I said to Sonzogno as soon as he came up. " I don't want him any more. He won't believe me, perhaps he'll believe you since you're a friend of his."

" Did you hear what the young lady said ? " asked Sonzogno.

" But I——" began Gino.

I supposed that they would continue arguing for some time, as usually happens ; and that at last Gino would become resigned and go away. Instead, I saw Sonzogno suddenly make a gesture I did not understand, and Gino stare at him for an astonished moment and then, without a single word, sag to the ground and roll off the pavement into the gutter. Or perhaps all I saw was Gino falling and guessed from that what Sonzogno's gesture had been. The movement was so swift and silent that I thought I had imagined it. I shook my head and took another look. Sonzogno stood in front of me, his legs wide apart, and he was looking at his clenched fist ; Gino, who was lying on the ground with his back to us, had come to himself again and had slowly lifted his head as he leaned on one elbow in the gutter. But he did not look as though he wanted to get to his feet ; rather it seemed as if he preferred to keep staring at a small scrap of white paper that could clearly be seen glimmering against the mud in the gutter.

" Come on," said Sonzogno at last, and I went with him towards my own place as in a dream.

He walked in silence, holding me by the arm. He was shorter than me and his hand gripping my arm was exactly like an iron clamp.

" You shouldn't have hit Gino like that," I said after a while. " He'd have gone away all the same without being hit."

" He won't worry you any more this way," he replied.

" But how did you do it ? " I asked. " I didn't even see what you did—I only saw Gino fall."

"It's a question of habit," he said.

He spoke as if he were chewing his words before uttering them, or rather, as if he were feeling their consistency between his clenched teeth, which I imagined fitting into one another like the teeth of feline animals. I longed now to squeeze his arm and feel his hard, taut muscles again beneath my fingers. He aroused more curiosity than attraction in me, and, above all, fear. But fear can be a pleasant and exciting feeling in a way, until the cause of it is known.

"What have you got here inside your arm?" I asked. "I can't believe it!"

"But I let you feel it once," he said with such earnest vanity that it sounded ominous.

"Not properly ... Gino was there ... Let me feel it again."

He stood still and flexed his arm, looking sideways at me with a serious and ingenuous air. But there was nothing child-like about his ingenuousness. I stretched out my hand and slowly felt his muscles, running my hand all the way down his arm from the shoulder. The sensation of feeling them, so alive and as hard as iron, was extraordinary. "You're very strong," I said in a ghost of a voice.

"Yes, I am strong," he affirmed grimly. And we began walking again.

I was sorry I had called him, now. I did not like him; besides, his seriousness and his behaviour frightened me. We reached my house without speaking again. I took out my key. "Thanks for seeing me home," I said, and held out my hand to him.

"I'm coming up," he said, and came closer to me.

I wanted to say no. But his way of staring into my eyes with incredible fixity overwhelmed and troubled me. "If you like," I said. And I did not realise until after I had spoken to him that I had made use of the intimate form of speech in addressing him.

"Don't be scared," he said, interpreting my distress in his own way. "I've got some money. I'll give you twice what the others give you."

"What's that got to do with it?" I said. "It's not because of the money——" But I saw a strange gleam flit across his face as if a threatening suspicion had struck him. Meanwhile I had opened the door. "I was only feeling a bit tired," I added.

Once in my room, he began to undress with the precise movements of a tidy person. He had a scarf round his neck, took it off with care, folded it up and put it into the pocket of his raincoat. He hung his jacket over the back of a chair and arranged his trousers so as not to spoil the creases. He put both his shoes under the chair with his socks tucked into them. I noticed that all his clothes were new, from head to foot, not de luxe quality, but hard wearing, good stuff. He did all this in silence, neither slowly nor hurriedly, with systematic, well-thought-out regularity, and he took no notice of me. I had undressed meantime and was lying naked on the bed. If he wanted me he certainly did not show it, unless the cease-less twitching of his jaw-muscles just under the skin meant he was in a state of excitement; but that could not be so, because he had had it before, when he did not seem to be thinking about me. I have already said that I like tidiness and cleanliness very much indeed because they seem to indicate corresponding mental qualities. But Sonzogno's tidiness and cleanliness aroused very different sensations in me that evening, something between horror and fear. That was the way surgeons got ready in a hospital, I could not help thinking, when they had to perform some bloody operation. Or worse, slaughterers, under the very eyes of the lamb they are about to kill. But lying there on the bed I felt as helpless and powerless as a life-less body about to undergo an experiment. His silence and indifference left me in doubt as to what he intended to do to me as soon as he had finished undressing. So when he came up to the head of the bed, stark naked, and placed his two hands on my shoulders as if to hold me still, I could not prevent a shudder of fear. He noticed it. " What's up ? " he asked me through his clenched teeth.

" Nothing," I answered. " Your hands are freezing."

" You don't like me, do you ? " he said, still gripping my shoulders as he stood by the head of the bed. " You prefer the people who pay you, don't you ? " As he spoke he stared at me, and the look was unbearable.

218

" Why ? " I said. " You're a man like all the rest. Besides, you said yourself you'd pay double."

" I know what I'm talking about," he said. " You and your like make love to the toffs, the gents. I'm only a man like yourself, and all you tarts only make love to toffs."

I recognised in his voice the same sinister, inflexible desire to stir up a quarrel which had made him insult Gino on the slightest pretext only a little while before. I had supposed at the time that he had his own reasons for bearing Gino a grudge. But I now realised that his grim, incalculable touchiness was always on the alert, and when he was possessed by such a devil you would be in the wrong no matter how you dealt with him.

" Why do you want to insult me ? " I asked, rather heatedly. " I've already told you all men are the same to me."

" If you were telling the truth you wouldn't be pulling such a face. You don't like me, do you ? "

" But I've already told you——! "

" You don't like me," he continued, " but I'm sorry, you've just got to like me."

" Oh, don't bother me ! " I said in sudden irritation.

" As long as I was useful in getting rid of your sweetheart," he went on, " you wanted me. Then afterwards you'd rather have sent me packing. But I came up instead. You don't like me, do you ? "

I was really frightened now. His hurried words, his calm, pitiless voice, the fixed stare in his eyes that seemed to have changed from blue to red, everything seemed to be carrying him on towards some fearful goal. I realised too late that any attempt to stop him on his path would be as hopeless a task as stopping a rock rolling down a precipitous slope. I merely shrugged my shoulders violently.

" You don't like me, eh ? " he went on. " You look disgusted when I touch you ; but I'll change your look for you, my sweet ! " He raised his hand as if to slap me. I was on the look-out for something of the sort and tried to protect myself with my arm. But he managed to strike me all the same, shockingly hard, first on one cheek and then, as I tried to turn my face away, on the other. This was the first time in all my life that anything of this kind had happened to me ;

and despite the sting of the blows I was more surprised than hurt at first. I uncovered my face. "Do you know what you are?" I said. "You're a wretched creature."

He seemed impressed by the phrase. He sat on the edge of the bed and rocked himself up and down, gripping the mattress with both hands. "We're all of us wretched creatures," he then said, without looking at me.

"You need real courage to hit a woman!" I said. But all at once I was unable to continue, for my eyes filled with tears, caused not so much by the blows I had received as by the nervous tension of the whole evening, with all its many unpleasant and distasteful episodes. I remembered Gino lying flat in the mud, remembered how indifferent I had been and how I had gone off cheerfully with Sonzogno, thinking only of testing the exceptional strength of his muscles, and I was overcome by remorse, pity for Gino and disgust at myself, and I realised I had been punished for my insensitiveness and stupidity by the same hand that had struck Gino down. I had delighted in violence and now that same violence had been turned against me. I looked at Sonzogno through my tears. He was sitting on the edge of the bed stark naked, white and hairless, his shoulders bowed, his arms that gave no hint of their strength hanging loosely. I felt an unexpected desire to lessen the distance between us.

"But won't you tell me why you hit me, at least?" I said with an effort.

"There was a look on your face," he said reflectively, the nerve in his jaw twitching.

I realised that if I wanted to get nearer to him I would have to tell him all I was thinking, hide nothing from him.

"You thought I didn't like you. Well, you were wrong," I answered.

"Perhaps."

"You were wrong. As a matter of fact, you frighten me, I don't know why. That's why I had that look on my face."

He turned round sharply at these words, looked at me suspiciously. But he calmed down at once and asked, with a hint of vanity: "So I frightened you, did I?"

"Yes."

" And do I still frighten you ? "

" No, you can kill me if you like, now—I don't mind any longer." This was the truth ; in fact I wanted him to kill me just then because I had suddenly lost all desire to go on living. But he grew angry.

" Who said anything about killing you ? " he said. " Why were you afraid of me ? "

" Who knows ? You frightened me. You can't explain these things."

" Did Gino frighten you ? "

" Why should he frighten me ? "

" But why do I frighten you ? " All his vanity had gone by now, there was a hint of fury in his voice once more.

" Well," I said to soothe him, " you frightened me because anyone can see you're capable of anything."

He said nothing and sat there pensively for a moment. Then he turned round. " All this means you want me to get dressed and get out ? " he asked me threateningly.

I looked at him and realised he was once more in a fit of rage. If I refused him I would be exposing myself to further violence, even worse. I would have to accept him. But I remembered his pale eyes and was filled with disgust at the idea that they would be fixed on mine during the act of love.

" No, you can stay if you like," I said feebly, " but put out the light first."

He stood up, small, white-skinned, but extremely well-proportioned except for his short neck, and went on tiptoe to switch the light off by the door. But I realised immediately that getting him to put the light out had not been a good idea ; for as soon as the room was plunged into darkness, the fear I thought had left me returned again, uncontrollably. It was as though there was in the room with me, not a man, but a leopard or some other wild beast, which might crouch down in a corner or leap on me and tear me to pieces. Perhaps he was slow finding his way among the chairs and other furniture in the dark ; or perhaps fear made his absence seem longer. I certainly had the sensation that ages had passed before he reached the bed, and when I felt his hands on me I could not repress another convulsive shudder. I hoped he had not noticed it, but his instincts were as delicate as an animal's and in fact I immediately heard his voice, close beside me.

" Are you still afraid ? " he asked.

My guardian angel must have been there in the darkness. Some nuance in his voice told me that he had raised his arm and was waiting to strike me according to whether I answered yes or no. I realised he knew he was terrifying, but wanted to be otherwise and to be loved like other men. But he knew no other means of achieving this end than by rousing a deeper fear. I lifted my hand and under the pretence of caressing his neck and right shoulder I discovered that his arm was indeed raised as I had supposed, ready to fall and strike me in the face. I spoke with an effort, trying to give my voice its usual calm and gentle intonation. " No," I said, " it's the cold this time, really. Let's get under the bedclothes."

" That's the way ! " he said. This reply, with its echo of a threat, only deepened my fear, if anything. I now experienced one of the worst moments of acute anguish in all my life, as he embraced and caressed me under the covers in the darkness surrounding us. Fear stiffened my limbs, which drew back and shuddered uncontrollably at the contact of his peculiarly smooth, sinuous, writhing body ; but at the same time I told myself it was ridiculous to be afraid of him at such a time and I tried with all the strength of my mind to overcome my fear and give myself to him fearlessly like a cherished lover. My fear lay not so much in my limbs, which still did as I bid them no matter how reluctantly, but more intimately in the depths of my womb, which seemed to close and reject his embraces with horror. At last he took me and I felt a pleasure made sinister and atrocious by fear and I could not restrain a long, wailing cry in the dark, as if the final clasp had been the clasp of death, not of love, and my cry was life departing from me, leaving behind a tortured, motionless body.

We lay there silent in the dark afterwards. I was exhausted and fell asleep almost at once. I soon felt a sensation as though I had a terrific weight on my chest, as if Sonzogno were squatting upon me, huddled up naked as he was, gripping his knees with his hands, his face leaning on his knees. He was seated on my chest, his bare, hard buttocks pressed against

222

my neck, his feet were on my stomach; as I continued to sleep his weight increased and although I was asleep, I tossed restlessly about trying to rid myself of him, or at least shift him. At last I felt as if I was suffocating and I tried to cry out. My voice stuck in my throat, crying out soundlessly for an endless period of time; at last I managed to force it out and woke up moaning aloud.

The light was lit on the night-table and Sonzogno was leaning his head on one arm and looking at me. " Did I sleep long ? " I asked.

" Half an hour," he said with clenched teeth.

I threw him a glance still filled with the terror of the nightmare I had had, because he asked me with a curious note in his voice, as if he wanted to start an argument: " Are you still afraid ? "

" I don't know."

" If you knew who I am," he said, " you'd be more afraid than ever."

All men feel inclined to talk about themselves and confide in a woman after they have made love. Apparently Sonzogno was no exception to the rule. His voice was unusually casual, lazy, affectionate even, with a touch of vanity and complacency. But I felt terribly afraid once again and my heart began to pound in my bosom as if it were going to burst. " Why ? " I asked. " Who are you ? "

He looked at me, not so much hesitating as savouring the effect of his words on me. " I'm the man of Via Palestro," he said slowly at last. " That's who I am."

He did not think it necessary to explain what had happened at Via Palestro and this time his vanity was right. Quite recently a horrible crime had been committed in a house in that street—all the papers had been filled with it, and all the people who get worked up over this kind of thing had discussed it. Mother, in fact, who spent a great part of the day spelling out the crime news in the papers had been the first to mention it to me. A young jeweller had been murdered in his flat where he lived alone. Apparently the weapon used by Sonzogno—for I was sure now that he was the murderer—was a heavy bronze paper-weight. The police had found no helpful clues.

Apparently the jeweller was also a receiver of stolen goods and the police imagined (quite rightly, as we shall see) that he had been killed during some illegal transaction.

I have often noticed that when a piece of news fills us with amazement or horror our minds become a blank and we fix our attention on the first thing our eyes fall upon, in a particular way, as if we wanted to strike through its surface and reach some undefined secret hidden within. This was what happened to me after Sonzogno had told me who he was. My eyes were wide open, my mind a complete blank, like a receptacle containing some liquid or fine powder which suddenly begins to leak—except that my mind, although blank, was ready and waiting to receive some other matter, and the sensation was painful because I longed to fill the void and could not. Meanwhile I was staring at the wrist of Sonzogno, who was stretched out beside me, leaning on one elbow. His arm was white, smooth, hairless, well covered, but gave no hint of his exceptional strength. His wrist, too, was smooth and white, and he wore a leather strap, like a watch-strap without a watch, the only object he had kept on in his nakedness. The dark, greasy colour of this strap seemed to give some significance not only to his arm but to the whole of his white, naked body and I played around this significance in my mind without being able to discover it. It was sinister meaning, it conjured up the idea of a ring in a convict's chain. But there was also something both charming and cruel about this leather strap, it was like an ornament that underlined the unexpected and feline character of Sonzogno's brutality. My blank state of mind lasted only a moment. Then my head was suddenly filled with a host of tumultuous thoughts beating about like birds in a crowded cage. I remembered I had been afraid of Sonzogno from the very first moment; I remembered I had made love to him; and I realised that by yielding to his embraces in the pitch dark I had learnt everything that he had concealed from me through my horrified body even before my ignorant mind had been aware of it, and that was why I had cried out as I had.

" Why did you do it ? " I asked. This was the first thing that came into my mind.

224

His lips hardly moved as he answered me. "I had something valuable to sell—I knew he was a dirty swine but he was the only dealer I knew. He offered me a ridiculous price. I already hated him because he had done me down before this. I told him I wanted the object back and also told him he was a cheat. He said something to me that made me lose my patience."

"What was it he said?" I asked. I now noticed with astonishment that as Sonzogno told me the story my fear began to diminish and despite myself a feeling of complicity thrilled me. In asking him what the jeweller had said I realised I was hoping it had been something so outrageous that the crime was excusable, if not completely justifiable.

"He said he would give me up to the police if I didn't go— so I thought: 'I've had enough'—and when he turned away . . ." he replied shortly, and did not finish the sentence but stared fixedly at me.

"What was he like?" I asked, and at the time my curiosity seemed purposeless and idle.

"Bald—rather short—a cunning face like a hare's," he answered precisely. But he spoke with an expression of unemotional dislike which brought the man before me and made me hate him, too, this receiver of stolen goods with a face like a hare's who had been deceitful and suspicious as he reckoned up the worth of the object Sonzogno had brought him. I was no longer afraid of anything, Sonzogno seemed to have transferred to me his hatred for his victim and I was not even sure that I condemned him. I actually seemed to understand what had happened so well that I felt I, too, might have been capable of the same crime. How well I understood his phrase: 'He said something to me that made me lose my patience'! He had lost all patience with Gino once and again with me, and it was only by a lucky chance that Gino and I were still alive. I understood him so well, I had penetrated into him so thoroughly that not only did I no longer fear him but I even felt a kind of horror-stricken attraction for him— the very attraction I had been unable to feel so long as I knew nothing of the crime and he was only one among my many lovers.

"Aren't you sorry?" I asked. "Don't you regret it?"

"It's done now," he replied.

I looked at him intently and was surprised to find myself nodding my head in approval at his reply. Then I remembered that Gino, too, in Sonzogno's words, was a dirty swine, and yet he was also a man and had loved me and I had loved him; I thought that in this way I might even find myself approving of Gino's murder in the near future; I thought that the jeweller was no better and no worse than Gino, after all, the only difference being that I did not know him, and I found his murder was justifiable merely because I had heard someone say in a certain tone of voice that he had a face like a hare. Remorse and horror filled me—but not for Sonzogno who was made that way and had to be understood before he was judged, but for myself, for I was not made that way like Sonzogno but nevertheless was infected by the contagion of hatred and blood. In a state of agitation I sat up on the bed, exclaiming: "Oh, my God! My God! Why did you do it? And why did you tell me about it?"

"You were so frightened of me," he answered simply, "yet you didn't know anything. I thought that was queer so I told you—luckily," he added, amused by his own idea, "luckily the rest aren't all like you, otherwise I'd have been caught out by now."

"You'd better go and leave me alone," I said. "Go on."

"What's up now?" he asked.

I could tell from his accent that he was growing angry. But I also thought I noticed a kind of distress at finding himself alone, condemned even by me when only a moment before I had given myself to him.

"Don't think I'm afraid of you," I added hastily; "I'm not at all afraid. But I've got to get used to the idea. I've got to think it over. Then you can come back and you'll find me changed."

"What is there to think over?" he said. "You aren't going to give me up to the police, are you?"

These words gave me exactly the same sensation I had had when Gino told me of his treachery towards the maid; as if I were living in a different world from Sonzogno. I made an effort to control myself. " But I'm telling you, you can come back!" I said. "Do you know what any other woman would have said? She'd have said she didn't want to have anything more to do with you, never see you again."

"But meanwhile you're telling me to get out."

"I thought you wanted to go. One minute more or less—— But if you want to stay, stay! Do you want to sleep here? If you like you can sleep with me and go away tomorrow morning. Is that what you want?" In point of fact I made these suggestions in a dull, sad, puzzled sort of voice and there must have been a lost look in my eyes. But nevertheless I made them and I knew I was glad to do so. Perhaps I was mistaken but I thought I saw a gleam of gratitude in the look he gave me.

"No, I was only talking," he said as he shook his head. "I've got to go." He stood up and went over to the chair where he had left his clothes.

"As you like," I replied, "but if you want to stay you know you can—and if you need somewhere to sleep one of these nights," I added with an effort, "you can come here."

He said nothing; he was dressing. I got up, too, and put on a dressing-gown. I felt crazy as I walked about, as if the room was full of voices whispering impassioned, insane words in my ear. Perhaps it was this sensation of being crazed which made me do something without understanding at the time why I did it. While I was wandering about the room, moving slowly although I felt frenzied, I saw him bend down to tie his shoelaces. I immediately knelt down in front of him. "Let me do it," I said. He was amazed but did not protest. I took his right foot, rested it on my lap and tied a double knot. Then I did the same with his left foot. He did not thank me and said nothing, probably neither of us understood why I had done such a thing. He slipped on his jacket. He then took out his wallet and made as if to give me some money.

"No, no," I snapped, "don't give me anything—it doesn't matter."

"Why? Isn't my money as good as another man's?" he asked angrily. I thought it was queer that he did not understand my instinctive disgust for money warm from the pockets of the dead man, probably. But perhaps he did understand it but wanted to compromise me by making me a kind of accomplice, and at the same time he wanted to discover what my feelings for him really were.

" No," I said, " it's not that. But I wasn't thinking about money when I called out to you. It doesn't matter."

He calmed down. " All right," he said. " But I'd like to leave you a souvenir." He pulled something out of his pocket and put it on the marble top of the night-table.

I looked at it without picking it up and saw it was the compact I had stolen some months earlier from Gino's employer. " What is it ? " I stammered.

" Gino gave me it, it's the thing I had to sell. He wanted to get it for nothing, but I think it's quite valuable, really—it's gold——"

" Thanks," I said, controlling myself.

" Not at all," he replied. He put on his raincoat and fastened the belt. " So long, then," he said from the doorway. Shortly afterwards I heard the front door close.

When I was alone I walked over to the night-table and picked up the compact. I felt bewildered and at the same time dully amazed. The compact glittered in my hand and the ruby set in the catch suddenly seemed to grow, become a round red drop that spread until it covered the gold. In the palm of my hand lay a round, glowing, bloody spot that weighed as much as the compact itself. I shook my head and the red spot disappeared, and once more all I saw was the gold compact with the ruby clasp. I then placed the compact on the night-table once more, lay on the bed wrapped in my dressing-gown, switched off the light and began to consider.

I supposed that if anyone had told me the tale of the compact I would have been as highly entertained as if I were being told of some almost incredible chain of circumstances. It was one of those tales that provoke the exclamation : " What a coincidence ! " and women like mother work out lottery numbers based on it—this number standing for the dead man, another for the gold, another for the thief. But this time it had happened to me, and to my astonishment I realised the difference between being on the inside of an event and being

228

only an outsider. In the manner of its occurrence, it was as if someone had planted a seed and then forgotten it : on re-discovering it he finds it has grown into a flourishing plant, covered with leaves and buds ready to burst into flower. Only—what a seed, what a plant and what buds were these ! I let my mind go back from one thing to another, but I could not find the starting-point. I had given myself to Gino because I hoped he would marry me, but he had betrayed me and out of pique I had stolen the compact. Then I had told him of the theft, he had become frightened, and to prevent him being dismissed I had returned the compact to him so that he could restore it to its owner. But instead of returning it he had kept it, and being afraid of being accused of the theft he had inculpated the maid who had been sent to prison, and the maid was innocent and in prison they beat her. Mean-while Gino had given the compact to Sonzogno to sell, Son-zogno had gone to the jeweller, the jeweller had offended Sonzogno, Sonzogno in a fit of rage had killed him, the jeweller was dead and Sonzogno was a murderer. I realised I could not trace the blame back to myself ; otherwise I would have been obliged to come to the conclusion that my desire to get married and set up a family was the prime cause of this chain of misfortunes ; but all the same I could not rid myself of a feeling of remorse and consternation. At last I was driven to conclude after much thinking that the whole fault was due to me, my legs, my hips, my breasts, all that beauty of which my mother was so proud, a quality in itself entirely innocent, like everything else given us by nature. But such thoughts were caused by my irritation and despair, as we allow one absurd thought to drive out others a hundred times as absurd. I knew in my heart that no one was really to blame and everything was as it had to be, although it was all intoler-able, and if guilt and innocence really must be attributed then each individual was equally guilty and equally innocent.

Meanwhile darkness gradually invaded me, like flood-water rising from the ground-floor to the upper storeys of a house. My faculty of judgment was the first to be submerged. But my imagination, on the other hand, dallied until the last with the fascination of Sonzogno's crime. The crime, however, was detached from any association of reproof or horror, like an inexplicable event that had its own strange charm. I imagined Sonzogno walking along Via Palestro, his hands in his raincoat pockets, then entering the house, standing in the jeweller's parlour awaiting him. I seemed to see the jeweller come in and shake Sonzogno's hand. He was behind his desk, Sonzogno held out the compact, the jeweller examined it and shook his head, feigning scorn for the object. Then he raised his hare-like face and made a ridiculous offer. Sonzogno looked at him fixedly, his eyes full of rage, and jerked the compact violently out of his hand. He then accused the jeweller of wanting to cheat him. The jeweller retaliated by threatening to denounce him to the police, warned him to get out. Then, as if to put an end to the discussion, he turned away or bent his head. Sonzogno picked up the bronze paper-weight and hit him once on the head. The jeweller tried to flee and then Sonzogno leapt on him and struck him repeatedly until he was quite sure he was dead. Then Sonzogno pushed him down on to the floor, searched the drawers, took what money he could find and made his escape. But before leaving he kicked the dead man in the face in an access of rage, I had read in the papers.

I lingered in fascination over all the details of the crime. I followed Sonzogno, fingering his gestures almost lovingly; I was the hand that held out the compact, picked up the paper-weight, struck the jeweller, I was the foot that crushed the dead man's face in fury when it was all over. There was no horror or blame in my fancied visions, but neither was there any approval. If anything, I experienced the same sensation of strange delight we feel when we are children listening to the tales our mothers tell; it is warm, huddled up near our mother, and we follow with rapt attention the adventures of those legendary heroes. Only my tale was grim and bloody, its hero was Sonzogno and helpless gloom mingled with my delight in it. Seeking to discover the hidden significance of the tale, I began to run through it again, to recapitulate all the stages of the crime, I experienced once more that same feeling of unaccountable pleasure and was face to face again with mystery. And then, like someone falling headlong into the gap between two precipices through a miscalculation of the distance, I fell asleep between two episodes in my mental wanderings.

I slept for about a couple of hours and then awoke. Or rather, I began to wake up physically while mentally I was still in a state of stupor. My hands were the first to wake, I stretched them out before me like a blind man in the dark without knowing where I was. I had fallen asleep lying at full-length on my bed; now I found myself standing upright in a narrow space between smooth, vertical, unbroken walls. It immediately suggested the idea of a prison cell to me, and at the same time I remembered the maid Gino had had arrested. I was the maid myself and in my heart I felt all the anguish she was suffering for the injustice done to her. This pain was transformed into the physical sensation that I was the maid herself; and her sorrow altered me, imprisoned me in her body, gave me her face, forced her gestures upon me. I put my hands to my face and wept and imagined myself wrongly imprisoned in a cell from which I could never escape. But at the same time I knew I was Adriana who had suffered no injustice, who had never been imprisoned, and I knew that one single gesture would free me, I would no longer feel I was the maid. But I could not imagine what this gesture must be— although I suffered indescribably through my desire to escape from my prison of pity and anguish. Suddenly Astarita's name flashed through my mind, shot through by the same spasmodic light and shade that dazzle the eyes of someone who has received a violent blow. "I'll go and see Astarita and get her freed," I thought; I stretched out my hands once more and discovered a narrow slit in the vertical walls of my cell— I could escape. I took a few steps in the dark, felt the switch under my fingers, turned it on with hysterical speed. The room leapt into light. I was standing near the door, naked, panting, my face and body were running with cold perspiration. The cell I had been imprisoned in was only the angle between the wardrobe, the corner of the room and the chest-of-drawers, a narrow space closed almost entirely by the walls and furniture. In my sleep I must have got up, walked about and forced myself into it.

I switched the light off once more, and went slowly back to bed. Before falling asleep I realised I certainly could not bring the jeweller back to life. But I could save or try to save the maid, and this was the only thing that mattered. It was all the more my duty now because I had discovered I was not as good as I had always believed myself to be. Or at least, my goodness did not exclude a taste for blood, admiration of violence and delight in crime.

The following morning I dressed carefully, put the compact into my handbag and went out to telephone to Astarita. I felt strangely light-hearted; the anguish Sonzogno's revelations had caused me the evening before had entirely vanished. I have many times in my life since noticed that vanity is the worst enemy of charity and moral reproof. What I now felt instead of fear and horror was a kind of vanity at the thought that I was the only one in town who knew how the crime had been committed and who had done it. I said to myself: 'I know who killed the jeweller,' and looked at people and things with different eyes from yesterday. I imagined there must even be something changed in my face, and I was afraid Sonzogno's secret could be read in the expression I wore. At the same time I felt a mild, pleasant, irresistible longing to tell someone what I knew. The secret overflowed from my heart like too much water from a small vessel, and I was tempted to pour it out to someone else. I suppose this is the chief reason why so many criminals tell their sweethearts or wives about the crimes they have committed, then the women tell it to their best friend and the best friend tells someone else, until it reaches the ears of the police and brings about the undoing of the whole lot. But I also suppose that in talking of their crimes the criminals are trying to free themselves of an intolerable burden by making others share it. Just as if guilt were something that could be parcelled out and borne by many until it becomes slight and unimportant, and not, as it really is, a load that cannot be transferred, whose weight is never lessened by being shared by others, but on the contrary increases with the number of those who bear it.

As I walked through the streets in search of a public telephone, I bought a couple of newspapers and looked for further details of the crime in Via Palestro. But some days had already passed; I could only find a few disappointing lines under the crosshead: 'No clues in jeweller's death.' I realised that unless he made some clumsy mistake Sonzogno would never be discovered. The illegal character of the victim's business made police enquiries extremely difficult. As the papers said, the jeweller had secret and inadmissible contacts with people of all classes and conditions; the murderer might have been someone he had never seen before, who had killed him on an impulse. This explanation was nearest to the truth. But since it was perfectly true for this very reason the police had obviously given up any hope of discovering the murderer.

I found a public telephone in a little restaurant and rang up Astarita. I had not phoned him for at least six weeks and I must have surprised him, because at first he did not recognise my voice and spoke to me in the business-like tones he used in the office. For a moment I even had an idea that he did not want to have anything more to do with me; and my heart missed a beat at the thought of the maid in prison and the ill-luck of Astarita ceasing to love me just when his intervention was most necessary in order to save that wretched woman. My dismay, however, was mixed with pleasure, because by bringing back to me the realisation of my goodness it made me see that the woman's release really mattered to me and that despite my intimacy with Sonzogno the murderer I was still the same gentle, compassionate Adriana I had always been.

In fear and trembling I gave Astarita my name and was relieved to hear the tone of his voice change on the instant and become uncertain and precipitate, stumbling over his words. I must admit that I felt an impulse of affection for him then, because a love of that kind, which is always flattering

233

to a woman, reassured me and filled me with gratitude at that moment. I made an appointment in caressing tones, he promised to come without fail, and I left the restaurant.

It had been pouring with rain all the time I had had my nightmare; often in my sleep I had heard the hiss of rain mingling with the howling of the wind to form a kind of wall of ill-weather round the house and increase the solitude and intimacy of the darkness in which I struggled. But the rain had stopped towards morning and the last gusts of wind had found strength to sweep away the clouds, leaving a limpid sky and the air clean and still. After 'phoning Astarita I began to walk along an avenue of plane-trees in the early morning sun. A slight dizziness was all that remained of my disturbed night and it soon passed in the cool air. I gloried in the lovely day, and everything I saw had a quality of charm about it that delighted and attracted me. I admired the patches of dampness that remained round the edges of the dry paving-stones; I admired the houses which bore traces of the night's downpour in great patches of damp on their façades; I admired the passers-by, men hurrying to their work, maids carrying shopping-bags, boys and girls with books and satchels, holding their parents' or elder brothers' hands. I stopped to give alms to an old beggar and while I hunted for some money in my bag I realised I was gazing fondly at his old military cloak and delighting in the patches at the elbows and round the collar. There were grey, brown, yellow, faded green patches and I realised how I loved observing the colours and seeing how well-sewn they were with big stitches in black cotton, and I surprised myself imagining how he must have worked one of those mornings, cutting away the worn parts with a pair of scissors, contriving a patch from some old rag, fitting it over the hole, sewing it lovingly. Those patches gave me as much pleasure as the sight of newly-baked bread gives a hungry man, and as I left him I could not help looking back at them again and again. I suddenly thought how wonderful it would be to live a life as limpid, clear and lovely as that morning was. A life that had been washed clean of all its muddy aspects, where even the humblest thing might be looked at fondly. My desire for a normal family life, so long dormant and unexpressed, with a husband and a new, clean, tidy, luminous house, was revived by the thought. I realised I did not like my profession, although by a queer contradiction I was designed for it by nature. It did not seem to me a clean profession; my body, my fingers, my bed, seemed to have a perpetual aura of musty sweat, impure warmth, sticky emanations, about them, no matter how much I washed myself and tidied up my room. And the very fact of dressing and undressing almost every day under the eyes of different men prevented me from looking upon my own body with the sense of pleasure and intimacy I would have enjoyed, which I remembered feeling when I looked at myself in the mirror or in the bath as a young girl. It is lovely to be able to look at your own body as at something new and unknown which grows, becomes stronger and more beautiful of its own accord; but in order to give my lovers this impression of novelty each time, I had deprived myself of it for ever.

In the light of these reflections Sonzogno's crime, Gino's wickedness, the maid's misfortunes and all the other intrigues I was involved in appeared to be the consequences of my own disorderly life. Consequences, however, without any particular meaning, which gave me no sense of sin and could be set aside as soon as I was able to satisfy my youthful desire for a normal life. I experienced an overwhelming desire to set my life in order in every way, and to come to terms with morality, which condemned a profession like mine, with nature which intended a woman of my age to bear children, with taste which designed a life lived among beautiful things, with new, charming clothes and light, clean, comfortable houses. Only, one thing excluded the others: if I wanted to be on good terms with morality I could not at the same time be on good terms with nature, and taste was overset by both morality and nature. The usual life-long irritation filled me at knowing myself to be in debt to necessity and incapable of satisfying its demands except by sacrificing my highest aims. But I realised once again that I had not yet accepted my fate entirely and this gave me some hope, because I was able to say to myself that as soon as I had an opportunity of changing my life I would not let myself be taken unawares, and I could take advantage of it consciously and decisively.

I had given Astarita an appointment for midday as soon as he left the office. I had an hour or two to wait, so having nothing to do I decided to go and see Gisella. I had not seen her for some time and I imagined someone must have taken the place in her life which had previously been filled by Riccardo, someone half-way between a fiancé and a lover. Gisella, too, hoped to put her life in order one day. I suppose this hope is common to all the women of my kind. But I was inclined to it by nature, whereas in Gisella, who thought worldly considerations of supreme importance, it was rather a matter of social decorum. She was ashamed for other people to take her for what she really was, although her vocation for her profession was far deeper than mine. I was not at all ashamed; I only felt an occasional sense of servitude and betrayal of my own nature.

On reaching Gisella's house I made as if to go upstairs. But the portress called out to me. " Are you going up to see Signorina Gisella ? She doesn't live here now."

" Where's she gone ? "

" Number seven, Via Casablanca." This was a new street in one of the new districts. " A fair young man with a car came and took up her stuff and she went away with him."

I realised immediately that this was just what I had come expecting to hear—that she had left with a man. I do not know why I suddenly felt tired, my legs were trembling, and I had to lean against the door-post to prevent myself falling. But I recovered and decided after a moment's thought to go and call on Gisella at her new address. I hailed a taxi and told the driver to take me to Via Casablanca.

As the taxi sped along, we left the centre of the town and its rows of old houses crowded close in narrow streets. The streets grew wider, branched off, converged in open squares, became wider and wider, the houses were new, and here and there I caught a glimpse of the green countryside between them. I realised that my journey had some hidden, extremely painful meaning, and I became sadder with every passing moment. I suddenly remembered the efforts Gisella had

236

made to deprive me of my innocence and make me like herself; and I began to cry as instinctively as a wound bleeds.

When I got out of the taxi at the end of the journey my eyes were shining, my cheeks wet. "You shouldn't cry, miss," said the driver. I only shook my head and went towards the entrance of Gisella's house.

It was a little white building, in modern style, evidently erected quite recently, as the barrels, tools and beams piled up in the barren little garden showed, and the splashes of whitewash on the bars of the gate. I entered a white, bare hall and saw a white stairway with opalescent windows which shed a peaceful light. The porter, a red-headed youth in workmen's overalls, quite different from the usual dirty old porters one sees, showed me into the lift: I pressed the switch and the lift began to ascend. The lift smelt pleasantly of new polished wood and spirit. There seemed to be something new in the very hum of the machinery, it was like a mechanism that had been functioning for only a short time. The lift rose to the top floor; as it went up the light increased, it was as though there was no ceiling and the lift was going right up into the sky. Then it stopped, I got out, and found myself on a dazzling white landing in brilliant light, standing in front of a handsome door with polished brass handles. I rang. A thin, dark little maid in a white lace cap and embroidered apron came and opened the door. "Is Signorina de Santis in?" I asked. "Please tell her it's Adriana."

She left me and went along the passage to a door with opalescent panes of glass like those on the staircase. The passage was all white and bare, too, like the rest of the floor; I supposed it must be a small flat, only four rooms. It was heated and the warmth from the radiators brought out the pungent smell of the new whitewash and paint. Then the glass-fronted door at the end of the passage opened and the maid returned to tell me I could go through.

I saw nothing when I first entered because the wintry sun was blinding as it flooded the room through a wide window that took up the whole of the wall facing the door. The flat was on the top floor and the only thing visible through those windows was a patch of blue sky glowing with the light of the sun. For a moment I forgot my visit and experienced a feeling of well-being as I shut my eyes in the sunshine, warm and golden like an old liqueur. But Gisella's voice made me start. She was seated in the front of the window and facing her across a low table covered with bottles was a little grey-haired woman, her manicurist.

"Oh, Adriana!" she said with assumed nonchalance. "Do sit down. I shan't be a moment."

I sat down near the door and looked around me. It was a long, narrow room. There really was not much furniture, only a table, a sideboard and a few chairs in some light-coloured wood, but everything was new and the sun was shining. The sun was really luxurious; sunshine like that was only to be had in wealthy houses, I could not help thinking. I shut my eyes deliberately in order to enjoy the delicious sensation and thought of nothing. Then I felt something soft and heavy on my lap, opened my eyes and saw a huge cat, a kind I had never seen before, long-haired, soft as silk, greyish-blue in colour, with a sulky, haughty expression I didn't like. The cat began to rub against me, mewing raucously and lifting the tip of its tail. Then it curled up on my lap and began to purr. "What a lovely cat!" I said. "What kind is it?"

"A Persian," said Gisella proudly; "it's very valuable. A cat like that costs anything up to a thousand lire."

"I've never seen one before," I said as I stroked it.

"Do you know who's got one just like it?" said the manicurist. "Signora Radelli. You ought to see how she looks after it! Better than a human being. The other day she sprayed scent all over it, even. Shall I touch up your toe-nails, miss?"

"It doesn't matter, Marta," said Gisella. "That'll do for today." The manicurist put her tools and little bottles away in a suitcase, said good-bye and left.

When we were alone we looked at one another. Gisella seemed all new, like the house. She was wearing a pretty red angora jumper and a brown skirt I had not seen her in before. She had put on weight, her bosom was fuller, her hips filled her skirt out more. I noticed her eyelids were

238

rather swollen, like a person who eats well, sleeps well, and has no worries. It was her eyelids that gave her a rather sulky look.

"Well—what do you think of my place?" she asked me as she examined her finger-nails.

I am not at all envious by nature. But at that moment I felt the sting of envy for the first time in my life; and I was amazed that there could be people in the world who nourished such a feeling in their hearts their whole life through, for I found it so extremely painful and unpleasant. My face was drawn, as though I had suddenly gone thin, and this made it impossible for me to smile at Gisella and say something complimentary as I would have wished. For Gisella herself I experienced a keen feeling of repulsion. I wanted to hurt her, say something spiteful to her, insult her, humiliate her, poison her happiness, in fact. 'What's come over me?' I thought in bewilderment while still continuing to stroke the cat. 'Aren't I myself any longer?' Luckily this feeling was of short duration. All the goodwill of which I was capable was already stirring and laying siege to envy. I reminded myself that Gisella was my friend and her good fortune was therefore mine, and that I ought to be glad for her sake. I pictured Gisella entering her new flat for the first time and clapping her hands with joy; and at that the icy paralysis of envy was struck from my face and I once more felt the warmth of the sun, but in a more intimate fashion, as though the sun had penetrated into my heart.

"How can you ask?" I said. "Such a gay, lovely place! How did it all happen?"

I thought I sounded sincere as I said these words, and I smiled, more as a reward to myself than at Gisella.

"Do you remember Giancarlo?" she replied with self-assurance, in the voice of one making a confidence. "That fair young man I quarrelled with straight away that first evening? Well, he came to see me again. He wasn't nearly as bad as he seemed at first sight. Then we met again, several times. A few days ago he said: 'Come on, I've got a surprise for you.' I thought he wanted to give me a handbag, a bottle of scent or some other little present, you know.

Instead he brought me here in the car, showed me in. The flat was empty, I thought it must be his own place. Then he asked me if I liked it, so I said yes, but without dreaming what he meant, of course ! Then he said : ' I've taken the flat for you.' You can just imagine what I felt ! "

She smiled with dignified complacency as she looked around her. I got up impulsively, went over to her. " I'm delighted," I said as I kissed her, " absolutely delighted, I really am."

This gesture dispelled all hostile feelings from my heart. I went up to the window and looked out. The house stood on a kind of rise with a vast landscape beneath it. It was a cultivated plain, traversed by a winding river, with woods, farms, clumps of rocks here and there. Nothing could be seen of the town but a few white buildings, the last blocks in a suburb, over in one corner of the view. A line of blue mountains stood out clearly on the horizon, against the background of the luminous sky.

" It's a magnificent view," I said, turning to Gisella.

" Isn't it ? " she answered. She walked over to the sideboard, took out two small glasses and a squat decanter and put them on the table. " Will you have a liqueur ? " she asked carelessly. Obviously all her gestures as mistress of a house of her own filled her with satisfaction.

We sat down at the table and sipped our liqueur in silence. I could see that Gisella was embarrassed and I wanted to do something to relieve her. " Still, it wasn't very nice of you," I said gently. " You ought to have let me know——"

" I didn't have time," she answered hurriedly. " You know what it is—a removal, and then I had such a job buying the things I needed most—the furniture, linen, crockery. I hadn't time to breathe. It's a business, setting up house." She pinched her lips together like a proper lady as she spoke.

" I see what you mean," I said, without a trace of spite or bitterness, as if the whole matter were none of my business. " Now you've got a place of your own and are better off, you don't want to have anything to do with me. You're ashamed of me."

" I'm not a bit ashamed," she replied with a touch of

annoyance, more irritated apparently by my reasonable tone of voice than by my words. "If you think that, you're being silly. Only we shan't be able to see one another now as we did before. I mean—go out together and all that. If he found out I'd be in the soup."

"You needn't worry," I replied gently. "You won't see anything more of me. I only came along today to find out what had happened."

She pretended she had not heard and this strengthened me in my belief. A short silence ensued.

"What about you?" she then asked with assumed eagerness.

Immediately, so spontaneously that it frightened me, I thought of Giacomo. "Me?" I repeated in a choked voice. "Nothing. Everything's the same."

"What about Astarita?"

"I've seen him from time to time."

"And Gino?"

"I'm through with him."

The memory of Giacomo wrung my heart. But Gisella interpreted in her own way the deep mortification she read in my face. She probably thought I was embittered by her own good luck and scornful manner.

"Still, no one will ever get it out of my head that Astarita is ready to set you up properly in a place of your own as soon as you say the word," she said, feigning an interest after a moment's reflection.

"I don't want him to," I said calmly. "Neither Astarita nor anyone else."

She appeared disconcerted by my reply. "Why not? Wouldn't you like to have a place like this?"

"I like the house," I said, "but I want to be my own mistress more than anything else."

"I am my own mistress!" she replied resentfully. "I'm more my own mistress than you are. I've got the whole day to myself."

"That's not the kind of freedom I meant."

"What did you mean, then?"

I realised I had offended her, if only by not showing enough

241

admiration for the flat she was so proud of. But she would have been even more deeply offended if I had explained to her that I didn't despise her and that actually I did not want to tie myself to any man I did not love. I preferred to change the subject.

"Show me over the flat," I said hurriedly. "How many rooms are there?"

"What do you care about the flat?" she said with childish disappointment. "You said yourself you didn't want a flat like this."

"That's not what I said," I replied calmly. "It's a lovely flat—I wish I had one like it."

She said nothing. She was gazing downwards with a sulky expression. "So," I went on weakly after a moment, "you don't want to show me over?"

She raised her eyes and I saw to my amazement that they were full of tears. "You aren't the friend I thought you were!" she exclaimed. "You're—you're bursting with envy and so you try to run the place down just to upset me." She was speaking at random, her face covered with tears. They were tears of rage and she was the one who was envious, this time, a pointless envy which was sharpened unconsciously by my hopeless love for Giacomo and the bitter sense of separation it gave me. But although I understood her so well, indeed, just because of this, I was sorry for her. I got up, went over to her, put my hand on her shoulder.

"Why say that?" I said. "I'm not a bit envious. I'd like other things—that's all there is to it. But I'm glad you're happy. So come on, show me the other rooms," I said as I embraced her.

She blew her nose and yielding to my persuasion said: "There are four rooms, all told—and they're practically empty."

"Come on, show me."

She got up, led the way into the passage, and opening one door after another showed me a bedroom with only a bed and an armchair at the foot of it, an empty room where she intended to put another bed for 'guests,' a little cubbyhole for the maid, with hardly room to swing a cat in. She showed me these rooms with a kind of spite, opening the doors and explaining what they were to be used for without any pleasure in them. But her ill-humour gave place to vanity when she showed me the bathroom and the kitchen, both tiled, with their new electric machines and shining taps. She explained how they worked, how much better they were than gas, how clean they were and how little they consumed, and although I was really not at all interested I pretended this time to be enthusiastic and exclaimed in admiration and surprise. She was so delighted with my attitude that when we had seen all over the flat she said : " Let's go back into the sitting-room and have another liqueur."

" No, no," I said hurriedly, " I've got to go."

" What's the hurry ? Stay a bit longer."

" I can't."

We were in the passage. She hesitated a moment. " But you must come again," she then said. " Do you know what we could do ? He often goes out of Rome—I'll let you know, and you bring along two friends of yours and we'll have some fun."

" Suppose he finds out ? "

" Why should he ? "

" All right, then," I said. I hesitated a moment and then took my courage in both hands. " By the way," I said, " did he ever mention that friend of his who was with him that evening ? "

" The student ? Why ? Did you like him ? "

" No, I only wondered."

" We saw him yesterday evening."

I could not conceal my agitation. " Listen," I said uncertainly, " if you see him tell him to come and call on me. But you know—casually, without insisting."

" All right, I'll tell him," she answered. But she was looking at me suspiciously and her glance embarrassed me because my love for Giacomo seemed written in large letters on my face. I understood from the tone of her voice that she would not give the message. In despair I opened the door, said good-bye, hurried downstairs without turning back. On the second landing I stopped and leaned against the wall, looking

243

up. " Why did I tell her ? " I thought. " What came over me ? " I went on down the stairs with bowed head.

I had given Astarita an appointment at my own place; when I got there I was worn out, I was no longer accustomed to go out in the morning and the sun and movement had tired me. I did not even feel unhappy. I had already paid for my visit to Gisella when I had cried in the taxi on my way to her new flat. Mother came and opened the door and told me someone had been waiting for me in my room for an hour. I went straight in and sat down on the bed, taking no notice of Astarita, who was standing before the window apparently staring down into the courtyard. I kept still for a moment, pressing my hand to my heart and panting because I had come upstairs so quickly. My back was turned to Astarita, I was gazing absently at the door. He had greeted me but I had not answered. Then he came and sat down beside me and put his arm round my waist, looking earnestly at me.

In all my worries I had forgotten his crazy desire that was always kindled and alert. " Oh, you're always wanting it ! " I said, thoroughly impatient, in a slow, disagreeable voice as I drew back from him.

He said nothing but took my hand and raised it to his lips, looking upwards at me. I thought I would go crazy and pulled my hand away. " You're always ready, aren't you ? " I went on. " Even in the morning ? After you've been working all morning ? Before you've had your lunch ? On an empty stomach ? You really are the limit, you know ! "

I saw his lips tremble and his eyes roll. " But I love you ! "

" There's a time for love and a time for other things. I made an appointment with you for one o'clock just to show you that I don't mean love and you—really, you are a one ! Aren't you ashamed of yourself ? "

He stared at me in silence. Suddenly I felt I understood him through and through. He was in love with me and had been waiting for this appointment for days. While I was struggling with so many difficulties, he had been thinking of nothing else but my legs, my bosom, my hips, my mouth. "So," I said, a little less angrily, "if I were to get undressed now——"

He nodded in agreement. I burst out laughing, not unkindly but bitterly. "It wouldn't occur to you that I might be unhappy or not feel like it—be hungry or tired—or have some worries—that wouldn't ever cross your mind, would it?"

He looked at me, then suddenly threw himself upon me and hugging me closely buried his face in the hollow between my neck and shoulder. He did not kiss me, he only pressed his face against me as if to feel the warmth of my flesh. He was breathing heavily and sighed from time to time. I was no longer irritated by him, his gesture roused my usual anxious pity; I only felt unhappy. When I thought he had had his fill of sighs I pushed him off.

"I asked you here upon a serious matter," I said.

He looked at me, then took my hand and began to stroke it. He was single-minded and for him nothing else existed in the world but his desire.

"You're in the police, aren't you?"

"Yes."

"Well, then—have me arrested, send me to prison." I said this quite firmly. I really wanted him to do it, at the time.

"Why? What's happened?"

"I'm a thief," I said aloud. "I've committed a theft and an innocent woman has been arrested in my place. So—arrest me. I'm quite willing to go to gaol. That's what I want."

He did not seem surprised, only annoyed.

"Come, come now!" he said with a grimace. "What happened? Tell me all about it."

"I've told you, I'm a thief." In a few words I told him about the theft and how the maid had been arrested instead of me. I told him of Gino's trick, but I did not mention his name, I only spoke of him as a servant. But I felt violently tempted to tell him about Sonzogno and his crime and I could hardly keep it back. At last I came to the end of my story.

245

"Now you must choose," I said. "Either you get that woman out of prison or I'll go and give myself up."

"Don't be in such a hurry," he said, raising his hand. "What's the need? For the time being she's in gaol—but she hasn't been sentenced yet. Let's wait."

"No, I can't wait! She's in gaol and they say she's been beaten up—I can't wait. You've got to make your mind up now."

He realised from my voice that I was speaking in earnest. He got up with a discontented look on his face and began to walk about the room. Then, as if speaking to himself, he continued: "There's the question of the dollars."

"But she's been protesting all along! The dollars were found again. We could say it was a personal revenge on the part of someone who hated her."

"Have you got the compact?"

"It's here," I said, taking it from my bag and handing it to him.

But he refused to touch it. "No, no, you mustn't give it to me," he said. "I could have that woman released," he went on after a moment's hesitation, "but at the same time the police would have to have some proof that she was innocent—this compact, for instance."

"Take it, then, and give it back to its owner."

He smiled disagreeably. "Obviously you know nothing about these matters! If I accept this compact from you I'm morally bound to have you arrested. Otherwise they'd say: 'How did Astarita get hold of the stolen object?—who gave it to him?—how did he get it?' and so on. No—you'll have to find some way of getting the compact to the police but without giving yourself away, of course."

"I might post it."

"No, that wouldn't do."

He paced about the room then came and sat down beside me. "This is what you'll have to do," he said. "Do you know any priest?"

I remembered the French monk I had confessed to when I came back from Viterbo. "Yes, my confessor," I said.

"Do you still go to confession?"

246

"I used to."

"Well—go to your confessor and tell him the whole story. Just as you told me. And beg him to take the compact and give it to the police on your behalf. No confessor could refuse to do this. He's not obliged to give any information to the police because he is bound by the seal of the confessional. I'll ring up a day or two later—and the maid you're so worried about will be released."

I was overcome by joy and could not help flinging my arms round his neck and kissing him. He continued in a voice already trembling with desire. "But you mustn't do these things, you know. When you need any money you've only got to ask me."

"Can I go and see the confessor today?"

"Of course!"

I stood there motionless for some time, staring fixedly in front of me, with the compact in one hand. I experienced a feeling of profound relief, as if I were the maid myself, and really, as I imagined her relief, so much greater than my own, at being released, I felt as if I were in her place. I was no longer unhappy, tired, disgusted. Meanwhile Astarita was stroking my wrist with his fingers and trying to insert them into my sleeve to touch my arm. I turned and spoke caressingly, gazing fondly at him.

"Do you really want to very much?" I asked.

He nodded, incapable of speech.

"Aren't you tired?" I continued tenderly and cruelly. "Don't you think it's getting late—and it would be better to put it off till another day?"

He shook his head.

"Do you love me so much?" I asked.

"You know I love you," he said in a low voice. He made as if to embrace me, but I avoided him. "Wait," I said.

He calmed down at once because he knew I had assented. I got up, went slowly to the door and locked it. Then I walked over to the window, opened it, drew the shutters together and closed the window again. I could feel his eyes on me the whole time as I walked about the room with slow, stately movements, and I could well imagine how wonderful my unexpected acquiescence must seem to him. When I had closed the shutters I began to hum softly in a gay, intimate voice, and still humming I opened the wardrobe, took off my coat and hung it up. Then, still singing, I looked at myself in the mirror. I thought I had never been so beautiful—my eyes were sparkling, my nostrils quivered, my mouth was half-open, showing my white, even teeth. I realised I was beautiful because I was pleased with myself and I felt I was a good girl, and I raised my voice a little as I sang, while at the same time I began to undo my jacket, beginning at the lower edge. I was humming a silly song that was going around about that time. It ran: *I'm singing the song I like so much that goes du-du, du-du, du-du.* The silly refrain was like life itself, obviously absurd, but fascinating and charming at moments. Suddenly, just as I had uncovered my bosom, someone knocked at the door.

"I can't come," I said calmly. "Later——"

"It's urgent," said mother's voice.

A suspicion crossed my mind; I went to the door and unlocked it, then peered out.

Mother beckoned to me to come out and shut the door.

"There's a man who wants to speak to you urgently," she whispered in the dark outer room.

"Who is it?"

"I don't know. A dark young fellow."

I opened the door of the living-room very quietly and peeped in. I then saw a man leaning against the table with his back to me. I recognised Giacomo immediately and shut the door again quickly.

"Tell him I'm just coming," I said to mother. "And don't let him leave that room."

She told me she would do as I wanted and I returned to my room. Astarita was still sitting on the bed, as I had left him.

"Quick," I said. "I'm sorry—but you'll have to go."

He became distressed and began to stammer some protest. But I cut him short. "My aunt's been taken ill in the street," I said. "I've got to go to hospital with my mother, as quickly as possible." It was rather a transparent lie but I could not think of anything else at the moment. He looked

248

at me stupidly, as if he could not believe his own ill-luck. I saw that he had removed his shoes and his feet in their striped socks were resting on the floor.

"Come on! What are you staring at me for? You've got to go!" I said in exasperation.

"All right—I'll go," he replied, and bent down to put his shoes on again. I stood in front of him to hand him his coat. But I realised I would have to promise him something if I wanted him to intervene in the maid's favour. "Listen," I said, as I helped him on with his coat, "I'm awfully sorry about this—but come back tomorrow evening after supper. We shan't be interrupted then. I'd have had to send you away again almost immediately today—in any case—it's better this way in the end."

He said nothing and I accompanied him to the door, leading him by the hand as if it were his first visit to the house. I was so afraid he might go into the living-room and see Giacomo.

"Mind—I'm going to see that confessor today," I said at the door. He replied with a nod as if to imply that it was an understood thing between us. He looked disgusted and frozen. I was so impatient I could not wait for his farewell and almost slammed the door in his face.

CHAPTER FIVE

When my fingers were on the handle of the living-room door, it struck me with sudden force, that short of a miracle I was bound to establish between Giacomo and myself the same unhappy relations I had with Astarita. I now saw that the mixture of subjection, fear and blind desire which Astarita felt for me was exactly what I felt for Giacomo; and although I knew that I ought to behave differently if I wanted to be loved, nevertheless I felt irresistibly drawn to place myself on a lower, dependent plane of anxious uncertainty with him. I could not have explained the reasons for my state of inferiority; if I could have done so, it would no longer have existed.

I only knew instinctively that we were made of different stuff, I was harder than Astarita but more fragile than Giacomo; and just as there was something which prevented me from loving Astarita so something prevented Giacomo from loving me; and my love for Giacomo had started badly and would end worse, as Astarita's for me. My heart was pounding, my breath came short even before seeing him and speaking to him; I was terribly afraid I would make some false step, show him my eagerness and desire to please him and so would lose him again once and for all. This is obviously the worst curse of love—that it is never requited, and when you love you are not loved in return, and when you are loved you do not love. Two lovers never meet on the same level of emotion and desire, although this is the ideal each human being strives for. I know without any shadow of doubt that just because I had fallen in love with Giacomo he had not fallen in love with me. And I also knew, although I did not want to acknowledge it to myself, that no matter what effort I might make I would never succeed in forcing him to fall in love with me. All this flashed through my mind while I stood hesitating outside the door, in a state of ghastly agitation. I felt dizzy, on the point of doing the most ridiculous things, and this irritated me extremely. At last I took my courage in both hands and entered the room.

He was still standing as he had been when I peeped at him through the crack of the door, that is leaning against the table with his back to me. But when he heard me come in he turned round. "I was just passing by," he said, looking at me with critical, calculating attention. "So I thought I'd drop in, perhaps I ought not to have done." I noticed he was speaking slowly as if he wanted to have a good look at me before committing himself to speech; and I could not help feeling anxious, wondering what I seemed like to him, perhaps different and less attractive than his memory of me which had led him to visit me after such a lapse of time. But I felt reassured as I remembered how handsome I had been when I gazed at myself in the mirror a little earlier.

"Not at all," I said, a little breathlessly. "You were

quite right—I was just going out to lunch. We might go together."

"Do you mean to say you recognise me ? " he asked ironically. "Do you know who I am ? "

"Of course I know you ! " I said stupidly. And before my will could control my gestures I had taken his hand and raised it to my lips, with a glance full of love. This embarrassed him and I was delighted.

"Why didn't you call, you naughty boy ? " I said fondly and anxiously.

He shook his head. "I've been very busy," he said.

I had quite lost my head. After kissing his hand I placed it on my heart below my breast. "Feel my heart ! " I said. But at the same time I told myself I was a fool because I knew I ought not to have done and said these things. He looked awkward so I hastily added, in alarm : "I'm just going to put my coat on. I'll come straight back. Wait for me——"

I felt so completely bewildered and was so afraid of losing him that when I was in the outer room I turned the key violently in the lock and removed it from the key-hole; in this way, if he tried to leave while I was dressing he would be unable to. Then I went into my own room, crossed over to the wardrobe mirror and removed all the paint from my eyes and mouth with the corner of my handkerchief. Then I picked up my lipstick and just lightly touched up my lips again. I went over to the coat-hanger, looked for my coat, could not find it, felt lost, then remembered I had hung it up in the wardrobe, pulled it out and put it on. I looked at myself in the mirror once more and thought my style of hairdressing was too showy. I hastily combed out my hair and arranged it as I used to wear it when I was engaged to Gino. Meanwhile, as I did my hair I swore to myself most solemnly that from that moment I would repress all the unconsidered impulses of my passion and would exercise a strict control over my words and gestures. At last I was quite ready. I went into the outer room and looked in at the door of the living-room to call Giacomo.

But as we were about to leave, the house-door, which I

had locked and in my confusion had forgotten to unlock, gave me away.

"You were afraid I'd run away," he murmured while I hunted for the key in my bag. He took the key from my hand and unlocked the door himself, looking at me and shaking his head with a kind of fond severity. My heart was filled with joy and I ran downstairs after him.

"You aren't annoyed, are you?" I asked him breathlessly, as I took his arm. He did not answer.

We walked along arm-in-arm in the sunshine, past the house-doors and shops down in the street. I was so happy walking beside him that I quite forgot my good resolutions; and when we passed the little villa with the tower it was as though someone took my hand and inspired me to press his. At the same time I realised I was leaning forward so as to have a better view of his face.

"Do you know—I'm awfully glad to see you again," I said.

He pulled his usual embarrassed face. "I'm glad, too," he said, but the tone of his voice was not exactly glad, I thought.

I bit my lips until they hurt and took my hand out of his. He did not seem to notice; he was looking round absent-mindedly. But when we reached the gateway in the walls he hesitated, stopped and spoke.

"Listen," he said in a reticent way, "I've got something I must tell you."

"Tell me then."

"I only came to see you by chance—and by the same chance I haven't a penny on me. So it'll be better for us to part." As he said this he held out his hand.

My first reaction was one of alarm. 'He's going to leave me,' I thought, and in my distress I saw no other remedy but to cling to him, beseeching him not to go, and weeping. But on second thoughts the very excuse that he had brought forward for leaving me seemed to me a good way out of the difficulty and my feelings underwent a change. I thought I would be able to pay for his lunch, and the idea of paying for both of us, just as so many had paid for me, delighted me. I have already mentioned the sensual pleasure I felt every time I received money. I now discovered that paying money out is no less thrilling a pleasure. And the mingling of love with money, whether the money is given or received, is not entirely a question of self-interest. "Don't think any more about it!" I exclaimed impetuously. "I'll pay. Look—I've got some money." And I opened my purse to show him some notes I had put into it the evening before.

"It isn't done," he protested, with a trace of disappointment.

"What does that matter? You've come back, it's only right that I should celebrate your return."

"No," he said. "It's better not." He again made as if to shake hands and leave me. This time I took his arm.

"Don't let's talk about it any more," and I started towards the restaurant.

We sat at the same table as before and everything was just as it had been, except for a ray of wintry sunlight that shone through the glass-fronted door and lit up the tables and the wall. The proprietor brought the menu and I gave my order in a firm, protective voice, just as my lovers did for me. He said nothing while I was ordering, his eyes were downcast. I had forgotten the wine because I don't drink; then I remembered he had had some wine last time we were together so I asked for a litre.

As soon as the proprietor had gone I opened my bag, took out a hundred-lira note, folded it in four, and after a rapid glance round I held it out to Giacomo under the table.

He looked at me questioningly.

"The money," I said. "Then you can pay afterwards."

"Oh, the money——" he said slowly. He took the note, opened it out on the table, looked at it, then folded it again, opened my bag and put it back, all this in ironical seriousness.

"Do you want me to pay?" I asked him, feeling rather disconcerted.

"No, I'll pay," he said calmly.

"Then why did you say you hadn't any money?"

He hesitated for a moment. "I didn't come to see you by chance," he then continued bitterly but sincerely, "the fact is—I've been thinking of coming for a month now. But every time I found myself outside your place I felt impelled to go away again. So I thought I'd say I hadn't any money, in the hope that you'd send me packing." He smiled and passed his hand over his chin. " Apparently I was mistaken."

So he had tried out a kind of experiment on me. He did not want to have anything to do with me. Or rather, his heart was torn in two between the attraction I had for him and an equally potent aversion he had for me. Later I was to discover that his capacity for feigning a part he did not feel sincerely was an essential part of his character. But at that time I felt utterly confused, I did not know whether I ought to be cheerful or to feel upset by his deceit and his defeat.

" But why did you want to leave me ? " I asked mechanically.

" Because I realised I felt nothing for you. Or rather, all I felt was the kind of desire my friend felt for your girl-friend that evening."

" Did you know they'd set up a flat together ? " I asked.

" Yes," he replied scornfully, " they're made for one another."

" You felt nothing for me," I said, " and you didn't want to come to see me—and yet you came ! " His lack of logic was something of a consolation in the disillusionment I had foreseen my love would cause me.

" Yes," he replied, " because I've got what's usually called a weak character."

" Still, you came, and that's enough for me," I said cruelly. I stretched my hand out under the table and placed it on his knees. Meanwhile I was watching him and saw that my touch troubled him, his chin began to quiver. I was delighted at seeing him so moved ; and I realised that although he wanted me very much, as he had confessed when he said he had been thinking about coming to see me for a whole month, there was a part of him that was hostile to me—I would have to do everything that lay in my power to destroy that part. I remembered his keen, cutting gaze at my naked back the first time we were together, and I told myself I had been wrong to let myself be frozen by such a look, and that if I had

254

persisted in my efforts to seduce him the look would have faded just as the convulsive dignity in his face was now breaking up and fading.

Leaning against the table as if I wanted to speak to him confidentially, I went on caressing him and at the same time saw with gay satisfaction the effects of my caresses as they were reflected in his face. He was looking at me with an offended, questioning air out of his large, dark, shining eyes with their long, feminine eyelashes.

"If you're content with my liking you this way, do as you like," he said at last.

I straightened myself immediately. And at that moment the proprietor put the knives and forks and plates on the table. We began to eat in silence, neither of us had any appetite.

"If I were you, I'd try to make me drunk," he said.

"Why?"

"Because I do as other people want me to more easily when I'm drunk."

His phrase, 'If you're content with my liking you this way, do as you like,' had already offended me. What he said about drinking was enough to convince me that my efforts were useless.

"I only want you to do what you feel like doing," I said in despair. "If you want to go, go—there's the door."

"I'd have to be sure that that was what I wanted if I were to go away," he said teasingly.

"Do you want me to go?"

We looked at one another. I was quite determined in my misery. And my determination seemed to trouble him as much as my caresses had done a moment earlier. "No," he said with an effort, "stay here."

We continued to eat in silence. Then I saw him pour out a large glass of wine and empty it at a breath. "You see," he said, "I'm drinking."

"I can see that."

"I'll soon be tight and then I might even make you a declaration of love."

His words pierced me to the heart. I really could not

255

continue to suffer in this way. "Listen," I said humbly, "stop torturing me."

"Am I torturing you?"

"Yes, you're making fun of me . . . the only thing I ask you is to take no notice of me. . . . I've taken a very strong liking to you . . . it'll pass . . . but let me be now."

He said nothing and drank off a second glass of wine. I was afraid I had offended him. "What's the matter?" I asked. "Are you cross with me?"

"Cross with you? Not at all."

"If you like making fun of me, it's all right . . . I was only talking . . ."

"I'm not making fun of you."

"And if you like saying cruel things to me," I insisted, driven on by the desire to humble myself before him, without any trace of calculation or cunning, "say them. I'll love you all the same . . . even more. Even if you hit me I'd kiss the hand that did it."

He was examining me attentively. He seemed extremely embarrassed, he obviously found my passion disconcerting. "Let's go, shall we?" he then said.

"Where?"

"To your place."

I was so hopeless that I had almost forgotten the cause of my hopelessness; and his unexpected suggestion, when we had only just finished the first course and half the wine was left in the carafe, astonished me more than delighted me. I supposed rightly that his embarrassment made him want to interrupt our meal.

"You're on tenterhooks to have done with me, aren't you?" I said.

"How did you guess?" he asked, but his reply, too cruel to be true, put new heart into me for some inexplicable reason.

"Some things go without saying," I said, lowering my eyes. "Let's finish our meal, though . . . then we'll go."

"As you like. But then I'll get drunk."

"Get drunk, then, as far as I'm concerned."

" But I'll get so drunk I'll be ill, and then instead of having a lover to love, you'll have a sick man to nurse."

I was simple enough to show my anxiety and stretched out my hand towards the carafe. " Don't drink, then ! " I said. He burst into laughter. " Caught you that time ! " he said.

" Why ? "

" Don't be scared. I don't get ill as easily as all that."

" I was thinking of you," I said, feeling humiliated.

" Of me—oh, oh ! "

He continued to tease me. But his innate kindness underlay all his teasing and therefore I did not mind very much.

" Why don't you drink, though ? " he added.

" I don't like it. Besides, a glass is enough to make me tight."

" What does that matter ? We'll be tight together."

" Women are awful when they're drunk. I don't want you to see me drunk."

" Why ? What's awful about it ? "

" I don't know. It's awful to see a woman stagger about, talk rubbish, make coarse gestures. It's sad. I'm an unfortunate woman, I know, and I know that's how you think of me. But if I were to drink and you saw me drunk you'd never look me in the face again."

" Suppose I ordered you to drink ? "

" You really want to see me humiliated," I said pensively. " The only good thing about me is that I'm not ungainly. Do you really want me to lose this good point as well ? "

" Yes, that's just what I want," he said emphatically.

" I don't know what sort of a kick you get out of it, but if it gives you one, pour me some wine." And I held out my glass.

He looked at the glass, at me, then burst into laughter again. " I was only joking," he said.

" You're always joking."

" So you aren't ungainly, aren't you ? " he went on after a moment, looking at me attentively.

" They say so, anyway."

" Do you think I agree ? "

257

"How do I know what you think?"

"Let's see. What do you suppose I think and feel about you?"

"I don't know," I said slowly and fearfully; "naturally you don't love me as I love you. Perhaps you like me well enough, as any man likes any woman provided she's not absolutely hideous."

"Oh, so you think you aren't absolutely hideous!"

"Yes," I said proudly. "In fact, I know I'm beautiful; but what use have my looks been to me, so far?"

"Beauty isn't meant to be of any use."

Meanwhile we had finished our meal and had nearly emptied two carafes. "You see," he said, "I've been drinking but I'm not drunk." But his shining eyes and trembling hands seemed to contradict him. I looked at him with a glimmer of hope. "You want to go home, eh?" he added. "*C'est Vénus toute entière à sa proie attachée . . .*"

"What's that?"

"Nothing. Only a line of verse I dragged in to fit the occasion. Waiter!"

He was still speaking emphatically but humorously. And humorously he questioned the proprietor to know what the bill was and chinked the money in his face, adding an exaggerated tip, as he said: "This is for you." Then he swallowed the rest of the wine and joined me outside the restaurant.

As soon as I was in the street I felt frantic to reach home. I knew he had come to see me against his will and I knew he hated and despised the feeling which had driven him to seek me out. But I had a great belief in my beauty and my love for him and was impatient to overcome his hostility with these weapons. A gay and aggressive will inspired me, and I felt sure my love would prove to be stronger than his aversion, and that at last in the heat of my own ardour the harsh, unyielding metal in him would be melted and he would reciprocate my love.

"Still," I said as I walked along beside him in the street, empty at that early hour in the afternoon, "you've got to promise you won't try to go away once we're home."

" I promise."

" And you've got to promise me something else."

" What ? "

I hesitated before answering. " The other time," I said, " everything would have gone all right if you hadn't looked at me in a certain way that made me feel ashamed. You've got to promise me you won't look at me like that again."

" Like what ? "

" I don't know . . . a nasty look."

" You can't master your way of looking," he replied after a moment. " But if you like I won't look at you at all. I'll shut my eyes. That'll be all right."

" No, it won't," I protested obstinately.

" How do you want me to look at you, then ? "

" How I look at you," I answered. I took hold of him by the chin while we were still walking and showed him how he ought to look at me. " Like this, meltingly . . ."

" Oh, I see, meltingly . . ."

When we were on the filthy sordid staircase that led to my flat I could not help remembering the block Gisella lived in, so clean and gleaming. " If I didn't live in a place like this," I said, as if speaking to myself, " and weren't the wretched creature I am, you'd think far more of me."

Quite unexpectedly he stood still, took hold of me by the waist with both hands. " If that's what you think," he said sincerely, " you can be quite sure you're mistaken." Something very like affection seemed to gleam in his eyes. At the same time he bent down and sought my mouth. His breath smelt strongly of wine. I never could stand the smell of wine ; but in his mouth at that moment it seemed innocent and charming, touching almost, as touching as it would have been in the mouth of an inexperienced boy. I also realised that my words had touched him on his most sensitive spot. I imagined I had awakened in his breast a spark of affection. Afterwards I realised it was, if anything, a flutter of self-love and that in embracing me he was submitting to a kind of moral blackmail rather than yielding to an amorous impulse. Subsequently I blackmailed him in the same way quite often : by accusing him of despising me because of my poverty and profession. And I always achieved the results my desire yearned after, although as my understanding of him grew this was peculiarly humiliating and disappointing.

But I did not know him so well then as I came to later on. And his kiss filled me with joy as if I had won a decisive victory. I merely touched his lips with mine, content with the gesture alone, and taking him by the hand I pulled him up the last flight of stairs, saying : " Come on, let's hurry ! " He let himself be dragged up without a word.

I entered my flat almost at a run, knocking him against the walls of the entrance as though he were a puppet. I entered my room violently and flung him on the bed. I then noticed for the first time that he was not only drunk, as I had foreseen, but was so drunk that he was on the point of vomiting. He was extremely pale, kept passing his hand across his forehead with a bewildered expression, had a dazed and wandering look in his eye. I noticed all this in a flash ; and immediately I began to be afraid he might really be sick, and for the second time our meeting would go up in smoke. I was filled with remorse as I walked about the room undressing, because I had not prevented him drinking—I was almost in despair. But it's worth mentioning that it never even crossed my mind to give up the idea of his love, for which I had been yearning for so long. I hoped for one thing only—that he would not feel so ill as to be unable to make love, and that if his qualms were really so bad their effects would not make themselves felt until after my desire had been satisfied. I was really in love with him, but I was so afraid of losing him that my love was unable to go beyond the limits of self.

So I pretended I did not notice his drunkenness and after removing my clothes I sat down on the bed beside him. He was still wearing his overcoat, just as when he had entered the room. I began to help him to get undressed and as I helped him I kept on talking in order to distract his attention and prevent it occurring to him to get up and leave me.

" You haven't told me how old you are, yet," I said. Meanwhile I was pulling off his overcoat and he was holding up his arms passively to make it easier for me.

" I'm nineteen," he said after a moment.

"You're two years younger than me."

"Are you twenty-one?"

"Yes, nearly twenty-two in fact."

My fingers fumbled clumsily with the knot in his tie. Slowly, with difficulty, he pushed me away and undid the knot. Then he let his arms fall and I slipped the tie off. "This tie's all worn," I said. "I'll buy you one—what's your favourite colour?"

He began to laugh and I loved him then because he had such a charming way of laughing. "You really mean to keep me!" he said. "First you want to pay for my meal, and now you want to give me a tie."

"Silly!" I said fondly. "What's it matter? If I like to give you a tie . . . it can't possibly make you cross!" Meanwhile I had taken off his jacket and waistcoat and he was sitting on the edge of the bed in his shirt.

"Can you tell I'm nineteen?" he asked. He always liked talking about himself. It didn't take me long to discover this.

"In some ways," I said, hesitating in a way I knew he would find flattering. "Your hair gives you away, mostly," I added, stroking his head. "Men's hair isn't so full of life. I couldn't tell from your face."

"How old would you say I am?"

"Twenty-five."

He was silent and I saw him shut his eyes as if overcome by his drunkenness. But I was seized once more by the fear that he might be sick so I hastened to take off his shirt. "Tell me more about yourself," I added. "Are you a student?"

"Yes."

"What are you reading?"

"Law."

"Do you live with your people?"

"No, they're in the country at S——"

"Do you live in a boarding-house?"

"No, a furnished room," he replied mechanically with his eyes shut. "Flat eight, number twenty, Via Cola di Rienzo, at Signora Amalia Medolaghi's—she's a widow."

His chest was bare now. I could not help running my

261

hand amorously over his breast and neck. "Why are you sitting there? Aren't you cold?" I asked.

He raised his head and looked at me. "Do you think I haven't noticed anything?" He laughed, his voice rather sharp.

"Noticed what?"

"That without seeming to you've been undressing me. I may be drunk but I'm not as drunk as all that."

"Well," I said, feeling rather disconcerted, "suppose I have, what harm is there in that? You ought to do it by yourself—since you don't, I've been helping you."

Apparently he did not hear what I was saying. "I'm drunk," he said, shaking his head, "but I know perfectly well what I'm doing and why I'm here. No, I don't need any help, thank you."

With unexpectedly violent gestures, that were made puppet-like by the thinness of his arms, he undid his belt and flung off his trousers and everything else he was wearing. "And I know what you expect from me, too," he said, clasping my waist with both hands. His strong, nervous hands gripped me and the drunken look in his eyes seemed to have faded, to be replaced by a kind of vigorous malice. I was to encounter this same malice in the very moments when he seemed most to abandon himself. It was a clear sign of the lucid consciousness he enjoyed at all times, whatever he was doing, and as I was to discover later to my sorrow, it prevented him from really loving anyone and getting into touch with them.

"This is what you want, isn't it?" he added, as he clutched me and dug his nails into my flesh. "This, and this, and this." Each time he said 'this' he made one of the gestures of love, kissing me, biting me, pinching me unexpectedly. I was laughing and wriggling and struggling, too happy at his sudden awakening to notice how forced and lacking in spontaneity his behaviour was. He really hurt me, as though my body was an object of hatred and not of love. And more rage than desire gleamed in his eyes. Then, his frenzy ceased as suddenly as it had begun. In a curious, inexplicable fashion, as though overcome once more by his feeling of drunkenness, he fell back full-length on the bed, shut his

262

eyes, and I found myself lying beside him with the strange sensation that he had never moved or spoken, had never touched me or embraced me. As if it all had yet to begin.

I remained there utterly still for some time, kneeling on the bed in front of him, my hair hanging over my eyes, looking at him and touching his long, thin, beautiful, innocent body with timid finger-tips. His skin was white and his bones stuck out, his shoulders were broad and thin, his hips narrow, his legs long, and he was hairless except for a few hairs on his chest, and his abdomen was flattened because of the way he was lying, so that his genitals appeared raised and offered. I do not like violence in love, and this was why I felt as if nothing had happened between us and everything was still to begin. So I waited for peace and silence to be restored after that forced, ironical moment of tumult, and when my heart was once more its usual serene and impassioned self I let myself down beside him, as if I were slowly slipping into the lovely waters of a motionless sea on a blazing day, and I twisted my legs round his and my arms round his neck and clung to him. This time he neither moved nor spoke to the end. I called him by the fondest names, panted in his face and wrapped him in the meshes of my impassioned embraces, while he lay as motionless and supine as if he were lifeless. I learnt afterwards that this detached passivity was the highest proof of love he could give.

After some little time, I raised myself on my elbow and gazed at him intensely in a way which is still, after so long, a precious, painful memory. He was sleeping with his head buried sideways in the pillow; his usual air of wavering dignity, which he tried to maintain at all times and at all costs, had left him; and nothing remained in the features sleep revealed in all their sincerity but his youthfulness, whose freshness and innocence can only be described as an expression mirroring some special quality or tendency in his soul. But I remembered I had seen him alternately spiteful, hostile, indifferent, cruel and desirous, and I was filled with melancholy and anxious discontent, because I knew that his spite, his hostility, his indifference, his desire, all these things differentiated him from me and everyone else, had their origin in some deep centre which was still secret and unknown to me. I did not want him to explain his attitudes by taking them down and examining them in words, like the parts of a machine can be taken down and examined; I would have preferred to come to know them in their subtlest manifestations through the act of love and unfortunately I had failed in this. The little of him that escaped me was all himself, and the greater part which did not escape me was unimportant and useless to me. Gino, Astarita, and even Sonzogno had been nearer to me and better known. I looked at him and felt anguished because the deeper parts of our beings had not been able to meet and join as our bodies had done only a little while before. My depths were mourning and weeping bitterly over the chance that had been lost. Perhaps there had been one moment while we were loving one another when he had let down his defences and by a gesture or a word I might have penetrated him and he would have been mine for ever. But I had not recognised the right moment and now it was too late, he was sleeping, and had gone away from me once more.

While I continued gazing at him he opened his eyes, but kept quite still, with his head buried sideways in the pillow. "Have you been to sleep, too?" he asked.

There was a different note in his voice, I thought, it was more trusting and confiding. I was filled with a sudden hope that during his sleep our intimacy had grown in some mysterious way. "No, I've been watching you," I said.

He was silent a moment. "I want to ask you a favour," he continued, "but can I rely on you?"

"What a question!"

"Will you do me the favour of keeping a parcel I'll give you for a few days? Then I'll come and collect it and perhaps bring you another."

At any other time I would have shown some curiosity over this matter of the parcels. But just then the only thing that mattered to me was Giacomo and our relationship. I thought it would give me another opportunity for seeing him; that I ought to do all I could to please him; and that if I were

264

to question him he might regret his suggestion and withdraw it. "If that's all!" I said lightly.

He was silent again for a long time as if he were meditating. "So you agree?" he then said.

"I've already told you so!"

"And don't you care to know what's inside the parcels?"

"If you don't want to tell me," I answered, doing my utmost to appear disinterested, "it means you have your reasons: so I don't ask you."

"But it might be something dangerous.—How do you know?"

"I'll have to risk it!"

"It might," he continued, lying flat on his back while his eyes gleamed with naïve amusement, "it might be stolen goods—I might be a thief."

I remembered Sonzogno who was not only a thief but a murderer; and my own thefts, the compact and the head-square; and I thought how queer it was for him to want to pass himself off as a thief to me, when I really was one and lived among thieves. "No, you're not a thief, I'm sure!" I said gently as I caressed him.

His face clouded over, his pride was always alert and the strangest and most unexpected things offended him. "Why not? I might be."

"You don't look like it . . . of course, everything's possible . . . but really, you don't suggest anything of the sort."

"Why? What do I look like?"

"What you are. A young man of good family, a student."

"I told you I was a student. But I might be something else; as, in fact, I am."

I no longer heeded him. I was thinking that I had not got a thief's face either; and yet I was one; and I longed to tell him so. This temptation was partly due to his own curious attitude. I had always thought stealing was something to be blamed; yet here was a man who not only did not blame an act of the same kind but seemed to find in it some positive aspect which I was unable to understand.

"You're right," I said, after a moment's hesitation. "I don't want to believe you're a thief, because I feel you aren't one; but as to what you look like—you might even be one—people don't always look what they are.—Do I look like a thief, for instance?"

"No," he replied without looking at me.

"And yet I am one," I said calmly.

"You are?"

"Yes."

"What did you steal?"

I had put my handbag down on the night-table, I picked it up and took out the compact. "This, in a house where I happened to be some time ago, and a silk head-square in a shop the other day, which I gave my mother."

You mustn't think I told him all this out of vanity. Actually, I was led to do it by a desire for intimacy, and emotional complicity: if nothing better offers, the confession of wrongdoing can draw people together and rouse love. I saw him become serious and look at me pensively; I was suddenly afraid he might think badly of me and might decide not to see me again. "Don't think I'm glad I stole," I said hastily; "I've decided to give the compact back; in fact, today. I can't give the head-square back, but I'm sorry and I've made up my mind not to do it again."

His usual malice gleamed in his eyes as I was speaking. He looked at me and suddenly burst into laughter. Then he gripped me by the shoulders and began to squeeze me and pinch me in his own unexpected fashion. "Thief! you're a thief, a great, big thief, a dear little thief, a thiefy-weefy," with a kind of sarcastically fond note which left me in doubt whether I ought to be offended or flattered. But his impetuousness excited and pleased me in a way. It was better than his usual deathly passivity, in any case. So I laughed and wriggled all over because I am very ticklish and he would insist on tickling me under the arms. But all the time I was twisting and laughing until the tears ran down my face I could see that the face bending over me so pitilessly was withdrawn and distant. Then he stopped, as suddenly as he had begun, and threw himself back upon the bed.

"I'm not a thief, though—nothing of the kind—and there won't be any stolen goods in those parcels."

I could see that he was bursting to tell me what the parcels contained and that the whole thing was a matter of vanity for him more than anything else—a vanity not vastly different from Sonzogno's, when he told me of his crime. Men have many things in common, despite all their differences; and when they are with a woman they love or with whom they have an amorous relationship they always tend to show off their virility by boasting of the dangerous, energetic things they have done or are going to do.

"You're dying to tell me what's in the parcels," I said gently.

He was offended. "You're a silly fool. I don't care a scrap. But I ought to tell you what's in them so that you can decide whether you're going to do me the favour or not. So—they contain propaganda."

"What do you mean?"

"I belong to a group of people," he said slowly, "who don't like the present government: they hate it, in fact, and want to get rid of it as soon as possible. The parcels contain a lot of matter printed secretly in which we explain why it isn't a good government and how it can be got rid of."

I had never had anything to do with politics. The question of the government did not touch me, or many other people, I believe. But I remembered Astarita and his occasional references to politics.

"But it's forbidden—it's dangerous!" I exclaimed in alarm.

He looked at me with evident satisfaction. At last I had said something he liked which flattered his egotism. "Yes," he agreed with extreme and slightly emphatic earnestness, "it is dangerous. Now it's up to you to decide whether you'll do me the favour or not."

"I wasn't speaking for myself," I retorted keenly. "I was meaning you. As far as I'm concerned, I'll do it."

"Mind," he said again, "it's really dangerous. If they find them you'll end up in gaol."

I looked at him and a flood of incontrollable emotion

267

swept over me, I do not know whether it was for him or for something else I could not define. My eyes filled with tears. "Don't you see it doesn't matter a scrap to me?" I stammered. "I'd go to prison . . . and what then?" I shook my head and the tears ran down my cheeks.

"And now whatever are you crying for?" he asked in astonishment.

"I'm sorry," I said. "I'm silly . . . I don't know why myself, perhaps because I wish you'd realise how I love you and am ready to do anything for you."

I had not yet learnt that I must not mention my love to him. At my words his face was filled with an expression of vague, distant embarrassment, as I was to see it so often in the future. "All right," he said hurriedly, "I'll bring you the parcel in a couple of days. We're agreed, then. And now I've got to go, it's getting late." As he spoke he leapt from the bed and began to dress quickly. I stayed where I was on the bed, in my emotion and tears, naked and a little ashamed, either because I was naked or because I had been crying.

He picked his clothes up off the floor where they had fallen and put them on. He went over to the hanger, got his overcoat, slipped into it and came over to me. "Feel," he said with the charming naïve smile I found so attractive.

I looked and saw he was pointing to one of the pockets of his overcoat. He had come near to the bed so that I could stretch out my hand without any effort. I felt something hard through the material of the pocket. "What is it?" I asked, without understanding.

He smiled in satisfaction, put his hand into his pocket and slowly drew a large, black revolver half out of it, staring at me fixedly all the while. "A revolver!" I exclaimed. "What are you going to do with it?"

"You never know," he said. "It may come in useful one day."

I was uncertain, did not know what to think, but he did not even give me time. He replaced the weapon in his pocket, bent down, brushed my lips with his, as he said: "All right, then—in a couple of days I'll be along." Before I could recover from my surprise he was gone.

268

Since then I have often thought over our first love-meeting and have reproached myself bitterly with not having foreseen the danger his passion for politics exposed him to. I know I never had any influence over him; but at least, if I had known a lot of things I have learnt since, I would have been able to advise him and when advice was useless, I would have been at his side, fully conscious and decided. The fault was entirely mine, due to my ignorance, which, however, was not my own fault but the fault of my condition. As I have already said, I had never had anything to do with political matters, which I did not understand and felt were entirely alien to me, as if they were happening on some other planet and not all around me. When I read a newspaper I always skipped the first page with the political news that didn't interest me and glanced through the reports of criminal cases, where certain incidents and crimes gave my mind something to feed on, at least. My condition was actually very like that of those transparent little creatures that live, they say, in the depths of the sea, in the dark, almost, and know nothing of what is happening on the surface in the sunlight. Politics, like many other things which people seem to think so important, reached me from a higher and unknown world, they were even weaker and more incomprehensible to me than the light of day to those simple little creatures in the depths under the sea.

But the fault was due not only to myself and my ignorance. It was his fault, too, in his vanity and lightness. If I had sensed anything else but vanity in him, as in fact there was, perhaps I would have acted differently and would have forced myself to understand and get to know all the things I was ignorant of: I cannot say with what success. And at this stage I would like to point out something else which certainly helped to make me behave nonchalantly—this was the fact that he always seemed to be burlesquing a part rather than acting seriously. He seemed to have built up an ideal character piece by piece, but was able to believe in it only up to a certain point, and was striving all the time to make his actions tally with his ideal character. This ceaseless comedy gave the impression that he was taking part in a

269

game he had mastered perfectly; but it also made what he was doing seem far less serious, as if it was only a game, and at the same time suggested that for him nothing was irreparable, that at the last moment even if he were to lose the game his opponent would return his losses to him and would shake his hand. Now perhaps he really was playing, like boys whose irrepressible instincts lead them to make a game of everything. But his opponent was in earnest, as we shall see. Therefore, when the game was up he found he was unarmed and helpless, held in a mortal grip, that had nothing of a game about it.

All these things and others far sadder and no less reasonable occurred to me later on when I thought over what had happened. But at the time, as I believe I have explained, the idea that this business of the parcels might influence our relationship in some way did not even cross my mind. I was glad he had returned to me, glad I could do him a favour, and at the same time have an opportunity of seeing him again, and I did not look beyond this double source of happiness. I remember that when I happened to think vaguely and dreamily about the odd favour he had asked me I shook my head as if to say: 'Schoolboy tricks!' and turned my mind to other things. In any case, I was so happy that even if I had wanted to, I would not have been capable of fixing my attention upon anything worrying.

CHAPTER SIX

Everything seemed to be going swimmingly: Giacomo had come back and at the same time I had contrived to have the maid who had been unjustly accused released from gaol, without being obliged to take her place. After Giacomo had left that day, I spent a couple of hours at least delighting in my happiness, as we delight in a jewel or some precious object which is still quite a novelty to us, in a puzzled, astonished, numb, way that does not, however, exclude profound enjoyment. Bells ringing for vespers aroused me from this sensuous contemplation. I remembered Astarita's advice, the urgent need to help the wretched woman who was in gaol. I dressed hurriedly and went out.

In winter when the days are short and we have passed the whole morning and the early hours of the afternoon at home, alone with our thoughts, it is lovely to go out and walk about the streets in the heart of the city, where the traffic is thickest, the crowds most numerous, the shops most brilliantly lit. The heart leaps up in the pure cool air, amid the noise, movement and glitter of city life, mists clear from the brain, and we are filled with joyous excitement and gay intoxication, as if all our difficulties had suddenly been solved and nothing was left to us but to wander lightheartedly and thoughtlessly among the crowd, content to follow any fleeting sensation suggested to our idle minds by the pageant of the streets. It really seems at such times as if all trespasses had been forgiven, as the Christian prayer says, without any merit or retribution on our part, merely by virtue of some mysterious, generous goodwill. Naturally we have to be in a happy or at least contented frame of mind ; because otherwise city life might give us nothing more than an acute sensation of absurd, aimless motion. But I was happy on that day, and I realised it most when I began to walk along the pavements in the heart of the town, among the crowds of people.

I knew I had to go to church to make my confession. But probably just because I knew that this was my purpose and I was glad I had suggested it, I was in no hurry and did not even think about it. I walked slowly from one street to another, stopping from time to time to look at the goods on show in the shop windows. If anyone who knew me had seen me then they would certainly have thought I was bent on picking up some man. But in fact nothing could have been further from my thoughts. I might have let some man I liked the look of stop me, but it would not have been for money, only out of an impulse of happiness and exuberance. But the few men who came up to me with the usual phrases and offers of company when they saw me standing still and looking in at the shop windows had nothing about them that attracted me. So I made no reply, did not even look at them and continued to walk along the pavement with my usual lazy, majestic steps as if they did not even exist.

The sight of the church where I had been to confession last time after the trip to Viterbo came upon me unawares, while I was in this gay and absent mood. The façade, sunk in darkness, of the baroque church that was built like a screen along a curve of the street, its high pediment topped by two trumpeting angels and streaked with violet rays from the electric sign on a neighbouring house, seemed to me like the dark, wrinkled face of an old woman beckoning to me confidentially from the shadow of an old shawl, among the lighted faces of the other passers-by, standing there as it did between the cinema placards and the hosier's window, which were both brilliantly lit. I remembered the handsome French confessor, Father Elia, and how I had been attracted by him, and I thought no one could perform the task of returning the compact better than he, for he was young, intelligent and a man of the world, different in every way from other priests. Besides, Father Elia already knew me, in a way, and so I would find it easier to confess to him the many terrible, shameful things which weighed so heavily upon my soul.

I climbed the steps, pushed aside the heavy covering over the door and entered, putting a handkerchief on my head. While I dipped my fingers in the holy-water stoup I was struck by a scene carved round its edge—it showed a naked woman, her hair streaming in the wind, her arms raised as she fled, pursued by a foul dragon with a parrot's beak that was standing upright on its hind legs like a man. I seemed to recognise myself in that woman and thought how I, too, was fleeing just such a dragon, except that the course of my flight was circular like hers and as I ran round in circles I sometimes found I was not fleeing but was gaily pursuing the ugly beast. I turned from the holy-water stoup to the church as I crossed myself and it seemed to have continued in the same darkness, squalor and untidiness I had noticed the first time I had visited it. Everything lay in darkness, as then, except the high altar with all its candles burning closely round the crucifix in a confused glitter of brass candlesticks and silver vases. The Lady Chapel where I had prayed so fervently and uselessly was also illuminated. Two vergers were standing on ladders fixing gold-fringed red hangings to the architrave. I found that Father Elia's confessional was engaged, so I went and knelt down in front of the high altar on one of the displaced straw-bottomed chairs. I was not at all moved, but was merely impatient to settle the matter of the compact. My impatience had something peculiar about it, it was gay, impetuous, self-congratulatory and rather vain, at heart, the kind you feel when you are on the point of doing some good deed you have been meditating for a long time. I have often noticed that this kind of impatience, which springs from the heart and is deaf to good advice, usually ends by compromising the good deed and does greater harm than would more calculated behaviour.

As soon as I saw the person who was confessing get up and go away I went straight to the confessional, knelt down and began to speak without waiting for the confessor to address me. " Father Elia," I said, " I have not come to make my confession in the usual way. I have come to speak to you of a very serious matter and to ask you a favour I am sure you will not refuse."

The confessor's low voice on the other side of the grill invited me to proceed. I was so sure Father Elia was on the other side that I almost imagined I could see his calm, handsome face outlined against the dark grill pierced with little holes. Then, for the first time since I had entered the church, an impulse of devout and trusting emotion swept over me. It was as though my soul felt impelled to free itself from my body and kneel down naked on the steps before the grill, with all its blemishes exposed. I felt for a moment as if I were a disembodied spirit, free, formed of light and air, like we are after death, they say. And I imagined Father Elia, too, whose spirit was so much more luminous than mine, had broken free of the prison-house of the flesh, had caused the grill, the walls, the darkness of the confessional to vanish and stood there in person before me, dazzling and comforting. Perhaps this is the emotion we ought to feel every time we kneel down to confess. But I had never felt it so intensely before.

I began to speak with my eyes closed, leaning my head against the grill. And I told him everything. I told him of

273

my profession, Gino, Astarita, Sonzogno, the theft and the murder. I told him my name, Gino's, Astarita's and Sonzogno's. I told him where the theft and the murder had taken place, told him where I lived. I even described what the different people looked like. I do not know what impulse swept me along. Perhaps it was the same impulse that a housewife feels when she finally decides to clean her house after a long period of neglect and is unable to rest until she has swept away the last speck of dust, the last bit of fluff under the furniture or in the corners. And in fact, as I went on telling my tale in all its particulars, I felt as if I were unburdening my heart and soul and felt lighter and cleaner.

I spoke in the same calm, reasonable voice the whole time. The confessor listened to me without interruption to the very end. When I stopped a moment's silence ensued. Then I heard a dreadful, slow, unctuous, dragging voice address me. "You have told me of terrible, fearful things, my child, the mind finds them hardly credible. But you did well to come to confession—I will do everything that lies in my power for you."

A long time had passed since my first and only confession in that church. And in the turmoil of my self-complaisant goodness I had almost forgotten Father Elia's most pleasing characteristic—his French pronunciation. The priest who was addressing me had no special accent, but he was undoubtedly Italian and had the peculiarly oily voice of many priests. I suddenly realised the mistake I had made and a cold shudder ran through me—as if my finger-tips had encountered the quivering, icy scales of a serpent when I had confidently stretched out my hand to pluck a lovely flower. The unpleasant surprise of being faced with a confessor I had not expected was enhanced by the sense of horror his deep insinuating voice aroused in me.

"Are you really Father Elia?" I stammered with an effort.

"Himself in person," replied the unknown priest. "Why? Have you been here before?"

"Once before."

The priest was silent for a moment. "Everything you have told me requires to be considered point by point. You

274

have told me not one, but many things, some of which concern yourself, and some other people. As far as you are concerned —do you understand that you have sinned grievously? "

" Yes, I know," I murmured.

" And do you repent? "

" I believe I do."

" If you are sincere in your repentance," he began, speaking in a confiding, paternal undertone, " you may certainly hope for absolution. Unfortunately you are not the only one. There are all the others, with their crimes and faults. You have come to know of a terrible crime : a man has been murdered in an appalling fashion. Do you feel no impulse in your heart to reveal the criminal's name and bring him to justice? "

In this way he suggested that I should denounce Sonzogno. I do not say he was wrong, as a priest. But the proposal, made in that insinuating voice at such a time, only increased my doubts and fears. " If I say who did it," I stammered, " I'll be put in gaol myself."

His reply was immediate. " Men, like God himself, will be capable of appreciating your sacrifice and repentance. The Law both punishes and forgives. But in exchange for some suffering you would have helped to re-establish justice which has been so foully overset. My child, do you not hear the voice of the victim vainly beseeching his murderer for mercy? "

So he continued to exhort me, choosing his words carefully and complacently from the conventional phrases proper to his function as a priest. But my only desire now was to get away, I felt almost hysterical.

" I'll think over the matter of denouncing him," I said. " I'll come back tomorrow and tell you what I've decided. Shall I find you here tomorrow? "

" Certainly, at any time."

" Very well," I replied in a dazed way. " All I ask of you for the time being is to hand over this object." I stopped speaking, and after a short prayer, when he had asked me once more if I really repented and had determined to change my way of life, he gave me absolution. I crossed myself and left the confessional. At the same time he opened his door and stood before me. All the fears his voice had roused in me were redoubled at the sight of him. He was short, with a huge head that hung sideways as if he had a perpetual stiff neck. I did not have time to examine him thoroughly, I was in such a hurry to escape and he filled me with such horror. I glimpsed a brownish-yellow face, a pale, high forehead, eyes sunk deep in their orbits, a flattened nose with wide nostrils, and a large, shapeless mouth with purplish, sinuous lips. He could not have been old, he was ageless. Clasping his hands on his breast and nodding his head he addressed me in heartfelt tones. " But why, my dear child, did you not come to me sooner ? Why ? How many terrible things you would have been spared ! "

I wanted to tell him what I believed : that God had not meant me to come any sooner, but I restrained myself, and taking the compact from my handbag I gave it to him. " Please be as quick as you can," I said earnestly. " I cannot tell you how distressed I am at the thought of that wretched woman in gaol on my account."

" I'll go this very day," he replied, as he clasped the compact to his breast and shook his head deprecatingly.

I thanked him in a low voice and having nodded to him I left the church as quickly as I could. He remained standing where he was beside the confessional, clasping his hands to his breast and shaking his head.

When I was once more safely in the street I tried to think collectedly over what had occurred. Now that I had shaken off my first confused terrors I realised that what I was most afraid of was that the priest would not keep the seal of the confessional; and I tried to discover what grounds I had for my fears. I knew, like everybody else, that confession is a sacrament and is therefore inviolable. I also knew it was impossible for any priest, no matter how corrupt he might be, to violate it. But his advice to me to denounce Sonzogno to the police made me fear he might take it upon himself to reveal the name of the perpetrator of the crime in Via Palestro. But his voice and appearance caused me the gravest fears. I am emotional rather than reflective and I have an instinct for danger, like some animals. All the reasons my mind marshalled to reassure me were nothing in comparison with my unreasoned presentiment. "It's a fact that the seal of the confessional is inviolable," I thought, "but only a miracle can prevent that priest from denouncing Sonzogno, me, and all the others."

Something else helped to give me the sensation of some impending disaster : the substitution of the second confessor for the first. Obviously the French monk was not Father Elia, although he had listened to me in the confessional that bore that name. Who was he, then ? I was sorry I had not asked the real Father Elia for news of him. But I was half afraid he might have told me he knew nothing of him, and this would have emphasised the phantom character the young monk had for me. There really was something of a phantom about him, both because he was so utterly different from other priests and because of the way he had appeared in my life and had then vanished. I actually began to doubt whether I had ever seen him; or, rather, whether I had ever seen him in the flesh, and I imagined I might have had an hallucination, because I now discovered that he undoubtedly resembled Christ himself as he is portrayed in sacred paintings. But if this was true, if Christ himself had appeared to me in my hour of sorrow and had heard my confession, his substitution now with the sordid, repellent priest I had just seen certainly boded ill. It meant, if nothing else, that religion had abandoned me in my worst spiritual distress. It was like opening a safe containing gold coins in order to meet some urgent need, and finding only dust, cobwebs and mice-dirt instead of the coins.

I returned home with the impression that some misfortune must result from my confession and went straight to bed, without supper, convinced that this would be my last night at home before being arrested. But I must admit that I was not at all afraid, now, and had no desire to avoid my fate. My first moment of terror, which may be attributed to a nervous weakness common to nearly all women, had been followed by the determination to accept the destiny that overhung me—it was something more than mere resignation. I felt a kind of voluptuous delight, in fact, in letting myself sink to the depths of what I imagined must be the last stage of despair. I felt protected in a sense by the excess of my misfortune; and I

277

found a certain pleasure in the thought that nothing worse could happen to me except death, which I no longer feared.

But next day I waited in vain for the expected visit from the police. The whole day and the next passed without anything occurring to justify my apprehensions. I never left the house, nor even my room, during the whole of this period and I soon tired of thinking over the consequences of my rashness. I began to think about Giacomo again and realised I was longing to see him at least once more, before the priest's inevitable denunciation had any effect. Towards evening on the third day I got up, dressed carefully and left the house.

I knew Giacomo's address and it took me twenty minutes to reach his house. But just as I was about to enter the main door I remembered I had not warned him I was coming and I suddenly felt shy. I was afraid he might be annoyed at seeing me and even send me packing. My impatient step slowed down, and I stopped outside a shop, with my heart full of sadness, wondering whether it would not be better to turn back and wait for him to make up his mind to call on me. I realised that at the beginning of our relationship, in particular, I ought to be very wary and subtle and never let him know that I was in love with him and could not live without him. But turning away seemed very bitter to me because I was uneasy on account of the confession and I needed to see him, if only to take my mind off my worries. My eye fell on the window of the shop in front of me ; it was full of shirts and ties and I suddenly remembered I had promised to buy him a new tie to replace his threadbare one. When people are in love their minds cease to function properly ; I told myself I could make the gift of a tie an excuse for my visit, without realising that it was the gift itself which emphasised the inferior, anxious nature of my feeling towards him. I went into the shop and after hesitating for some time over my choice I bought a grey tie with red stripes, the handsomest and most expensive of them all. The man behind the counter asked me, with the somewhat indiscreet courtesy of salesmen who think they can influence their customers in their choice, whether the tie was for a fair or a dark man. "He's dark," I replied slowly, and realised I pronounced the word 'dark'

278

in a caressing tone, and I blushed at the thought that the salesman might notice it.

The widow Medolaghi lived on the fourth floor of a gloomy old palace whose windows looked out on to the Tiber embankment. I walked up eight flights of stairs and rang the bell at a door hidden in the shadows, without even waiting to recover my breath. The door opened almost immediately and Giacomo himself appeared on the threshold. " Oh, it's you ! " he exclaimed in surprise. He was obviously expecting someone.

" Can I come in ? "

" Of course. Come this way."

He led me from the dim hall into the sitting-room. It was dark there, too, because the windows had little, round, red, leaded panes, like a church. I glimpsed a quantity of black furniture inlaid with mother-of-pearl. A round table with a blue crystal decanter of an old-fashioned shape stood in the middle. There were several carpets and a worn, white bear-skin rug. Everything was old, but clean and tidy and well-preserved within the deep silence that had apparently reigned in the house since time immemorial. I went and sat down on a sofa at the other end of the room.

" Were you expecting anybody ? " I asked.

" No. But why have you come ? " The words were not very welcoming, I must say. But he did not seem angry, only surprised.

" I've just come to say how do you do," I smiled. " Because I think this'll be the last time we'll see one another."

" Why ? "

" I'm positive that tomorrow at the latest they'll come for me and carry me off to gaol."

" To gaol ? What the devil do you mean ? "

His voice and expression changed and I realised he was afraid on his own account, perhaps he thought I had denounced him or compromised him in some way by talking to someone about his political activities. " Don't worry," I smiled again. " It's nothing in the least to do with you."

" No, no," he replied hurriedly, " but I can't understand, that's all. Why should you go to gaol ? "

"Shut the door and come and sit here," I said, pointing to the sofa beside me.

He went to shut the door and then sat down beside me. I then told him the true story of the compact, very calmly, including my confession. He listened with his head bowed, without looking at me, biting his nails, which was always a sign that he was interested. "So I'm sure, that that priest will play a dirty trick on me. What do you think?" I concluded.

He shook his head and spoke, not looking at me but at the leaded panes in the windows. "He ought not to, in fact, I don't think he will. Simply because you didn't like his face you can't say."

"But you should have seen him!" I interrupted eagerly.

"He may be hideous, but that doesn't justify your saying he'd do any such thing! But of course, anything may happen," he added, laughing.

"So you think I needn't be afraid."

"Yes. All the more so, since you can't do anything—it doesn't depend on you."

"That's a nice way to talk! People feel afraid because they're afraid!—it's something stronger than yourself."

He suddenly made a fond gesture typical of him. He put one hand on my neck and laughed as he gave me a little shake. "You aren't afraid, though, are you?" he said.

"I tell you I am!"

"You aren't afraid, you're a brave woman!"

"I tell you I was terrified! I even went to bed and didn't even stir for a couple of days."

"Yes, but then you came to see me and tell me everything with the utmost calm. You don't know what it is to be afraid."

"What should I have done?" I asked, smiling against my will. "I can't cry out in terror!"

"You aren't afraid."

A moment's silence followed. Then he suddenly asked me a question in an odd tone of voice that surprised me. "What about this friend of yours—let's call him your friend!—Sonzogno?—What sort of a man is he?"

280

"Like a lot of others," I answered vaguely. I could not think of anything in particular to say about Sonzogno at that moment.

"But what's he like? Describe him."

"Why? Do you want to have him arrested?" I asked, laughing. "If you do I'll be put into gaol, too, remember! He's fair," I added, "short, broad-shouldered, with a pale face, blue eyes, nothing special, in fact. The only outstanding fact about him is that he's terrifically strong."

"Strong?"

"You wouldn't think it to look at him. But if you touch his arm it's like iron." Seeing that he was interested I told him the story of the incident between Sonzogno and Gino. He made no comment. "So you think Sonzogno's crime was premeditated," he said at the end. "I mean, that he thought it all out and then did it in cold blood."

"Not at all!" I answered. "He never plans anything. A moment before laying out Gino flat on the ground with one blow he probably wasn't even dreaming of such a thing. It must have been like that in the goldsmith's case, too."

"Then why did he do it?"

"Because! Because it's something stronger than himself . . . like a wild beast. One moment it's calm, the next it hits out at you with its paw, and no one knows why." I then told him the whole story of my relationship with Sonzogno, how he had struck me and threatened to murder me in the dark. "He never thinks," I concluded. "At a certain moment a force stronger than his will takes hold of him—it's best to keep your distance at such times! I'm sure he went to the gold-smith's to sell him the compact, then the goldsmith insulted him and he murdered him."

"He's a kind of brute, then."

"Call him what you like. It must be an impulse," I added, trying to define in my own mind the feeling Sonzogno's homi-cidal mania inspired in me, "like the one that impels me to love you. Why do I love you? God knows. Why does Son-zogno feel an impulse to murder? God only knows this, too. I don't think there's any explanation of such things."

He pondered a while. Then he raised his head. "What

281

sort of an impulse do you think I feel towards you ? " he then said. " Do you think I feel any impulse to love you ? "

I was terrified that I might hear him say he did not love me. So I covered his mouth with my hand. " Please," I begged him, " don't tell me anything of what you feel for me."

" Why not ? "

" Because I don't care to know . . . I don't know what you feel for me and don't want to know. . . . It's enough for me to love you myself."

He shook his head. " It's a bad thing to love me," he said. " You ought to love a man like Sonzogno."

I was really amazed. " What on earth do you mean ? A criminal like that ? "

" Suppose he is a criminal, he still has the impulses you mentioned. Just as Sonzogno has the impulse to kill, I'm sure he'd have an impulse to love, quite simply, without any complications. But I——"

I did not let him continue. " You can't compare yourself with Sonzogno," I protested, " you are what you are. He's a criminal, a monster. And, anyway, it isn't true that he might have an impulse to love. . . . A man like that can't love. It's nothing more than a satisfaction of the senses, for him. . . . It's all the same to him whether it's me or any other woman."

He did not seem convinced, but he said nothing. I took advantage of his silence and slipped my fingers under his cuff, over his wrist, trying to reach his arm. " Mino," I said.

I saw him start. " Why do you call me Mino ? "

" It's short for Giacomo. Can't I ? "

" No, no, it doesn't matter, of course you can. Only it's what they call me at home, that's all."

" Is that what your mother calls you ? " I asked, letting go of his wrist and slipping my hand under his tie and stroking his bare chest between the edges of his shirt with my finger-tips.

" Yes, it's what my mother calls me," he said impatiently. " It's not the only thing you say which my mother says, too," he continued in a voice that was partly sarcastic and partly scornful. " You share the same opinions about everything, at heart."

282

" What, for instance ? " I asked. I was excited and hardly heard what he was saying. I had unbuttoned his shirt and was trying to reach his gracefully boyish shoulder with my hand.

" This, for instance," he replied. " When I told you I busied myself with politics you immediately exclaimed in a frightened voice : ' But it's illegal ! It's dangerous ! ' Well, that's exactly what my mother would have said, in the same tone of voice."

I was flattered at the idea that I resembled his mother, first of all because she was his mother and then because I knew she was a lady. " Silly boy ! " I said tenderly. " What's the harm ? It means your mother loves you as I do. It's quite true that it's dangerous to have anything to do with politics. A young man I knew was arrested and has been in gaol two years now. And what's the good ? They're stronger, anyway, and as soon as you do anything they clap you into prison . . . I think you can get along very well without politics."

" Just like my mother ! " he exclaimed, jubilantly sarcastic. " That's exactly how she talks."

" I don't know what your mother says," I replied, " but I'm sure that whatever it is it's for your good. You ought to leave politics alone. It's not your profession. You're a student. A student's job is to study."

" Study, get a degree, and make a position for yourself," he murmured as if speaking to himself.

I did not answer, but putting my face up to his I offered him my lips. We kissed and then drew apart and he seemed sorry he had kissed me and looked at me with a hostile and mortified expression. I was afraid I had annoyed him by interrupting his political outburst with my kiss. " But anyway," I added hastily, " do what you like, I've nothing to do with your affairs. As a matter of fact, since I'm here you might as well give me that parcel, and I'll hide it for you, as we arranged."

" No, no," he said quickly, " not at all, it wouldn't do—not with your friendship with Astarita—suppose he found out ! "

" Why ? Is Astarita so dangerous ? "

" He's one of the worst," he replied earnestly.

I felt a mischievous impulse to wound him in his pride. Not spitefully, but almost affectionately. " As a matter of fact," I said gently, " you never really meant to give me that parcel."

" Then why did I mention it to you ? "

" Because—well, don't be offended, now—I think you mentioned it in order to cut a good figure with me—to let me see you did dangerous, illegal things in real earnest."

He grew angry and I realised I had struck home. " What nonsense ! " he said. " You really are a silly girl. But what makes you think so ? " he asked awkwardly, suddenly calm once more.

" I don't know," I answered with a smile, " it's your whole manner. Perhaps you don't notice it yourself, but you never give the impression that you really mean what you say."

He made a queer gesture, as if in criticism of himself. " And yet it's an extremely serious matter . . ." he said. He stood up, and stretching out his thin arms began to recite emphatically in a falsetto voice :

> " *My sword, give me my sword!*
> *I alone will fight, alone will fall.*"

He was so funny, waving his arms and legs about, he looked rather like a marionette.

" What does that mean ? " I asked.

" Nothing," he replied. " It's a line out of a poem." His excitement suddenly gave way to a strangely depressed and reflective mood. He sat down again and continued earnestly. " . . . and yet—I'm so much in earnest in everything I undertake. I really hope I'll be arrested. And then I'll show everyone whether I'm in earnest or not."

I said nothing but took his face between the palms of my hands and began to stroke it. " Your eyes are so beautiful," I said. It was true, his eyes really were exceptionally beautiful, large and gentle, with an innocent expression. He was troubled, his chin began to tremble. " Why don't we go into your room ? " I murmured.

" It's out of the question—it's next to the widow's own room—and she's in her room the whole day long, with the door open, watching the passage——"

284

" Let's go home to my place, then."

" It's too late.   You live too far away.   I'm expecting some friends before long."

" Here, then."

" You're crazy ! "

" You're scared, you mean ! " I insisted. " You aren't afraid to go in for political propaganda—at least, that's what you say—but you're afraid of being caught in this sitting-room with the woman who loves you. What could happen, anyway ? The widow might send you away, and then you'd have to look out for another room."

I knew that if I made it a matter of pride I could get anything out of him.   And in fact he seemed to be persuaded. Actually, his desire must have been at least as strong as mine. " You're crazy ! " he repeated, " it might be more of a bother to be sent away from here than to be arrested.   Besides, where can we lie ? "

" On the floor," I said, softly and amorously.   " Come, I'll show you."   He now seemed to be in such a state that he could not speak.   I got up from the sofa and slowly stretched myself on the floor.   The floor was covered with rugs and in the middle of the room stood the table with the carafe.   I stretched myself on the rugs, my head and bosom under the table ; then I pulled Mino down by one arm, forcing him to lie reluctantly upon me.   I threw my head back, shut my eyes, and the ancient smell of dust and fluff in the carpet seemed as intoxicating as if I were lying in a field in springtime and the smell was the scent of flowers and grass, not dirty wool.   Mino lay on me and his weight made me conscious of the delightful hardness of the floorboards and I was happy because he did not feel it and my body was his pallet.   Then I felt he was kissing my neck and my cheeks and I was filled with joy, because he never did this.   I opened my eyes, my head was turned sideways, one cheek rubbed against the rough wool of the carpet and I could see a wide stretch of wax-polished mosaic flooring beyond the carpet and the lower part of the double folding-doors beyond that.   I heaved a deep sigh and closed my eyes again.

Mino was the first to get up ; I stayed for some time as he

had left me, flat on my back with one arm over my face, my dress disordered, my legs apart. I felt happy and blank in my happiness, and I imagined I could have stayed there for hours, feeling the pleasant hardness of the floor under me, and the smell of dust and fluff in my nostrils. Perhaps I even dropped off into a light, rapid sleep for a second, and I seemed to be dreaming that I really was in a flowery meadow, stretched out on the grass with the sunny sky over me instead of the table. Mino must have thought I was feeling ill, because I suddenly felt him shake me. " What's the matter ? " he said under his breath. " What are you doing ? Get up, quick ! "

With an effort I removed my arm from my face, slowly came out from under the table and stood up. I felt happy and I was smiling. Mino looked at me in silence as he stood with his back against the sideboard, still panting, his expression hostile and bewildered. " I never want to see you again," he said at last. At the same time his bowed body gave a strange, involuntary shudder as though he were a puppet and a spring had suddenly snapped in him.

I smiled. " Why ? " I said. " We love one another— we'll meet again." And going up to him I caressed him. But he turned his white, distressed face away from me. " I never want to see you again," he repeated.

I knew his hostility was chiefly due to his remorse at having given way to me. He never resigned himself to making love to me without a feeling of reluctance and deep regret. He was like a man who decides to do something he does not want to do, and knows he ought not to do. But I was sure his ill-humour would be short-lived and that his desire for me, however he might struggle against it and hate it, would always be stronger in the end than his queer longing for chastity. So I took no notice of his words and remembering the tie I had bought for him I went over to the ledge where I had put my gloves and handbag.

" Come on, now," I said. " Don't be so cross ! I won't come here again. Will that do ? "

He made no reply. At that moment the door was flung open and an elderly parlourmaid showed two men into the room. " Hullo, Giacomo," said the first, in a deep, thick voice.

286

I realised these must be his political comrades and looked at them curiously. The one who had spoken was a giant—he was taller than Mino, broad shouldered, and looked like a professional boxer. He had fair, ruffled hair, blue eyes, a flattened nose, a red, shapeless mouth. But his expression was open and pleasant, with a mixture of shyness and simplicity I found attractive. Although it was winter he had no overcoat, but a white polo-sweater underneath his jacket emphasised his sportsmanlike appearance. His red hands, with their thick wrists, which stuck out of the rolled cuffs of the sweater, struck me at once. He must have been very young, about Giacomo's age, probably. The other man was about forty, and had the clothing and appearance of someone out of the middle-classes as opposed to his companion, who was apparently a working-man or a peasant. He was short, and looked tiny beside his friend. He was very dark and his face was eclipsed by a huge pair of tortoiseshell-rimmed spectacles. A snub nose peered out from under his spectacles and a wide mouth that was a slit stretching from ear to ear. His thin, unshaven cheeks, his threadbare collar, his creased and spotted suit in which his wretched little body floated loosely, everything about him gave an impression of deliberate, aggressive negligence, of complacent poverty. As a matter of fact I was astonished at the appearance of these two men, because Mino always dressed with a kind of careless elegance and there were many indications that he belonged to a different social class from theirs. If I had not seen them greet Mino, and Mino return their greeting, I would never have imagined they were friends of his. But I instinctively liked the tall one and disliked the short one.

" Perhaps we've come too early ? " the tall one asked with an embarrassed smile.

" No, no," said Mino, pulling himself together. He was dazed and seemed to find some difficulty in recovering himself. " You're very punctual."

" Punctuality is the courtesy of kings," said the short man, rubbing his hands together. Suddenly, as if he found his phrase extremely funny, he burst into a fit of unexpected laughter. Then, just as he had laughed, with the same disagreeable suddenness, he grew serious once more, so serious that I doubted whether he had ever laughed.

"Adriana," said Mino, with an effort, "let me introduce two friends of mine—Tullio," he said, pointing to the short one, "and Tommaso."

I noticed he did not mention their surnames and I thought the names he gave were probably false. I held out my hand with a smile. The tall man shook it so hard that he hurt my fingers; but the little one made them moist with the sweat that bathed the palm of his hand. "Delighted," said the little one, with burlesque heartiness. "Pleased to meet you," said the tall one simply, as if he liked me, I thought. I noticed he had a slight dialect intonation in his voice.

We looked at one another in silence for a moment. "We can go away, Giacomo, if you like," said the tall man. "If you're busy we can come back tomorrow."

I saw Mino start and look at him, and I realised he was about to tell them to stay and to ask me to leave. I knew him well enough by now to understand that he could not have done otherwise. I remembered that I had given myself to him only a few minutes before—the sensation of his lips kissing me was still warm on my neck and the feeling of his hands clinging to me was in my flesh. It was my body, not my soul—which was always ready to yield and be resigned—which rebelled as if against a treatment unworthy of the gift it had made and of its beauty. I took a step forward. "Yes, you'd better go," I said violently, "and you can see one another tomorrow—I've still got a great deal to say to Mino."

Mino objected with an air of startled displeasure.

"But I've got to talk to them!"

"You can talk to them tomorrow."

"All right," said Tommaso good-naturedly, "make up your mind—if you want us to stay, say so—if you want us to go, we'll go."

"We ask nothing better," intervened Tullio with his usual laugh.

Mino still hesitated. My body, despite itself, felt another aggressive impulse. "Listen," I said, raising my voice, "a few minutes ago Giacomo and I were making love here on the

288

floor, on this carpet—what would you do in his place? Would you send me away?"

I believe Mino blushed. He certainly became confused and turned his back peevishly and went over to the window. Tommaso looked sidelong at me and then said, without smiling: "I see—we'll go. Bye-bye, Giacomo—we'll see you tomorrow at the same time."

But my words seemed to have upset little Tullio. He gaped at me, his eyes wide open behind his thick lenses. Certainly he had never heard a woman speak so frankly and at that moment a thousand dirty thoughts must have crossed his mind. But the tall man called to him from the doorway. "Come along, Tullio," he said, and the short man, without taking his lustful, astonished eyes off me, walked backwards to the door and left.

I waited for them to be out of the house and then walked over to Mino, who was still standing by the window, his back to the room, and put an arm round his shoulders.

"Now you can't stand me."

He turned slowly and looked at me. His eyes were full of anger, but at the sight of my face, which must have had an innocent, loving expression, his look changed and he spoke in rather a sad, reasonable voice. "Are you happy now? You got what you wanted."

"Yes, I'm happy," I said, embracing him. He let me do so.

"What was it you wanted to say to me?" he then asked.

"Nothing," I replied. "I wanted to spend the evening with you."

"But I'm going in to eat soon," he said. "Here—with the widow Medolaghi."

"Very well, invite me too."

He looked at me and smiled slightly at my boldness. "Very well," he said resignedly, "I'll go and tell them. How am I to introduce you?"

"As you like . . . as a relation."

"No, I'll introduce you as my fiancée—will that do?"

I did not dare to let him see how delighted I was at his suggestion. "It's all the same to me," I said, pretending to

289

be indifferent, " as long as we can be together, as fiancés or anything else."

" Wait here, I'll be back at once."

He went out and I walked over to a corner of the sitting-room, pulled up my dress and hastily buttoned my cami-knickers which had become disarranged in the confusion of love-making and the unexpected arrival of his friends. A mirror on the wall facing me showed me my long, perfect leg, clothed in silk, and it made a curious impression upon me among all that old furniture, in that silent, secluded atmosphere. I remembered the time when I had made love to Gino in his mistress's villa and had stolen the compact, and I could not help comparing that distant moment in my life with the present one. At that time I had felt a sense of emptiness, bitterness and a desire to revenge myself if not upon Gino directly at least upon the world, which by means of Gino had hurt me so cruelly. Now instead, I felt happy, free, light. Once more I realised I really loved Mino and it did not matter much that he did not return my love.

I smoothed my dress, went over to the mirror and tidied my hair. The door opened behind me and Mino returned.

I hoped he would come up to me and kiss me from behind while I was looking at myself in the mirror. But he went to sit down on the sofa at the end of the sitting-room instead. " That's done," he said, as he lit a cigarette. " They've laid another place—we'll go into supper soon."

I left the mirror and came to sit beside him and put my arm through his and pressed against him. " Those two were your political friends, weren't they ? " I said at random.

" Yes."

" They can't be very rich."

" Why ? "

" Judging by the way they dress, at any rate."

" Tommaso is our bailiff's son," he said, " and the other one's a schoolmaster."

" I don't like him."

" Who ? "

" The schoolmaster. He's dirty-minded and gave me such a look when I said I had been making love to you."

290

"He must have liked you, obviously."

We were silent for some time.

"You're ashamed to introduce me as your fiancée," I then said. "If you like I'll go."

I knew this was the only way to wring an affectionate gesture out of him : by blackmailing him with the accusation that he was ashamed of me. And in fact he immediately put his arm round my waist.

"I suggested it !" he exclaimed. "Why should I be ashamed of you ? "

"I don't know. I can see you're in a bad temper."

"I'm not in a bad temper, I'm dazed," he answered in a tone of voice that was almost scientific, "and that's because we've made love. Give me time to get over it."

I noticed he was still very pale and was smoking with disgust.

"You're right," I said. "I'm sorry. But you're always so cold and off-putting that you make me lose my head. If you were different I would not have insisted on staying a moment ago."

He threw his cigarette down.

"I'm not cold and off-putting," he said.

"And yet..."

"I like you immensely," he continued, looking at me attentively, "and in fact I didn't resist you a little while ago as I meant to." This phrase delighted me and I lowered my eyes without speaking. "Still, I suppose you're right, really, and this can't be called love."

My heart stood still and I could not help murmuring, "What do you mean by love, then ? "

"If I had loved you," he replied, "I would not have wanted to send you away a moment ago. And then I wouldn't have been angry when you wanted to stay."

"Were you angry ? "

"Yes—and now I'd be chatting to you, I'd be cheerful, gay, witty, amusing—I'd be making plans for the future— isn't that how love is ? "

"Yes," I said softly. "At least, these are the effects of love."

He was silent for some time and then spoke without any feeling of complacency, with arid humility. "I do everything in the same way; without loving what I'm doing or experiencing it in my heart—knowing mentally how to do it and occasionally even doing it, but always coldly and externally. That's how I am and apparently I can't be otherwise."

I made a great effort to control myself.

"I like you as you are," I said. "Don't worry." And I embraced him most affectionately. Almost at the same instant the door opened and the old servant looked in to tell us dinner was ready.

We left the sitting-room and went along a passage to the dining-room. I remember all the details of that room and the people in it perfectly, because I was as sensitive to impressions at that time as a photographic plate. I felt I was not so much acting as watching myself act, with wide, melancholy eyes. Perhaps this is the direct result of the feeling of rebellion we experience when faced with a reality that causes us to suffer while at the same time we wish it were otherwise.

I don't know why, but Signora Medolaghi, the widow, seemed to me to resemble closely the furniture in her parlour, in black ebony with mother-of-pearl inlay. She was a middle-aged woman, imposingly tall, with a voluminous bosom and massive hips. She was dressed entirely in black silk, had a broad, flabby face, whose pallor was like mother-of-pearl, framed in black hair that was obviously dyed, and had huge, dark shadows under her eyes. She was standing in front of a flowered soup-tureen and was serving the soup with a kind of disdain. The weighted lamp that had been pulled down over the table lit up her bosom, which was extremely like a large, black, shiny parcel, and left her face in shadow. In that shade her white face with its black-ringed eyes recalled the little silk masks worn during carnival. The table was small, and four places were laid, one on each side. The daughter of the house was already seated in her place and did not get up when we entered.

"The young lady can sit here," said the widow Medolaghi, "What's your name?"

"Adriana."

" Just like my daughter," said the mistress without thinking what she was saying. " We've got two Adrianas." She spoke self-consciously without looking at us and obviously she did not at all welcome my presence there. As I have already said, I use hardly any paint, I never peroxide my hair and in fact give no hint of my profession. But anyone could see that I was a simple, uneducated girl of the people, and I took no trouble to conceal the fact. " What strange people you bring to my house ! " the lady must have been thinking at that moment. " A common girl."

I sat down and looked at the girl who bore the same name as I did. In everything she was precisely the half of me—her head, her bosom, her hips ; she was thin, with scanty hair, and had a refined, oval face with huge, dull eyes whose expression was half-dazed. I looked at her and noticed that my beauty made her lower her eyes. I thought she may be shy. " Do you know," I said in order to break the ice, " it seems so odd that someone else should have the same name as me and yet be so different ? "

I had spoken at random, in order to start the conversation flowing ; and it was a silly phrase. But to my surprise I received no reply. The girl looked at me with wide-open eyes and then bent her head over her plate and began to eat in silence. Suddenly the truth dawned upon me : she was not shy but terrified. And I was the cause of her terror. She was terrified by my beauty which burst upon the dusty, faded air of her dwelling like a rose in a cobweb, by my exuberance which could not pass unnoticed even when I was silent and motionless, but chiefly by the fact that I was a common girl. A rich man certainly has no love for a poor man, but neither does he fear him, and he knows how to keep him at a distance by his own pride and conceit ; but a poor man who by education or by nature is possessed of the soul of a rich man is absolutely terrified by a genuinely poor man, as though he felt he had a tendency to catch a certain illness from someone who has already been infected. The two Medolaghi women were certainly not rich, otherwise they would not have let rooms ; being conscious of their poverty but unwilling to admit it, my presence as a poor girl wearing no mask seemed both dangerous and insulting to them. Who can say what passed through the daughter's mind as I addressed her? 'This girl here is talking to me, she wants to be friendly, I shan't be able to get rid of her.' I realised all these things in a flash and decided not to utter another word until the end of the meal.

But her mother, who was possibly more curious and had an easier manner, did not want to give up all idea of some conversation. " I didn't know you were engaged," she said to Mino. " How long have you been? "

Her voice was affected and she spoke from behind the mass of her bosom as if from behind a protective trench.

" About a month," said Mino. This was true, we had known one another for only a month.

" Is the young lady a Roman? "

" Indeed she is, seven generations back."

" And when is the wedding to be? "

" Soon—as soon as the house we are to live in is free."

" Oh, you've already got a house in mind? "

" Yes, a little villa with a garden—and a little tower. It's charming."

This was the sardonic way in which he described the little villa I had pointed out to him on the main road near my own flat.

" If we wait for that house," I said with an effort, " I am afraid we'll never get married."

" Nonsense," said Mino cheerfully. He seemed quite recovered and even had more colour in his cheeks. " You know it's to be free on the day we fixed."

I do not like jokes, so I said nothing. The maid changed the plates. " Villas, Mr. Diodati," said Signora Medolaghi, " are all very well, but they aren't convenient. You need a lot of servants."

" Why? " said Mino. " That won't be necessary. Adriana will be cook, parlourmaid, housekeeper, won't you, Adriana? "

Signora Medolaghi summed me up with a glance. " Really," she said, " a lady has something else to do besides thinking of cooking and sweeping and making beds. But if the young lady is accustomed to do it, in that case . . ." She did not finish her sentence and turned her attention to the plate the

294

parlourmaid was offering me. "We didn't know you were coming, we could only add another egg or two."

I was angry with Mino and with the lady and was almost tempted to reply: 'No, I'm accustomed to walking the streets.' But Mino, who was bubbling over with a crazy kind of gaiety, poured himself out a generous glassful of wine, poured some for me (Signora Medolaghi's eyes followed the bottle uneasily), and continued. "Oh, but Adriana's not a lady! And she never will be—Adriana's always made beds and swept floors. Adriana's a common girl."

Signora Medolaghi looked at me as if she were seeing me for the first time. "Exactly—as I was saying, if she's accustomed," she repeated with offensive politeness. Her daughter bowed her head over her plate.

"Yes, she is," went on Mino, "and I'm certainly not going to be the one to make her give up such useful habits. Adriana's a shirtmaker's daughter and a shirtmaker herself—aren't you, Adriana?" He stretched his arm across the table, seized my hand and turned it over, palm upwards. "She paints her nails, I know, but it's the hand of a working-girl—big, strong, unaffected—like her hair—it's curly, but rebellious, coarse at the roots." He let my hand fall and pulled my hair hard, like an animal's. "Adriana, in fact, is in everything and everywhere a worthy representative of our fine, healthy and vigorous people."

There was an echo of a sarcastic challenge in his voice; but no one took it up. The daughter looked through me, as if I were transparent and she were looking at some object behind me. The mother ordered the maid to change the plates, then, turning to Mino asked him in an entirely unexpected fashion: "So, Mr. Diodati, did you go to see that play?"

I almost burst into laughter at such a clumsy way of changing the subject. Mino, however, did not lose face. "Don't talk of it!" he exclaimed. "It was rotten."

"We're going tomorrow. They say it's an excellent company."

Mino replied that the actors were not as good as the papers said, though; the mistress was astonished that the papers should lie; Mino replied calmly that the papers were one lie from beginning to end; and from that moment the conversation dealt with similar matters. As soon as one of these themes of conversation was exhausted Signora Medolaghi started another, with poorly concealed haste. Mino, who seemed highly amused, acted up to her and replied smartly. They talked of actors, night-life in Rome, cafés, cinemas, theatres, hotels and so on. They were like two ping-pong players intent on returning the ball to one another without letting it drop. But while Mino did it out of his usual love of comedy, which was so highly developed, Signora Medolaghi did it in fear and disgust at me and anything connected with me. She seemed to imply by her formal, conventional talk that: 'This is my way of telling you how shocking it is to marry a common girl, and in any case how shocking it is to bring her to the house of the widow of the civil servant, Medolaghi.' The daughter said nothing; she was terrified, and seemed to be longing quite openly for the meal to come to an end and for me to be gone as quickly as possible. For a while I found some amusement in following the conversational skirmish, but I soon got tired of it and was utterly overwhelmed by the sadness in my heart. I realised that Mino did not love me, and the knowledge was bitter. Besides, I noticed that Mino had made use of my confidence in him to build up his comedy of an engagement, and I could not quite understand whether he wanted to make a fool of me, of the two women, or of himself. Perhaps all of us, but chiefly himself. It was as if he, too, had nourished in his heart the same aspirations towards a normal, decent life as I had, and had given up all hope of being able to fulfil them, for different reasons from mine. On the other hand, I understood that his praise of me as a girl of the people in no way flattered me or the common people—it had been nothing more than a means of making himself unpleasant to the two women. These observations brought home to me the truth of what he had been saying shortly before—that he was incapable of loving with his heart. Never as at that moment had I understood so well that everything is love, and that everything depends on love. This love either was, or was not. If there was love, then one loved not only one's own lover but all people and all things,

296

as I did; but if there was no love, one loved nobody and nothing—as in his case. And the lack of love in the end causes incapacity and impotence.

The table had been cleared by now and in the circle of light, shed by the chandelier on to the tablecloth sprinkled with crumbs, stood four coffee-cups, a tulip-shaped terra-cotta ash-tray, and a large mottled hand, adorned with several cheap rings, which held a burning cigarette, Signora Medolaghi's hand. My bosom suddenly swelled with impatience and I rose to my feet. "I'm sorry, Mino," I said, deliberately exaggerating the Roman accent I had, "but I'm busy . . . I've got to go."

He crushed out his cigarette in the ashtray and rose to his feet, too. I bade them a ringing, "Good-evening," just like any girl of the people would, made a slight bow which Signora Medolaghi returned stiffly and the daughter ignored, and then I left. In the entrance I spoke to Mino. "I'm afraid Signora Medolaghi will ask you to look out for another room after this evening."

He shrugged his shoulders. "I don't think so. I pay her well, and very punctually."

"I'm going," I said. "This meal has made me unhappy."

"Why?"

"Because I've become quite convinced at last that you can't love."

I said this sadly, without looking at him. Then I raised my eyes and thought he looked humiliated. But perhaps it was the shadow in the hall on his pale face. I suddenly felt full of remorse. "Are you cross?" I asked.

"No," he said with an effort, "it's the truth, after all."

My heart overflowed with affection for him, I embraced him impulsively. "It isn't true . . . I only said it out of spite. And anyway, I love you so much all the same . . . Look . . . I brought you this tie." I opened my bag, took out the tie and offered it to him. He looked at it.

"Did you steal it?" he asked.

It was only a joke and revealed more fondness for me at heart than the warmest thanks could have done, I understood later. But at that moment it pierced me to the heart. My

297

eyes filled with tears. " No, I bought it—in a shop just down below," I stammered.

He noticed my humiliation and embraced me. " Silly ! " he said. " I was only joking. But in any case, I'd like it even if you had stolen it, perhaps even more."

" Wait, I'll put it on for you," I said, feeling a little consoled. He lifted his chin and I undid his old tie, turned back his collar and knotted the new one for him.

" I'm going to take this horrid old worn-out tie away," I said. " You mustn't ever wear it again." What I really wanted was to have some memory of him, something he had worn.

" I'll see you soon, then," he said.

" When ? "

" Tomorrow, after supper."

" Very well." I took his hand and made as if to kiss it. He pulled it away but was not in time to prevent me brushing it with my lips. Without looking back, I ran hastily down the stairs.

CHAPTER SEVEN

After that day, I went on leading my usual life. I really loved Mino and more than once I felt tempted to give up my profession, so complete a contrast to real love. But despite the fact that I had fallen in love, my condition remained unaltered, I was still at the same point : that is to say, I had no money and no possibility of earning any except in that way. I did not want to accept money from Mino ; but in any case he had only a limited amount, since his family only sent him barely enough to pay for his keep in town. I must admit at this point that I always felt an irresistible desire to pay the bill myself in all the places, cafés and restaurants we frequented. He always refused my offers and every time I was disappointed and embittered. When he had no money he took me to the public parks and we sat together chatting on a bench and watching the passers-by, like two poor people.

"But if you haven't any money," I said to him one day, "let's go to a café all the same. I'll pay . . . what difference does it make?"

"It's out of the question."

"Why? I want to go to a café and have a drink."

"Go by yourself, then."

As a matter of fact, I was not so keen on going to a café as on paying for him. I had a deep, obstinate and painful desire to do so; and I would have liked to have handed all the money I earned straight over to him, rather than do all the paying myself, little by little as I received it from the birds of passage who were my lovers. I imagined that in this way only could I show him my love; but I also supposed that if I kept him financially I would bind him to me with a bond stronger than that of mere affection. "I'd be so pleased to give you some money," I said to him on another occasion. "And I'm sure it would give you some pleasure to have it!"

He began to laugh. "Our relationship, as far as I'm concerned at least, is not based on pleasure!"

"Oh what, then?"

He hesitated. "On your will to love me," he then replied, "and on my weakness in the face of this will of yours; but that doesn't mean my weakness has no limits."

"How do you mean?"

"It's very simple," he said calmly, "and I've explained it to you over and over again: we're together because you willed it so. I, on the contrary, did not, and even now, in theory, at least, I would rather not——"

"That'll do," I interrupted, "don't let's talk about our love. I shouldn't have mentioned it."

Often since, when thinking over his character, I have come regretfully to the conclusion that he did not love me at all, and that I was only the object of some experiment of his. In point of fact, he was interested only in himself; but within these limits his character was extremely complicated. He was a lad of a well-to-do provincial family, as I believe I have already said, delicate, intelligent, cultured, well-mannered, serious. His family, as far as I could make out from the little he told me, for he was not fond of talking about it, was one of those families I would have liked to have been born into, in my vain dreams of a normal life. It was a traditional family: his father was a doctor and landowner, his mother was still young and stayed at home most of the time, thinking only of her husband and children; there were three younger sisters and an elder brother. The father was admittedly a busybody and an authority in local affairs, his mother was extremely bigoted, his sisters rather frivolous and his elder brother quite a young man about town, like Giancarlo. But when all was said and done these faults were all bearable, and for me, who had been born among people whose way of life was so different in every way, they did not even seem to be faults. It was an extremely united family and all of them, parents and children, were devoted to Mino.

My own impression was that he had been very lucky in being born into such a family. But he seemed, on the contrary, to feel an aversion, a dislike and disgust for his family which I found quite incomprehensible. And he seemed to feel the same aversion, dislike and disgust for himself, what he was and what he did. But this hatred of himself appeared to be only a reflection of his hatred for his whole family. In other words, he seemed to hate in himself all that part of him which had remained attached to his family or had in any way come under the influence of the family circle. I have said he was well-mannered, cultured, intelligent, delicate, serious. But he despised his intelligence, manners, culture, delicacy, seriousness, merely because he suspected that he owed them to the milieu and the family into which he had been born and where he had grown up. "But really," I said to him once, "what would you like to be? These are all fine qualities—you ought to thank your lucky stars that you have them."

"Oh, for all the use they are to me!" he said, scarcely moving his lips. "Speaking for myself, I'd have preferred to be like Sonzogno."

He had been deeply impressed by the story of Sonzogno, I can't imagine for what reason. "How dreadful!" I exclaimed. "He's a monster, and you want to be like him!"

" Obviously I wouldn't want to be like Sonzogno in every respect," he explained calmly. " I mentioned Sonzogno merely to make my meaning clear. Sonzogno is acclimatised to life in this world of ours, and I'm not."

" Do you want to know what I would like to have been ? " I then asked him.

" Tell me."

" I would have liked," I said slowly, savouring the phrases in each of which one of my most cherished dreams seemed to be embodied, " to have been just what you are and what you are so unhappy at being—I would have liked to have been born into a family as well-to-do as yours, which would have given me a good education—I would have liked to have lived in a lovely, clean house like yours—I would have liked to have had good teachers, foreign governesses, as you had—I would have liked to have spent the summer at the seaside or in the mountains—and to have had good clothes, and be invited and to receive guests—and then I would have liked to marry someone who loved me, a decent fellow who worked and was well-to-do, too—and I would have liked to live with him and bear his children."

We were lying on the bed as we talked. Suddenly he leapt upon me, as was his way, clutching me and shaking me as he repeated : " Hurray, hurray, hurray ! In fact, you'd have liked to be like Signora Lobianco."

" Who's Signora Lobianco ? " I asked, both offended and disconcerted.

" A terrible harpy who often invites me to her receptions in the hope that I'll fall in love with one of her horrible daughters and marry her, because I'm what's called a good match."

" But I wouldn't like to be at all like Signora Lobianco ! "

" But that's what you'd certainly be if you had all the things you mentioned. Signora Lobianco was born into a wealthy family that gave her an excellent education, with good teachers and foreign governesses, sent her to school and even to the University, I believe—she, too, grew up in a lovely, clean house—she, too, went to the seaside or the mountains every summer—she, too, had beautiful clothes and was invited out and gave parties—lots of invitations and lots of parties—she, too, married a decent fellow, Lobianco the engineer, who works and brings a great deal of money into the house—and she has had a number of children by this husband of hers, to whom I even believe she has been faithful —three daughters and a son—but despite all this she's a terrible harpy, as I said——"

" She must be a harpy quite independently of her surroundings ! "

" No, she's one like her friends are and the friends of her friends."

" Maybe," I said, trying to break away from his sarcastic embrace, " but everyone's got their own character. Maybe Signora Lobianco is a harpy, but I'm sure that in those conditions I'd have turned out far better than I am."

" You'd have turned out no less horrible than la Lobianco."

" Why ? "

" Because."

" But, look here, do you think your family's horrible, too ? "

" Of course, loathsome."

" And are you horrible, too ? "

" Yes, in everything I've got from my family."

" But why ? Tell me why ! "

" Because."

" That's not an answer."

" It's the same answer Signora Lobianco would give you if you asked her certain questions," he replied.

" What questions ? "

" We needn't mention them," he said lightly. " Embarrassing questions—a ' because ' said with conviction shuts the mouth of even the most curious person—' because,' for no reason—' because '——"

" I don't understand."

" What does it matter if we don't understand each other, as long as we love each other—which is true ? " he concluded, embracing me in his ironical and loveless fashion. And so the discussion ended. For just as he never gave himself up completely, emotionally speaking, and always seemed

302

to keep something back, perhaps the most important part, so that his rare outbursts of affection were valueless, in exactly the same way he never revealed the whole of what he was thinking, and every time I believed I had reached the very core of his intelligence he repelled me with some joke or amusing trick, to distract my attention. He really was elusive in every sense. And he treated me like someone inferior, almost as a kind of object for an experiment. But perhaps it was for this very reason that I loved him so much and in such a helpless and submissive fashion.

Sometimes, though, he seemed to hate not only his own family and his own milieu, but all mankind. One day he remarked—I cannot remember in what connection: "The rich are appalling, but the poor certainly aren't any better, if for different reasons."

"You'd be a bit nearer the mark, if you admitted frankly that you hate all mankind without exception."

He began to laugh. "In the abstract," he replied, "when I'm not among them I don't hate them; at least, I hate them so little that I believe in their progress. If I didn't believe this I wouldn't trouble myself with politics. But when I'm among them they horrify me. Really," he added sadly, "mankind is worthless."

"We're people, too," I said, "and therefore we're worthless, too, and therefore we have no right to judge."

He laughed again. "I don't judge them," he replied. "I smell them—or rather, I sniff them—like a dog sniffs the scent of a partridge or a hare. But does the dog judge them? I sniff them and I find they're malicious, stupid, selfish, petty, vulgar, deceitful, shameful, full of filth, I smell them. It's a feeling; but we can't suppress feelings, can we?"

I did not know what to reply and contented myself with saying: "I haven't got that feeling."

On another occasion he spoke to me in the following manner. "Men may be good, or bad, I don't know—but in any case they're certainly useless, superfluous——"

"What do you mean?"

"I mean that the whole of mankind could very well be wiped out. It's only an ugly excrescence on the face of the

303

earth—a wart. The world would be far more beautiful without mankind, their cities, streets, ports, all their little arrangements. Think how beautiful the world would be if there were nothing but sky, sea, trees, earth, animals."

I could not help laughing. "What queer ideas you have!" I exclaimed.

"Mankind," he continued, "has neither a beginning nor an end—it's something decidedly negative, therefore. The history of mankind is nothing but one long yawn of sheer boredom. What need is there of it? Speaking for myself—I'd have done very well without it."

"But you're part of mankind yourself," I objected. "Would you have done without yourself, then?"

"Especially without myself."

Chastity was another of his obsessions, all the more singular in that he did not try to practise it and the idea served only to spoil his pleasure. He sang its praises continually, especially just after we had made love, as if out of pique. He used to say lovemaking was only the silliest and easiest way of shelving all questions, by forcing them out below, secretly, without anyone noticing, like embarrassing guests shown out by the back-door. "Then, when the operation has been performed, you go out for a stroll with your accomplice, wife or mistress as the case may be, wondrously disposed to accept the world as it is, even the worst of all possible worlds."

"I don't understand you," I said.

"And yet you ought to understand this, at least," he said, "isn't it your speciality?"

I felt offended. "My speciality, as you call it," I said, "is to love you. But if you like we won't make love any more—I'll love you all the same."

He laughed. "Are you quite sure?" he asked; and that day we argued no more. But he came back to the same things repeatedly; so that in the end I took no further notice, but accepted this as I did so many other traits in his contradictory character.

He never talked to me about politics, though, except for an occasional reference. Even today I have no idea what he was aiming at, what were his ideas, what party he belonged to. My ignorance is partly due to his secretiveness over this aspect of his life, and partly to the fact that I understood nothing about politics and my shyness and indifference prevented my asking him for all the explanations which might have enlightened me. I was wrong; and God knows I regretted it later on. But at the time I thought it was very convenient not to be involved in things I believed were no concern of mine, and to think only of love. I behaved, in fact, like so many other women, wives and mistresses, who often do not even know how their men earn the money they bring home. Quite often I met his two companions, whom he used to see almost every day. But they did not mention politics in my presence; they either joked or talked of indifferent matters.

And yet I was unable to shake off a constant feeling of apprehension, because I realised that plotting against the government was dangerous. What I feared most was that Mino might be drawn into some act of violence; in my ignorance I was unable to separate the idea of a plot from that of weapons and blood. In this connection I must relate a fact which shows to what extent I felt it was my duty, however dimly, to intervene in order to ward off the dangers that threatened. I knew that the carrying of arms was illegal; and a man might be sentenced to gaol merely for carrying arms without a permit. On the other hand, it is extremely easy to lose one's head at certain times, and the use of arms has often compromised people who otherwise would have got off scot-free. For all these reasons I thought that the pistol Mino was so proud to own was not only quite unnecessary, but was positively dangerous, for he might be obliged to use it or it might be discovered on him. But I did not dare to mention it to him, because I realised it would have been quite fruitless. In the end I decided to act secretly. On one occasion he had explained to me how the weapon worked. One day while he was asleep I took the pistol from his trouser pocket, pulled out the magazine and removed the bullets. Then I closed it again and replaced it in his pocket. I hid the bullets in a drawer underneath my lingerie. I did all this in an instant and then went to sleep again beside him. Two days later I put the bullets into my handbag and went to throw them into the Tiber.

One of these days Astarita came to see me. I had almost forgotten him; and as far as the matter of the maid went, I believed I had done my duty and I did not want to think any more about it. Astarita told me the priest had delivered the compact to the police and that the owner, on the advice of the police themselves, had withdrawn her accusation and the maid had been set free without a stain on her character. I must admit that this news delighted me, especially since it dispelled the feeling of foreboding I had had ever since my last confession. I thought nothing of the maid who had been set free at last, but only of Mino and told myself that now, since there was no further danger of the denunciation I had anticipated, I had nothing more to fear for either of us. In my delight I could not help embracing Astarita.

"Were you so very keen on getting that woman out of gaol, then?" he asked me with a doubtful expression.

"It may seem strange to you," I lied, "who send so many innocent people to gaol every day with the lightest of hearts—but it was real agony to me."

"I don't send anyone to gaol," he muttered, "I only do my duty."

"Did you see the priest yourself?" I asked him.

"No, I didn't see him; I rang up. They told me the compact had in fact been given up by a priest who had received it under the seal of the confessional. So then I recommended her liberation."

I remained pensive; I did not know why myself.

"Do you really love me?" I then asked him.

This question put him into a state immediately and he embraced me. "Why do you ask me?" he stammered. "You ought to know by now."

He wanted to kiss me but I avoided him. "I wanted to know," I said, "because I wonder whether you'll always help me—every time I ask you—as you did this time."

"Always," he replied, shuddering all over. "But you'll be kind to me?" he said, putting his face up to mine.

Now I had decided after Mino had returned to me that I

306

would not have anything more to do with Astarita. He was different from my usual fleeting lovers; and although I did not love him and indeed felt a positive aversion for him at times, perhaps for this very reason I felt that giving myself to him would be a betrayal of Mino. I was tempted to tell him the truth—" No, I shall never be kind to you "—but then I suddenly changed my mind and controlled myself. I remembered what power he had, how Giacomo might be arrested at any time, and if I wanted Astarita to intervene to free him it was unwise to irritate him. I resigned myself therefore. " Yes, I'll be kind to you," I whispered.

" Tell me," he insisted, feeling emboldened, " tell me—do you love me a little ? "

" No, I don't love you," I said frankly, " and you know it —I've already told you so time and again."

" Won't you ever love me ? "

" I don't think so."

" But why ? "

" There isn't any reason."

" You love someone else."

" This can be of no interest to you."

" But I need your love," he said in despair, looking at me with his bilious eyes. " Why, why won't you love me a little ? "

That time I allowed him to remain with me until late into the night. He was inconsolable because of my inability to love him and seemed quite unconvinced of the truth of what I said. " But I'm no worse than other men," he protested, " why couldn't you love me instead of someone else ? " Really, I felt quite sorry for him; and since he insisted on questioning me about my feelings for him and on trying to find some fuel for his hopes in my replies, I felt almost tempted to lie to him, if only to give him the illusion he longed for. I noticed that he was more mournful and disgusted that evening than he usually was. It was as though he wanted his gestures and attitudes to awaken in me, from without, the love my heart denied him. I remember that at a certain moment he requested me to sit naked in an armchair. He knelt down in front of me and put his head in my lap, crushing

307

his face against my belly and remaining motionless like this for some time. Meanwhile I had to stroke his head again and again with a light, incessant caress of the hand. This was not the first time he had obliged me to perform a kind of mimicry of love; but he seemed more desperate that day than usual. He pressed his head violently into my lap as if he wanted to enter into me and be swallowed up, and groaned occasionally. At such times he no longer seemed like a lover, but rather a baby seeking the warmth and darkness of his mother's lap. And the thought occurred to me that many men would have preferred never to have been born; and that this movement of his unconsciously expressed that dim longing to be engulfed once more in the shadowy vitals from which he had been painfully expelled into the light.

That night he remained kneeling so long that I became drowsy and fell asleep, with my head flung back against the chair, my hand resting on his head. I do not know how long I slept, and at a certain moment I woke up and caught a glimpse of Astarita, who was no longer kneeling at my feet but was seated in front of me, already dressed, and was gazing at me with his mournful, bilious eyes. But perhaps it was only a dream, or an hallucination. The fact is that I suddenly awoke in earnest and found that Astarita had gone, leaving the usual sum of money in my lap where he had lain his head.

About a fortnight passed, and these were among the happiest days in my life. I saw Mino almost every day and although there was no change in our relationship yet I contented myself with the kind of habit we had established, which seemed at last a common ground between us. It was silently taken for granted between us that he did not love me, that he never would love me, and that in any case he would always have preferred chastity to love. It was equally taken for granted that I loved him, that I always would love him despite his indifference to me, and that in any case I preferred a love like that, incomplete and wavering though it might be, to any other love. I am not made like Astarita; and having once resigned myself to the fact that I was not loved I found much pleasure all the same in loving. At the bottom of my heart perhaps I nursed a hope that my submissiveness, patience and affection might one day make him love me. But I did nothing to encourage this hope; and it was, more than anything else, the rather bitter condiment to his uncertain, grudging caresses.

But I certainly did all I could to enter unobtrusively into his life, and since I could not do so by the main door I exercised my ingenuity in trying to enter by the back door. Despite his explicit and I believe sincere hatred of mankind some curious contradiction gave him an irresistible impulse to preach and act in support of what he thought was for the good of mankind. This impulse was almost always checked by sudden regrets and sarcastic disgust, certainly, but it was sincere. At that time he appeared to become passionately heated over what he ironically referred to as my education. As I have said, I tried to bind him to me and therefore I favoured this inclination of his. But the experiment ended almost immediately in a way I think it worth while recalling. He came to see me for several evenings running and brought some books of his with him. After he had explained briefly what the subject was he began to read a passage here and there. He read well, with a great variety of expression in his voice according to the subject-matter, and with a passion that made him flush and gave his features an unusual animation. But I was unable to understand what he read however hard I tried; and I soon gave up listening to him and contented myself with watching the different expressions that flitted across his face while he was reading, a pleasure I never tired of. During these readings he really abandoned himself completely without any fear or irony, like someone in his own element who is no longer afraid of showing his sincerity. This fact struck me, because until then I had always thought that love, not literature, was the most favourable condition in which the human soul could blossom. Apparently in Mino's case the opposite was true; certainly I never, not even in his rare moments of affection, saw such enthusiasm and candour in his face as there was when, raising his voice in curiously hollow tones or lowering it to the level of conversation, he read me passages from his favourite authors.

At such times he entirely lost his air of theatrical, burlesque artificiality, which never left him even in his most serious moments, and gave the impression that he was always acting a superficial, premeditated part. I even saw his eyes fill with tears, quite often. Then he shut the book. " Did you like it ? " he asked me abruptly.

I usually answered that I had liked it, without specifying why, a thing I would have been unable to do because, as I have said, from the very outset I gave up all effort to grasp the meaning of such obscure stuff. But one day he insisted. " Tell me why you liked it," he said, " explain why."

" To tell you the truth," I replied after a moment's hesitation, " I can't explain because I didn't understand a word."

" Why didn't you tell me ? "

" I didn't understand anything—or only very little—of what you were reading."

" And you let me go on reading without warning me ! "

" I saw you enjoyed reading and I didn't want to spoil your pleasure—but in any case, I'm never bored—you're very amusing to watch while you're reading."

He leapt to his feet in a rage. " What the deuce ! You're a fool, an idiot. Here am I, wasting my breath— you're a half-wit ! " He looked as though he were going to fling the book at me but controlled himself in time and continued to insult me in this way for a good while. I allowed him to let off steam for some time and then spoke. " You want to educate me," I said, " but the first condition for my education would be to free me of the necessity of earning my living as I do—I certainly don't need to read poetry or reflections about morality in order to attract men. I might even be quite incapable of reading or writing but they'd pay me all the same."

" You'd like to have a lovely house, a husband, children, clothes, a car, wouldn't you ? " he said sarcastically. " The trouble is that not even the Lobianco women read—for different reasons from yours but no less justifiable, from their point of view."

" I don't know what I'd like," I said peevishly, " but these books don't suit my condition of life. It's like giving a beggar a most expensive hat and expecting her to wear it with her usual rags."

"Maybe," he said, "but this is the last time I'll ever read you a line."

I have mentioned this slight tiff because it is so characteristic of his way of thinking and behaving. I doubt whether he would have continued in his effort to educate me, even if I had not confessed my inability to understand him. It was not only his inconsistency that made me think this, but also his singular inability to persist in any effort which demanded sincere, sustained enthusiasm; this inability was probably physical in origin. He never spoke of it in so many words, but I realised that the burlesque quality his words expressed often corresponded in fact to a spiritual condition. He got worked up, as it were, over any aim and as long as the fire of his enthusiasm lasted he saw that aim as something concrete and attainable. Then suddenly the fire died down and all he felt was boredom, disgust and above all a sensation of utter absurdity. Then he either abandoned himself to a kind of dull, inert indifference, or acted in a conventional and superficial way, as if the fire had never died down—in one word, he pretended. I find it rather difficult to explain what happened to him in such a conjuncture—it was probably a sharp interruption in his vitality, as if the heat of his blood had suddenly cooled, leaving only an arid void in his mind. It was an immediate interruption, complete and unforeseeable, comparable only to the interruption of an electric current, which plunges a house into sudden darkness that only a moment earlier had been gaily illuminated; or to a motor when every little wheel ceases to move and remains still, on the sudden cessation of electric power. This constant ebb and flow of his deepest vitality was first revealed to me by the frequent alternation in him of states of ardour and enthusiasm with others of apathy and inertia; but in the end it was shown to me fully by a curious incident to which I attributed little importance at the time being, but which later appeared highly significant.

"Would you like to do something for us?" he asked me one day, quite unexpectedly.

" For whom ? "

" For our group. Help us distribute our leaflets, for instance ? "

I was always on the alert for anything that might bring me nearer to him and strengthen our bonds.

" Of course," I replied sincerely ; " tell me what I have to do and I'll do it."

" Aren't you afraid ? "

" Why should I be ? If you do it——"

" Yes, but first I must explain what it's all about," he said. " First of all you have to understand the ideas for which you run such a risk."

" Explain them, then."

" But you're not interested."

" Why ? I'm sure to be interested—and then, everything you do interests me, if only because you do it."

He looked at me and suddenly his eyes sparkled and his cheeks grew flushed in a most unexpected manner. " Very well," he said hurriedly, " it's too late today—but I'll explain everything tomorrow—myself, since books bore you. But mind, it'll be a long business, and you'll have to listen and follow me—even if you think you don't understand sometimes."

" I'll try to understand," I said.

" You ought to," he replied, as if speaking to himself. And he left me.

Next day I waited for him but he did not come. Two days later he arrived and as soon as he was in my room he sat down on the armchair at the foot of the bed without saying a word.

" Well," I said gaily, " I'm ready—I'm listening."

I had noticed his downcast expression, his dull eyes, and his flagging, exhausted manner, but I did not want to remark on it.

" It's no good listening," he said at last, " because you won't hear anything."

" Why ? "

" Because."

" Now tell me the truth," I protested. " You think I'm

too stupid or too ignorant to be able to understand certain things, don't you? Thanks!"

"No, you're wrong," he said seriously.

"Why, then?"

We continued like this for some time, with me insisting on knowing why and he refusing to explain. "Do you really want to know why?" he said at last. "Because I wouldn't know how to express these ideas to you, myself, now."

"Why not?—since you think about them all the time!"

"I do think about them the whole time, I know. But since yesterday, and the Lord knows how long I'll feel like this, those same ideas have become incomprehensible to me, and to tell you the truth, I don't understand a thing."

"You don't mean what you're saying!"

"Try to understand," he said. "Two days ago, when I suggested that you should work for us, I'm quite sure that if I had explained our ideas to you I'd have done it vigorously, clearly and persuasively, and you'd have understood them perfectly. But today I might pronounce certain series of words with my tongue and my lips, but it would be quite mechanical, something I had no share in. Today," he repeated, emphasising each syllable as he spoke, "I don't understand a thing."

"You don't understand a thing?"

"No, I don't understand a thing. Ideas, concepts, facts, memories, convictions, everything has been transformed into a kind of mass—a mass which fills my head—" he tapped his forehead with his fingers—"my whole head—and disgusts me as if it were excreta."

I looked at him in puzzled suspense. A quiver of exasperation seemed to run through him at this.

"Try to understand," he cried, "today everything seems incomprehensible. Not only ideas, but even anything written or said or thought, it all seems absurd. For instance, do you know the Lord's Prayer?"

"Yes."

"Say it, then."

"Our Father, Who art in Heaven," I began.

"That'll do," he interrupted. "Now just think how many ways this prayer has been said during the centuries, with how many different emotions! Well, I don't understand it at all, in any way. You might say it backwards, it'd be all the same to me."

He was silent for a moment. "But it isn't only words that have this effect on me," he continued, "but things, too—people. There are you sitting on the arm of this chair beside me, and perhaps you think I can see you? But I don't see you because I can't understand you—I might even touch you and not understand you all the same—I will touch you, in fact"—as he spoke he pulled my dressing-gown and uncovered my breast, as if he were seized by a sudden frenzy. "I touch your breast—feel its shape, warmth, form, see its colour, its outline. But I don't understand what it is. I say to myself: here's a round, warm, soft, white, swelling object, with a little, round, dark knob in the middle—which gives milk and gives pleasure if it is caressed. But I don't understand a thing. I tell myself it's beautiful, that it ought to fill me with desire, but I still don't understand a thing. Do you see what I mean, now?" he repeated furiously, clutching my breast so hard that I could not repress a little cry of pain. He let me go at once. "Probably," he observed reflectively after a moment, "it's just this kind of incomprehension that makes so many people cruel. They are trying to find contact with reality through other people's pain."

Silence followed. Then I spoke. "If this is true, how do you manage when you have to do certain things?"

"What, for instance?"

"I don't know—you tell me to distribute your leaflets—and that you write them yourself. But if you don't believe in it how can you write them and distribute them?"

He burst into a fit of sarcastic laughter. "I behave as if I did believe."

"But that's impossible."

"Why impossible? Almost everyone does it, except in the case of eating, drinking, sleeping and love-making.

Almost everyone does things as if they believed in them. Hadn't you noticed that ? "

He laughed nervously.

" I don't," I replied.

" You don't," he replied, almost insultingly, " because you content yourself with eating, drinking, sleeping and love-making whenever you feel like it. It isn't necessary to pretend in these things, I believe—which is already saying a great deal. But at the same time, it's not much." He laughed, suddenly slapped me hard on the thigh and then took me into his arms, as he usually did. " Don't you know this is the world of ' as if ' ? " he said, squeezing me and shaking me. " Don't you know that everyone, from the king to the meanest beggar, behaves ' as if '—it's the world of ' as if, as if, as if '."

I let him have his way because I knew that at such moments it was better not to be offended or to protest but to wait for his ill-humour to die down. But at last I said firmly : " I love you—that's the only thing I know and it's enough for me."

" You're right," he said simply, suddenly growing calm again. The evening finished in the usual way, without our speaking any further about politics or his incapacity to discuss the question.

When I was alone again I concluded after much reflection that perhaps things were as he said ; but that it was far more likely that he was unwilling to talk to me about politics because he thought I might not understand and also because he was probably afraid I might compromise him through some carelessness of mine. Not that I thought he was lying ; but I knew from experience that a day comes in everybody's life when the world seems to fall to pieces, or, as he said, when you do not understand a thing, not even the Lord's Prayer. I, too, when I was ill or in a bad-temper for some reason, had experienced more or less the same sensation of boredom, disgust and dullness. There must obviously be some other motive behind his refusal to let me share his most secret life ; mistrust, as I have said, either of my intelligence or of my discretion. I realised too late that I had been

315

mistaken, and that in his case such morbid states of mind assumed a special gravity, either through his youthful inexperience or weakness of character.

But at the time I thought it would be wiser to retreat and not pester him with my curiosity; and I did so.

CHAPTER EIGHT

I do not know why, but I remember perfectly even the weather we were having at that time. February had come and gone, cold and rainy, and with March began the first milder days. A close network of white gossamer clouds veiled the whole sky and dazzled the eyes as soon as one stepped from the darkness of the house into the street. The air was mild but still quite numbed from the rigours of the winter. I walked along in that drowsy, tenuous and half-awakened light with stupefied pleasure, and every now and again slackened my pace and closed my eyes; or stood still in amazement to gaze at the most insignificant things: a black and white cat licking itself on a doorstep, a hanging branch of oleander shrivelled by the wind but which perhaps would flower all the same, a tuft of green grass springing up between the slabs of a pavement. The moss which the rain of the past months had sprinkled along the interstices at the base of the houses filled me with a deep sense of peace and trust: I thought that if such lovely emerald velvet could flourish in the sparse soil between the jagged edges of bricks and cobble-stones, then my life, which had roots no deeper than those of wood-moss and which also throve on the most meagre nourishment and was really nothing more than a kind of lichen growing at the foot of a building, had perhaps some likelihood of continuing and flourishing. I was convinced that all the unpleasant matters of the immediate past were now settled once and for all; that I would never see Sonzogno again or hear his crime mentioned; and that from now on I could peacefully enjoy my relationship with Mino. And with these thoughts I seemed to taste to the full the real savour of life for the first time, composed as it was of tempered boredom, opportunity and hope.

I even began to see opening up before me some possibility of changing my way of life. At heart my love for Mino made me cold towards other men, and therefore I no longer had the incentive of curiosity and sensuality in my casual affairs. But I also thought that one way of life was as good as another, and that it was not worth while making much of an effort to change, and that I would only do so if I acquired new habits, affections and interests and became quite a different girl from what I had been so far, but without any abrupt shock or interruption, merely through the effect of circumstances and independently of my own will. I saw no other means of changing my way of life; for the time being I was not at all ambitious for material success and progress, and I did not think that by changing my mode of life I would be able to better myself in any way.

One day I imparted these ideas to Mino. "I think you're contradicting yourself, aren't you?" he said, after listening to me attentively. "Aren't you always saying you'd like to be rich, have a fine house, a husband and children? It's quite right that you should, and you may still have them some day—but you never will if you go on thinking in that way."

"I didn't say I'd like them," I replied, "but that I would have liked them—that is to say, if I could have chosen before I was born I certainly wouldn't have chosen to be what I am. But I was born in this house, with this mother, in these conditions, and after all, I am what I am."

"And that is?"

"That is, it seems silly to me to long to be another person. I'd long to be another person only if I could continue to be myself at the same time; that is to say, if I could really delight in the change, but it isn't worth while being a different person just for the sake of change."

"It's always worth while," he said under his breath, "if not for yourself, then for other people."

"And then," I continued without noticing his interruption, "the facts are what matter most. Do you think I could not have found a rich lover like Gisella? Or even have got married? If I haven't it means that at heart, despite all my talk, I didn't really want to."

"I'll marry you," he exclaimed embracing me playfully; "I'm rich—when my grandmother dies, which won't be long now, I'll inherit acres and acres of land, not to mention a villa in the country and a flat in town. We'll set up house properly, you'll invite the ladies of the district to your ' at homes ', we'll have a cook, a parlourmaid, a one-horse carriage or a car. One day we might even, with a little effort, discover that we're of noble birth and be called count or marquis——"

"It's impossible to have a serious conversation with you," I said, pushing him away. "You make a joke of everything."

One afternoon I went to the cinema with Mino. On our way back we got into a crowded tram. Mino was to come home with me and we were to dine together at a tavern near the walls. He took the tickets and made his way ahead through the crowd that packed the gangway. I tried to keep close to him but lost sight of him when the crowd lurched forward. While I was looking for him, standing crushed against one of the seats, I felt someone touch my hand. I lowered my eyes and there, seated right below me, was Sonzogno.

I gasped, felt myself grow pale and my expression change. He was looking at me with his usual intolerable stare. Then, half-rising in his seat he spoke to me between clenched teeth. "Do you want to sit down?" he asked me.

"Thanks," I stammered. "I'm getting down soon."

"Sit down."

"Thanks," I repeated, and sat down. If I had not done so perhaps I would have fainted.

He remained standing beside me, as if he were keeping guard over me, holding on to the back of my seat and the one in front with both hands. He had not changed in the least; he was still wearing the same waterproof coat with a tight belt, his jaw still twitched in the same mechanical way. I closed my eyes and tried momentarily to put my thoughts in order. It was true that he had always looked like that, but this time I thought I saw a harder expression in his eyes. I remembered my confession and it occurred to me that if the priest had spoken, as I believed he must have done, and Sonzogno had come to know of it, my life wasn't worth much.

This thought did not frighten me. But he, as he stood there stiffly beside me, did frighten me indeed—or rather, he fascinated me and dominated me. I felt I could refuse him nothing, and that there was a bond between us far stronger than the bond between myself and Mino, although it was not love. He, too, must have felt it instinctively and his whole attitude to me was one of masterfulness. "Let's go to your place," he said to me after a while.

"If you like," I replied docilely without the slightest hesitation.

Mino came up, making his way with some difficulty through the crowd and stood just beside Sonzogno, clinging on to the same seat as he did and actually brushing Sonzogno's thick, short fingers with his own long, slim ones. The tram gave a jerk and they were thrown against one another and Mino politely begged Sonzogno's pardon for having knocked into him. I began to feel upset at seeing them together, so close and yet so unknown to one another, and I suddenly turned to Mino deliberately in such a way that Sonzogno would not think I was addressing him. "Look, I've just remembered I've got an appointment with someone for this evening— it'd be better to say good-bye now."

"If you like I'll see you home."

"No—I'm being met at the tram-stop."

This was nothing new. I still took men home and Mino knew it. "As you like," he said calmly, "I'll see you tomorrow, then." I nodded in agreement and he went off through the crowd.

As I watched him making his way among the people I was overcome for a moment by an attack of violent despair. I thought I was seeing him for the last time, but not even I knew why I had this impression. "Good-bye," I murmured to myself, as I followed him with my eyes, "Farewell, love." I wanted to cry out to him to stop, to turn back, but my voice

319

stuck in my throat. The tram stopped and I thought I could see him getting down. The tram started off again.

During the whole journey Sonzogno and I kept silent. I felt calmer now and told myself the priest could not possibly have spoken. On the other hand, I did not really regret having met him, after I had thought the matter over for some time. In this way I would get rid of my doubts once and for all concerning the results of my confession.

I stood up at the tram-stop, left the tram and walked on a little without looking back. Sonzogno was beside me and I could see him if I turned my head slightly. "What do you want with me?" I asked him at last. "Why have you come back?"

"You told me to come again yourself!" he said with a touch of astonishment.

This was true; but in my terror I had forgotten it. He came up close to me and took my arm, gripping it tight and almost holding me up. I began to tremble all over despite myself.

"Who was that?" he asked.

"A friend of mine."

"Have you seen anything more of Gino?"

"Never."

He looked around him rapidly. "I don't know why, but I've had a queer feeling lately that I'm being followed. There are only two people who could have given me away, you and Gino."

"Why Gino?" I asked in a whisper. But my heart had begun to beat violently.

"He knew I was going to take that thing to the jeweller's, I'd even told him the name. He doesn't exactly know I killed him, but he could easily have guessed it."

"Gino hasn't anything to gain by giving you away—he'd be giving himself away, too."

"That's what I think," he muttered.

"As for me," I went on in my calmest voice, "you may be sure I've said nothing. I'm not a fool—I'd be arrested, too."

"I hope so, for your own sake," he replied threateningly.

"I saw Gino for a moment," he then added; "he told me by

way of a joke that he knew a whole heap of things. I don't feel easy in my mind. He's a bad lot."

"You treated him very rough that evening, and of course he hates you now," I said. I realised while I was speaking that I almost hoped Gino had really given him away.

"It was a beauty," he said with grim vanity. "My hand hurt for two days afterwards."

"Gino won't denounce you," I concluded, "it wouldn't suit his book. Besides, he's too frightened of you."

We were walking along without looking at one another as we spoke, our voices lowered. It was twilight, a bluish mist enveloped the dark walls, the white branches of the plane-trees, the yellowish houses, the distant view of the main road. As we reached the street door I felt for the first time that I was actually being unfaithful to Mino. I had wanted to delude myself into thinking that Sonzogno was only one of many men; but I knew this was not true. I entered the courtyard, pulled the door to behind me, and there in the dark I stood still and turned towards Sonzogno.

"Look here," I said, "you'd better go away."

"Why?"

I wanted to tell him the whole truth, despite the fear that possessed me. "Because I love another man and don't want to be unfaithful to him."

"Who is it? The man who was with you in the tram?"

I was afraid on Mino's account. "No, someone else," I replied hastily, "you don't know him. And now please, do leave me—go away."

"Suppose I don't want to go away?"

"But don't you understand that there are some things you can't get by force?" I began. But I was unable to finish. I do not know how it happened, but without seeing him or his movements in the dark I suddenly felt him give me a terrible blow on my cheek with the back of his hand. "Get along," he said.

I hurried upstairs with my head bent low. He had seized me by the arm again and supported me on every step. I felt almost as if he raised me off the ground and that I was flying. My cheek was smarting; but what dismayed me most of all was a sensation of grim foreboding. This blow, I felt, had interrupted the happy rhythm of recent days and once more the difficulties and fears of the past were about to return. I was filled with utter desperation and decided on the spot to fly from the fate I foresaw. I would run away from home that very day, I would go somewhere else, either to Gisella's or some furnished room.

I was thinking so intently about all these things that I hardly noticed I was in the flat, and had passed through the outer room into my own. I found myself—I might almost say I awoke to find myself—seated on the edge of the bed, while Sonzogno was removing his clothes one by one and placing them methodically on a chair with the precise, self-satisfied gestures of an essentially tidy person. He had quite recovered from his fit of rage. " I would have come before," he said calmly, " but I couldn't. I've been thinking about you all the time, though."

" What were you thinking about me ? " I asked mechanically.

" That we're made for each other," and he stood up, holding his waistcoat in his hand. " In fact," he added in a strange tone of voice, " I came to make you a proposal."

" What ? "

" I've got some money. Let's go to Milan together, where I've got several friends. I want to start up a garage. And we could get married in Milan."

I felt as if I were melting inside and such a sensation of weakness overcame me that I closed my eyes. This was the first time, since Gino, that anyone had proposed marriage to me, and it was Sonzogno who made this proposal. I had longed so intensely for a normal life, with a husband and children, and now it was being offered to me—but with the normality reduced to a kind of empty covering, inside which everything would be abnormal and terrifying. " But why ? " I said feebly. " We hardly know one another, you've only seen me once———"

He sat beside me and put his arm round my waist. " No one knows me better than you do," he said ; " you know everything about me."

It occurred to me that he was probably deeply stirred and

wanted to show me that he loved me and that I ought to love him. But this was only imagination on my part, for nothing in his behaviour warranted the assumption.

"I know nothing about you," I said in a low voice, "I only know that you killed that man."

"And then," he said, speaking as if to himself, "I'm so tired of living alone. When you live alone, you end by doing something crazy."

After a moment's silence I spoke again. "I can't say yes or no point-blank like this," I said. "Give me time to think it over."

"Think it over, do," he said to my astonishment. "There's no hurry." Then he left my side and continued undressing.

I had been struck chiefly by the phrase; 'We're made for each other,' and I now asked myself whether he was right, after all. What could I hope for now but a man like him? And was it not true that a hidden bond, which I recognised and feared, existed between us? I found I was repeating submissively to myself the words, 'Run away, run away,' and was shaking my head despondently.

"Did you say go to Milan?" I said in a clear voice, and my mouth was full of saliva. "Aren't you afraid they'll be on the look-out for you?"

"I only said that for the sake of something to say. Actually no one even knows of my existence."

The weakness which made my limbs as heavy as lead suddenly vanished and I felt strong and determined. I stood up, took off my coat and went to hang it on the coat-hanger. As usual I turned the key in the lock and then walked slowly over to the window to close the shutters. Then, standing straight up in front of the mirror, I started to unbutton my blouse, beginning at the hem. But I stopped almost immediately and turned towards Sonzogno. He was sitting on the edge of the bed and was bending over to untie his shoe-laces. "Just a minute," I said with assumed casualness, "someone was supposed to be coming this evening, I must go and warn mother to send him away." He made no reply, had not even time to do so. I left the room, closing the door behind me, and went into the living-room.

Mother was at the sewing-machine near the window. She had taken up her work again some little time before in order to relieve the monotony of her existence. " Ring me up at Gisella's or at Zelinda's," I said hurriedly, under my breath. " Tomorrow morning——" Zelinda was a woman who hired out rooms in the centre of the town ; I used to go there sometimes with my lovers, and mother knew her.

" Why ? "

" I'm going out," I said. " When that man in there asks after me tell him you don't know where I am."

Mother sat there gaping at me while she removed a hook from a worn old fur jacket that had been mine years before.

" Above all, don't tell him where I've gone," I added. " He'd murder me."

" But——"

" The money's in the usual place . . . Take care, then . . . don't tell him anything and ring me up tomorrow." I went out hurriedly, crossed the hall on tiptoe and began to go downstairs.

When I was in the street I began to run. I knew that Mino was at home at that time and I wanted to reach him before he went out with his friends after supper. I ran as far as the square, took a taxi, gave Mino's address. While the taxi sped along, I suddenly knew that I was fleeing not so much from Sonzogno as from myself, for the good reason that I felt myself to be attracted by his strength and violence in some obscure way. I remembered the piercing cry of mingled horror and delight he had wrung from me the first and only time he had possessed me, and I told myself that on that day he had conquered me once and for all, as no other man had since known how, not even Mino. Yes, I could not help concluding, we really were made for one another ; but simply in the way a body may be said to be made for the precipice that causes its head to spin dizzily, and its eyes to become misted until finally it is dragged down towards the giddy depths.

I climbed the stairs two at a time, arrived out of breath, and gave Mino's name to the elderly parlourmaid who came to open the door.

She looked at me as if scared out of her wits ; then, without a single word she hurried away, leaving me on the threshold.

I thought she had gone to tell Mino, so I went into the hall and closed the door.

Then I heard a kind of whispering behind the curtain that separated the hall from the passage. The curtain was raised and the widow Medolaghi appeared. I had forgotten her entirely since the first and only time I had ever seen her. Her heavy, black figure, her white, deathly face with the black mask of her eyes, filled me with a sense of terror as she rose up before me, it was as if I were in the presence of some frightening apparition. She halted at some distance from me and addressed me.

" Did you want Signor Diodati ? "

" Yes."

" He's been arrested."

I did not understand at first, for some unknown reason I imagined his arrest was connected in some way with Sonzogno's crime. " Arrested ! " I stammered. " But he's got nothing to do with it."

" I know nothing about it," she said. " I only know they came here, searched the house and arrested him." I understood from her expression of disgust that she would not tell me anything.

" But why ? " I could not help asking her.

" Signorina, I've already told you I don't know anything."

" Where did they take him ? "

" I don't know anything."

" But tell me at least whether he left any message."

This time she did not even reply, but turning away in stiff and offended majesty called out : " Diomira ! "

The old parlourmaid with the scared look reappeared.

Her mistress pointed to the door, and said, as she raised the curtain and turned to go, " Show the young lady out," and the curtain fell back into its accustomed position.

Only after I had gone downstairs and was out in the street did I realise that Mino's arrest and Sonzogno's crime were two separate facts, independent of one another. The only link between them in fact was my own fear. This unexpected flood of misfortunes was proof to me of the lavishness of destiny which poured out all her tragic gifts for me at one and the same time; just as a good season makes all kinds of different fruits ripen together. It is a fact that trouble never comes single-handed, as the proverb says. I felt this, rather than thought it, as I walked from one street to the next, with my head and shoulders bowed under a kind of shower of imaginary hailstones.

Naturally the first person I thought of turning to was Astarita. I knew the phone number of his office by heart, went into the first café I came across and rang him. His number was disengaged but no one replied. I rang several times and at last became convinced that Astarita was absent. He must have gone out to supper and would be back later. I knew all this, but I had hoped that this time I would find him in, as an exception to the rule.

I looked up at a clock. It was eight o'clock in the evening and Astarita would not be back in his office before ten. I came to a halt on a corner of the street. The curved surface of a bridge lay before me, with its unending flow of foot-passengers, alone or in groups, and they rushed towards me, dark and hurrying, like dead leaves driven by a ceaseless wind. The rows of houses beyond the bridge created an impression of peace with all their gleaming windows and people moving up and down among the tables and other furniture. It occurred to me that I was not very far away from the central police-station where I imagined Mino must have been taken, and although I knew it was a desperate undertaking I decided to go straight there to ask for news of him. I knew in advance that I would not obtain any; but that did not matter, I wanted to feel that I was doing something for him.

I followed the side-streets, keeping close to the walls, reached the police-station, mounted the steps and entered. A policeman who was leaning back on a chair in the porter's lodge reading a newspaper, with his feet on another chair and his cap on the table, asked me where I was going. "Aliens' Office," I replied. This was one of the many departments at the police-station and I had heard Astarita refer to it on one occasion, I do not remember why.

I did not know where I was going, but I began to climb at random up the dirty, badly-lit staircase. I kept on running into clerks or uniformed policemen who were going upstairs or coming down, their hands full of papers, and I kept close to the wall on the darkest side with my head bent. On every landing I had a glimpse of low, dark, dirty passages with people moving to and fro, scanty lighting, open doors, for room after room. The police-station seemed to be like some kind of an extremely busy bee-hive, but the bees who inhabited it certainly did not alight on flowers, and their honey, of which I was tasting the flavour for the first time in my life, was rank and black and most bitter. When I reached the third floor I felt so desperate that I chose one of the passages hap-hazard. No one looked at me, no one troubled about me. Door after door, mostly open, stood on each side of the corridor and uniformed policemen were sitting in the door-ways on straw-bottomed chairs, smoking and chatting. The view inside each room was always the same—shelf upon shelf of files, a table, and a policeman seated behind the table with a pen in his hand. The corridor was not straight but curved slightly so that after a short time I had lost my way. Every now and again it led down into a lower passage and I had to descend three or four steps—or else it crossed other corridors that were identical in every particular, with their lights, their rows of open doors and policemen seated in the doorways. I felt bewildered, at a certain moment I had the impression that I was retracing my own steps and was following a corridor I had already traversed once. A messenger passed by, so I asked him for the chief constable and without speaking he pointed to a dark passage nearby, between two doors. I went towards it, descended four steps and entered a low and ex-tremely narrow little corridor. At the same moment a door opened at the end, where this kind of entrail of a corridor formed a right-angle, and two men appeared; they were walking away from me towards the corner. One of them was holding the other by the wrist and for a moment I thought it was Mino. " Mino ! " I cried, and hurled myself forward.

I did not manage to reach them because someone seized me by the arm. It was a young policeman with a thin, dark face,

327

his cap perched sideways on his mass of curly, black hair. "Who do you want? Who are you looking for?" he asked me.

The two men had turned at my cry and I could see I was mistaken. "They've arrested my friend," I panted. "I wanted to know whether he's been brought here."

"What's his name?" asked the policeman without letting me go, with an air of peremptory authority.

"Giacomo Diodati."

"What does he do?"

"He's a student."

"When was he arrested?"

I suddenly realised he was questioning me in this way to give himself an air of importance and that he knew nothing. "Instead of asking me so many questions," I replied angrily, "tell me where he is."

We were alone in the corridor. He looked round and then pressing close to me whispered in a fatuous tone of understanding: "We'll see to the student—but give me a kiss in the meantime."

"Let me go! Don't waste my time!" I shouted furiously. I pushed him away, ran off, entered another corridor, saw an open door and beyond the door a larger room than the others, with a desk at the end where a man was seated. I went in. "I want to know where Diodati, the student, has been taken—he was arrested this afternoon," I said, without pausing to get my breath.

The man raised his eyes from his desk where a newspaper lay open before him and looked at me in astonishment. "You want to know——"

"Yes, where Diodati the student, who was arrested this afternoon, has been taken."

"But who are you? Who let you in?"

"That's none of your business—just tell me where he is."

"Who are you?" he shouted, and hammered with his fist on the table. "How dare you? Do you know where you are?"

I suddenly realised that I would learn nothing and that I was in danger of being arrested myself, and then I would be unable to talk to Astarita and Mino would not be set free. "It doesn't matter," I said, withdrawing. "I made a mistake —I beg your pardon."

My apologies made him even more furious than the questions which had preceded them. But by now I was near the door. "You make the Fascist salute on entering and leaving this room," he cried, as he pointed to a notice which hung above his head. I nodded as if in agreement—it was quite true, one ought to enter and leave the room with the Fascist salute; and I left the room, retreating backwards. I crossed the whole length of the corridor, wandered about for some time, and at last, having chanced upon the staircase, I hurried down it. I passed the porter's lodge and came out into the open once more.

The only result of my visit to the police-station was that it had helped the time to pass. I reckoned that if I were to walk very slowly towards Astarita's Ministry it would take me about three-quarters of an hour, or even an hour. When I got there I could sit in a café near the Ministry and ring up Astarita after about twenty minutes, in the hope of finding him in.

While I was walking along, it occurred to me that Mino's arrest might be a kind of revenge on Astarita's part. He held an important post in the branch of the political police force which had arrested Mino; obviously they must have been keeping an eye on Mino for some time and knew of my relations with him; it was not at all unlikely that the papers had passed through Astarita's hands and that he had given orders for Mino's arrest out of jealousy. At this thought a kind of rage against Astarita overwhelmed me. I knew he was still in love with me and I felt quite capable of making him pay bitterly for his cruel deed if my suspicions turned out to be well-founded. But at the same time I realised with a sense of misgiving that perhaps this was not the case and that I was preparing, with my feeble weapons, to fight a hidden foe who had no features and whose properties were rather those of an ingenious mechanism than of a sensitive man swayed by his emotions.

When I reached the Ministry I gave up the idea of going to sit in a café and went straight to the telephone. This time someone lifted the receiver as soon as the bell started to ring and it was Astarita's voice that answered me.

" It's Adriana," I said impetuously, " and I want to see you."

" At once ? "

" Yes, immediately, it's urgent. I'm down here outside the Ministry."

He paused to think for a moment, then said I could come. This was the second time I had climbed the stairs in Astarita's Ministry ; but I now did so in a very different state of mind from the first time. The first time I had been afraid Astarita might blackmail me, afraid that he might upset my marriage with Gino, afraid of the vague threat all poor people feel hanging over them where the police are concerned. I had gone there with a tremulous heart, a quivering spirit. Now, on the contrary, I was going there in an aggressive mood, with the idea of blackmailing Astarita in my turn, determined to use every means in my power to have Mino freed. But my aggressiveness could not be explained only by my love for Mino. My scorn for Astarita formed part of it, too—for his Ministry, for political matters and for Mino himself inasmuch as he troubled himself with politics. I understood nothing at all about politics, but perhaps it was my very ignorance that made politics seem a ridiculous, unimportant matter compared with my love for Mino. I remembered the way Astarita's speech was impeded by his stammer every time he saw me, or even when he only heard my voice, and I thought complacently that he certainly did not stammer when he faced one of his chiefs, even if it was Mussolini himself. With these thoughts in my mind I hurried along the huge corridors of the Ministry and noticed I was looking scornfully at all the clerks I happened to meet. I longed to snatch the red and green folders they were carrying and throw them away, to scatter to the winds all their papers full of prohibitions and iniquity. " I have to speak to Dr. Astarita at once—I have an appointment and can't wait," I said imperiously to the usher who came towards me in the ante-room. He looked at me in amazement but did not dare to protest and went to announce me.

As soon as Astarita saw me he hurried forward, kissed my

330

hand and led me towards a divan at the end of the room. This was the way he had greeted me the first time, too, and I suppose it was the way he behaved to all the women who came to his office. I restrained the impulse of anger that I felt swelling within me. "Look," I said, "if you've had Mino arrested—have him set free at once. Otherwise you'll never see me again."

An expression of profound astonishment mixed with some unpleasant afterthought was painted on his face, and I realised he knew nothing about the whole matter. "Just a moment—what on earth !—What Mino ?" he stuttered.

"I thought you knew about it," I said. And then I told him as shortly as possible the whole story of my love for Mino and how he had been arrested that afternoon. I saw him change colour when I said I loved Mino, but I preferred to tell him the truth, not only because I was afraid of harming Mino if I lied but also because I longed to proclaim my love for Mino to the whole world. Now, after having discovered that Astarita had had nothing to do with Mino's arrest, the rage which had kept me going so far had died down, and once more I felt utterly weak and disarmed. For this reason I began my tale in a firm, excited voice and ended almost in tears. In fact my eyes were overflowing. "I don't know what they'll do to him," I said in anguish. "He says they beat them."

Astarita interrupted me immediately. "Don't worry. If he were a working man—but since he's a student——"

"But I don't want him to be shut up !" I cried tearfully.

Then we were silent. I tried to master my emotion and Astarita looked at me. For the first time he seemed reluctant to do me the favour I was asking him. But his unwillingness to satisfy me must have been due in part to his disappointment at finding that I was in love with another man. "If you get him out," I said, as I placed my hand over his, "I promise I'll do anything you want."

He looked at me irresolutely and although my heart was not in it I bent forward and offered him my lips. "Well—will you do me this favour ?" I asked.

He gazed at me, torn between the temptation to kiss me

and the consciousness of the humiliation of a kiss offered by a tear-stained face as a mere bribe. Then he pushed me away, leapt to his feet, told me to wait and disappeared.

I was certain now that Astarita would have Mino freed. I was so inexperienced in these matters that I imagined Astarita telephoning in angry tones to a servile warder and telling him to free Giacomo Diodati immediately. I counted the minutes impatiently, and as Astarita re-appeared I rose to my feet, thinking I would thank him and then hurry away to meet Mino.

But there was a singularly unpleasant expression on Astarita's face, a mixture of disappointment and malicious anger. "What do you mean by saying he's been arrested?" he said shortly. "He fired on the police and ran off—one of the policemen is dying in hospital. If they catch him now, as they most certainly will, I can't do anything for him."

I stood there gasping with astonishment. I remembered I had removed the bullets from the revolver—but of course, he might have re-loaded it without my knowing. Then, on second thoughts, I was filled with joy and my joy was due to different emotions, as I realised at once. There was the joy of knowing Mino was free; the joy, too, of knowing he had killed a policeman, which was an action I had thought him incapable of performing and which profoundly modified the idea I had had of him until that moment. I wondered at the aggressive, urgent force with which my heart, usually so opposed to all forms of violence, applauded Mino's desperate action; it really was the same kind of irresistible pleasure I had felt when I had reconstructed Sonzogno's crime in my own mind, but this time it was accompanied by a form of moral justification. Then I began to think how I would soon discover where he was and we would run away and hide together; we might even go abroad where I knew political refugees were welcomed; and my heart swelled with hope. I also imagined that perhaps a new life was really about to begin for me, and I told myself that I owed this renewal of my life to Mino and his courage and I was filled with gratitude and love for him. Meanwhile Astarita was pacing furiously up and down the room, stopping from time to time only to shift some object on his desk. " Obviously he took his courage in both hands after he was arrested," I said calmly, " so he fired and made off."

Astarita stood still and looked at me, twisting his face into an ugly grimace. " You're glad, aren't you ? " he said.

" He was right in killing the policeman," I said sincerely, " since he was trying to carry him off to gaol—you'd have done the same yourself."

" I've nothing to do with politics," he answered unpleasantly, " and the policeman was only doing his duty, he had a wife and children."

" If Mino busies himself with politics he must have his own good reasons for it," I replied, " and the policeman might have known that, rather than let himself be carried off to gaol, a man will do anything. So much the worse for him. . . ."

I felt peaceful at heart because I imagined I could see Mino going freely about the streets of the city, and I was enjoying in anticipation the moment when he would summon me from his hiding-place and I would see him again. Astarita seemed to lose all his self-control at the sight of my calm. " But we'll find him," he cried, " do you think we shan't be able to ? "

" I don't know anything about that. I'm glad he got away, that's all."

" We'll find him and then he may be sure he won't get away with it so easily."

" Do you know why you're so angry ? " I asked him after a moment.

" I'm not at all angry."

" Because you hoped he'd been arrested so that you could show off your generosity to me and to him—and instead he slipped out of your hands. And that makes you angry."

I saw him shrug his shoulders furiously. Then the telephone rang and Astarita lifted the receiver with the air of relief of a person who has succeeded in finding some excuse for breaking off an embarrassing discussion. At the very first words his face, like a landscape gradually illuminated by a sudden ray of sunshine on a stormy day, changed from grim annoyance to a more serene expression ; and I interpreted this as a bad sign, though I could not say why. The call was a lengthy one, but Astarita never said anything except yes or no, so that I could not tell what the discussion was about. " I'm sorry for your sake," he said as he hung up the receiver, " but the first report about that student's arrest was wrong. Police headquarters had sent their men both to his house and to yours, in order to make absolutely sure of him, and in fact they did arrest him in the widow's house where he rented a room. But they found someone else at your place, a short, fair man with a Northern accent who, as soon as he saw them shot at them and escaped instead of showing his papers as they asked. It was obviously someone who had an account to settle with the police."

I felt faint. So Mino was in gaol; and Sonzogno was convinced I had denounced him. Anyone, seeing me disappear and then seeing the police arrive immediately afterwards, would have thought the same. Mino was in gaol and Sonzogno was looking for me in order to wreak his revenge upon me. I was so dazed that I could only murmur: " Oh dear, oh dear," as I made towards the door.

I must have gone very pale because Astarita immediately lost his triumphant, sullen look of satisfaction and came up to me. " Sit down," he said anxiously, " let's talk it over—nothing is irrevocable."

I shook my head and put my hand out to the door. Astarita stopped me. " Look here," he stammered, " I promise you I'll do all I can. I'll question him myself—and then, if there's nothing serious I'll have him set free as soon as possible. Is that all right ? "

" Yes, that's all right," I said dully. " Whatever you do," I added with an effort, " you know I'll be grateful."

I knew by now that Astarita really would do all that lay in his power to free Mino, as he had said. And I had only one desire,—to go away, to leave his dreadful Ministry as quickly as I could. But he was addressing me again with professional anxiety. " By the way—if you have any reason to fear that man they found at your place—tell me his name. That'll make it easier for us to lay our hands on him."

" I don't know his name," I said, and made as if to leave.

" In any case," he insisted, " you'd better go of your own

334

accord to the commissioner of police. Tell him what you know—they'll tell you to keep yourself at their disposal and then they'll let you go. But if you don't go it'll be worse for you."

I replied that I would and said good-bye. He did not close the door at once but stood watching me from the doorway while I went across the ante-room.

CHAPTER NINE

Once I was outside the Ministry I walked hastily to the nearest piazza, as if I was running away. Only when I had reached the middle of the square did I realise that I had no idea where to go and I began to wonder where I could take shelter. At first I had thought of Gisella; but her house was a long way off and my legs were giving way under me through sheer exhaustion. On the other hand, I was not at all sure that Gisella would be willing to take me in. Zelinda, the lodging-house keeper whom I had mentioned to my mother on my way out, was the only other solution. She was a friend of mine, and, besides, her house was near at hand; I decided to call on her.

Zelinda lived in a yellowish building, one of many of the same kind, situated on the station square. This house of Zelinda's was remarkable, among many other particulars, in that it had a staircase that was immersed, even in the mornings, in an all but impenetrable obscurity. There was no lift, there were no windows, and as you climbed up in almost total darkness you were liable to bump into the shadowy form of anyone who was coming down while clinging to the same handrail. A perpetual stench of cooking poisoned the air; but it was cooking that might have been done years before, the various odours of which had been decomposing in the dank and chilly air. My legs trembled, I was sick at heart as I mounted the stairs that I had climbed so often before, followed closely by some impatient lover. "I want a room . . . for the night," I said to Zelinda, who came to open the door.

Zelinda was a stout woman, no more than middle-aged, perhaps, but looking old beyond her years on account of her fatness. For all her corpulence, her blotchy unhealthy cheeks, her dull bleary blue eyes, and her scant fair hair, which was always dishevelled and fell in rat's-tails as if made of tow, she still retained, above all in her features, some signs of graceful charm, just as some lingering rays are still reflected in unruffled water some time after the sun has gone down. "I've got a room," she said. "Are you alone?"

"Yes, I'm alone."

I went in and she closed the door. She stumbled along in front of me, broad and dumpy, in her old dressing-gown, with her knot of hair hanging down half-undone on her shoulders, and all her hairpins sticking out. The flat was as chilly and dark as the stairway. But here the smell was of recent cooking and conjured up a vision of good and clean food being prepared at that very moment. "I was just getting supper," she explained, turning round and smiling at me. Zelinda, who let out rooms by the hour, was fond of me, I did not know why. She often kept me there after my usual visits, chatting and offering me sweets and liqueurs. She was unmarried and probably no one had ever been in love with her, because she had been deformed by her stoutness ever since childhood—her virgin state could be deduced from the shyness, curiosity and clumsiness with which she questioned me about my affairs. I imagine that since she was utterly lacking in envy and malice she regretted in her heart that she had never done what she knew was being done in her rooms; and her occupation as a landlady letting rooms by the hour satisfied not so much her business sense as her unconscious desire not to feel entirely excluded from the forbidden paradise of love-affairs.

There were two doors that were extremely familiar to me at the end of the corridor. Zelinda opened the left-hand one and preceded me into the room. She lit the three-branched lamp with its glass tulip bulbs and went to close the shutters. It was a large, clean room. But the cleanliness seemed to throw into pitiless relief the poor condition of the furnishings— the threadbare carpets by the bed, the darns in the cotton coverlet, the coruscating mirrors, the chips on the jug and basin. She came towards me. " Don't you feel well ? " she asked me as she looked at me.

" I feel quite well."

" Why don't you sleep at your own place ? "

" I didn't want to."

" Let's see if I can guess what's the matter," she said with a fond, knowing air. " You've had a disappointment—you were expecting someone and he didn't turn up."

" Perhaps——"

" And let's see if I'm right this time, too—it was that dark, young officer you came with last time."

This was not the first time that Zelinda had asked me questions of this kind. " You're quite right—and then ? " I replied, almost choking with anguish.

" Oh nothing—but you see, I understand you at once ! I guessed what was the matter immediately. But you mustn't be upset—if he didn't come, he must have had some reason for it. Soldiers aren't their own masters, you know——"

I did not reply. She looked at me for a moment. Then she addressed me again in her fond, hesitant, coaxing voice. " Do you want to keep me company at supper ? There's something nice."

" No thanks," I replied hastily. " I've already eaten."

She looked at me once again and gave me a little tap on the cheek in place of a caress. " Now I'll give you something you won't refuse," she then said, with the promising, mysterious expression of an old aunt talking to a young boy, some young nephew. She pulled a bunch of keys out of her pocket, went over to the chest-of-drawers and opened one of the drawers with her back to me.

I had undone my coat and now, leaning against the table with one hand on my hip, I watched Zelinda rummaging about in the bottom of the drawer. I remembered that Gisella often came to that room with her men-friends and I remembered Zelinda did not like Gisella. She liked me for myself and not because she liked everyone. I felt consoled. After all, I thought, there was something else in the world besides police, ministries, prisons and other such cruel, heartless things. Meanwhile Zelinda had finished rummaging in her drawer.

337

She shut it carefully and came over to me, repeating: "Here, you certainly won't refuse this," and put something down on the mat on the table. I looked and saw five cigarettes, good ones, gold-tipped, a handful of sweets wrapped in coloured papers and four little coloured fruits made of almond-paste. "Is that all right?" she asked, giving me another little pat on the cheek.

"That's fine, thanks," I stammered in embarrassment.

"Don't mention it, don't mention it—if you need anything, just call me, don't be afraid."

When I was alone once more I felt chilled to the marrow and in a state of great indecision. I was not sleepy and I did not want to go to bed; but in that cold room, where the chill of winter seemed to have been preserved for years as it is in churches and cellars, there was nothing else to do. I had never had to face this problem on the other occasions when I had come there—both the man accompanying me and I myself longed only to get beneath the sheets and warm one another; and although I had no fondness for those pickup lovers, nevertheless the act of love itself absorbed me and overwhelmed me in its spell. It now seemed incredible to me that I had made love and had been made love to among such squalid furniture, in such a chill atmosphere. The ardour of the senses must certainly have created an illusion for me and my companions each time, making those ridiculously alien objects both pleasant and familiar. It occurred to me that my life, if I were never to see Mino again, would be just like this room. If I looked back at my life objectively without any illusions, I saw that it contained nothing beautiful or intimate, indeed, it was entirely made up of ugly, worn, chilly things, like Zelinda's room. I shuddered and began to undress slowly.

The sheets were icy and seemed clammy with dampness; I had the impression when I stretched myself in the bed that I was imprinting the shape of my body on wet clay. For a long time I remained lost in thought while the sheets gradually grew warmer. I went off on a side-track thinking about Sonzogno and analysing the motives and the consequences of all that obscure business. Sonzogno certainly believed by now that I had betrayed him and appearances were all against

338

me. But only the appearances? I remembered his phrase: 'I've a queer feeling I'm being followed,' and I asked myself whether the priest had talked, after all. It did not seem likely, but so far nothing went to show that he had not.

With my mind still on Sonzogno I began to imagine to myself what must have happened at home after I had left. I imagined Sonzogno waiting, getting impatient, dressing, the entrance of the two policemen, Sonzogno pulling out his gun, shooting without warning and running away. These imaginary pictures of what had occurred caused me an obscure, insatiable sense of pleasure, as they had done when I had reconstructed Sonzogno's crime. Time and again I went over the scene of the shooting, dwelt lovingly on all the details; and undoubtedly in the struggle between Sonzogno and the police I was heart and soul on Sonzogno's side. I trembled with joy at seeing the wounded policeman fall to the ground, I heaved a sigh of relief when Sonzogno escaped, I followed him anxiously down the stairs, my peace of mind was restored only when I saw him disappear in the darkness of the distant main road. At last I grew tired of this kind of mental cinema, and put out the light.

I had already noticed on other occasions that the bed stood against a door that communicated with the next room. As soon as I had put out the light I saw that the two halves of the door did not meet properly and a ray of light shone through the gap. I pulled myself up on to the pillows on my elbows, slipped my head between the iron decorations at the end of the bed and peeped through the slit. I did not do this out of curiosity, since I already knew what I would see and hear through the slit, but I was afraid of my thoughts and my loneliness, and my fear led me to seek for companionship in the next room even if I could do so only by eavesdropping. But for some time I could see no one at all—there was a round table in front of the slit in the door and the light from the chandelier poured down on to the table, beyond which I caught a glimpse of a wardrobe-mirror gleaming in deep shadow. But I could hear voices—the usual talk that was so familiar to me, about one's home town, one's age and name. The woman's voice was calm and reserved, the man's hurried and excited. They were talking in some corner of the room, perhaps they were already in bed. I began to have an acute pain in my neck through gazing so long without seeing anything and I was about to turn away when the woman appeared beyond the table, in front of the dim mirror. Her back was towards me; she stood up straight, naked, but visible only from the waist upwards, because the table hindered my view. She must have been very young; her back, under her mane of curly hair, was thin, hard, ungraceful, and of an anæmic whiteness. She was probably not even twenty years old, but her bosom was flaccid and probably she had already had a child. She must be one of those half-starving young girls, I thought, who hang around the clumps of trees near the station, hatless and often coatless, badly painted and ragged, their feet thrust into enormous wedge-shoes. When she laughed she must show her gums, I thought. All these things occurred to me quite spontaneously, without reflecting, because the sight of that miserable, naked back comforted me and I felt I loved her and understood only too well the feelings she was experiencing at that moment while looking at herself in the mirror. But the man's voice called out roughly: "What on earth are you up to?" and she left the mirror. For a moment I saw her sideways, with her bent shoulders and scraggy chest, just as I had imagined her. Then she vanished and a second later the light was extinguished.

The vague affection I had felt for the girl while I could see her was extinguished, too, and I found myself all alone once more in the great, cold bed, in that darkness filled with worn, chilly objects. I thought of the two of them there on the other side of the wall: they would fall asleep together in a short while, and she would lie at her companion's back with her chin resting on his shoulder, her legs entwined in his, her arm round his waist, her hand on his groin and her fingers falling languidly across his belly—like roots seeking for nourishment in the deepest earth—and I suddenly felt I was like an uprooted plant myself, thrown out upon a smooth paving-stone where I would wither and die. I missed Mino; and if I stretched out my hand I became conscious of an enormous, empty, frozen space that surrounded me on all sides, while I lay there huddled up in the middle without any protection or companionship. My longing to embrace him was painfully acute, but he was not there, and I felt widowed and began to weep with my arm underneath the sheets, pretending to myself that I was holding him. At last I fell asleep, I know not how.

I have always slept well and deeply, sleep for me is like an appetite, easily satisfied without any particular effort or interruption. So when I awoke next morning I was almost surprised to find myself in Zelinda's room, stretched out in that bed, in a ray of sunshine that slipped through the shutters and fell on to the pillow and the wall. I had hardly realised where I was when I heard the phone ring in the corridor. Zelinda answered, I heard her say my name and then she knocked at the door. I leapt out of bed and ran to the door as I was, in my nightdress, with bare feet.

The passage was empty, the receiver lay on a ledge, Zelinda had gone back into the kitchen. I heard mother's voice at the other end of the line.

" Is that you, Adriana ? "

" Yes."

" What made you go away ? . . . If you only knew what's been happening here ! . . . You might have warned me. . . . I've had such a scare ! "

" Yes, I know all about it," I said hurriedly. " It's no good talking about it."

" I was so worried about you," she went on, " and then there's Signor Diodati."

" Signor Diodati ? "

" Yes, he came along very early this morning . . . he wants to see you very urgently . . . he says he'll wait here."

" Tell him I'll be along at once. Tell him I'll be there in a minute or two."

I hung up the receiver, ran into my room and dressed as quickly as I could. I had not even hoped for Mino to be set free so quickly and I felt less happy than I would have done if I had waited for his liberation for a few days or a week. I mistrusted such a speedy release, and I could not help feeling vaguely apprehensive. Every fact has a meaning, and I was unable to grasp the meaning of that rapid return to freedom. But I calmed down when I thought that possibly Astarita had managed to have him set free immediately as he had promised. In any case, I was impatient to see him again, and my impatience was a pleasant sensation, although it was also rather painful.

I finished dressing, put the cigarettes, sweets and almond-paste into my bag so as not to hurt Zelinda's feelings, since I had not touched them the evening before, and went into the kitchen to say good-bye to her.

"Feeling more cheerful?" she asked. "Got over your bad mood?"

"I was feeling tired. Bye-bye for the present."

"Now, now! Do you think I didn't hear you on the telephone? Signor Diodati, eh? Here, wait a minute—have a cup of coffee——" She was still talking when I was already out of the flat.

Perched on the edge of the seat in the taxi, with my hands gripping my bag, I was quite ready to leap out as soon as it stopped; I was afraid I would find a crowd in front of the house on account of Sonzogno's shooting. I wondered whether I was wise in going home—Sonzogno might turn up to revenge himself upon me—but I realised I did not care. If Sonzogno wanted to take his revenge on me he could, I longed to see Mino and was determined I would never hide myself for something I had not done.

I met no one at the street door, no one on the stairs. I rushed into the living-room and saw mother sitting at the sewing-machine by the window. The sun struggled in through the dirty window-panes, the cat was sitting on the table licking its paws. Mother stopped sewing immediately. "So there you are!" she exclaimed. "You might at least have told me you'd gone out to get the police!"

"What police? What on earth do you mean?"

"I'd have gone with you—if you only knew how frightened I was."

"I didn't go out to get the police," I protested angrily. "I went out, that's all. The police were looking for someone else. This man must have had something on his conscience."

342

"So you won't even tell me," she said, looking at me reproachfully.

"Tell you what?"

"I won't go and gossip. But you'll never get me to believe you went out for nothing. The police came a few minutes after you'd left."

"But it isn't true, I——"

"You were quite right, anyway. There are some dreadful people about. Do you know what one of the policemen said? 'I've seen that face before,' he said."

I saw that there was no way of convincing her; she thought I had gone out on purpose to denounce Sonzogno and there was nothing more to be said about it. "All right, all right," I interrupted her brusquely. "What about the wounded man? How did they take him away?"

"What wounded man?"

"I was told a man was dying——"

"No, no, they told you wrong. One of the policemen got his arm grazed by a bullet. I bandaged it for him myself. But he went away quite all right. Still, if you'd heard the shots! They were shooting on the stairs. The whole house was in an uproar. Then they questioned me, but I said I knew nothing about it."

"Where is Signor Diodati?"

"In your room."

I had lingered with mother for a little while because I now felt almost reluctant to go to Mino, as though I foresaw some bad news. I left the living-room and went towards my own room. It was plunged in darkness, but even before I put my hand out to the switch I heard Mino's voice. "Please don't put the light on," he said.

The peculiar tone of his voice struck me; it did not sound at all cheerful. I shut the door, groped my way to the bed, sat down on the edge of it. I could feel he was lying on his side near me. "Don't you feel well?" I asked him.

"Perfectly well."

"Aren't you tired?"

"No, I'm not tired."

343

I had expected quite a different kind of meeting. But it is a fact that joy and light are inseparable. In the dark like that my eyes seemed unable to sparkle, my voice was incapable of breaking into exclamations of joy, my hands could not recognise his beloved features. I waited for some time. "What do you want to do?" I then asked him as I bent towards him. "Do you want to go to sleep?"

"No."

"Do you want me to go away?"

"No."

"Do you want me to stay here beside you?"

"Yes."

"Do you want me to lie on the bed?"

"Yes."

"Do you want to make love?" I asked casually.

"Yes."

This reply was a surprise to me, because as I have already said he never really felt inclined to love me. I suddenly felt myself growing excited. "Do you like to make love to me?" I asked him affectionately.

"Yes."

"Will you always like it from now on?"

"Yes."

"Shall we always be together?"

"Yes."

"Don't you want me to put the light on?"

"No."

"It doesn't matter, I'll get undressed in the dark."

I began to undress with the intoxicating sensation of having won a complete victory. I imagined that the night he had spent in prison had unexpectedly shown him that he loved me and needed me. I was wrong, as I shall relate; and although I was right in thinking that there was a connection between his arrest and his unexpected submissiveness I did not understand that the change in his attitude had nothing flattering or even encouraging for me in it. But on the other hand, I could not very well have been more clear-sighted at that moment. My body urged me impetuously towards him, like a horse that has been curbed too long, and I was impatient to give him the ardent, joyous welcome his attitude and the dark-ness had prevented me giving him earlier.

But when I drew close to him and bent over the bed to stretch myself beside him, I suddenly felt him grip my knees with his arms and then bite me savagely on the left hip. I felt an acute spasm of pain while at the same time I realised absolutely that the bite expressed some indefinable despair he was experiencing; it was as though we were two cursed souls driven by hatred, rage and sadness to bury our teeth in one another's flesh in the depths of some new hell, rather than two lovers about to make love. It seemed an endless bite, it was as though he wanted to tear out a piece of my flesh with his teeth. At last, although I half wanted him to bite me and his biting gave me a feeling of pleasure, while at the same time I sensed that there was little love in it, I could not stand the pain any longer and I pushed him away. "No, no," I said in a humble, broken voice, "what are you doing? You're hurting me. . . ."

And so my illusion of victory came to an end. After this we said not one word more all the time we were making love; but nevertheless I was able from his behaviour to guess dimly at the real meaning of his abandonment, which he later ex-plained to me in detail. I understood that until that moment he had wanted not so much to ignore me as to ignore that part of himself which desired me; now, on the contrary, he gave this part of himself free rein, whereas hitherto he had fought against it—that was all. I had nothing to do with it, and he no more loved me now than he had done before. It was all the same to him whether he had me or another girl. I was nothing more than a means he adopted to punish or reward himself. I was not so much conscious of thinking these things while we lay in the dark together, as of feeling them in my flesh and my blood, just as some time before I had sensed the fact that Sonzogno was a monster although I had known nothing of his crime. But I loved him; and my love was stronger than my knowledge.

But nevertheless I was amazed at the violence and indefatig-able quality of his desire, which had once been so grudging. I had always thought that he restrained himself for reasons of health, since he was delicate. Therefore, when he began all over again after he had already made love to me I could not help whispering to him : "Do as you like, as far as I'm concerned—but mind it doesn't hurt you."

I believe he laughed. "Nothing can ever hurt me now," he murmured in my ear.

That 'ever' gave me a ghastly sensation and therefore the pleasure I felt in his embraces was almost completely obliterated, and I waited impatiently for the moment when I could talk to him and find out what had actually happened. After we had finished making love he seemed to drop off but perhaps he did not really fall to sleep. I waited for a reasonable length of time before speaking to him. "And now tell me what happened," I said in a low voice, with an effort which made my heart miss a beat.

"Nothing happened."

"But something must have happened."

He was silent for a moment and then spoke as if to himself. "I suppose you'll have to know, too. Well, this is what happened. At eleven o'clock yesterday evening I became a traitor."

An icy chill gripped me at these words, not so much on account of the words themselves as for the tone in which he uttered them. "A traitor ? " I stammered. "Why ? "

The tone of his reply was cold and grimly humorous. "Il signor Mino, among the comrades of like political faith, was known for the intransigence of his opinions and the violence of his reactions. Il signor Mino was considered by them to be cut out for their future leader. . . . Il signor Mino was so sure that he would do himself credit in any circumstances that he almost hoped he would be arrested and put to the test . . . because, you see, il signor Mino thought that arrest and imprisonment and other sufferings of that kind are an essential part of the life of a political man, just as long cruises, hurricanes and shipwrecks form part of the life of a sailor. But at the first heavy seas the sailor felt as sick as the most wretched little school-girl ! Il signor Mino no sooner found himself in the presence of an ordinary little policeman, than he blurted out everything without even waiting to be threatened

346

or tortured . . . in fact—he's a traitor. . . . So from yesterday il signor Mino said good-bye to his political career and entered upon that of—shall we say—informer ? "

" You were afraid ! " I exclaimed.

" No," he answered immediately. " Perhaps I wasn't even afraid. Only the same thing happened to me as happened that evening I was with you—when you wanted me to explain my ideas to you. They suddenly didn't seem to matter at all. I took a kind of liking to the man who was questioning me. He wanted to know certain things ; I didn't trouble at the moment to conceal them from him and I told him them. Quite simply, like I'm talking to you now—or rather," he added after a moment's thought, " not so simply—carefully, hurriedly, eagerly you might say. A little more, and he would have had to moderate my enthusiasm ! "

I thought of Astarita and I found it queer that Mino should have taken a liking to him. " Who questioned you ? " I asked.

" I don't know. A very well-dressed young man, with a sallow face, bald head, dark eyes. He must have been one of the high-ups."

" And you liked him ! " I could not help exclaiming, since I recognised Astarita from the description.

Mino began to laugh in the dark with his mouth on my ear. " Come, come ! Not him personally, but his job. You know—when you give up being what you know you ought to be, or don't even know what you ought to be, what you really are comes to the surface. Aren't I the son of a rich landowner ? And wasn't that man protecting my interests, in the light of his job ? We recognised that we belonged to the same kind, that we were really united in the same cause. What did you think ? That I liked him for himself ? No, no, I liked the job he had—I realised that it was I who was paying him to do what he did, it was I who defended him, I who stood behind him as his master even though I stood facing him in the position of an accused man."

He laughed, or rather gave a coughing sort of laugh which grated horribly on my ears. I only realised that something very tragic had happened and that my whole life was once

347

more in question. " But perhaps I'm doing myself an injustice," he added after a moment. " Perhaps I only talked because it didn't matter to me whether I did or not—because everything suddenly seemed absurd and unimportant and I didn't understand any of the things I ought to have believed in."

" You didn't understand ? " I repeated mechanically.

" No, or rather—I only understood the words themselves, but not the facts underlying them. Now how can you suffer for mere words ? Words are sounds, it would have been like going to prison for the braying of an ass or the creaking of a wheel. The words I heard had no value, they seemed all alike and worthless, he wanted words and I gave him them, as many as he wanted."

" Well then," I could not help objecting, " since they were only words what does it matter ? "

" Yes, but unfortunately, as soon as I'd pronounced them they ceased to be mere words and became facts."

" Why ? "

" Because I began to suffer. Because I was sorry I had said them. Because I realised, I felt, that in saying them I had become myself that fact which is known by the word traitor."

" But why did you talk, then ? "

" Why do people talk in their sleep ? " he said slowly. " Perhaps I was asleep. But now I've woken up."

And so he went round and round but always returned to the same point. I felt pierced to the heart. " But perhaps you're mistaken," I said with an effort. " You think you said all sorts of things—but actually you didn't say a thing."

" No, I'm not mistaken," he said briefly.

I was silent for a moment. " What about your friends ? " I then asked him.

" What friends ? "

" Tullio and Tommaso."

" I don't know anything about them," he said, deliberately assuming an air of indifference. " They'll be arrested."

" No, they won't ! " I exclaimed. I thought Astarita certainly would not take advantage of Mino's momentary

348

weakness. But at the idea of their being arrested the gravity of the whole matter began to dawn upon me.

"Why not?" he said. "I gave their names. There's no reason why they shouldn't be arrested."

"Oh, Mino," I could not help exclaiming painfully. "Why did you do it?"

"That's what I keep on asking myself."

"But if they aren't arrested," I went on after a moment, clinging to the only hope I had left, "it isn't so desperate. They'll never know that you——"

"But I know it!" he interrupted me. "I'll always know it. I'll always know that I'm not the same person as I was but someone else, someone I have given birth to as surely as a mother gives birth to her child. But unfortunately, it's not a person I like. That's the trouble. Some men kill their wives because they can't bear to live with them. Now just imagine what it must be like to be two people in one body, when one of them hates the other like death. Anyway, as far as my friends are concerned they're sure to be arrested."

I could not restrain myself any longer. "Even if you'd never spoken," I said, " you'd have been released all the same. And your friends aren't in any danger." Then I hurriedly told him the story of my relationship with Astarita, my intervention on his behalf, and Astarita's promise. He listened to me in silence. "Better and better!" he said at last. "So I don't owe my release to my eagerness as an informer, but to your love-affair with a policeman."

"Don't talk like that, Mino!"

"But anyway," he added after a moment, "I'm glad my friends will get off lightly—at least I shan't have this on my conscience."

"Look," I said eagerly, " what's the difference between you and your friends? They owe their freedom to me, too, and to the fact that Astarita's in love with me."

"I beg your pardon! There is a difference! They haven't talked."

"How do you know?"

"I hope not, for their sakes. But in any case it doesn't help at all to be in the same boat."

"But you've only got to behave as if nothing had happened," I insisted again. "Go and see them, without saying anything. What does it matter to you? Anyone might have a moment's weakness like that."

"Yes," he replied, "but not everyone dies and yet is obliged to go on living. Do you know what happened to me in that instant when I spoke? I died—just died. Died for ever."

I could no longer bear the anguish which wrung my heart and I burst into tears. "Why are you crying?" he asked.

"Because of what you're saying," I answered, sobbing harder than ever. "That you're dead. I'm so frightened."

"Don't you like being with a dead man?" he asked jokingly. "It's not as dreadful as it seems. In fact, it isn't at all dreadful. I died in a very special way. My body's quite alive still. Feel if I'm not alive," and he took my hand, made me feel him. "You can feel I'm alive." He pulled my hand, made me press it against him, pulled it down to his groin, crushed it against his penis. "I'm alive all over. And as far as you're concerned, I'm more alive than ever I was. Don't be scared, if we didn't make love very much while I was alive, we'll make up for it thoroughly now I'm dead."

He flung my lifeless hand away from him with a kind of angry disdain. I put both hands to my face and sobbed out my wretchedness noisily. I wanted to cry for ever, to go on crying endlessly, because I was afraid of the moment when I would stop weeping and would be left empty, dazed, and still confronted by the same unchanged situation which had provoked my outburst. But the moment came, however, and I dried my wet face with the sheet and stared into the darkness with wide-open eyes. Then I heard him address me in a gentle, affectionate voice. "Let's see what you think I ought to do," he asked.

I turned round violently, clung to him as hard as I could and spoke with my mouth on his. "Don't think any more about it. Don't worry about it any more. What's done's done. That's what you ought to do."

"And then?"

"And then begin studying again. Take your degree.

350

And after that go back to your own home-town. I don't mind if I don't see you again as long as I know you're happy. Begin to work, when the time comes marry a girl from that part of the world, who loves you, a girl of your own class. What have you got to do with politics? You weren't made for politics, you were wrong ever to take it up. It was a mistake, but everyone makes mistakes. One day you'll think it extraordinary that you ever bothered your head about it all. I really do love you, Mino, another woman in my place wouldn't want to leave you, but if it's necessary, go away tomorrow, if you think it's necessary we'll never meet again. As long as you're happy——"

"But I'll never be happy again," he said in a clear, deep voice. "I'm an informer."

"It's not true!" I answered in exasperation, "you're not an informer at all. And even if you were, you could be happy all the same! There are heaps of people who have even committed crimes and yet they're perfectly happy. Take me, for example. When people talk of a street-walker the Lord only knows what they imagine. But I'm a woman like all the rest, and I'm often happy. I was so happy these last few days," I added bitterly.

"You were happy?"

"Yes, very. But I knew it couldn't last, and in fact "— at these words I felt like crying again, but I controlled myself —" you imagined yourself as something quite different from what you are," I added, "and then we know what happened. Now you must accept yourself as you really are, and everything will fall into place. What's making you so unhappy over what happened is the fact that you feel ashamed, and are afraid of what other people, your friends, will think. Give up seeing them, then, see other people, the world's a big place! If they aren't fond enough of you to understand it was only a moment's weakness, stay with me. I love you and understand you and don't sit in judgment on you— really!" I exclaimed forcefully at this stage. "Even if you had done something a thousand times worse you'd still be my Mino."

He kept silent. "I'm only a poor, ignorant girl, I know,"

I went on, "but I understand some things better than your friends and better even than you. I've had just the same feeling as you have now. The first time we met and you didn't touch me I got it into my head that it was because you despised me, and I suddenly lost all desire to go on living, I felt so unhappy. I wanted to be someone else and at the same time I realised that was impossible and that I'd have to go on being what I was. I felt a sticky, burning kind of shame, despair, heartsickness, I felt shrivelled, frozen, bound hand and foot. I even wanted to die, or so I thought at times. Then one day I went out with mother and we happened to go into a church and there, as I prayed, I felt I understood that at heart I had nothing to be ashamed of, if I was made as I was, it meant it was the will of God, I ought not to rebel against my fate but accept it submissively and trustfully, and if you despised me it was your fault and not mine. In fact, I thought a great many things and at last my humiliation passed over and I felt gay and lighthearted again."

He began to laugh, a laugh that froze me. "That is," he answered, "I ought to accept what I've done and not struggle against it—I ought to accept what I've done and what I've become and not judge myself. Well, maybe such things can happen in church, but out of church——"

"Go to church, then," I suggested, clinging to a new hope.

"No, I won't. I don't believe in it and I'm only bored in church. Besides—what a way of talking!" He began to laugh again, but suddenly stopped short and, seizing me by the shoulders, started to shake me violently. "Don't you understand what I've done?" he shouted. "Don't you understand? Don't you understand?" He shook me so hard that he made me lose my breath before flinging me backwards with one final outburst, and then I heard him leap out of bed and begin to dress in the dark. "Don't put the light on," he said threateningly. "I've got to get used to being looked at. But it's too soon yet. Look out for yourself if you switch the light on!"

I did not even dare to breathe. "Are you going?" I asked him at last.

" Yes, but I'll come back," he said, and I believe he laughed again. " Don't be afraid, I'll come back. In fact, here's a piece of good news for you—I'll come and live here with you."

" Here with me ? "

" Yes, but I shan't be a nuisance. You'll be able to carry on with your usual way of life. As a matter of fact," he went on, " we could both of us live on what my family sends me. I was paying full board, but it would be enough for the two of us, living at home."

I found the idea that he might come and live with me strange rather than delightful. But I did not dare to make any comment. He finished dressing in silence in the pitch-dark. " I'll be back tonight," he then said. I heard him open the door, go out, shut the door. I lay there in the dark, my eyes staring wide open.

CHAPTER TEN

That very afternoon I followed Astarita's advice and went to the local police-station to make a statement about Son-zogno's case. I went most reluctantly, because after what had happened to Mino anything that was remotely connected with the police inspired me with mortal dread. But by now I was almost resigned. I realised that life had lost almost all its savour for me for some time to come.

" We expected you this morning," said the commissioner of police as soon as I had told him the reason for my visit. He was a fine fellow, I had known him for some time, and although he was the father of a family and over fifty years old I had realised much earlier that his feelings for me were more than friendly. What stands out in my memory of him is his large nose, like a sponge, giving him a melancholy expression. His hair was always standing on end and his eyes were always half-shut as if he had only just got out of bed. His sharp blue eyes seemed to be peeping out from behind a mask, his thick, pink, wrinkled face was like the skin of those huge oranges, the last of the season, which contain nothing but a shrivelled core.

I said I had been unable to come sooner. The blue eyes behind the orange-peel skin of his face looked at me for a moment and then he addressed me confidentially. " Well, what's his name ? "

" How should I know ? "

" Come, come, of course you know ! "

" I give you my word of honour," I said with my hand on my heart. " He stopped me in the Corso—I remember thinking there was something queer about him. But I didn't take any notice."

" But how was it you left him alone in your flat ? "

" I had an urgent appointment, so I left him."

" But he thought you'd gone out to call the police. Did you know that ? And he shouted out that you'd given him away."

" Yes, I know."

" And that he'd pay you back."

" What then ? "

" But don't you realise he's a dangerous man," he added, looking at me intently, " and might even fire at you tomorrow for having given him away, just as he fired at the police ? "

" Of course I realise it."

" Then why won't you tell us who he is ? We'll have him arrested and you needn't worry any more."

" But I've told you I don't know his name ! Am I supposed to know the names of all the men I take home ? "

" But we know who he is ! " he suddenly declared, in a higher, more theatrical tone of voice as he leaned forward.

I knew he was only pretending. " If you know," I answered coolly, " why bother me about it ? Arrest him and don't let's hear any more about the whole thing."

He looked at me in silence for a moment. I noticed that his restless, worried eyes were examining my figure rather than my face, and I understood that despite himself his professional sense of duty had been overcome by his desire for me. " We also know that if he fired and then ran off he must have had good reason for doing it," he went on.

354

" Oh, I'm quite sure of that ! "

" But you know what his reasons are."

" I don't know anything.   If I don't know his name how could I know the rest ? "

" We know the whole business," he said.   By now he was speaking quite mechanically as if he was thinking about something else and I felt sure that in another moment he would get up and come over to me.   " We know all about it and we'll get him.   It's just a question of days—perhaps hours."

" So much the better for you."

He stood up as I had foreseen he would, walked round the table, came up to me, and cupping my chin in his hand, spoke to me.   " Come, come, you know all about it and won't tell us.   What are you afraid of ? "

" I'm not afraid of anything," I answered, " and I don't know anything.   And now keep your hands to yourself."

" Come, come," he repeated.   But he sat down again behind the table before continuing.   " You're lucky because I like you and know you're a good girl.   Do you know what another man would have done in my place, to make you talk ? He'd have had you kept in custody for a long time.   Or sent to San Gallicano."

I got up.   " Well, I'm busy," I said.   " If you haven't anything else to tell me . . ."

" Go along.   But be careful what company you keep— political and otherwise."

I pretended I had not heard these last words, which he pronounced meaningly, and I escaped as hurriedly as I could from those sordid little rooms.

As I walked along, I began to think about Sonzogno again. The commissioner of police had strengthened me in what I had already suspected.   Sonzogno wanted to revenge himself upon me because he was sure I had denounced him.   I was terrified ; not for myself but for Mino.   Sonzogno was raving mad ; if he found Mino with me he would not hesitate to kill us both.   I must confess that the idea of dying with Mino was curiously attractive.   I imagined the whole scene : Sonzogno would shoot and I would throw myself between him and Mino in order to shield Mino and then be wounded

355

in his place. But I quite liked the idea that Mino, too, should be wounded and that we would die together, mingling our blood. But I thought that being killed by the same murderer at the same moment would not be as wonderful as committing suicide together. A suicide pact seemed a worthy conclusion to a passionate love-affair. It was like cutting a flower before it had withered ; like shutting oneself up in silence after having heard some celestial music. I had often pondered over this kind of suicide, which interrupts the passage of time before it can corrupt and spoil love and is deliberately planned through an excess of joy, rather than through an inability to bear suffering. At those moments when I felt I loved Mino so intensely that I would never be able to love him so much in the future, the idea of a suicide pact occurred to me quite naturally, with the same impulsiveness with which I kissed and caressed him. But I had never mentioned it to him because I knew that if two people commit suicide together they have to be in love to the same degree. And Mino did not love me ; or if he loved me, it was not so much that he wanted to die with me.

I was pondering over all these things as I walked home. But all of a sudden an attack of giddiness, accompanied by a wave of sickness and a ghastly feeling of weakness in all my limbs, overcame me and I just had time to go into a milk-bar nearby. I was not far from home, but I knew I had not got the strength to cover that short distance without falling down.

I sat down at one of the little tables behind the glass-fronted door and shut my eyes, feeling shattered. I still felt very sick and giddy and this sensation was increased by the puffs of steam from the coffee-machine, which were extremely upsetting although strangely remote. I could feel the warmth of the closed, heated room on my hands and face, but despite this I felt very cold. " A cup of coffee, Miss Adriana ? " called the man behind the counter, who knew me well, and without opening my eyes I nodded assent.

At last I recovered and sipped the coffee which the man had placed on the table in front of me. As a matter of fact, it was not the first time I had felt the same kind of sickness, but it had always been very slight, scarcely noticeable. I had not paid any attention to it because the extraordinary and distressing events in which I had been involved had prevented me. But now, thinking it over and associating my feeling of sickness with a significant interruption in my physical life, which had occurred in the previous month, I became convinced that the vague suspicion I had had recently, but had always pushed into the darkest background of my consciousness must be founded on fact. " There can be no doubt about it," I suddenly found myself thinking, " I must be expecting a child."

I paid for the coffee and left the place. What I felt was extremely complicated and even now, after such a lapse of time, I do not find it at all easy to express it. I have already remarked that misfortunes never come singly; and this new fact which I would have greeted joyously at any other time and on another occasion seemed to me to be a real piece of bad luck in the present circumstances. But, on the other hand, my temperament is such that an inexplicable and irresistible instinct always leads me to discover an attractive side even in the most unpleasant circumstances. This time it was not at all difficult to find the attractive side; it was the same feeling which fills the hearts of all women with hope and satisfaction when they learn that they are pregnant. Certainly my child would be born in the least favourable conditions imaginable; but he would still be my child and I would be the one who had given him birth and I would educate him and delight in him. A child is always a child, I thought; and no woman, however poor she is, however terrible her circumstances and uncertain her future, however abandoned and unprovided for, can help being happy at the idea of giving birth to a child.

These thoughts restored my calm, so that after a moment's fear and despair I once more felt as placid and trustful as ever I was. The young doctor, who had examined me some time before when mother had dragged me to the chemist's in order to find out whether Gino and I had been making love, had his consulting-room not far from the milk-bar. I made up my mind to go and be examined by him. It was early, there was no one in the waiting-room. The doctor, who knew me very well, greeted me cordially.

"Doctor, I'm almost sure I'm pregnant," I announced calmly as soon as he had closed the door.

He began to laugh because he knew what my profession was. "Are you sorry?" he asked me.

"Not at all. I'm glad in fact."

"Let's see."

After he had put me several questions about my sickness he made me lie down on the oil-cloth sheet spread on the couch and examined me. "You've hit the right nail on the head this time," he said cheerfully.

I was glad to have my suspicions confirmed without any shadow of doubt. I was perfectly calm. "I knew I was," I said. "I only came here really to make quite sure."

"You can be absolutely sure."

He rubbed his hands together as joyfully as if he were the father himself and swayed from one foot to the other, cheerful and pleasantly disposed towards me. Only one thing troubled me and I wanted to make certain. "How far gone am I?" I asked.

"About two months, I should say, more or less. Why? Do you want to know who it was?"

"I know already."

I made for the door. "If you need anything come and see me," he said as he opened the door for me. "And when the time comes we'll see that the child is born in the best conditions possible." He, like the commissioner of police, was very fond of me. But I liked him, too, whereas I had no liking whatsoever for the commissioner. I have already described him once. He was a handsome young man, very dark, strong and vigorous, with a black moustache, bright eyes and white teeth, as cheerful and lively as a gun-dog. I often went to him to have myself examined, at least once a fortnight, and once or twice I had let him make love to me, out of gratitude because he did not make me pay him a fee, on the same couch with the oil-cloth where he had examined me. But he was very tactful and except for an occasional playful gesture he never tried to force his desire on me. He gave me advice, and I think he was a little bit in love with me in his own way.

I had told him I knew who was the father of my child. In point of fact at that moment I felt I knew it instinctively rather than by mechanically counting the days—it was an idea I had. But when I was out in the street once more, reckoning up the time and looking back into my memories of the past, the idea became a certainty. I remembered the long, plaintive cry of anguish and pleasure wrung from me in the darkness of my room by the mixture of terror and attraction I had felt for him, and I was sure that the father of my child could be no other than Sonzogno. It was dreadful to know that one had had a child by a brutal, murderous wretch like Sonzogno, particularly because there was always the danger that the child might take after his father and reproduce his characteristics. On the other hand, I could not help feeling there was something peculiarly just in Sonzogno being the father. Sonzogno was the only one of all the many men who had loved me who had really possessed me in the darkest and most secret depths of my being. The fact that he horrified and frightened me and that I was persuaded to give myself to him against my will did not alter the fact that his possession of me had been complete and profound; it confirmed it, rather. Neither Gino nor Astarita nor even Mino, for whom I felt quite a different kind of passion, had aroused in me the sensation of such a legitimate possession, even though I loathed it. All this seemed strange and terrifying; but so it was. Feelings are the only things one cannot reject or deny or even analyse, in a certain sense. I came to the conclusion that some men are made for love and some for procreation; and if it was only right that I should have a child by Sonzogno it was no less right for me to detest him and flee from him and to love Mino, as I really did.

I climbed the stairs slowly, thinking of the living weight I now bore within me; when I was in the hall I heard voices in the living-room. I went to the door and was surprised to see Mino sitting at the head of the table talking calmly to mother, who was seated near him sewing busily. Only the central light was burning and most of the room was in darkness.

"Good-evening," I said lazily as I came forward.

"Good-evening, good-evening," said Mino in a grating, hesitant voice. I looked at his face, saw how bright his eyes were and I felt sure he was drunk. One end of the table was spread with a napkin and knives and forks for two, and knowing that mother always ate on her own in the kitchen I realised that the second place was for Mino. "Good-evening," he repeated, "I've brought my suitcases. They're in the other room. And I've made friends with your mother We understand one another perfectly, don't we ? " he said to her.

I felt faint at heart as I heard his sarcastic and grimly playful voice. I slumped down into a chair and shut my eyes for a moment. I heard mother reply to him. "That's what you say. But if you speak badly of Adriana we'll never get along together."

"But what have I said ? " exclaimed Mino, feigning astonishment. "That Adriana was born for the life she leads. That Adriana thinks life's wonderful. What's wrong about that ? "

"It isn't true," retorted mother. "Adriana wasn't born for the life she leads. She deserved something far better, with all her beauty. Don't you know she's one of the handsomest girls in the neighbourhood, if not in all Rome ? I see lots of other girls who aren't nearly as good-looking as she is, who strike lucky. But Adriana, who's as lovely as a queen, never gets anywhere. But I know why."

"Why ? "

"Because she's too good, that's why. Because she's beautiful and good. If she were beautiful and bad you'd see how differently everything would run."

"Come, come," I said, feeling embarrassed by this discussion and more particularly by Mino's tone of voice, for he seemed to be making fun of mother. "I'm hungry. Isn't dinner ready yet ? "

"It's ready now." Mother put her sewing on the table and went out hurriedly. I followed her into the kitchen.

"Are we setting up a boarding-house?" she grumbled. "He walked in as if he were master of the house, put his suitcases in your room and gave me some money to go out shopping."

"Well, aren't you glad?"

"I liked it better before."

"Well, pretend we're engaged. Anyway, it's only a temporary arrangement, he's only here for a few days—he can't stay for ever." I said one or two things of the same nature in order to put her into a good humour, hugged her, and then went back into the living-room.

I shall remember that first meal of Mino's in my own home, with mother and me, for a long time to come. He kept on joking and had an excellent appetite. But his jokes seemed colder than ice and more bitter than a lemon. Obviously he had only one thought in his head and it was like a thorn in the flesh and his jokes only irritated it and drove it deeper to renew the agony. It was the thought of all he had said to Astarita, and really, I never saw anyone so deeply repentant. As a child the priests had taught me that repentance washes away sin; but in Mino's case the repentance seemed endless and led to no beneficent result. I realised that he was suffering dreadfully and I suffered for him to the same extent and perhaps even more, because my suffering was increased by my inability to help him or lighten his burden.

We ate the first course in silence. Then mother, who was standing up to serve us, said something about the price of meat. "Don't worry," said Mino, raising his head. "From now on it'll be my business to keep you supplied. I'm going to get a good job."

I felt almost hopeful as he made this announcement. "What job?" asked mother.

"A job with the police," said Mino with exaggerated seriousness. "A friend of Adriana's is getting me the job—a Mister Astarita."

I put down my knife and fork and stared at him. "They've found out that I've got the very qualities they're looking for in the police."

"Maybe," said mother, "but I never liked the police

myself. The son of the laundress who lives below us is a policeman, too. Do you know what the young fellows who work next door in the cement-works said to him? 'Keep off, we don't want anything more to do with you.' And anyway, the work's badly paid." She made a face and changed his plate, then offered him the dish of meat.

"That's not what I mean," retorted Mino as he helped himself; "what I mean is an important job, something very delicate, very secret. What the devil! I haven't studied for nothing! I've almost taken my degree. I know modern languages. Poor people become mere policemen, not people like me."

"Maybe," repeated mother. "Take this," she added, pushing the largest piece of meat on to my plate.

"Not maybe at all," said Mino, "it really is as I say."

He was silent for a moment. "The government knows that the country's full of people opposed to it, not only among the poor but among the rich, too. They need educated people to spy on the rich, people who speak like they do, dress like they do, have the same manners and inspire confidence. That's what I'll do. I'll be well-paid, I'll live in first-class hotels, travel in a sleeper, eat in the best restaurants, get my clothes from a fashionable tailor, visit fashionable seaside resorts, famous holiday-places in the mountains. What on earth did you take me for?"

By now mother was gaping at him. She was dazzled by such splendour. "In that case," she said at last, "I've nothing to say."

I had finished my meal. I suddenly found it was quite beyond me to go on watching such a kind of heart-rending comedy. "I'm tired," I said brusquely, "I'm going into the other room." I got up and left the living-room.

When I was in my own room I sat on the bed and huddled myself up, then began to cry silently through my fingers which concealed my face. I thought of Mino's distress, the baby that I was going to have, and both these things, the distress and the baby, seemed to be growing by themselves independently of me, without my control, and they were living and there was nothing more to be done about it. After a while Mino came in, and I got up at once and turned away from him so that he would not see my eyes full of tears before I had time to dry them.   He had lit a cigarette and lay flat on the bed.   I sat down beside him.   " Mino," I said, " please— don't talk like that to mother ever again."

" Why ? "

" Because she doesn't understand a thing.   But I understand and every word you say is like a needle piercing my heart."

He said nothing and went on smoking in silence.   I took a nightdress out of the drawer, picked up a needle and reel of silk and began to sew without speaking, sitting on the edge of the bed near the lamp.   I did not want to speak because I was afraid that if I did he would begin to discuss the usual thing, and I hoped that if I kept silent his thoughts would wander and he would drive it out of his mind.   Sewing requires a lot of attention but leaves the mind free, as all women know who sew for a living.   While I was sewing my thoughts whirled round in my head, or rather, I felt as if I were mending a tear or stitching a hem in my mind as I was in the work I held in my hands, pushing the needle rapidly in and out.   I, too, shared Mino's obsession and could not help thinking of what he had said to Astarita and the consequences it would have.   But I didn't want to think about it, because I was afraid that if I did some mysterious influence would set him thinking about it too, and I would be responsible in some way, despite myself, for having increased his sorrow and kept it alive.   I therefore tried to think about something else, something clear, something light and cheerful, and I concentrated with the whole strength of my mind on the baby I was going to have, which was, in fact, the only joyous aspect in my life, now so full of terribly tragic prospects.   I imagined what he would be like at two or three years of age, the best time of all, when children are at their most charming and beautiful, and as I thought of all the things he would do and say and the way I would bring him up, I grew cheerful again, as I had hoped I would and forgot Mino and his distress for a moment.   I had finished mending my nightdress and as I took up another piece of work I reflected upon the way in which I would relieve the tension of the long hours spent with Mino by making the baby's layette. Only I would not have to let him discover what I was doing, or I would have to find an excuse. I thought I would tell him that I was making it for a neighbour of ours who was actually expecting a baby, and I thought it would be a good excuse, since I had already mentioned her to Mino and had referred to her poverty. I was so taken up with these ideas that without noticing it, almost, I began to hum softly. I have a very good ear although my voice is not very strong, and my accent is extraordinarily sweet, even in my speaking voice. I began to sing a song that was popular just then : *Villa triste*. When I raised my eyes, as I bit the thread in two with which I was sewing, I saw Mino looking at me. I thought he might blame me for singing at a time that was so grave for him, so I stopped.

"Sing some more," he said, looking at me.

"Do you like me to sing ? "

"Yes."

"But I can't sing well."

"It doesn't matter."

I took up my sewing again and began to sing for him. Like most girls I knew quite a number of songs, in fact I had quite a good repertoire because my memory is excellent and I could even remember the songs I had learnt as a child. I sang a little of everything and as soon as I had finished one song I began another. At first I sang softly and then, as it grew on me, I sang aloud with all the feeling I could muster. One song followed another, and they were all different, and as I sang one I was already thinking of the next. He listened to me with a serious expression on his face and I was glad I was able to distract his attention from the remorse he felt. But at the same time I remembered that once when I was a child I had lost some toy I was very fond of, and since I could not stop crying on account of the loss, mother had sat down on my bed and had begun to sing the few things she knew. She sang badly, out of tune, but nevertheless at first I had listened to her just as Mino was listening to me. But after a while the idea of the toy I had lost had slowly begun to distil bitterness into the cup of forgetfulness that mother offered me and at last it had poisoned everything and had made it, by contrast, utterly intolerable. So at last I had suddenly burst into tears again and mother, out of patience with me, had switched off the light and had gone away, leaving me to cry my heart out in the dark. I was sure that when the deceptive sweetness of my singing had vanished he would inevitably feel the same anguish, which would be even sharper and more acute by contrast with the sentimental superficiality of my songs; and I was not mistaken. I had been singing for nearly an hour when he interrupted me brusquely. "That'll do," he said. "Your songs bore me stiff." Then he curled up as if he meant to go to sleep, with his back turned to me.

I had foreseen that he would behave in this rude way so I was not too deeply pained. In any case, I did not expect anything else now but unhappiness, and the contrary would have astonished me. I got up from the bed and went to put away the linen I had mended. Then, still in silence, I took off my clothes and slipped into the bed on the side Mino had left free. We lay for some time in silence like that, back to back. I knew he was not asleep and was thinking all the time of one thing; and this knowledge, together with the sharp sense of my own helplessness, provoked a storm of confused, desperate thoughts in my head. I was lying on my side and staring in front of me, into a corner of the room as I thought. I could see one of the two suitcases Mino had brought with him from Signora Medolaghi's house, an old yellow leather case covered with the coloured labels of different hotels. Among the rest there was one that showed a square of blue sea, a huge red rock and the word: Capri. In the half-light, among the dull, opaque furniture, that blue spot seemed luminous, seemed something more than a mere spot, it was a hole through which I caught a glimpse of that strip of distant sea. I had a sudden longing for the sea, so sparkling and lively, in which even the most corrupt and shapeless object is purified, smoothed, rounded, fashioned into something beautiful and clean. I have always loved the sea, even the tamed and crowded beach of Ostia; and the sight of the sea always gives me a sense of liberty which intoxicates my ears even more than my eyes, as if I were listening to the notes of a wondrous, timeless music floating eternally on its waves. I began to think about the sea, yearning acutely for its transparent waves, which seem to wash not only the body but also the soul, making it light and full of joy with its liquid contact. I told myself that if I could take Mino to the sea perhaps the immensity, the perpetual motion and sound would produce on him the effect my love alone could not achieve.

"Have you ever been to Capri?" I suddenly asked him.

"Yes," he said, without turning round.

"Is it beautiful?"

"Yes—very."

"Listen," I said, turning round in the bed and putting an arm round his neck. "Why don't we go to Capri? Or some other seaside place? As long as you stay here in Rome you won't be able to think about anything pleasant. If you have a change of air I'm sure you'll see everything differently. You'd see lots of things that escape you for the moment. I'm sure it'd do you good."

He did not answer at once and seemed to be thinking. "I don't need to go to the sea," he then said. "I could see things differently even here, as you say. All I have to do is to accept what I've done, just as you advised. And I'd begin to enjoy the sky, the earth, you, everything, at once. Do you think I don't know that the world is beautiful?"

"Well then," I said anxiously, "accept it. What does it cost you?" He began to laugh. "I ought to have thought of that first. I ought to do as you do—accept right from the beginning. Even the beggars that sit warming themselves in the sunshine on the church-steps have accepted everything from the beginning. It's too late for me."

"But why?"

"There are some who accept and some who don't. Obviously I belong to the second group."

I did not know what to say, so I remained silent. "Now put out the light," he added after a moment. "I'll get undressed in the dark. It must be time to go to sleep."

I obeyed, and he undressed in the dark and got into bed beside me. I turned towards him as if I wanted to embrace him. But he pushed me away wordlessly and curled himself

366

up on the edge of the bed with his back to me. This gesture filled me with bitterness and I too huddled myself up, awaiting sleep with my spirit mourning. But I began to think about the sea again and was overcome by the longing to drown myself. I imagined it would only be a moment's suffering, and then my lifeless body would float from wave to wave beneath the sun for ages. The gulls would peck my eyes, the sun would burn my breast and my belly, the fish would gnaw my back. At last I would sink to the bottom, would be dragged head downwards towards some icy, blue current that would carry me along the sea-bed for months and years among submarine rocks, fish and seaweed, and floods of limpid salt water would wash my forehead, my breast, my belly, my legs, slowly wearing away my flesh, smoothing and refining me continually. And at last some wave some day would cast me up on some shore, nothing but a handful of fragile, white bones. I liked the idea of being dragged to the bottom of the sea by my hair; I liked the idea of being reduced to a little heap of bones one day, without human shape, among the smooth stones of a shore. And perhaps someone without noticing it would walk on my bones and crush them to white powder. With these sad, voluptuous thoughts I fell asleep.

CHAPTER ELEVEN

The following day, although I tried to force myself to believe that rest and sleep had changed Mino's feelings, I noticed immediately that he was the same as ever. In fact, if anything, he seemed to me rather worse. He kept passing from periods of long, gloomy, obstinate silence to outbursts of rambling, sarcastic chatter upon indifferent matters in which, however, the same dominant thought was always apparent, like the watermark in some kinds of paper. As far as I could see, his deterioration consisted chiefly of a kind of wilful inertia, apathy, carelessness which were something quite new in him, for he had always been extremely active and energetic; it was a kind of progressive detachment from all the things he

367

had done so far. I opened his suitcases and put his suits and other clothes in my wardrobe. But when it came to the books he needed for his studies, and I suggested putting them in a row on the marble-topped chest-of-drawers underneath the mirror, he replied : " Leave them in the case. They aren't any use to me any more, anyway."

" And why not ? " I asked. " Haven't you got to take your degree ? "

" I'm not going to take my degree."

" Don't you want to go on with your studies ? "

" No."

I did not insist in case he began to talk about the usual thing which was distressing him and I left the books in the suitcase. I noticed he did not shave and did not wash himself. Now, he had always been very clean and finicky in his person. He spent the whole of the second day in my room, either lying on the bed smoking or walking thoughtfully up and down with his hands in his pockets. But he did not say anything more to mother at lunch, as he had promised me. When evening came he said he would dine out and left the house by himself, without my daring to suggest that I should accompany him. I have no idea where he went, I was just going to bed when he came in and I noticed immediately that he had been drinking. He embraced me in a burlesque and exaggerated manner and insisted on possessing me and I had to give in to him, although I realised that making love for him was now like drinking, something unpleasant which he forced himself to do in order to tire and numb himself. I told him so. " You might as well go with some other woman," I told him. He laughed. " I might as well," he replied, " but you're there, within easy reach." I was offended by these words and hurt even more than offended because they proved he had so little affection for me.

Then I had a sudden gleam of comprehension. " Look," I said, " I know I'm only a poor girl of no importance . . . but try to love me. It's for your own good. If you can love me I'm sure you'll be able to love yourself in the end." He looked at me then repeated " Love, love," in a loud, mocking voice and switched out the light. I lay there in the dark with staring eyes, feeling bewildered and embittered, not knowing what to think.

There was no change in the days that followed and everything went on in the same way. He merely seemed to have formed new habits to replace the old ones. Previously he had studied, gone to the University, seen his friends at some café, had read. Now he lay on the bed smoking, strolled about the room, kept on making the same crazy, rambling hints, got drunk and made love. On the fourth day I really began to feel quite desperate. I could see that his anguish was as bitter as ever and I thought it must be impossible to continue living with such anguish. My room, which was always full of cigarette smoke, seemed like a factory working day and night to produce anguish, without a moment's break; and the very air I breathed had by now become a thick gelatinous mass of sad, insistent thoughts. At such times I often cursed my ignorance and pettiness and the fact that mother was even more petty and ignorant than I was. One's first impulse in moments of difficulty is to turn to someone older and more experienced for advice. But I did not know anyone who possessed these qualities, and asking mother for help would have been like asking one of the many children who used to play in the courtyard. On the other hand, I was unable to penetrate to the very depths of his sorrow; many things escaped me; little by little I came to the conclusion that what tormented him most of all was the thought that everything he had said to Astarita was written down in the police report and kept in the archives, as a perpetual witness to his weakness. Some things he said strengthened me in this conviction. So one afternoon I spoke to him about it. " If you're sorry they wrote down everything you said to Astarita—well, Astarita would do anything I asked him. I'm sure if I ask him he'll have the report on you destroyed."

" What makes you think so ? " he said, giving me a strange look.

" You said so yourself the other day. I told you that you ought to try to forget and you told me that even if you forgot the police wouldn't."

" But how could you set about asking him ? "

369

"That's easy enough! I'll simply phone him and go and see him at the Ministry."

He would not say what he wanted. "Well—do you want me to ask him?" I insisted.

"Do what you like as far as I'm concerned."

We went out together and phoned from a milk-bar. I got hold of Astarita at once and told him I had to speak to him. I asked him if I might come to the Ministry. "Either at your place or not at all," he replied in a strange stuttering voice.

I realised that he wanted to be paid for the favour I was going to ask him to do; and I tried to avoid the point. "Let's meet in a café," I said.

"No, either at your place or not at all."

"Very well, then," I said, "at my place." I added that I would be at home that very day, late in the afternoon.

"I know what he wants," I said to Mino as we returned home, "he wants to make love to me—but no-one has ever been able to force a woman to make love against her will, and he's only blackmailed me once, when I was still inexperienced, but he won't be able to bring that off again."

"But why don't you want him to make love to you?" asked Mino indifferently.

"Because I love you."

"But perhaps he'll refuse to destroy the reports if you don't let him make love to you—and what then?" he asked, still in a casual tone.

"He'll destroy them, don't worry."

"But suppose he didn't want to except on this one condition?"

We were on the stairs. I stood still. "I'll do what you decide," I said.

He put his arm round my waist. "Well," he said slowly, "this is what I want—I want you to get Astarita to come to your place and go into your room with you with the idea of making love. I'll be waiting behind the door and as soon as he comes in I'll kill him with a revolver. Then we'll shove him under the bed and make love ourselves, all night."

His eyes were shining, for the first time for days they were clear of the oppressive mist that had obscured them. I grew

370

frightened because I could see that there was a certain logic in what he suggested; and because by now I was resigned to the idea of a worse and more final disaster and it seemed just the kind of crime that might happen. "For God's sake, Mino!" I exclaimed. "Don't say such things even for fun."

"Not even for fun," he repeated. "I was joking, as a matter of fact."

I thought he probably had not been joking at all; but I was reassured by the thought that the revolver he might use was unloaded, although he did not know this, since I had taken out the bullets myself, as I have already said. "Don't worry," I continued. "Astarita will do anything I want. But don't talk like that any more. You frightened me so."

"Oh, one can't even joke any more!" he said lightly as he went indoors.

I noticed that a sudden fit of restlessness possessed him as we entered the living-room. He began to walk up and down with his hands in his pockets as usual. But he moved in a different manner, more energetically than usual, with an expression on his face which showed that he was thinking clearly and profoundly and had shaken off his usual disgust and apathy. I attributed the change to the relief of knowing that the compromising papers would soon be destroyed. "You'll see everything will come right soon," I said, hope springing once more within my breast.

He shuddered deeply, looked at me as if he did not recognise me and then repeated mechanically: "Yes—everything will come right."

I had sent mother out with the excuse of doing some shopping for supper. I suddenly felt optimistic. I thought everything really would come right, perhaps even better than I expected. Astarita would do what I wanted, if he had not already done so; and day by day Mino would become detached from his remorse, would begin to enjoy life again and look confidently towards the future. In time of trouble all men content themselves with merely surviving; but as soon as the wind changes they begin to construct ambitious, far-reaching plans. Two days earlier I had thought myself quite capable of giving Mino up for his own happiness; but now that I had persuaded myself into believing that I might be able to restore his happiness I not only gave up all idea of leaving him, but tried to work out how I could bind him even more strongly to me. It was not my reason which urged me to form these plans; it was an obscure impulse within my spirit, which needed hope and could not bear humiliation and sorrow for long. It seemed to me that there were only two possible solutions for us, as things were : either we must separate or be bound to one another for life; and since I did not even want to consider the first solution, I began to wonder whether there was not some means by which I could achieve the second. I hate lying and I think I may count an exaggerated kind of sincerity among my few positive qualities. If I lied to Mino at that moment it was because I did not feel as though I was lying at all; I seemed to be telling the truth. It was a truth that was truer than truth, a spiritual and not a material truth. As a matter of fact, I did not think at all; it was, if anything, a kind of inspiration.

He was walking up and down as usual and I was sitting at one end of the table. "Listen," I said suddenly, "stop walking about. I've got something I must tell you."

"What is it ?"

"I haven't been feeling well lately. I went to see a doctor a few days ago—I'm pregnant."

He stood still and looked at me. "You're pregnant ?" he repeated.

"Yes. And I'm absolutely sure it was you."

Mino was intelligent, and although he could not guess that I was lying, he immediately understood the real purpose of my announcement. He took a chair, came and sat down beside me, caressed my cheek fondly. "I suppose this ought to be one more reason, the chief reason, in fact, which should make me forget what has happened and go ahead. Isn't that so ?"

"What do you mean ?" I asked, pretending I had not understood him.

"Since I'm going to become a *pater familias*," he continued, "I ought, for the sake of this innocent creature, as you women say, to do what I wouldn't do for love of you."

" Do what you like," I said, shrugging my shoulders, " I've told you because it's the truth. That's all."

" After all," he went on, as if he were thinking aloud, " a child could be a reason for living. Many people ask for nothing more. A child is a justification. You might even steal or murder for a child."

" Who on earth wants you to steal or murder ? " I interrupted him indignantly. " I only want you to be glad. If you aren't . . . then there's nothing more to be said."

He looked at me and stroked my cheek again fondly. " If you're glad I'm glad. Are you glad ? "

" I am, yes," I said proudly and firmly. " First of all because I like children and then because it's yours." He laughed. " You're a sharp one," he said.

" Why ? what's sharp about being pregnant ? "

" Nothing. But you must admit it's a good stroke just at this moment. ' I'm pregnant and therefore——' "

" Therefore ? "

" Therefore you must accept what you've done," he shouted unexpectedly at the top of his voice as he leapt to his feet, waving his arms wildly, " therefore you must live, live, live ! "

The tone of his voice was indescribable. I felt pierced to the heart and my eyes filled with tears. " Do what you like," I stammered ; " if you want to leave me, leave me, then. I . . . I'll go away."

Apparently he regretted his outburst, for he came up to me and caressed me again. " I'm sorry," he said. " Don't take any notice of what I say. Think about your child and don't worry about me."

I took his hand and pressed it to my face, bathed it with my tears and stammered : " Oh, Mino . . . How can I help worrying about you ? "

We remained silent like this for some time. He was standing beside me, I pressed his hand against my cheek, kissed it and wept. Then we heard the front-door bell ring.

He broke away from me and became very pale, but at that moment I could not understand why and did not trouble to ask him. I leapt to my feet. " Go on," I said, " here's Astarita ! Quick ! Go away."

He went out by the kitchen door, leaving it ajar. I dried my eyes quickly, put the chairs back in their places and went out into the hall. I felt perfectly calm and sure of myself once more; and in the darkness of the hall it occurred to me that I might even tell Astarita I was pregnant; in this way he would let me be and if he was disinclined to do me the favour I asked him out of love for me, he would do it out of pity.

I opened the door and stepped hastily back. Instead of Astarita, I saw Sonzogno on the threshold.

His hands were in his pockets and as I tried, almost mechanically, to shut the door in his face he shoved lightly against it with his shoulders, flung it wide open and came in. I followed him into the living-room. He went and stood by the table near the window. He was hatless as usual and as soon as I entered I felt his insistent, unwinking eyes fixed upon me. I closed the door and then spoke to him, pretending to be quite indifferent.

"Why have you come?"

"You went and denounced me, didn't you?"

I shrugged my shoulders and sat down at the head of the table. "I didn't denounce you," I said.

"You left me, went out and called the police."

I felt quite calm. If I felt anything at all at that moment it was anger rather than fear. He did not frighten me any longer and I felt anger rising within me against him and against all those who prevented me from being happy, as he did. "I left you and went away," I said, "because I love another man and I don't want to have anything more to do with you. But I didn't call the police. I'm not an informer. The police came of their own accord. They were looking for someone else."

He came up to me, took hold of me and pinched my two cheeks so cruelly that I had to unclench my teeth as he raised my face to his. "You can thank God that you're a woman," he said.

He continued to pinch my cheeks, forcing me to make a painful grimace that was both hideous and ridiculous. Rage overcame me and I leapt to my feet. "Get out, you fool!" I cried.

He put his hands back into his pockets and came even nearer to me, staring into my eyes as usual. "You're a fool!" I cried once more. "With your muscles, your little blue eyes, your bald head! Get out, clear off, idiot!"

He really was a fool, I thought, as I saw him standing there in silence with a slight smile on his thin, crooked mouth, his hands in his pockets, staring at me as he came even nearer. I ran to the other end of the table, gripped an iron, a heavy tailor's iron, and shouted: "Get out, idiot! Or I'll smash your face in with this."

He hesitated a moment and stood still. At the same instant the door of the living-room opened behind me and Astarita appeared in the doorway. Obviously he had found the door open and had walked in. I turned towards him. "Tell this man to get out," I cried. "I don't know what he wants. Tell him to get out."

I do not know why the smartness of Astarita's clothes on this occasion gave me such pleasure. He was wearing a new-looking double-breasted, grey overcoat. He had a silk shirt, with red stripes on a white background. A silvery grey shot-silk tie was tucked into the folds of his navy-blue suit. He looked at me as I stood there waving the iron, looked at Sonzogno. "The young lady told you to go away," he said calmly. "What are you waiting for?"

"The young lady and I have several things to talk over. It would be better if you went," said Sonzogno in a very deep voice.

As Astarita came in he had taken off his hat, a black felt with a silk edge. He put it down on the table in a leisurely fashion and went towards Sonzogno. His attitude amazed me. His eyes, which were usually so black and melancholy, seemed to gleam belligerently, his large mouth curled upwards in a pleased, defiant smile. He showed his teeth. "Oh, so you don't want to go," he said, emphasising each syllable, "but you see, I'm telling you you're going, at the double."

Sonzogno shook his head in refusal, but, to my astonishment, took a step backwards. And then I remembered precisely who Sonzogno was. And I was afraid, not for myself but for Astarita, who was provoking him so boldly, without

375

knowing who he was. I had the same feeling of anguish I had experienced as a child at the circus when I saw a little lion-tamer armed with a whip facing a huge, roaring lion, and teasing it. " Look out ! " I wanted to shout, " he's a murderer, a brute ! " But I had not got the strength to speak. " Well, are you going—or aren't you ? " said Astarita once more.

Sonzogno shook his head again and took another step backwards. Astarita moved one step forward. They were face to face, almost touching, both of the same height. " Who are you, anyway ? " asked Astarita with the same twisted grimace. " Tell me your name—out with it ! "

Sonzogno made no reply. " So you don't want to, eh ? " repeated Astarita almost voluptuously, as if Sonzogno's silence was a source of pleasure. " You don't want to say who you are and you don't want to get out, eh ? Is that it ? "

He waited for a moment then raised his hand and slapped Sonzogno hard, first on one cheek, then the other. I put my fist to my mouth and buried my teeth in it. " Now he'll kill him," I thought as I shut my eyes. But I heard Astarita's voice. " And now clear off. Quickly, get a move on ! " I reopened my eyes and saw Astarita pushing Sonzogno towards the door, dragging him by his coat-collar. Sonzogno's cheeks were still crimson from the blows he had received, but he seemed docile. He let himself be dragged along as if he were thinking about something else. Astarita pushed him out of the living-room and then I heard the front-door slam violently, and Astarita reappeared.

" Who was he ? " he asked, mechanically removing a piece of fluff from the revers of his overcoat and looking himself over as if he were afraid he had spoilt his elegance by the violent effort he had made.

" I never knew his surname. I only know him as Carlo," I lied.

" Carlo," he replied with a snigger, shaking his head. Then he came up to me. I was standing in the window-embrasure and was looking out through the panes of glass. He put his arm round my waist. " How are you ? " he asked me, and his voice and expression were already quite different.

"I'm quite well," I said without looking at him. He gazed at me and then pressed me to him, close, without speaking. I pushed him away gently. "You've been very kind to me," I said. "I telephoned to ask you to do me a favour."

"Let's see what it is," he said. He was still gazing at me and did not appear to be listening.

"That young man you questioned——" I began.

"Oh, yes," he interrupted, pulling a face. "The same fellow again. He didn't turn out to be very heroic."

I was curious to know the truth about Mino's interview. "Why?" I asked. "Was he afraid?"

Astarita shook his head. "I don't know if he was afraid or not. I only know that at the first question I put him he blurted everything out. If he had denied it I couldn't have done anything to him. I hadn't any proofs."

So it really had gone as Mino had said, I thought. It had been a kind of sudden absence, a plunge, unreasoned, unasked for and unprovoked. "Well," I went on, "I suppose you wrote down what he said. I want you to destroy all traces of everything you wrote."

He grinned. "He sent you, didn't he?"

"No, it's my idea," I replied. "I wish I might be struck dead this very moment if I'm not saying the truth," I added impressively.

"They all want the records to disappear. The police archives represent their uneasy consciences. If the record disappears their remorse disappears, too."

"I wish it were true," I said, remembering Mino. "But I'm afraid you're wrong this time."

He drew me to him again, my body pressed to his. "What will you give me in exchange?" he stammered, trembling with desire.

"Nothing," I replied simply. "Nothing at all this time."

"And suppose I refuse?"

"You'd make me very unhappy because I love him, and everything that happens to him seems to be happening to me."

"But you told me you'd be nice to me."

"I did so. But I've changed my mind."

377

" Why ? "

" Because. There isn't any reason."

He drew me to him again and stammering and speaking with his mouth to my ear he began to beg me to yield for the last time to his desperate longing for me.   I cannot repeat all the things he said because he mingled his supplications with the kind of atrocious things I could not write down, the things men say to women like me, the things women like me say to their lovers.   He said them in meticulous, precise detail ; but not with the usual boundless gaiety which accompanies outbursts of this kind, but with grim pleasure, as if he were obsessed.   I once heard a homicidal maniac describe to his nurse the tortures he would inflict upon him if he chanced to have him in his power, and he spoke in the same scrupulous, serious, balanced tone of voice with which Astarita whispered his obscenities to me.   What he was really describing in this way was his love, which was both tragic and lustful ; anyone else might have thought it was nothing but lust but I, on the contrary, knew it was as deep, utter and pure, in its way, as any other love.   I felt stirred to pity for him, as I always did, because underneath his obscenities I could guess his loneliness and his absolute incapacity to shake it off.   I let him pour it all out before speaking to him.   " I didn't want to tell you," I then said, " but you force me to.   Do what you like.   But I can never again be what I was.   I'm pregnant."

He was not astonished, he never deviated for one single moment from his fixed purpose.   " Well—what then ? "

" I'm going to change my way of life.   I'm getting married."

My chief reason for telling him of my condition had been to console him for my refusal.   But I realised as I spoke that I was saying what I really thought and that my words came from my heart.   " When you first knew me I wanted to get married," I added with a sigh.   " And it wasn't my fault if I didn't."

His arm was still round my waist but he had loosened his hold of me.   This time he drew right away from me.   " I curse the day I met you ! " he said.

" Why ? "

He spat, turning his head sideways from me, then con-

378

tinued. "I curse the day I met you and the day I was born."
He spoke quietly and did not seem to be giving vent to any
violent emotion. He spoke calmly and surely. "Your
friend needn't be afraid," he added. "The interview wasn't
written down, and the information he gave was not acted
upon. He's only noted in our archives as still being dangerous
from the political standpoint. Good-bye, Adriana."

I remained by the window and returned his farewell as he
went off. He picked up his hat from the table and left without
turning round.

The door leading into the kitchen opened immediately and
Mino came in with his revolver in his hand. I gazed at him in
astonishment, feeling empty and speechless.

"I had made up my mind to kill Astarita," he said with a
smile. "Did you really think I minded whether the papers
dealing with my case disappeared or not?"

"Then why didn't you do it?" I asked in a dazed voice.

"He cursed the day he was born so deeply : let him go on
cursing for a year or two yet," he said, shaking his head.

I felt that something was worrying me, but however hard
I tried I was unable to discover what it was. "In any case,"
I said, "I've got what I wanted. There's nothing written
down."

"I heard him," he interrupted me, "I heard everything. I
was standing behind the door, and the door was ajar. I saw
what he did, too. He's brave," he added carelessly, "your
Astarita's brave. The way he slapped Sonzogno was quite
masterly ! There are ways of doing these things, even cuffing
someone. He hit him like a superior hits an inferior being,
like a master hits a servant. And the way Sonzogno swallowed
it ! He didn't say a word." He laughed and put his revolver
back into his pocket.

I was rather disconcerted by his strange praise of Astarita.
"What do you think Sonzogno will do?" I asked tremulously.

"Who knows?"

It was nearly night by now and the living-room was immersed in deep shadow. He leaned over the table, switched
on the central light and it was dark all around. Mother's
spectacles and her patience cards lay on the table. Mino sat

down, picked up the cards and shuffled them. " Want a game of cards while we wait for supper ? " he then said.

" What an idea ! " I exclaimed. " A game of cards ! "

" Yes, beggar-my-neighbour. Come on."

I obeyed him, sat down and mechanically took up the cards he dealt me. My head was dazed and my hands were trembling for some unknown reason. I began to play. The figures on the cards seem to possess a malicious, disturbing character of their own : the jack of clubs was black and sinister with his black eye and a black flower in his hand ; the queen of hearts lustful, excited, shapeless ; the king of diamonds paunchy, cold, impassive, inhuman. I felt we were playing for some immensely important stakes, but I did not know what. I was deathly sad and every now and again, even while I was playing, I heaved a sigh in order to see whether the weight that was oppressing me was still there. And I could feel that not only was it still there but was becoming heavier.

He won the first game and then the second. " What's the matter ? " he asked, shuffling the cards. " You're playing so badly ! "

I threw the cards down. " Don't torture me like this, Mino ! I really don't feel like playing at all."

" Why ? "

" I don't know."

I got up and walked about the room, wringing my hands together without him seeing. " Let's go into the other room, shall we ? " I then suggested.

" If you like."

We went out into the hall and there in the dark he put his arm round my waist and kissed me on the neck. For the first time in my life I felt that love was what he thought it was ; that is to say, a means for numbing oneself and driving out thought, but no more pleasurable or important than any other means. I gripped his head with my hands and kissed him violently. We went into my room clinging together. It was plunged in darkness but I did not notice. A glowing light as red as blood filled my eyes and every movement we made had the splendour of a flame leaping rapidly and unex-

380

pectedly out of the fire that consumed us. There are times when our bodies seem possessed of a sixth sense and the shades become as familiar as the light of the sun. But it is a vision which goes no further than the bounds of physical contact; and all I could see were our two bodies projected against the darkness like the bodies of two drowned people cast up on the shore from some black eddy.

Suddenly I found I was lying on the bed with the light from the lamp reflected on my naked belly. I squeezed my thighs together, I don't know whether from cold or shame, and covered myself with my two hands. Mino looked at me. "Now your belly will begin to swell," he said, "more and more each month and one day pain will make you open those legs you're pressing together so closely now, and the baby's head, already covered with hair, will appear and you will thrust it out into the light of day and they'll pick it up and put it in your arms, and you'll be happy, and there'll be another man in the world. Let's hope it won't say what Astarita said——"

"What did he say?"

"Cursed be the day on which I was born."

"Astarita's a wretched man," I said. "But I'm sure my son will be happy and lucky."

Then I wrapped myself up in the blanket and I believe I fell asleep. But Astarita's name had reawakened in my heart the same feeling of anguish which I had felt after his departure. Suddenly I heard an unknown voice shouting : "Pam, pam !" aloud in my ear, as if imitating the noise of two revolver-shots ; and I sat up sharply in bed in my terror and anxiety. The lamp was still alight, I got out of bed quickly and went towards the door to make sure it was properly shut. But I ran into Mino, who was standing fully dressed near the door smoking. I went back and sat down on the edge of the bed in a state of bewilderment. "What do you think?" I asked him. "What will Sonzogno do?"

"How should I know?" he replied, looking at me.

"I know him," I said, succeeding at last in finding words to express the anguish I experienced. "The fact that he let himself be pushed out of the room without protesting doesn't mean anything. He's quite capable of killing him. What do you think?"

"May be. It's quite likely."

"Do you think he'll kill him?"

"I wouldn't be surprised if he did."

"He ought to be warned," I cried, getting up and beginning to dress myself without further ado. "I'm sure he'll kill him. Oh, why didn't I think of it before?"

I dressed rapidly while talking of my fear and my presentiments. Mino said nothing, he was smoking and walking about. "I'm going to Astarita's house," I said at last. "He's at home now. Wait here for me."

"I'm coming, too."

I did not insist; at heart I was glad of his company because I was in such a state of agitation that I was afraid I might be ill. "We must get a taxi at once," I said as I put on my coat. Mino put on his coat, too, and we went out.

I began to walk hurriedly along the street, almost running, and Mino lengthened his stride to keep pace with me, his arm in mine. After a while we found a taxi and I hurried into it, shouting Astarita's address. It was a street in the Prati neighbourhood. I had never been there but I knew it was near the Law Courts.

The taxi began to gather speed and as if I were crazy I began to follow its route, leaning forward and watching the roads over the driver's shoulder. At a certain moment I heard Mino say softly: "And what if he has? One serpent has devoured another, that's all," but I did not register it. As soon as we were outside the Palace of Justice, I stopped the taxi and got out and Mino paid the fare. We ran across the little formal garden, following the gravel paths, between the trees and benches. The street where Astarita lived unfolded itself unexpectedly before me, long and straight as a sword, lit up far into the distance by a row of large, white lamps. It was a street of orderly, massively built houses, without any shops, and seemed deserted. From the number I guessed that Astarita's house must be towards the end. The street was so calm that I said: "Perhaps it's all my imagination... Still I couldn't do otherwise."

382

We passed three or four buildings and cross-roads and then Mino spoke. " Still, something must have happened," he said calmly, " look there." I raised my eyes and saw a black crowd gathered in front of one of the front doors, not so far away. A row of people stood lined up on the opposite pavement, gazing up towards the dark sky. I felt sure that must be Astarita's house, and I began to run, and I believe Mino was running, too. " What is it ? What's happened ? " I panted to the first member of the crowd pressing round the doorway.

" It's not altogether clear," said the person I had addressed, a fair young lad, hatless and coatless, who was holding a bicycle by the handle-bars. " Someone threw himself down the well of the stairs. Or he was thrown down. The police have gone up on to the roof and are looking for someone else."

I made my way through the crowd and elbowed myself into the entrance-hall, which was vast and well-lit and full of people. A white stairway with an iron railing rose in a wide curve over the heads of the crowd. As I pushed ahead, lifted up almost by my own impetus, I was able to see, over all those heads and shoulders, an open space on the floor underneath the stairway. A round white marble column supported a naked, winged figure in gilded bronze, one upraised arm held a frosted glass torch with an electric bulb inside it. A human body covered with a sheet lay immediately underneath the column. Everyone was looking in the same direction, and I looked, too, and then I saw that they were gazing at a foot in a black shoe which stuck out from under the sheet. At that moment I heard several people begin to shout imperatively. " Get back, get back ! " they were saying, and I was pushed back with all the others into the street.

" Mino, let's go home," I said faintly to someone just behind me, and I turned round. I saw an unknown face looking at me in astonishment. After having protested and hammered in vain on the shut door the people began to disperse and make their comments on what had happened. Others kept running up from other directions ; two cars and a number of cyclists had stopped for information. I began to wander through the crowd in a state of increasing anxiety, looking into each face without daring to speak to anyone. Some shoulders or heads seen from the back seemed like Mino's, I pushed my way impetuously into the middle of each group and then saw a number of unknown faces looking at me in surprise. The crowd was still at its densest around the doorway, they knew there was a body and they still hoped to catch a glimpse of it. They were closely-packed, with patient, serious faces, it was as though they were queueing outside a theatre. I went on wandering about but at a certain moment I realised I had looked into every face and kept coming across the same ones. I thought I heard Astarita mentioned in one of the groups and I realised I did not care at all about him, but that all the anguish I felt was concentrated on Mino. At last I convinced myself that he was no longer there. He must have gone off when I pushed my way into the hall. I imagined I ought to have foreseen that he would run off, I don't know why; and I was astonished at not having thought of it before. Pulling myself together I dragged myself as far as the piazza, got into a taxi and gave my home address. I thought that perhaps Mino had lost me and had gone home on his own. But I was almost certain this was not true.

He was not at home and did not come back that evening nor the day after. I shut myself up in my room, overwhelmed by such a strong feeling of uneasiness and anxiety that I could not prevent myself from trembling all over. I had not got a temperature, but I seemed to be living outside myself, in an abnormal, excessive atmosphere in which every sight, every noise, every contact hurt me and made me faint. Nothing could distract my thoughts from Mino, not even the new crime Sonzogno had committed, which filled all the papers mother brought me. This crime bore Sonzogno's unmistakable imprint : perhaps they had struggled with one another on the landing outside Astarita's front door for a moment, then Sonzogno had bent Astarita back against the railing, had lifted him up and thrown him down the well of the stairs. Such brutality was extremely expressive : only Sonzogno could have thought of murdering a man that way. But, as I have said, I had one thought only and was unable to rake up any interest even in the articles which told how Sonzogno had been shot dead later that night as he was escaping across the roofs like a cat. Any form of occupation, distraction or meditation, even, which was unconnected with Mino filled me with nausea, and at the same time the thought of Mino caused me unbearable anguish. Two or three times I happened to think of Astarita, and as I remembered his love for me and his melancholy, I experienced a strong feeling of helpless pity for him and told myself that if I had not been so anxious on Mino's account I would have wept for him and prayed for his soul, which had never been gladdened by any light and had been cut off from his body in such a barbarous and unexpected fashion.

This was how I passed the whole of the first day, the night and the whole of the day and night following. I lay on my bed, or sat in the armchair at the foot of the bed. I clutched in my hands one of Mino's jackets which I had found hanging up and every now and again I kissed it passionately or bit it to calm my restlessness. Even when mother forced me to eat something, I ate with one hand only and continued to grip the jacket convulsively in the other hand. Mother wanted to put me to bed on the second night and I let her undress me passively. But when she tried to take the jacket from me I gave such a shrill scream that she was terrified. Mother did not know anything for certain but she had guessed more or less that Mino's absence had driven me to desperation.

On the third day I managed to work out an idea and I stuck to it all morning tenaciously, although I felt obscurely how ill-founded it was. I imagined Mino had become scared at knowing I was pregnant and had wanted to escape the duties incumbent upon him and had gone home to his place in the provinces. It was an unpleasant supposition but I preferred to think him thus vile rather than to accept the other hypotheses I could not help imagining to explain his disappearance. They were such tragic ones and were suggested to me by the circumstances accompanying his flight.

At noon that day mother came into my room and threw a letter on the bed. I recognised Mino's writing and my heart leapt with joy. I waited for mother to leave the room and then waited for my excitement to die down a little. Then I opened the letter. Here it is.

Dearest Adriana,

By the time you receive this letter I shall be dead. When I opened the pistol and found it unloaded, I realised at once that you had done this and I thought of you very affectionately. Poor Adriana, you don't know anything about guns and you didn't know there was another bullet in the chamber. The fact that you didn't notice it strengthened me in my decision. And anyway, there are so many ways of killing oneself.

As I told you, I am unable to accept what I did. I have realised in these last few days that I love you; but if I were logical I ought to hate you; because you are everything I most hate in myself, to the highest degree, everything that interview revealed in me. What really happened at that moment was that the character I ought to have been collapsed, and I was only the man I really am. It wasn't a question of cowardice or treachery but only a mysterious interruption of the will. Perhaps it wasn't even so very mysterious—but that would be taking me too far. All I need say is that in killing myself I am putting things back into the order in which they ought to be.

Don't be afraid, I don't hate you; in fact I love you so much that only by thinking of you I become reconciled to life. If it had been possible I would have lived and would have married you and we'd have been very happy together, as you so often said. But it really isn't possible.

I have remembered the child that is to be born and have written two letters concerning him, one to my family and one to a lawyer friend. They're decent people, after all, and although one can't have any illusions about their feelings towards you, I am sure they will do their duty. If they should refuse, which I think most unlikely, don't hesitate to go to law. My lawyer friend will come and see you and you can trust him. Think of me sometimes. I kiss you.

Mino.

PS. My lawyer's name is Francesco Lauro, Via Cola di Rienzo, 3.
386

As soon as I had read this letter I buried myself in the bed-clothes, pulled the sheet over my head and cried bitterly. I cannot say how long I cried. Every time I thought I had finished a kind of piercing, painful laceration in my breast made me burst out sobbing again. I did not cry out loud as I longed to because I was afraid of attracting mother's attention. I wept silently and felt that this was the last time I would ever cry in my whole life. I wept for Mino, for myself, for all my past and all my future.

At last I got up, still crying, and feeling dazed and stupid with my eyes blinded by tears I began to dress hurriedly. Then I washed my eyes in cold water, painted my red, swollen face as best I could and went out quietly without telling mother.

I went to the local police station and had myself shown in to the commissioner. He listened to my story and then said sceptically : " As a matter of fact, we haven't had any information. You'll find that he's thought twice about it."

I longed for him to be right. But at the same time he irritated me, I don't know why. " You talk like that because you don't know him," I said sharply. " You think they're all like you."

" But look here ! " he asked. " Do you want him alive or dead ? "

" I want him to live," I shouted, " I want him to live ! But I'm terribly afraid he's dead."

He reflected. " Pull yourself together," he then said. " When he wrote that letter perhaps he wanted to kill himself. But he might have changed his mind afterwards. He's a human being. It might happen to anyone."

" Yes, he's a human being," I stammered. I did not know what I was saying any longer.

" In any case, come back this evening," he concluded, " and by then I'll be able to give you some news."

I went straight from the police station to church. It was the church where I had been held up to be baptised, where I had been christened, and where I had made my first com-munion. It was a very old church, long and bare, with two rows of beige stone columns and a dusty floor of grey paving-stones.   But in the darkness of the naves on each side, beyond the two rows of columns, were a number of richly gilded chapels like deep grottoes filled with treasure.   One of these chapels was dedicated to the Madonna.   I knelt down on the floor in the darkness before the bronze screen which shut off the chapel.   The Madonna was shown in a big dark picture behind a number of vases of flowers.   She held her Baby in her arms and a saint knelt at her feet with clasped hands, adoring her.   I bent down to the ground and beat my head against the paving-stones.   As I covered the stone with kisses I made a sign of the Cross in the dust and then called upon the Virgin and made a vow within me.   I promised I would never let another man touch me, all my life, not even Mino. Love was the only thing I cared about in the whole world, the only thing I enjoyed, and I thought I could make no greater sacrifice for Mino's salvation.   Then, still bent double with my forehead on the pavement I prayed, from my heart without words and without thoughts.   But when I got up I was dazzled, the deep shadow which engulfed the chapel seemed to split in sudden brightness and in this light I distinctly saw the Madonna looking at me sweetly and kindly, but neverthe-less shaking her head as if to say she did not accept my prayer. It lasted only an instant and then I found myself standing once more in front of the screen facing the altar.   Feeling more dead than alive, I crossed myself and went home.

I waited the whole day, counting the minutes and the seconds, and towards evening I went back to see the police commissioner.   He looked at me in a queer way; I felt as if I were going to faint and said in a ghost of a voice : " It's true then, he did kill himself."

The commissioner of police picked up a photograph from the table and held it out to me.   " A man who has not yet been identified killed himself in a hotel near the station," he said.   " Have a look and see if it's your man."

I took the photo and recognised him at once.   They had photographed him from the waist up, stretched out on a bed, apparently.   Little black lines of blood ran across his face from the temple where he had shot himself.   But his face was serene beneath these lines, as I had never seen it during his lifetime.

I identified him in a faint voice and got up. The police officer wanted to say something more, perhaps to console me; but I would not listen to him and went out without turning round.

I went home and this time I threw myself into mother's arms, but without crying. I knew she was stupid and did not understand a thing, but she was the only person I could confide in. I told her everything, about Mino's suicide, our love and how I was with child. But I did not tell her Sonzogno was the father of my child. I told her about the vow I had made, too, and said I had decided to change my way of life and that I would help her with her shirt-making or would go into service. After trying to console me with a number of silly but sincere phrases, mother said I ought not to make any rash decisions—what I had to do now was to see what the family would do for me.

" That's a matter which concerns my child," I said. " Not myself."

Next morning Mino's two friends, Tullio and Tommaso, called unexpectedly on me. They, too, had received a letter in which, after telling them he was going to commit suicide, Mino informed them of his betrayal and warned them of the consequences it might have.

" Don't worry," I said sharply. " If you're scared, you needn't be. Nothing at all will happen to you." And I told them about Astarita and how Astarita, who was the only one to know anything, had died and the interview had never been written down and they had never been denounced. It looked as though Tommaso was sincerely upset about Mino's death; but Tullio had not yet recovered from his fear. After a moment he spoke. " Still, he got us into a fine mess," he said. " Who can trust the police? You never know. It was a real piece of treachery," and he rubbed his hands together with one of his usual exaggerated bursts of laughter, as if it had been something really amusing.

I got up in indignation. " It wasn't anything of the kind ! " I said. " He killed himself—what more do you ask of him ? Neither of you would have had the courage to do likewise. And I can tell you another thing, too—you're quite worthless,

389

even if you aren't traitors! And do you know why? Because you're two unfortunates, two poor wretches, two penniless creatures who'll never have a penny to call their own, and if things go well you'll get what you've never had so far in all your life, and you and your families will be all right. But he was rich, he was born into a wealthy family, he was a gentleman, and if he got mixed up in it it was because he believed in it, and not because he expected to get anything out of it! He had everything to lose, but you, on the contrary, have everything to gain! That's what I can tell you—and you ought to be ashamed to come here and talk to me about treachery."

Little Tullio opened his enormous mouth as if he wanted to reply, but Tommaso, who had understood what I had said, stopped him with a gesture. "You're right," he said to me, "but don't worry—I'll never think anything but good of Mino, myself." He seemed moved and I felt drawn to him because obviously he had really been fond of Mino. Then they said good-bye and left me.

When I found myself alone once more I felt that what I had said to those two had to some extent relieved my sorrow. I thought about Mino and then I thought about my child. I thought how he would be the child of a murderer and a prostitute; but any man in the world might happen to kill someone and any woman might sell herself for money, and what mattered most of all was that he should have an easy birth and grow up strong and healthy. I decided that if it was a boy I would call him Giacomo in memory of Mino. But if it was a girl, I would call her Letitia, because I wanted her to have what I had not had, a gay, happy life, and I was sure that, with the help of Mino's family, that was just what she would have.